ELVIS PRESLEY:

MY SECOND CHANCE

By Bruce Portmann

Copyright

Acknowledgements

Special thanks to first my sister, Claire J. Portmann, for her encouragement, putting up with my constantly asking her how to spell words and my need for her help with my computer. Claire also did the final edit on the book, and I can't thank her enough for her contribution to the cause.

I also want to give a special thanks to Mary Watson for her belief and support.

Others that added their help and support are; Ilania Frazier, my dear friend who spent three weeks helping to edit the book. Lt. John Bradley - PBC Fire Station #18, Renee Robitailla M.S.CCC-SLP and Raymond A. Beane PT from Jupiter Medical Center with their kind explanations of medical information; Joan Conning Afman my first editor and Jennifer Fitzgerald of www.MotherSpider.com for the cover design, fellow Jupiter author Traci Hall, Al & Jan Feinstein and the people at CDS #093, Sharon Menear, Caryn Gross-Devincenti and the Palm Beach County Writer's Group, Katherine Nolan Conner, and all the other people that gave me words of encouragement along my journey writing this book.

Thank you all.

Introduction

I was as shocked as everyone else at the early demise of Elvis Presley. After Elvis' death, I heard of Elvis sightings that happened every so often. Stories circulated that Elvis was seen at a Wendy's ordering cheeseburgers or he was spotted sailing in the Caribbean. These stories and others help keep Elvis' memory alive and in the consciousness of the world, along with a great collection of recorded music, movies, concerts, and TV performances for generations to come.

Over thirty-three years later, I was given the idea to make a movie about Elvis by Russell Calkins. My first instinct was to say, "No, it's already been done." Then he suggested, "What if he didn't die, what might have happened?" I sat there in silence for three or four minutes, my brain was going a million miles an hour. Yes, what might have happened if Elvis had lived and been able to turn his life around, giving himself a second chance at life? That's when the idea for this book was born.

While this alternate biography is a fictional story, it incorporates a great deal of research and a bit of history into the story line. It also includes imagining what real and fictional people might have said and done. I hope you enjoy this fantasy about what might have happened.

Contents

Chapter 1

August 16, 1977

My name is Elvis Aaron Presley. This story is what happened to me August 16, 1977, but it's certainly not what you might have expected.

There is a lot of activity going on at Graceland today. It's a bright, sunny, humid day, about 98 degrees at 2:00PM.

Everyone is busy, from my household staff to the group of friends, associates, and employees whose main function is to provide services as bodyguards and take care of tour logistics. This is the group that has been nicknamed the Memphis Mafia. They are getting things ready for me to fly up to Portland, Maine tonight. Tomorrow night is the opening night of my upcoming tour.

Joe Esposito, a short stocky guy from Chicago, is sharp and an all-around good friend. He has dark hair like mine. We first met in the Army in 1958 and he came to work for me right after we were discharged in 1960. Joe has a great personality, a dynamite smile and everyone seems to like him as soon as they meet him. He fit right in with the Memphis Mafia and was one of the two best men at my wedding.

Joe has become my go-to-guy for handling a lot of business details, such as scheduling, keeping track of my expenses and organizing my career. He deals with everyone from Concert West, RCA Records, Vernon, and even Colonel Parker. They all were very happy to work with someone who

1

took on a more defined work role and is more accessible than me.

At the moment, Joe is in his office here at Graceland. It's located in the building behind the mansion.

A little background about my home: Graceland is located in Memphis, Tennessee. It was originally called Graceland Farms and owned by S.C. Toof, who made his fortune in the commercial painting business. The grounds were named after Toof's daughter, Grace who inherited the farm from her father. Grace later gave the land designated as Graceland to her niece Ruth Moore. In 1939, Ruth and her husband Dr. Thomas Moore, built the American colonial style mansion on the property.

In early 1957, I decided we had outgrown our $40,000 home at 1034 Audubon Drive in East Memphis. My parents, Gladys and Vernon, found Graceland near the Tennessee-Mississippi border. The house was empty and badly needed work. It is located on 13.8 acres and constructed of limestone with twenty-three rooms, including eight bedrooms and eight bathrooms. The entrance boasts four Corinthian columns. Once the property was mine, I purchased two large cement lions from a local resident for $1,000. They are now perched on each side of the portico.

The mansion is my security blanket. I love the seclusion that Graceland provides me. It is where I can breathe and recharge my batteries. And, most of my oldest friends live nearby, in or around the Memphis area.

~ * ~

2

Joe is sitting at his desk. He is talking to the three guys standing in front of his desk. They are the flight crew for my personal jet, the *Lisa Marie*.

I use the *Lisa Marie* to fly anywhere I want to go, when I want to go. She's a Convair 880 jet that I bought from Delta Airlines for $250,000. It took another $350,000 or so to refurbish her to my specifications.

Joe says to Captain Elwood David, my personal pilot, "You'll need to be ready to leave by 11:00PM.tonight. That's when Elvis, the Memphis Mafia and his other guests will be at the airport."

"We'll be ready," replies Elwood. He is accompanied by his co-pilot, Ron Strauss, and the flight engineer, Jim Manny. "I'll have Ron and Jim make sure the *Lisa Marie* is fueled, stocked up, and ready to go."

Joe continues, "I'll call you with the passenger list as soon as I know who will be with us. I can tell you that Vernon is coming with us tonight for the opening."

"Good, it will be nice to have him with us on the trip." Elwood says with a grin.

We'll be ready!" exclaims Ron, who is never at a loss for words.

After taking a swig from his can of Pepsi Cola, Jim asks, "We're flying to Portland, Maine tonight right?"

"Yep, I've already checked and the 1209 mile flight should take us 2 hours and 42 minutes, give or take, to get there." Elwood replies.

"Colonel Parker is already up there and will have ground transportation at the airport waiting to take everyone to their hotels," Joe tells them.

"I'll file the flight plan as soon as I get back to the airport," Ron assures Joe.

"Okay! Now get out of here. I have a lot of work to do before we leave, and you have to get the *Lisa Marie* ready." The three crew members file out and head back to the airport.

~ * ~

I have a sixteen-by-twenty foot wardrobe room dedicated to storing all my jumpsuits and stage clothes I wear on stage when I am touring. Al Strada is packing my wardrobe cases for the tour. He will also pack street clothes I'll wear while we're out on the road.

I originally hired Al back in 1972 through Pacific Palisades Security in California. He started out, part time, guarding my Trousdale Estate and then guarding my Monovale Estate when I was living in Los Angeles. His duties were to guard the house at night when my wife and my daughter were in residence while I was out on the road. Al began working for me full time in January 1974. He's very shy and looks somewhat like me. So much so, sometimes he even gets mistaken for me.

Nancy Rooks is helping Al. She is making sure all the jumpsuits are pressed and ready to go. I hired her in May of 1967 as a cook/housekeeper and she's been with me ever since. Nancy also keeps an eye out for my daughter, Lisa Marie, when she is here without her mother, my now ex-wife, Pricilla.

4

As they are finishing up, the intercom rings and Nancy picks it up.

"Hello?"

"Nancy, who's on duty down there?" a voice asks frantically. Ginger Alden, my fiancée, is on the other end of the line.

"Al is. Do you want to talk to him?"

"Yes, let me talk to him! Quick!"

"Just a minute," Nancy hands the phone to Al, "It's Ginger."

"Hello Ginger," Al says, "What's up?"

"Al, there's something wrong! I can't wake Elvis up. He's fainted or something."

"What?"

"I can't wake him up," Ginger says with panic in her voice.

Chapter 2

All right, I'll be right up."

Al runs up the flight of stairs to the second floor of the mansion. At the top, he turns right and opens the doors to my bedroom suite. As he comes through the doors, he moves quickly past my office on his left. Straight ahead are the blue Naugahyde padded double doors that lead into the bedroom area.

The room that Al enters is decorated in red plush, velour and velvets. Light in the room comes through the windows, from table lamps and from a fixture that hangs from the ceiling. The hanging lamp is near my side of the bed, over a foot locker that holds books I'll read when I'm out on the road. The ceiling is soundproofed and has a TV hanging from it in the corner.

Just inside the doors, on the left, Al passes the four foot tall statue of Jesus, a Christmas gift I received from my Memphis Mafia. He notices how cool it is in the bedroom. The central air conditioner is always set at 68 degrees and there is a large window unit that blows cool air right on my custom made 9 foot by 9 foot bed.

Al checks the bed, that has a Naugahyde headboard with a built in arm rest that allows me to sit up in bed to read. But he doesn't see anyone in the bed, although it appears to have been slept in.

Not seeing Ginger or me, he calls out, "Where are you?"

Ginger answers "Here! We're in the bathroom."

Al moves toward her voice, past the large bed and the bank of security monitors sitting on a wooden table against the right wall. I keep them there so that I can see everything going on around Graceland while I'm in bed.

Between the bedroom and the bathroom, Al passes the small refrigerator in an alcove on the right that has an accordion door to hide it from view. He continues to the right, into the bathroom which is decorated with gold and black tiles.

The bathroom is big enough so that it has a black leather chair and reading light next to it. The large circular shower is made with small black, brown and white tiles. There is one window and dressing-room lights around the large mirror over the gold sink with gold faucets provide the lighting. On the twelve foot counter top, Al sees Brut cologne, Colgate toothpaste, hair dye, deodorant, combs, brushes, hair gel, constipation medication, cotton balls, lotion, Neutrogena soap and other various make-up products and brushes.

Looking closer he sees that last thing he ever expected: me, curled up on the red shag carpet between the toilet and the shower. Next to me is the book that I was reading, "A Scientific Search for the Face of Jesus." I am wearing a blue top and yellow pajama bottoms.

Ginger is kneeling next to me with a frantic look on her face. "Al, I can't wake him up!" she cries.

Al moves closer and kneels down to see for himself. "That's okay, it will be alright," he says in a reassuring way. He checks to see if I'm still breathing. I am. Then he checks my neck for a pulse which, while rapid, I still have. He thanks God that I'm still alive.

Picking up the intercom, Al calls Joe.

"Come up here, I need you right away!" he says with great urgency.

"Where are you?"

"Ginger and I are in Elvis' bathroom. Get up here quick!"

"Why? What happened?"

"Joe, Elvis is unconscious. I need your help!"

"I'll be right there."

Joe bolts out of his office, through the back door of the mansion and up the stairs. He runs in and sees me lying on the floor.

Ginger says as he comes in, "Joe is Elvis going to be alright?"

"Yes, I'm sure he's going to be fine." Joe says "Have either of you called for an ambulance yet?"

Al answers, "No."

Joe says, "We better get one here right away."

Joe snatches up the phone hanging on the wall and calls the operator. "Can you put me through to the fire department? I need an ambulance, right away!"

The operator puts the call through. He raps his fingertips on the counter until the dispatcher answers the phone. He then yells into the receiver, "Hello! We need an ambulance here at Graceland, now! Can you get someone here really quick, please?"

"Yes, sir, I've dispatched one right now. What seems to be the problem? Who is it that needs help?"

Joe says, "He's a forty-two year old male, who has apparently fainted and is not responding very well."

"Is he unconscious?"

"Yes"

"OK. Is he breathing?"

"Yes and he has a pulse."

"That's good. Stay with him. The ambulance will be there in a few minutes."

"Great, thank you," Joe says.

"Will there be someone there to open the gate and let the ambulance on to the grounds?"

"Yes someone from the front guard house will let them in. Just have them come up the driveway and come in through the front door."

The dispatcher reassures Joe, "The ambulance will be there in just a few minutes. Is that all I can do for you now?"

"Yes, thanks for your help," he says and hangs up the phone.

He immediately picks the phone back up and calls the front gate where he speaks to my cousin, Harold Lloyd. "Harold, it's Joe."

"Hey, Joe."

"Listen. There is an ambulance on the way. I want you to let it in as soon as they get here."

Harold asks, "What's going on?"

"Just let them in and I'll talk to you later. Just do it, please!" Joe says with a great deal of urgency.

Harold is startled at Joe's abruptness, "Yeah, sure, Joe, but I just…"

Joe cuts him off. "Harold, I have to go now, goodbye." He hangs up the phone.

Harold hangs up the phone at his end. He is wondering what is going on at the mansion, but keeps an eye out for the ambulance.

Joe then calls my father, Vernon Presley, who is in his office, "Vernon, Elvis has fainted up here in his bathroom."

"What happened?"

"I don't know exactly, Vernon. But, I wanted to let you know."

"I'll be right there, Joe!"

As he hangs up the phone, Vernon summons Charlie Hodge, who is working on the guest list for tomorrow night's show. Charlie is an energetic fun loving guy who performed with the Foggy River Boys on "Ozark Jubilee" before coming to work for me.

"Charlie, I need you to come with me, right now!" They both head out of Vernon's office, located in a smaller house behind the mansion. They rush through the back door of the mansion, passing the kitchen on the right hand side to go into the foyer and up the stair case to the second floor.

~ *~

In the mean time, Al suggests to Joe, "Shouldn't we give Dr. Nick a call, and tell him we need him right away?"

George Constantine Nichopoulos, also known as "Dr. Nick" is an American doctor of Greek descent who earned his MD at Vanderbilt University Medical School in 1959. This was after studying at the University of the South, Birmingham-Southern College in Alabama, and the University of Alabama in Tuscaloosa. Dr. Nick first treated me in 1967 for pain brought on by horseback riding. He then took the full time position as my personal physician in 1970.

Joe reaches Dr. Nick on his mobile phone. "Hello, Dr. Nick, it's Joe. Elvis is unconscious, on the floor in his bathroom and we need your help right away."

"I'm already in my car and on my way over. I'll be there in a couple of minutes. So what is going on?"

"Ginger found Elvis on the floor and we have called for an ambulance. Elvis is unconscious. He has a weak pulse and he is breathing is very slowly. Dr. Nick, get here as soon as you can."

"It sounds like you've done what you can. Like I said, I'm on my way and I'll be there in few minutes."

"Please get here quick. I don't know what else to do!"

"Just hang on Joe, I'm almost there!" Dr. Nick disconnects his brand new mobile phone and hits the gas pedal. His green Mercedes is traveling well over the speed limit in order to get to Graceland as quickly as possible.

Vernon comes into the bathroom with Charlie close behind to see what the commotion is all about. Joe sees that Vernon is frightened to find me lying on the floor being attended to by Al and Ginger. He asks frantically, "What's going on up here?"

Joe replies, "Ginger found Elvis like this. He is unconscious, but he is breathing and he has a pulse."

Vernon cries out in an agonized voice, "Elvis, Elvis don't leave us. Hang in there Elvis."

As he tries to move closer, Charlie holds him back. Ginger gets up from the floor and goes over to Vernon and says, tearfully, "Vernon, I'm scared. What if he doesn't make it?"

He puts his arm over her shoulder, saying "Oh God, little girl, don't even talk like that. Come on guys, do something to help my boy. You *have* to save him."

"We have already called Dr. Nick and the ambulance is on the way, Vernon. Elvis is going to be alright." Joe responds.

In his agitation, Vernon blurts out, "We are supposed to be doing a show tomorrow night."

Joe says "I know, I know. We have to get Elvis to the hospital and find out what going on. We're may have to cancel the shows."

Vernon pleads, "My God, boys, do something to make my boy better!"

Al says, "We will, Vernon, as soon as Dr. Nick gets here and the ambulance can get Elvis to the hospital."

My 9 year old daughter, Lisa Marie suddenly appears in the midst of all the confusion. From the doorway she sees me lying on the floor. "What's wrong with my Daddy?" she asks as Ginger escorts her out of the bathroom and closes the door.

"Something is wrong with my daddy and I'm going to find out what it is," she shouts as she runs through the bedroom to the second door into the bathroom, only to find it locked. She starts pounding on it demanding to be let in.

Joe comes out of the bathroom to comfort Lisa Marie.

"What wrong with my daddy, Joe. Why is he lying on the floor?"

Joe calmly tells her, "Lisa Marie, your daddy is sick. We just need to take him to the hospital."

"I know, but what's wrong with him?"

"We don't know what is wrong, but we're going to take him to the hospital to find out. Okay?"

Joe turns to Ginger, "Ginger, please take Lisa Marie back down stairs. We're going to need room up here for the EMT's to get Elvis down stairs. Have her stay with Minnie Mae in her room, please."

"Okay, Lisa Marie, let's go downstairs," Ginger says to Lisa. "Joe and everyone will let you know what's going on, but you need to go back down stairs to stay out of the way."

Lisa Marie says reluctantly "Alright, but I want to see my daddy before he goes."

"You'll see him, I promise," Joe reassures her.

Ginger and Lisa Marie go back down stairs and are met at the bottom of the stairs by Nancy.

Ginger updates her, "Oh my God, Nancy, Elvis is lying up there on the bathroom floor. Joe had to call for an ambulance to come get him and Dr. Nick is on his way over."

"My goodness, what happened?" Nancy asks.

Lisa Marie announces, "My daddy doesn't feel well."

"I know darling. I know," Nancy says reassuringly to Lisa Marie.

Ginger' answers "I just found Elvis on the floor in the bathroom, and I couldn't wake him up."

"Oh my goodness child, I hope that Mr. Elvis will be okay."

"The guys seem to think so, Nancy. Joe asked me to have Lisa Marie stay with Minnie Mae in her room. I'm going to take her over there."

Ginger takes Lisa Marie by the hand to her great grandmother's bedroom to keep her out of the way. Ginger explains to Minnie Mae what is happening and asks if she would keep an eye on Lisa Marie.

"Sweetheart, come sit here with Granny Minnie Mae," as she pats a space next to her on the bed. Leaving Lisa Marie with her great grandmother, Ginger returns to where Nancy is standing in the foyer.

In the distance, they hear the siren of the ambulance coming from Engine House No. 29 in Whitehaven, just minutes from Graceland. The siren shuts off once the ambulance approaches the property. Harold has the gates open for them. They pass through, up the driveway and stop at the front door. The EMT's jump out and race to pull out the gurney and their medical bags from the back of the ambulance. They hurry up the four steps from the drive way to the front door. It is 2:33 PM.

Nancy meets the EMT's at the door, saying, "I'm so glad you're here."

Ginger says urgently "Go upstairs quickly! It's Elvis, please help him! Upstairs, on your right."

Ulysses Jones, one of two EMT's says, "We will ma'am." They make their way up the stairs, into the bedroom. They are met by Charlie who guides them into the bathroom. Joe, Al, and Vernon back out to make room for the EMT's.

Ulysses and his partner, Charlie Cosby enter the bathroom and start their 'head to toe inspection.' Ulysses tells Charlie to do an 'ABC check.' As Charlie gets into position, Ulysses asks, "Is this how you found him?"

Al says, "No we found him in a fetal position so we rolled him on his back."

Charlie crouches down with my head between his knees, places his hands on each side of my head and tilts it backwards. He then opens my mouth with his thumbs to check the airway. He reports "His airway is clear." Ulysses starts writing things down in his chart.

Then Charlie moves to my right side and puts his left cheek near my mouth to feel for any breath and to look down my torso to see if I am breathing. "Yes, I feel his breath on my cheek."

At the same time he is also checking for my pulse. "His heart rate is 105." Charlie then pulls my eyelids open to look at his pupils, "There's a delayed response to my light."

"Is there any sign of vomit or diarrhea?"

"No, but there is a small amount of drooling out of the right side of his mouth with some facial drooping on the same side."

Ulysses asks, "How old is Elvis?"

Al answers, "He's 42 years old"

"Is he on any kind of medication?"

"Yes, he is on--" Al starts to reply, but is interrupted by Vernon.

"No, he isn't on them anymore."

Al tries again, "Vernon you know that--."

Vernon sternly reinforces his position, "I said he's not on any pills anymore!"

"Alright, Vernon, he is not taking anything," Al concedes with reluctance in his voice.

Joe raises an eyebrow and exchanges looks with Ulysses. They both know that once they get me to the hospital, there will be blood work done that will tell what medications I have been taking.

Charlie Cosby suggests that they 'load and go' and Ulysses agrees. Charlie pulls me up into a sitting position on the floor, putting his arms under

16

my armpits and crosses his arms in front of me, and Ulysses grabs under my knees. Ulysses says, "On the count of three, 'one, two, and three," They pick me up, carry me out of the bathroom and place me onto the gurney that had been left in the bedroom.

As the EMT's work to stabilize me on the gurney, Joe asks, "Where are you going to take Elvis? To Baptist Memorial Hospital?"

Ulysses says, "Yes, it's the closest, so we'll take him there."

The EMT's have strapped me onto the gurney. They lower it and carry me down the stairs.

Nancy and Ginger are standing at the bottom of the stairs in the living room. Lisa Marie is holding Minnie Mae Presley's hand and they are looking into the foyer to see what's going on.

Behind them is Sam Thompson, another member of my security team, who is supposed to take Lisa Marie back to her mother on the *Hound Dog II* today.

Even though I am still unconscious, Ginger leans in and gives me a kiss on my forehead and says, "I'll come to the hospital to see you, Elvis. I love you. We'll see you soon."

She turns to Lisa Marie, "Don't worry. I'll take you to see your daddy, as soon as the doctors let us visit."

The EMT's pop the gurney up to wheel me out the front door and down to the ambulance.

~ * ~

Meanwhile, Joe picks up the phone and calls another of my cousins, Billy Smith. "Hello Billy, it's Joe. Listen, I have some urgent news. Elvis is being taken to Baptist Memorial Hospital."

Billy, his voice full of concern, says "Oh, my God, Joe, what's going on? We were playing racquetball earlier today."

"Listen Billy, all I know so far is Ginger called Al, and Al called me. Ginger found Elvis on the bathroom floor unconscious. He is breathing and he has a pulse. The EMT's are taking "E" over to the hospital now."

"Wow. Do you want me to meet you at the hospital?"

"Yes. They're taking him downstairs on the gurney now, so meet us at Memorial."

"Where is Dr. Nick?"

"I called him and he is on the way over here."

"All right, I'll head out now and I'll see you at the hospital."

"Thanks. I'll see you there."

Joe hurries downstairs to catch up with me and make sure things are organized.

~ * ~

Dr. Nick pulls into the driveway just as the EMT's are loading me into the back of the ambulance. Getting out of his car, he hurries directly to the ambulance and announces, "My name is Dr. George Nichopoulos. What do we have here?"

Charlie Cosby answers, "We have a white male, age 42. His blood pressure is 210 over 110 and his pulse is 105."

Ulysses reports, "His breathing is shallow, but we have him stabilized the best we can for now."

Dr. Nick is a take charge kind of guy. As they put me into the ambulance, he climbs into the back and instructs Joe, "Come with me so you can deal with the press at the hospital." Dr. Nick then addresses the EMT's, "Let's get going!"

As Joe climbs into the ambulance, he tells Al and Charlie Hodge, "Meet us at the hospital."

Charlie says, "We're right behind you, Joe." He closes the back doors of the ambulance and pounds on them with his fist three times in rapid succession to let Ulysses, the driver, know that it's okay to pull out.

By this time, the normal group of fans that wait outside the gates of Graceland has gotten even larger, having been drawn by the sight of the ambulance entering the property. It is difficult for the ambulance to get through them before making the frantic trip to Baptist Memorial Hospital.

In the back of the ambulance, Dr. Nick says, "His breath looks slow, about 5 breaths per minute. Where is your oxygen mask?"

Charlie Cosby hands Dr. Nick the mask and he applies it to my face while urging me to, "Hang in there Elvis, we are on the way to the hospital. We'll be there soon. Elvis, you're going to be all right!"

Chapter 3

"This is George Klein from WHBQ-AM with a Special Report. I just got word that my good friend, Elvis Presley, has been loaded into an ambulance. We are assuming that he is being taken to Baptist Memorial Hospital.

"I don't have any word on his condition at this time, but from what I have been told, there has been a lot of activity around Graceland this afternoon. That's not unusual because Elvis was scheduled to leave today to open his current tour tomorrow night in Portland, Maine.

"As soon as I can find out anything more about the King's condition I will break in and let you know. This is George Klein for WHBQ-AM, and now it's back to your regularly scheduled program already in progress back at the studio."

~ * ~

The ambulance backs into the gloomy gray emergency room entrance of one of the city's most respected hospitals, Baptist Memorial. The arrival is noted at 2:55PM, just 22 minutes after the EMT's arrived at Graceland.

The emergency room staff has prepared Trauma Room # 1 for my arrival and a team of doctors and nurses are standing by. Ulysses, George, and Dr. Nick with Joe's assistance maneuver the gurney out of the ambulance and roll me into the ER entrance. The staff stops Joe a as he tries to enter Trauma Room #1 with everyone else. For privacy, a staff member ushers him to Trauma Room #2 where they let him wait for news.

~ * ~

Al and Charlie enter through the front doors of Memorial Hospital, and work their way back to the Emergency Room. They are directed by the nursing staff to the Trauma Room #2.

Billy arrives at the hospital a few minutes later and is also sent to join Joe, Al and Charlie. As he enters the room, Billy asks, "Hey, guys what's going on? How is Elvis?"

"We don't know. They wouldn't let us in with him. So we're here just sitting around waiting to hear," Joe replies.

Charlie asks Billy, "So what do you know? Did I hear that you played racquetball with Elvis and Ginger this morning?"

"Yes, we did. Elvis had a dental appointment with Dr. Lester Hoffman at 10:30 last night. He had his teeth cleaned and two small cavities filled. At about 2:15AM, Elvis' stepbrother, Ricky Stanley, drove to the all-night pharmacy here at Baptist Memorial Hospital and came back with six Dilaudid pills. But, I don't know if or when Elvis took them."

"Then about 4:00AM Elvis woke me up and asked me and my wife, Jo, if we would come over and play a game of racquetball with him and Ginger. Elvis, as usual, played the game barely moving around the court and playfully tried to hit me with the ball. We called the game off when Elvis hit himself with his racquet, bruising his leg.

"He then decided to play a couple of gospel songs, and then 'Blue Eyes Crying in the Rain' on the piano. The four of us came back into the house around 5: 00 AM.

"Ginger and Jo went into the kitchen to talk, while Elvis and I went upstairs. I noticed that he took one of his pre-packaged packets of pills, made up by Dr. Nick, upstairs with us. Elvis ask me to wash his hair and we talked about the tour. He was nervous like he always is, but he was looking forward to doing it. He loves working the audience."

"Forty-five minutes later, Ginger came upstairs. Elvis told me to go home to get some rest and that he would see me later this evening on the flight to Portland. I went back downstairs, got Jo and we left."

Al said, "Well, Ginger told me that Elvis called downstairs about 7:00AM and had Nancy bring up some banana pudding, vanilla ice cream and three Pepsis. He put two of the Pepsis in the 'fridge. After eating, Elvis took a pack of pills and they went to bed.

"But Elvis was restless and thinking about the upcoming tour. At 8:00AM he still wasn't able to sleep. So he called his Aunt Delta Mae Biggs to bring up another packet of pills.

"At about 9:30AM Elvis picked up the book he had been reading and went into the bathroom. Ginger said she told Elvis 'Don't fall asleep in there,' knowing his tendency to nod off."

"He replied, "Okay, I won't."

"Ginger fell asleep and when she woke up about 1:45PM, she realized that Elvis wasn't in bed. She went across the hall to her bathroom to put on her makeup and get dressed in one of her two-piece jogging suits.

"Then she went to Elvis' bathroom door and knocked. There was no answer. That's when she went in and found him lying on the floor in front of the toilet. She called down stairs for help. Joe and I were the first to get up there." Al continued.

"Man, I was scared, seeing Elvis lying on the floor like that. I couldn't tell if he was breathing or not at first," Al recalls.

Joe nods, "Well, we did what we had to do. We called for the ambulance. Dr. Nick arrived just as the ambulance was ready to leave."

"What is going on back at Graceland? Has anyone talked to them since we've been here?" Billy asks.

"Ginger and Vernon are there. Lisa Marie is with Nancy, who is probably feeding them, and everyone else. I'll give them a call after Dr. Nick tells us what's up," Al said. After a short pause he adds, "So Joe, what's going to happen to the tour?"

"I don't know Al, but I'm sure we will have to make a decision soon."

"Has anyone called Priscilla yet?" Charlie asks.

"No, I don't think so. Not unless Vernon has, but I don't think he would have called her yet," Joe says.

Billy exclaims, "Look, here's Dr. Nick with another doctor."

Dr. Nick walks into the room, "Hey guys. This is Dr. Jerry Francisco."

"Good afternoon, gentlemen. We've checked Mr. Presley out and have determined that he has suffered a stroke." Dr. Francisco, wearing a very serious expression on his face, informs them.

Everyone starts asking questions at the same time. Joe, "Damn! Is he going to be all right?"

Al, "How bad is it?"

Billy, "How long will he be here in the hospital?"

"Slow down, gentlemen," Dr. Francisco says. "Dr. Nichopoulos and I are here to tell you what we know, as of now."

Dr. Nick starts out, "Here's what we know so far. Elvis has developed a serious drug problem. He thought things were okay because the drugs he took were all prescribed for him. But there have been too many prescriptions written by too many different doctors, much to my dismay. The combination has been too much for him. I know yesterday alone, he saw his dentist and got pain pills from him."

Dr. Francisco interjects, "From the blood work-up and his history, it appears that Elvis is addicted to Codeine, Valium, Morphine and Demerol. That is why his health has declined and he has put on the weight. And, it is a major factor contributing to his stroke."

Billy jumps to Elvis' defense, "Elvis was just taking his prescriptions like the doctors told him to. He never even drinks alcohol. He only experimented with recreational drugs; you know pot, one time with Priscilla, George and Barbara Klein. He certainly didn't get hooked on it. From what I understand none of them ever tried smoking again."

Dr. Francisco responds, "Yes, but he was seeing four or five or more different doctors in different locations and getting prescriptions from each of them. He just over did it, and that is why he's in the condition he is in."

Charlie asks with great concern, "Dr. Francisco, what's really going to happen to Elvis now?"

Dr. Nick says cautiously, "Listen guys, Elvis will live. But and it is a big but, we don't know the full extent of damage done by the stroke yet. It's going to take time for him to recover, maybe a very long time. If ever."

Joe says, "What do you mean by that?"

"It's going to take a lot of rehabilitation. It could take as much as a year or more before Elvis is fully functioning. We'll have to wait and see how well he responds. We don't know if he will ever be able to perform again," Dr. Nick responds. The looks on everyone's face turned to a mix of astonishment and alarm as they realize that Elvis is a mortal man.

"Damn! If he can't do that, it will be worse than back when he was in the service." says Billy. "Elvis was so frustrated when the Colonel wouldn't let him perform while he was serving our country in the Army. Elvis loves to perform. The thought of him not performing… I can't imagine that."

"Excuse me," Maurice Elliott, the public relations spokesperson for the hospital walks in on the group. The focus in the room instantly shifts.

He says, "Is someone here going to make a statement to the press, or, do you want me to do it? There are radio, TV and newspaper people outside, all wanting to know what is going on."

Joe shakes his head, as if coming out of a dream, and says "Uh, that would be me. Give me a moment; I'll come up with some sort of statement."

"Joe, please wait," says Dr. Nick, "I want to go back to Graceland and tell Vernon before he hears it on the radio or sees it on the TV news. I'm not sure his heart will be able to take the news."

Billy offers, "I'll give you a ride back to Graceland, Doc. I have my car here."

"Thanks, Billy."

"I'll ride back with you, too," Joe says to Billy. "Give me a few minutes to write out a statement. Al, will you read it to the press after we have notified the family back at Graceland?"

Al says "Sure. You know I'll do whatever needs to be done."

"Charlie, can you stay here, with Al, so if anything else needs to be done you can handle it?" Joe asks, "Is that all right with you guys?" Charlie and Al both nod in agreement.

Maurice finds Joe a pen and some paper. He starts writing out what he wants Al to read to the press. As he writes, he tells Al, "Please wait until we get back to Graceland, I'll call and let you know when you can give the statement."

"Ok, I'll stay with Maurice, so call and have him paged so you can get me here," Al agrees.

"Sounds like a plan, Al." Joe says, "Oh, Dr. Francisco, please make sure that only people from our group can get in to see Elvis besides your staff. Charlie and Al will be here to make sure only those allowed will be able to get into his room."

Dr. Francisco replied, "Yes we will have our security guards patrolling the floor, no one without authorization will get past them."

Joe nods and extends his hand, "Thanks, Dr. Francisco."

Al brings the conversation back to his main concern. "So, Dr. Nick, Elvis won't be able to perform any time soon?"

"That's right. The best we can tell, at this point, is that Elvis has had a stroke. He has paralysis in his right arm; his speech is slurred and he has facial drooping on the right."

Everyone's jaw drops upon hearing that Elvis is paralyzed and slurring. Joe says, "No wonder you want to get back to Graceland before Vernon hears what condition Elvis is in."

"Yes, boys, Elvis' condition *is* very serious. It's going to take quite a while for him to recover."

"Wow!" Charlie exclaims, "What is this going to do to Elvis' image?"

Dr. Francisco says, "You guys saved Elvis' life today! That is the most important thing. At least he is still with us. Imagine what it would be like if we had to send him to the morgue?"

A shocked silence fills the room. Everyone becomes very somber, reflecting for themselves what the world might be like without Elvis.

Billy breaks the silence, "Oh shit, that would be a very sad day, not only for us, but for the whole world," he says with a terrible sadness.

Joe gives Al the hand written statement he wants him to read to the press. "Here, wait for my phone call, and then have Maurice introduce you to the press. Let the press know that you have a statement to be read on behalf of the Presley family in regard to Elvis' condition, and there will be no questions at this time."

"I've got it, Joe."

"Ok, so we all know what we need to do. Let's get going." Billy, Joe, Charlie, Al and Dr. Nick all come together and hug each other. As they let go of each other, they spontaneously, in unison, quietly exclaim "TCB!" the short version of their motto: "Taking Care of Business."

~ * ~

Billy, Joe and Dr. Nick leave the hospital. They pile into Billy's new black and gold 1977 Pontiac Trans Am, 200-hp, 6.6-liter V-8 with a three speed manual transmission. Billy starts the car up with a great roar of the engine. The back tires squeal as they pull out of the hospital parking lot in a cloud of white rubber smoke.

Billy drives up I-55 N to I-240 E to get back to Graceland. It is a trip of a little more than the 12 miles. He maneuvers carefully through the mass of fans at the property entrance, ignoring the questions they call out.

After passing through the gates of the estate, they see Lisa Marie riding around in one of the paddocks on her custom made miniature electric golf cart. Billy drives up close to her, rolls down the window, calling, "Hey, Lisa Marie, what are you doing?"

"I'm trying to get Snoopy to stop chasing the horses through the field." Snoopy is a Great Dane, one of the many gifts I had given Priscilla.

"Well, come back inside the house now honey, I want to talk to you."

"I'll be right there Uncle Billy. How is my daddy?"

"Come on in and I'll let you know."

Billy pulls up to the front door and Lisa Marie drives the golf cart up behind the Trans Am. She calls Billy 'Uncle', even though he is actually a cousin. As she comes running up, Billy puts his arm around her shoulder, pulls her to his. They all walk up the front stairs to enter through the front door.

Lisa Marie pipes up, "Uncle Billy, how is my daddy?"

"He's doing well Lisa Marie. But, he's going to be in the hospital for a while. "

"When can I see him?"

Dr. Nick tells her, "Maybe as soon as tomorrow, sweetheart."

"Is he going to get better?"

"Yes, he is going to get better," Dr. Nick tells her.

Lisa Marie and Billy go into the kitchen, while Joe and Dr. Nick head out the back door to the smaller house that Joe and Vernon work from.

Vernon's office is a room with a drop ceiling, florescent lighting and brown wood-paneled walls. It is furnished with a couple of drab green metal desks, filing cabinets and wooden book shelves. It is a rather utilitarian place from which to work.

There is a sign on the office door:

"Please read & observe. No loafing in office. Strictly for employees only! If you have business here please take care of it and leave. Vernon Presley"

As they enter, Joe goes to his desk while Dr. Nick goes into Vernon's office to break the news to him.

Dr. Nick greets Vernon as he walks in, "Hello Vernon."

Vernon's face is creased with worry lines. "Hello Dr. Nick, how is my son?"

"Well, Vernon the good news is that Elvis is still alive and it looks like he will stay that way. But, the not so good news is, Dr. Francisco and I have checked Elvis out and determined that he has had a stroke. Dr. Francisco also says that his recovery is going to take a while."

The doctor pauses briefly before he adds. "You know that Elvis has been taking uppers to stay awake, and downers to go to sleep, and that he's been doing this for years. His eating habits aren't the best either. That is why he has been packing on weight and it has taken its toll on him. Not to mention that Elvis is over 42, so he's not as young as he used to be."

Vernon says impatiently, "Yes, yes, yes. But is Elvis going to be all right?"

"We will have to wait and see. But, if he wants to get well, Elvis is going to have to change his ways. He has to get off the pills, start eating right and exercise."

"Yes, I know. I've told him that those God damn pills were going to cause him problems," Vernon states, shaking his head. "Can I go see him?"

"It would not be a good time right now. They are still doing tests and the therapists are evaluating his status. Give him a call tomorrow.

"What I think you need focus on right now is writing a press statement about what has happened to Elvis. Rumors are bound to start spreading. Newspapers, radio stations and TV stations from here and out of town are sending reporters to Graceland and to the hospital."

"Let me get with a couple of the Memphis Mafia and together we'll come up with a statement," Vernon replies.

"Joe wrote out a statement for Al to read after you make a statement from here. You know, Vernon, the sooner the better."

"I'll get with Joe and have him help me write something up since he's already done that at the hospital. Thanks, Dr. Nick, for letting me know about Elvis' condition."

The doctor nods, "You're welcome, Vernon."

~ * ~

While Vernon and Dr. Nick are talking in Vernon's office, Joe is calling Priscilla Beaulieu Presley, born Priscilla Ann Wagner, mother of Lisa Marie and my now ex-wife.

Michelle, Priscilla's sister answers the phone. Joe asks, "Hello, Michelle, is Priscilla there?"

"No, she's not, Joe. I'm not sure when to expect her home."

"I need to talk to her. Do you know where I can reach her?"

"No, I don't. Why, what's going on?"

"I just need to talk to her. It's very important."

Michelle hears the front door of the house opening, "Oh wait a minute. I think she is coming in the door now. Priscilla, is that you? Joe is on the phone and needs to talk to you," she hollers out.

Only a few seconds pass as Priscilla walks into the living room were Michelle is sitting on the couch. She puts down her shopping bags as Michelle hands the phone to her.

"Here, it's Joe." Priscilla takes the phone and flashes her sister a 'what does he want' kind of look. Michelle shrugs.

"Thanks Michelle," Priscilla puts the phone to her ear, "Hello, Joe."

"Hello Priscilla, listen I have some disturbing news to tell you."

"What is it?" With panic rising, she quickly adds, "Is Lisa Marie all right?"

"Yes, yes she is fine. But, I have just come from the hospital where Elvis has been admitted because he had a stroke."

Priscilla is beside herself and starts to shake, sitting down next to Michelle. "A stroke! What happened? Is he all right? Oh, my God. Is Lisa Marie okay? Who is taking care of her?"

Concerned about what she has gathered from Priscilla's side of the conversation, Michelle reaches out and takes her sister's hand to comfort her.

Joe, in a calming voice, tries to reassure Priscilla. "Lisa Marie is fine, don't worry, she's with Billy, Jo, and Nancy right now. And yes, Elvis should be all right, but the doctors said it's going to take some time and effort on his part to recover from this."

Priscilla asks Joe, "How long is some time? What exactly is wrong with Elvis?"

"Dr. Francisco, the doctor at Baptist Memorial Hospital and Dr. Nick checked Elvis out. They are saying it could take a year or more for him to recover."

"A year for him to recover? Oh my!" Priscilla exclaims.

"This has all just happened, Priscilla. I wanted to tell you before you heard it on the news. You know how cruel and insensitive the tabloids can be. I figured you would want to have a statement prepared."

"Oh yes, I'll have to come up with something, won't I. But you know... I don't like Dr. Nick. I think he bends over backward to give Elvis what he wants, just to be able to hang out with him."

"Yes, I know how you feel about him, and I agree with you, Pricilla. You know I love Elvis too, and I'll do whatever I can for him. I'm not into the drugs that Elvis uses to function, so I try to stay away from that part of his life."

"I know you love him, Joe. You have been a good friend ever since we met in Germany. You've always taken good care of us."

"Elvis is in the best hands possible right now. If it is okay with you, may Lisa Marie stay on here, so that she can see her Dad, for herself, as soon as possible? And, if you want to see him I can make arrangements for *Hound Dog II* to come and get you whenever you want."

"Okay, Joe, Lisa Marie can stay. I know that she is in good hands there. Since Elvis is in the hospital, and you tell me he is going to be all right, I'll come back in a few days. I'll call Lisa Marie and let her know what my plans are and make sure she is okay. Once the craziness settles down, I'll be there to see them. Tell Elvis I love him and I'll call him soon. I'll call to let you know when I can get there."

"All right, Priscilla, I'll wait to hear back from you. If anything changes here, I'll keep you informed."

"Thanks for the call, Joe. I really appreciate you letting me know what's going on."

"That's okay. Take care of yourself and I'll talk to you later."

Chapter 4

Joe hangs up the phone just as Vernon and Dr. Nick walk into his office.

Vernon says, "Joe, Dr. Nick says that you wrote out a statement for Al to read once he gets the okay from us here. Will you help me to write one?"

"Sure, I'd be happy to help you."

"Can you do that now?"

"Yeah sure, Vernon, but shouldn't we call the Colonel and let him know what's going on? Do you want to do that, or should I?"

"No. I'll do that after I make the statement. I can make it from the front steps. Let Dick know to open the gates and let the press and fans in at 6:15PM."

"Here, I wrote this out for Al and made a copy for you, too. Change anything you want to."

"Thanks. Let me read this over a few times before I do this."

"Sure. I'll call Dick and get things organized for you."

Joe calls Dick Grob, who was a Sergeant in the Palm Springs, CA, police force when he first met me in 1969. Three years later, Dick joined me full time as the head of my security staff because of his training with the FBI and the CIA.

"Hello, Dick. Listen, Vernon is going to make a press statement from the front steps at 6:30PM. He wants you to open the front gates at

35

6:15PM and let the press and visitors come in for his announcement."

Dick wanting to confirm that he heard Joe correctly. "You said to open the gates at 6:15PM right?"

"Yep, 6:15PM, I'll talk to you later, Dick. I have to go now."

"Okay, consider it done."

~ * ~

Vernon walks from Joe's office to the foyer of the mansion, going over the statement that Joe has given him.

Everyone in the world, by now, knows that something has happened to Elvis and wants to know what it is. Hundreds of fans have been lining up outside the front gates of Graceland and on both sides of Elvis Presley Boulevard. The press corps has also arrived in great numbers to report on what has happened to the King of Rock and Roll.

At the appointed time, Dick opens the gates and there is a mad rush up the left side of the semicircular driveway as hundreds of fans and media converge on the front steps to hear what is going to be said.

A little after 6:30 PM, an emotional Vernon emerges from the mansion. Standing at the top of the stairs, he makes the following announcement to the world:

"My son, Elvis Aaron Presley, is in the Baptist Memorial Hospital here in Memphis. He is being attended by Dr. George Nichopoulos and Dr.

Jerry. Earlier today, he suffered a stroke here at his home, Graceland.

"Due to these circumstances, I'm sorry to tell you that Elvis' scheduled concert tour has been cancelled. There will be no other statement about my son's condition at this time, and, I will not answer any questions. I hope you will respect the privacy of the family and friends during this period of Elvis' recovery. Thank you."

Vernon turns and goes back into Graceland. He is even more emotional now, and tells Joe, "That was the hardest thing I've had to do. I can't talk to the Colonel right now, so would you please call him and tell him what is going on?"

"Sure Vernon, I'll do that for you, but I should call Al first and have him read the statement to the press there."

"Good, thanks Joe, I'm going to lie down now. I can't handle this pressure. Please tell Dr. Nick to come see me in my room? I think I might need a sedative."

"Yes, sure, Vernon I'll have him come right over to see you and I'll make those calls for you."

Joe heads back to his office. Once there he picks up the phone and dials the hospital. "Hello this is Joe Esposito can you page Maurice Elliot."

The Baptist Memorial Hospital Receptionist says, "Yes sir. Just a moment, please."

"Thank you."

The call is picked up by Maurice and soon Joe is speaking with Al. "Hello, Al. Dr. Nick has brought Vernon up to speed. He has just now read the announcement to the people gathered at Graceland. So, go ahead and read the statement to the press there. But, don't answer any questions."

"Ok, I'll do that now. What's happening there?"

"Vernon's pretty upset and has gone to lie down. I have to call the Colonel after I finish talking to you and let him know what's going on. There's crying and confusion, but I think it will calm down soon,"

"Okay, okay, I got it; I'll go do it now."

"Thanks for doing this, Al."

"Sure, that's okay. Do you want Charlie and me to stay here after I finish reading the statement?"

"Yes, please. I'll be in touch with you guys again soon. Be sure to keep everyone but the staff and family out of Elvis' room."

"Got it, I'll talk to you later."

~ * ~

Al finds Maurice Elliott outside in the hall. Together they exit the hospital through the Emergency Room to find several newspaper, radio & TV reporters, and numerous fans waiting to hear the latest update on Elvis. The press corps has set up several microphones to record any statements made during Elvis' stay at the hospital.

Elliott announces, "I will not be making a formal statement, about Elvis Presley. That being said, I would like to introduce Mr. Al Stratus who will be making a statement on behalf of the Presley family."

Al steps up to the bank of microphones. He then reads the same statement Vernon gave at Graceland. There is a slight easing of the tension in the crowd as if they let out the breath they had been collectively holding. While there is still a general feeling of worry in the crowd, it is now mixed with relief that Elvis is still alive. The fans, mostly young girls are sobbing and the news people push forward, eager to get the scoop.

Al and Elliott turn and walk back into the hospital as the reporters start shouting. Bob Ford yells out, "Al, what is Elvis' prognosis at this time?"

Clark Porteous from the Memphis Press-Scimitar waves his hand wildly. "Al! Al! When can we talk to the doctors about Elvis' condition?"

Alanna Stills, an aggressive young reporter calls out loudly, trying to be heard. "Is Ginger Alden here?"

Bob Ford tries again. "What is Elvis' prognosis?"

Nash Tamara, a young guy, obviously wanting to be the first to get back to his desk with the story, jumps into the air, vying for attention, "How long will...Elvis be in the hospital?"

Alanna, Ms. Pushy yells out, "What will be his recovery time Al?"

Bob Ford is persistent. "How did the stroke affect Elvis physically?"

Al and Elliot ignore the hubbub as they disappear back into the hospital.

Once they are back inside, Bob Ford turns back to the camera and says, "Well, you heard it here first from us at WHBQ-TV.

"Apparently, Elvis Presley was brought here to Baptist Memorial Hospital just hours ago from "Graceland. We have been told that the King has had a stroke. Just how severe it is, is unknown at this time. We are trying to get further word from Elvis' personal doctor, Dr. George Nichopoulos, better known as Dr. Nick, or Dr. Jerry Francisco, the attending physician here at Memorial.

"We have also just been informed that the scheduled concert tour that was to open tomorrow night in Portland, Maine has been cancelled. As we continue live coverage of this shocking event we will bring you more information from family members, either here or back at Graceland.

"Stay tuned for our updates to hear more about what is happening with the King of Rock and Roll. I'm Bob Ford, here at Baptist Memorial Hospital. Now back to you in our studios at WHBQ-TV."

Chapter 5

Thomas Andrew Parker, better known to the world as Colonel Tom Parker, was born Andreas Cornelis van Kuijk in Breda, Netherlands. The Colonel, best known as my manager, structured his deals so that he received much more on record deals than the traditional 10 to 15 percent a manager usually earns. It was his masterminding that created the success of my career and enabled the Colonel's percentage to reach as high as 50 percent on merchandising.

Tom Parker received his rank of "Colonel" from a member of the Louisiana State Militia, Governor Jimmie Davis, who was also a former country singer. Through fund-raising efforts for the Governor's charities, the Colonel met stars such as Minnie Pearl and Eddy Arnold and got himself involved in music promotion.

In 1945, the Colonel became Eddy Arnold's full time manager, contracting Arnold to 25 percent of his earnings for helping secure hit songs, TV appearances and live tours. Arnold fired the Colonel in 1953 because of the Colonel's involvement with the singer Hank Snow. The Colonel and Snow worked together and formed Hank Snow Enterprises and Jamboree Attractions, a successful promotional company to help upcoming country singers.

In early 1955, the Colonel first became aware of me. Bob Neal was my current manager at that time. That February, following a meeting with the Colonel, Bob agreed to let the Colonel take some control of booking and tours. Snow and the Colonel promoted me as the opening act for the Hank Snow Tour which helped to move my career to a new level.

By the summer of 1955, the Colonel became my "Special Advisor". Then on October 29, 1955 he became my official manager, signing me to Hank Snow Enterprises. Bob Neal gradually became less and less involved and by the end of his contract in early 1956, it was the Colonel who was in total control of my career. My feeling early on were that I didn't think I would have been very big with another manager, because he's a very smart man.

Joe calls Colonel Parker in his hotel room at the Dunfey Sheraton in Portland, Maine. George Parkhill, assistant to Colonel Parker, answers the phone in the Colonel's suite, "May I help you?

Joe, "Hello George, I need to talk to the Colonel."

"Sure. Just a minute, Joe." George puts his hand over the phone receiver and announces to the Colonel, "Colonel, it's Joe on the phone for you."

The Colonel takes the phone out of George's hand, "Do you have the list of who is coming up tonight?"

"Ah… no, I don't Colonel. Plans have changed. I've just come from the Baptist Memorial Hospital; we had to take Elvis in this afternoon. Ginger called us when she found him unconscious on the floor in his bathroom."

The Colonel is stunned into silence for a moment, and then says, "I can't believe it." He slumps in his chair, and mutters to himself, 'Oh, dear God. Joe, you know its Elvis' image that needs to be protected. So what happened?"

"Yes sir, I understand about Elvis' image," Joe said. "After talking to the doctors at the hospital though, it appears that Elvis has had a stroke."

"Is the boy going to be all right?" inquires Colonel Parker, with a note of anxiety in his voice.

"Yes sir, he's going to live but it's the recovery time. It's going to take quite a while, could be even as much as a year or more."

"What! A year to recover? What are we going to do? I've got to think of something. Okay, do what you have to do down there. I'll be down as soon as I can. Has there been a press release yet?"

"Yes sir, we have issued a statement from the hospital and Vernon made a statement from the front steps here at Graceland."

"I'll call the promoter and let him know that there won't be a show tomorrow or any time in the near future," the Colonel says. "And I'd better call Tom Hulett and Pat Kelleher and let them know. Where is Vernon?"

"Like I said, Vernon just made a statement to the press. He went to lie down because the stress was getting to him. Dr. Nick is with him now."

"All right, I need to get a flight down there and I have to make a few phone calls. Thanks for calling, Joe. I'll talk to you soon."

"Yes sir, Goodbye."

"Goodbye." The Colonel turns and yells to his assistant, "George, get me a flight to New York

City to arrive early tomorrow morning. I need to meet with the merchandising associates and with RCA executive, Pat Kelleher. They are going to want to know that they need to prepare for a huge demand in Elvis products. Then I've got to get down to Memphis later that evening to take care of business."

George asked, "What's going on?"

The Colonel said, "They took Elvis to the hospital because he had a stroke.

"Whoa! What are you going to do now, Colonel? "

The Colonel responded, "Why I'll just go right on managing him!"

The Colonel calls and gets Tom Hulett at Concerts West in L.A on the phone.

"Good afternoon Colonel, how are you?"

"Hello Tom, I'm fine, but I just got off the phone with Joe Esposito. Elvis has been taken to the hospital."

"Damn! What happened? Is he OK?"

"Well, he's had a stroke and as of now he is out of commission, and will be for quite some time. No more shows until he gets better. We're cancelling tomorrow night's show and the rest of the tour. I need to get hold of the venues for the tour and inform them right away. If you need more information you can get the details from Joe yourself. He is in his office at Graceland right how. Get him to give you the press release they have already put together."

Tom's brain goes into neutral for moment and he asks the only thing that comes to mind. "Wow, cancelling the tour on such short notice?"

"Well, what the hell do you expect me to do, Tom?" Colonel Parker yells at Tom. "There is nothing else we can do. It has to be done!"

"Oh, I understand that Colonel, it's just such a surprise. I'll get on it right away."

"Do what you have to do," the Colonel tells Tom a little more calmly but with stern authority. "Call Joe and talk to him for more information," the Colonel hangs up before Tom can say goodbye.

The Colonel dials the phone again, placing a call to Pat Kelleher at RCA Records.

"Hello Colonel, how are you today?"

"I'm not doing too well, Pat. I just got off the phone with Joe Esposito and he told me that Elvis has been hospitalized with a stroke."

"Oh my God, Colonel, how bad is he?"

The Colonel goes into all the details again and tells Pat to contact Joe for his version of the press release.

"I'll talk to Joe and then put out our release. I'll take care of that right away."

"Listen Pat, I'm coming into New York in the morning and I want to meet with you and make sure we have merchandise available."

Pat tells the Colonel, "Let me know when you get into the city, we'll send a car for you and be ready to meet. I'll have everything organized. Believe me nothing will fall through the cracks."

"Ok, I'll call you when I get in. I want RCA to get ready for sales to go through the roof. I want you to triple the inventory you have in the warehouse, because you know we will get all kinds of air play. And, I'm not just talking about Top 40 radio playing the Boy's music. Major media will pick up on this story and there will be weeks of free publicity for us. I don't want you to miss any sales while this is in the public eye."

"I'll take care of it as soon as we hang up, Colonel. I'll get the pressing plants going 24 hours a day to make sure we have enough product to cover all the bases. At least this time we won't have to lease production time from other label's plants, like we did when "Heart Break Hotel' came out.

"Seriously, Colonel, I'm sorry to hear about Elvis. If there is anything I or the company can do, just let me know."

"I'll keep you informed and if there is anything we need, I'll let you know."

"We'll do whatever it takes from this end." Pat said, "Please give Elvis our best wishes and we hope that he has a speedy recovery."

"Thanks Pat, I'll be in Memphis tomorrow night and pass along your good wishes to Elvis. I have things to do so I'll see you in the morning."

~ * ~

Meanwhile, Tom Hulett calls Joe at Graceland. Tom says in a subdued voice, "I just got off the phone with the Colonel. I understand that Elvis has had a stroke. He asked me to call you for more information about what's going on. I need to

46

put together a press release making an announcement from our office."

"Sure thing, Tom. Ok, let's see. It should be short and to the point. Let me give you what I wrote out for Al to read at the hospital. Vernon basically just read the same statement here at Graceland." Joe then reads to Tom the statement he had prepared and adds, "Tom you should mention that the tour has been cancelled in what you put together."

"Yes, I'll do that and I may change some of the wording but I'll get the point across."

"I know you'll do a fine job, you always do. I know that Elvis and Vernon are thankful for your help as always Tom."

"Sure, that's no problem. You know that Elvis is my favorite client. I'll do whatever I can. Just keep me in the loop."

"I sure will, Tom."

Tom asks, "Has Priscilla been called yet?"

"Yes, I talked to her about an hour ago. She is in L.A. and will be coming back here in a few days. She was concerned about Lisa Marie, but I assured her that she is all right. It would be like Elvis is off on tour and everyone else is here for Lisa Marie. But, we want her to be able to see her dad as soon as she can, for both their sakes."

"I'll give Pricilla a call and see how she is doing. If there is something I can do I'd be glad to take care of it for her."

"Thanks again, Tom."

"All right then, let me get going on this right away. I'll talk to you later, Joe."

Joe remembers that the flight crew is getting the *Lisa Marie* ready to take Elvis and his entourage to Portland tonight. He picks up the phone and makes another phone call to Elwood at the airport to let him know the change in plans. "Hello, Elwood, its Joe."

"Yes, Joe. Do you have the guest list?"

"No I don't, we have a change of plans," He then fills Elwood in on the news.

"I'll have the crew stand down and wait to hear what to do next."

"Thanks Elwood, I'll stay in touch. Let the other guys know, will you?"

"I sure will Joe, take care."

Joe takes a deep breath and rubs his face and eyes with his hands. He's realizing how this day is taking its toll but knows he has to keep pushing. Joe knows that I need him more than ever. He will do whatever it takes to make things go well for the man who is his boss and, more importantly, his friend.

After taking another deep breath Joe calls Al at the hospital. Once he gets through, Al answers, "Hello Joe, how are you holding up?"

"It's been crazy here. I've been on the phone with Colonel Parker, Priscilla, Elwood, and Tom from Concert West. And…Vernon had to lie down after reading the statement because he couldn't handle the stress. So, how is Elvis doing?"

"They have taken him up to the 12th floor and put him in a private room. He's stabilized and they tell me he is resting comfortably now."

"Well thanks for staying there, Al," Joe says. "Can you get the room across the hall from his?"

"Yeah, I'm sure I can, why?"

"I just want to make sure that the fans, or more importantly, reporters, can't get to Elvis."

"The security here is pretty good. They have the place pretty well locked down, Joe."

"All right then. Do you and Charlie want to go home and get some rest?"

"No, I think I'll stay. I'll let Charlie know and see if he wants to go home. But I think he's going to want to do the same. If not, I'll send him home,"

"You and Charlie have been a big help today. Thanks so much."

"Sure. You know Joe, we are all brothers and we will do whatever we need to for the King."

"All right then, I'll see you and Charlie there tomorrow morning."

"OK, till then."

~ * ~

Bob Ford, the good looking reporter for WHBQ-TV is standing at the makeshift news set outside the emergency room entrance at Baptist Memorial Hospital. Looking into the TV camera Bob makes this announcement:

"Late this afternoon, Elvis Presley was brought here to Baptist Memorial Hospital. We haven't had any word since the statement that was given out earlier to inform us that Elvis has had a stroke. Other than that, we don't know what the King's condition is.

"What we have learned is that the concert tour that was to start tomorrow in Portland, Maine has been cancelled. As soon as we get more details we'll pass it along to you.

"Reporting from Baptist Memorial, this is Bob Ford saying good evening from WHBQ-TV."

Chapter 6

It's early in the morning. Dr. Francisco comes into my room with Marion Cocke, a registered nurse and the unit supervisor. Dr. Nick first requested Marion to do private duty care for me here at Baptist Memorial Hospital during a previous stay back in the second week of January 1975. Later, Dr. Nick also requested she become my personal nurse at Graceland, even though she was still fulfilling her duties at Memorial. Marion refused to accept pay for her private duty nursing. She said that everything she did for me was because she wanted to.

I have thanked Marion several times over the years; once giving her gold filigreed cross with 13 diamonds and flecks of black onyx. She tried to refuse the gift but I said, "Yes, ma'am, this is for you," and put it around her neck.

The last time I checked in here at Baptist Memorial Hospital, I told Marion, "I've ordered you a new car.

Marion told me "That's really nice of you Elvis, but I don't need a new car."

"Well, it will be here tomorrow whether you need it or not." As promised, the next day I told Marion to look out the window where she saw a white 1976 Gran Prix. I was standing there next to her, dangling the keys from my hand. Marion grabbed the keys and went racing down stairs to see the new car I had bought for her.

As Dr. Francisco and Marion enter my room, they find me semi-awake. I am pale and look tired; the expression in my eyes reflects my questions and concerns. "Good morning," Dr. Francisco says in a soft voice, so as not to startle me.

"What, um… oh… hi, Doc," I say, trying to focus on Dr. Francisco and also noticing my old friend Miss Marion, as I was in the habit of addressing her.

Dr. Francisco remarks, "Well you seem to be doing a little better than when we saw you yesterday."

"I remember… um… something about… riding… in ah… ambulance. I remember… being… ah… in the… emergency… room?" I am having trouble getting the words out.

Dr. Francisco sees that I am trying to remember.

"Yes, you had quite a day yesterday. Once you were stabilized we brought you up here to the 12th floor," says the doctor.

"I'm not… in Portland? I guess… the show… um… has been… canceled?"

"Yes, but that was up to your people to deal with. My main job is to get you better," Dr. Francisco says.

"Where are… um… my guys?"

"Al and Charlie are here. They spent the night across the hall from you and I guess everyone else is back at Graceland," The doctor continues, with obvious concern, "So how are you feeling this morning?"

"Slow… and ah… sluggish. Hungry… and ah… sounds… like I'm… um… having trouble… talking," I slur.

"After examining you, it appears that you have had a stroke."

"Is that… why um… my right arm... ah… doesn't seem… to um… do what… I want it… to do?"

"Yes. You are lucky the EMT's got you here as soon as they did, otherwise you might have made the trip to the morgue instead," the doctor says patting me on the shoulder.

"Was… I… um… that bad?" I ask.

"Yes, I'm afraid so, but we have you stabilized now and it's up to you to keep yourself that way."

I reflect a moment on what Dr. Francisco has told me. "I… um… think you're… right Doc. This is… ah… big… wakeup… call …for me."

The doctor nods, "I'm going to have a physical therapist work with you later on today, to help with your bed mobility, sitting and standing and to check your balance."

"K… Doc… um… how bad… am I?" I want to know.

The doctor rubs his chin. "It's hard to say yet. We will be doing a series of tests to determine your level of ability. I'll also have the physical therapist work with you on your upper extremities for weakness, and to check your motor control and the muscle tone in your arms. What we don't know yet, is if you have any problems in your lower torso and extremities."

A worrisome thought penetrates my foggy brain... "Ah… you don't… know… um… if I… can walk?" I ask concerned.

Dr. Francisco slightly shrugs his shoulders, and tries for a reassuring tone. "You might need a walker or a cane for stability if you have a problem walking."

"Doesn't… um… sound good. How long… ah… to recover?"

"That depends on how much damage has been done by the stroke. The rest is up to you, the most important thing of all is how hard you are willing to work at getting back into shape. I'm making a guess right now, but depending on what the test show it could be a year or more."

I draw in a deep, ragged breath, and let out a long sigh. "Well Doc… um… that's not ah… very pretty picture… ah… I have… ah lot… um… hard work… ahead… ah me."

I'll have the speech therapist come in as soon as she can make some time, but it won't be too long." Dr. Francisco pauses, "Do you have any questions for me before I go?"

"No… I think… um… you have… told me… enough… ah… for now… um… let's… see how… treatments go."

"Okay then, I guess that's it for now. They're going to be serving breakfast soon."

"Thanks… for… um… coming, Doc." I manage a tight lopsided smile. "Now… we have… um… business… out of… the way… ah… how are… you… Miss Marion?"

Marion is dressed in her perfectly starched and pressed white uniform, with white shoes and cap. "I'm doing fine, Babe." She smiled, using her nickname for me.

"Ah… how's… Bob?" I ask, referring to Marion's husband.

"He's doing fine also, thanks. But I'm so sorry to see you in this condition. Like Dr. Francisco said, with your help, Babe, we should be able to get you back to prime health," she lays a reassuring hand on my arm and gives me another smile.

"With… your um… help… I can… make ah… comeback… ah… more important… I want to… um… stay… that way."

Marion attempts to enlighten me, gently. "Babe, this is going to be a team effort. The doctors and the therapists are all going to work together right alongside you to help you get back again, just like 'Humpty Dumpty, all together!"

Dr. Francisco says, "Okay, rest for now. As I said, breakfast will be served soon. The physical therapist will be coming in later this morning to evaluate you and I'll see you again this afternoon."

"Thanks Doc… ah... see you… later… too… Miss Marion," I stutter as Dr. Francisco and Marion leave the room. Marion waves goodbye.

~ * ~

55

Larry, who doesn't waste any words, arrives at my hospital room to find me awake, with an IV stuck in my arm. "Man, you look a mess!"

Larry Geller, born August 8, 1939 in Elmira, New York began his association with me in Los Angles in 1964, as my personal hairstylist. Over the years, as our friendship grew, he became my confidant and spiritual mentor. From countless personal appearances, hundreds of concert engagements, to multiple Las Vegas appearances, Larry's always been by my side. He was the one who groomed me into the image of "The King."

Larry's responsibility goes beyond the caring for the outer me. Because Larry has been on his spiritual path for most of his life, he has become something of a spiritual guide for me. He has my sacred trust of nurturing and guiding the inner me, the soul and spirit of me. He realized that I am obsessed with religion and psychic powers, including my own. He brought into my life books and ideas that have expanded the way I think. We have shared in countless intimate conversations over the course of our time together. Larry has become my spiritual Guru. I gave him the nick name of "The Swami."

Larry says to me, "Boy, I'm glad to see you alive."

"You're not… the… um… only one… son," giving my little laugh.

"Yeah, I'm told the stroke has affected the speech area of your brain. Seems like your mind is sharp but it's hard for you to get the words out."

"Yeah… having… ah… hard time… talking. My… right hand… um… arm… not doing… good… either."

Larry pulls up a chair close to the bed then says encouragingly, "Rehab will help improve your speech. It will help with your arm, also. They are doing marvelous thing in rehab these days. You should get most, if not all of your mobility back."

"Um… doctors… tell me… ah… it's going… take… ah… long… um…time… um… to recover."

"Yeah, you're going to need some time off to take care of yourself, you know. We talked about you going back to Hawaii to get off the drugs, but now you're going to have to do rehab to get yourself back together. Looks like Spirit has arranged for you to do it all at one time."

I attempt to raise my head from the pillow to tell Larry, "Yeah… um… your… right… bout that. Ah… Larry… you ah… will…. Understand... I saw… ah… white light… um… when on… bathroom floor… ah… was… wondering… was I to… ah… make it… or not. I heard… um… Mama's voice… ah… she was… talkin'… to me… She said… um… "It's not… your time… um… son. You're not… done… yet… ah… you must… go… um… back… finish… your work."

"That's truly amazing, Elvis. There are a lot of people that step into the light and then get sent back to finish what they came here to do when their works not done."

I nod, wincing as it hurts. "Um… I… know… have read… ah… bout that… with… other… um… people. Yeah… guess… wasn't…

my time… um… would have… gone to… ah… light … the other side. Comfort… ah… to hear… Mama's voice… and… what she said."

"I'm sure it was. This was an early wake up call for you, my friend, and it's time for you to decide how you want your future to go."

I am confused, "Larry… ah… what is… my work? What… am I… supposed… to be doing…? Ah… been on tour… years… um… making records… movies. Ah… feel I've been… um… on ah… merry-go-round."

Larry nods. "I understand."

"They… tell me… um… the medicine… ah… I was… taking… is what… um… caused ah… stroke. Want to… get… off… ah… pills." I admit to Larry, almost pleading with him. "I know… ah… got to… diet… um… get back… in shape."

"That sounds like a good place to start. You need to focus on getting back to your 'karate kid' self again. It will be a step by step process, and I know you can do it."

"I was… um… thinking this… ah… before yesterday… um… I want to… live… um… in Hawaii… um… get me…ah… back together… yeah… um… take just… ah… couple… um… Mafia… with me."

Larry agrees, "Yes, you need to do the rehab and focus on yourself. And yes, you don't need a bunch of the Mafia hanging around watching you get better. You only need professional help to get your health back. You need to go within, and clean out your system. That means just like you said, getting off the pills.

"I think Hawaii is a great place to get yourself back together. You're also going to have to change your diet. You can eat a lot better there by getting fresh organic food from the land and you've always loved the islands."

I attempts a smile which droops on the right, "I want… um… to work… on… um… an album… when… ah… over there… new… um… song…writers… producer… ah… create… new sound. This time… um… want to ah… put together… ah… 'World… Come Back… Tour.' Yeah… tour the… world! Can't do… that… um… while Colonel… is… manager." I struggle to get the words out, and it takes a lot out of me. I close my eyes briefly.

"That sound like a good idea, Elvis. Breathe new life into your performances. Take the time to put together a world class tour and a whole new stage show. You know what I mean. New lights and sound system would completely revamp the show. Larry pauses, thinking. "But you've been with the Colonel for a long time and he has done a lot for your career."

"Yeah… you know… we… um… have… our problems. Part is… ah… my fault… Colonel has… um… over… stepped… bounds ah… many times… ah… not delivered… um… a good script."

Larry nods and waits for me to continue.

"I'm, um… to make… one… ah… more… great movie. Yeah, ah… to be… ah… serious actor… um… like… um… Marlin… um… Brando… James… Dean… ah… Paul… Newman. Tired of making… um… cookie cutter… movies… um… just to… keep the… ah… Colonel happy."

59

"You're holding yourself up to pretty high standards there buddy," Larry says with a grin. "But, you're a great enough actor to be able to pull it off. It sounds like you have your future life pretty much figured out. Could it possibly be that is what your work is? That is what you need to finish doing."

"Yeah… um… you're right… sounds like… ah… plan; need to get… my… um… health back… ah… to do… what… um… talkin' about."

Larry sits up straight in his chair. "I know you can do it! I also know that you voraciously read the books I bring you on religion, spirituality and mysticism, so I brought you a new book, "Cheiros Book of Numbers," Larry says pulling it out of his bag.

I smile my, now lopsided, smile, "Thanks… ah… I'm looking… into… um… numerology."

"I know that, that's why I got it for you. It's a pretty good book."

"I need… to figure… um… out. Got to be… a reason... um… why… ah… I chose… to be… Elvis Presley. What's… his plan… um… for me? What… am I… um… supposed… to do?" I am having trouble getting out the words, but Larry is patient.

"That's what your search is all about my friend, that's what your search is all about. It may take you a lifetime to figure that out. You're in God's hands, as always."

I close my eyes again, "You're… um… right… Larry… I'm… um… tired now… ah…

Thanks for… um… the book." I feel like drifting off.

Larry nods and grips my hand. "Oh that's alright; I'd better get going."

"We'll talk… um… soon. Um… you're not… going back… to… um… L.A. yet… are you?"

Larry shakes his head. "No, I'll be here for a while."

"Good… I… ah… want to… talk… again, um… soon."

"I'll see you again."

The encounter with Larry has tired me out so I drift off to sleep as Larry leaves the room.

Twenty minutes later an orderly comes into my room with breakfast. A thin young black man with a worshipful expression, says "Excuse me Mr. Presley, your breakfast is ready."

I slowly open his eyes and take a moment to focus on the young man standing there at attention, with a tray in his hands, as if he was standing in line for chow in the Army. "Hello… soldier," I greet the young man.

"Hello, sir," the young man replies with great respect.

"What… have they… um… prepared… for me… this morning?" attempting a jovial tone.

"It's scrambled eggs, dry toast and orange juice sir."

"What's… your um… name… soldier?" Elvis asks.

"William, sir."

"William… um… put down… the tray… ah… on the…um… table… I'll get to… it… in ah… minute."

"Yes sir," and William, puts the tray down on the over bed table and pushes the table over to my bedside.

"Can you… um… help me… sit up?"

"I'm not supposed to do that, sir," William answers.

"Just find… um… the controls… to raise… um… my head… ah… up… so I can… see um… what I'm… eating."

William gives me a nervous look.

"If I could… um… find… the controls… ah… I can… push… the button… myself. Ah… will you… um… help… me find… ah… the controls?"

William looks around the room as if to see if anyone else is in the room. He comes over to the right side of the bed and finds the controls and pushes the button up so the head of my bed rises up into a sitting position.

"Thanks… um… William… good job. I'm going… to… ah… promote you… to… um… adjusting beds… and… ah… delivering… um… food trays," I say, in my usual kidding manner.

William gives me a shy grin, "Thank you sir."

I try to remove the cover from the eggs with my right hand and realize I can't do it. "Looks like… I'm ah… going to… become… a lefty." So, I use my left hand and remove the cover. "Ah… looks like… um… military food," I complain.

"That's what we're serving this morning sir," William apologizes.

"Guess… that's um… what… I'll be… having then." I reply while trying to pick up my fork with my right hand. I realize again this is going to be a problem. "Damn! I really… am… um… going to… have… to become… ah… lefty." It's awkward but I manage to get two small bites of eggs down using my left hand. I have a hard time swallowing the bites because they tend go down the wrong way, causing me to choke and cough on the slippery morsels.

I find it impossible to spread the strawberry jam on my toast so I just left it on my plate.

William says "I have to go and make my rounds to the other patients. See you, sir," William says as he leaves the room.

"Thanks… for your… um… help… um… William. See yah."

I then struggle with using my fork left handed and get about three more small bites of egg down.

"Hey there, Mr. Presley," announces a gorgeous young woman who introduces herself as A.E. Tucker, "I'm your physical therapist." A.E., a five foot ten inch, slender young woman, with long straight blond hair, well-endowed and with great legs comes walking into my room. As my gaze locks with her deep blue eyes, I realize, they're as blue as mine. I am arrested by the beauty of this 29 year old Scandinavian. The sexual energy that she brings into the room has my interest peaked even in my present condition. At least that part of me is still working.

I say, "You going… to um… make my… arm… work again?"

"We will give it our best," she replies.

I smile at my new therapist with a twinkle in my eye.

"Dr. Francisco, has asked me to evaluate the level of affect the stroke has had on you and to determine your degree of weakness. Then we'll begin to treat the musculoskeletal deficits that the stroke has created for you. The most important goal is to have you resume as many, if not all of your pre-stroke activities and functions as possible."

Nodding my head, I understand, yet I am quite distracted by A.E.'s sexual energy.

"Your stroke may have involved permanent loss of some brain cells but a total return of your pre-stroke status may be a realistic goal. And, in your case, a return to an independent life is very possible.

"It's my job to help you become independent in your daily living activities. I'll begin by evaluating your ability to control the movement you have in your arms and legs."

A.E. pauses and, consults her chart. "First, I'll test your sitting and standing balance. Then we'll work on your bed mobility, transferring you from the bed to a chair and back. Once you've mastered that we will begin to ambulate you with the aid of a walker or a cane as needed."

She explains the different treatments that will be used, such as Proprioceptive Neuromuscular Facilitation (PNF), Movement Therapy, Compensatory Approach, Rehabilitation Approach, Adaptation Approach and Cognitive Behavioral Approach.

I nod, and think, "If I have to undergo all this therapy, I'm going to enjoy looking at A.E. while I'm doing it."

A.E. continues, "By using these different treatments and following the strategies we develop for you, we will set you up for a quicker return to your normal, self-reliant lifestyle."

"You're very… ah… intense," I say smiling.

"Yes, I am. I know what you need to do and I'll show you how to do it."

"Okay… A.E., um… I'm in… your hands… ah… I look… forward… to um… being… in them. Can't… ah… use my… right hand… um… arm… don't have… um… strength to ah..." I use my left hand to pat my almost useless right arm.

A.E. reaches over and lays her hand on top of mine and softly says, "That's why I'm here, to help you gain the strength back in that arm and hand. We'll get you back to using it as if nothing has happened."

"You really… think… um… I can?"

"Yes, from what I've read in your case file, you've had a mild stroke. Believe me; I've seen people in a lot worse shape than you are in. This is your first stroke and I hope your last, and this is all new to you."

"Yes... but... I um... have this... stutter."

"Well, Cathy, your speech therapist will work with you on that."

"I'm... having... um... trouble... swallowing. Eating... my eggs... this morning... um... it... went down... um... the wrong... pipe... made... me cough."

"That's called 'dysphagia' and Cathy will help you with that too,"

I nod, as she continues. "What I'm going to focus on is your muscle coordination, both basic and your fine motor skills. We need to reteach you new ways to performing the basic activities, like eating, dressing yourself, moving from place to place, and self-grooming."

"I usually... have... um... help... with that."

A.E. raises her eyebrows. "You do?"

"Well... not always." I say, embarrassed. "I do... um... before... a show, ah... but... at home... um... I usually... take care... of... um... myself. I'm willing... um... to let... you... teach me... how... to get... undressed... and... ah... dressed." I say suggestively, with a smile on my face.

But, A.E. doesn't seem amused. "I am going to ignore that statement. Let's stick to the work we're here to do, thank you," she says sternly.

My attention is distracted by another attractive young woman as she walks into the room. Her chestnut hair is done up in a bun and she has a great smile. Cathy Robitaille is a speech-language pathologist from the Baptist Memorial Hospital

Rehabilitation Unit. "Hello A.E., how's it going?" Cathy greets her.

A.E. turns, "Hi Cathy, how are you doing?"

"I'm doing great, thanks. Is this our new patient?"

I speak up, "Yes… um… I guess… I am."

"My name is Cathy, and I'll be doing your speech therapy while you are here at Memorial." Cathy says standing by the bed, "It's an honor to meet you, Mr. Presley."

I smile at her. "You can… call me… ah… Elvis."

"Okay, Elvis."

"I don't want to rush you two, but, have you done your evaluation and explained the protocol to Elvis yet?" Cathy says looking at A.E.

"I've informed him of what I expect of him, to get the results we are looking for." A.E. says with a raised eyebrow as her blue eyes penetrate mine once again. "I'll let you take over so you can work your magic on him. I'll come back later and do the evaluation."

"While we were talking, he mentioned that he was having trouble swallowing when he was eating his scrambled eggs this morning. I told him that you would work with him on that."

"Don't worry, we will address that," Cathy tells me.

"Elvis, I'll be back later this afternoon to work with you. And, Cathy, I'll see you later and we'll talk then."

"Okay, sweetie, see you later," Cathy replies as A.E. picks up her chart and heads out the door.

"So you're having troubles swallowing?" Cathy inquires.

"Yes… when I… um… swallow… seems to… go… down… ah… the wrong…um… pipe… makes me… cough."

"Okay, you still have some eggs here, so I want you to take a bite while I observe the muscles around your mouth and throat to see how they've been affected. This will help me to understand what is happening when you swallow," Cathy explains.

I pick up my fork with my left and fumble to take a small bite of egg. I chew a few times and begin to swallow; once again, I choke and cough up about half of the eggs.

"Okay, you all right?" Cathy asks, as she pats me on the back.

"This is… one way… ah… to… lose weight," I joke.

Cathy directs me how to do three exercises. They will strengthen my throat muscles, which will allow me to eat soft foods without choking. As she is teaching me the Shaker Exercise she says, "This will improve your ability to swallow."

Next, Cathy teaches me the Mendelsohn Maneuver exercise. "This is a simple exercise that will improve your swallowing reflex," she explains. "I want you to use a different head and mouth position to help you swallow safely. It will help the swallowing muscles work better."

She writes a note in my chart. "This last exercise is called the Effortful Swallow. The exaggerated retraction of the tongue will increase your tongues driving force," Cathy says as she directs me to squeeze hard with my throat and neck muscles while I swallow. "This helps to get food past the uvula," After working on these exercised until she felt I was comfortable doing them, Cathy moves on to a new skill building set.

"Now, I want to address your communication skills. It appears you have what is call dysarthria, which is causing the dysphagia or difficulty swallowing and dysphasia or speech difficulty. Are you experiencing the muscles in your face, lips, and tongue feeling heavy or sluggish? You tend to run out of breath when you talk, and I'm sure your voice sounds different to you. Have you noticed that you are drooling because of the muscle weakness in your face and mouth?"

I blink at the rapid fire questions and nod yes.

"While I have been here talking with you, I've been listening to your speech. I have observed how your muscles are moving and how they affect your voice. We're going to have to retrain the breath pattern of your speech so you can talk in full sentences again."

"What about… um… people who… ah… can help… me… ah… when you're… not here?"

Cathy gives me a quick nod as she slides her notes into a pocket of her white lab coat. "I can talk to your family members, and other caretakers to give them tips on how to help you with your exercises."

"You'll have… to talk… um… to… my dad… and ah… members of… ah… Memphis Mafia."

"Yes, I'd be glad to talk to all of them. I would like to work with them as soon as possible to follow through with these techniques I have taught you today."

"Talk… to Joe… ah… he… can work… out ah… schedule… for you… to meet… everyone."

She glances at me with a question in her dark eyes. "Who is Joe?"

"My… number one… um… guy. Joe… um… Esposito… ah… he'll… be here… um… today. I'll… have him… ah… look… you up… to get… um… your… information."

"Okay, I look forward to meeting him. This has been a good first session. I'll come back tomorrow, and we'll continue to work on your swallowing exercises and your speech pattern. Is there anything else we need to work on?"

"No… I think… that's it… um… thanks Cathy. I'll be…um… sure… to do… the exercises,"

Cathy leaves a sheaf of papers on my bedside table. "Here are copies of the instructions for the exercises I've given you," Cathy says, then slips out of the room.

I, lie back with a deep sigh, feeling tired, drift off into a restful nap.

~ * ~

As Cathy walks down the hall toward the nurse's station, she sees Marion and A.E. talking to

70

each other. "Well, hello ladies! What are we talking about?" Cathy asks as she reaches them.

Marion answers, "A.E. was telling me about the sexual energy between her and Elvis she was feeling when she was in the room with him."

A.E. tells the women, "He isn't as beautiful as he once was, but he still has the good looks and the sexual appeal that he has always had even in the condition he in now. Wow. I never expected I would ever have the chance to work with him."

"I know what you mean. Trying to keep your professionalism is difficult when around Elvis. Besides rich and famous, he's so good looking," Cathy tells them.

Marion cuts in, "I know that when Elvis was here about four months ago… Let's see that would have made it ah… early April, I think. He was real disappointed when the remainder of that tour had to be canceled. The nurses were sneaking in his room every chance they got to try to cheer him up! Or, should I say, to take a peek at him?"

Cathy grins and claps her hands. "Well I guess we have had our dream come true. We have met Elvis Presley!"

"Yes, but I've got to keep a lid on this sexual tension that's between us. I mean it's not just me. He definitely let me know that he felt it too. I know that he's engaged, but he's Elvis, and if I wasn't working on him, I'd be banging him or at least giving him a blow job him right now," A.E. says with a smirk.

Marion and Cathy giggle in surprise at A.E. bold comment.

Then Marion asserts her professionalism. "Well, we need to keep our professional decorum, ladies."

"Can you imagine how many of my friends and other people are going to ask me about Elvis? You know, what kind of guy he is, how he's feeling and if he's going to be alright?" A.E. says as she puts on more lip gloss. "Too bad we can't talk about it outside the hospital!"

Cathy nods in agreement. "You're right and I'll do my best to keep it professional."

A.E. says, "How about giving him a hand job, do you think that would be alright?" She says laughing, "No. No. I'm just kidding; I'll keep myself under control." They all laugh again.

They bid each other goodbye and get back to work with their other patients.

~ * ~

Joe is sitting in his office at Graceland drinking a cup of coffee he picked up from Nancy on his way through the mansion. He calls the hospital and hears the now familiar voice of the receptionist at the other end of the phone.

"Good morning, Baptist Memorial Hospital. How may I help you?"

"Hell. This is Joe Esposito. Will you put me through to Marion Cocke on the 12th floor, please?"

The receptionist cheerfully replies, "Yes, I can. Just a moment, please."

"Hello, This Is Marion. How may I help you?"

"Good afternoon, Marion, it's Joe."

"Hello Mr. Esposito, how are you?"

"I'm fine thanks. But, I want to know how Elvis is doing this morning."

"What I can tell you is that Elvis slept well through the night. He has seen Dr. Francisco, his physical therapist and the speech therapist. Also, Larry Geller was in this morning. He is resting comfortably right now."

"Good, that's all I needed to know. I'll be in later on today to see him and I'll check in with you too, Marion."

"That would be fine, Mr. Esposito. I'll look forward to seeing you then."

Joe thanks Marion for all her help. As they end the conversation, he wonders if she is sugar-coating the truth about Elvis. He thinks, "I'll just have to see for myself."

Chapter 7

The usual crowd of customers is eating their breakfast at the south east corner of 540 S. Main Street and G. E. Patterson Avenue. This is the Arcade Restaurant, the oldest café in Memphis, established in 1919. Patrons are sitting on black Naugahyde seats, as they eat from mismatched plates using mismatched silverware. The waitresses seem to glide across the black and white square tile, moving between the kitchen, and the Formica topped tables and booths.

At the booth near the front window, a waitress serves plates of food to a family of four as they look out on the bright sunny day in downtown Memphis. The smell of fried eggs, bacon, grits, toast and coffee fills the air. This particular mix creates a wonderful aroma that gives that down home feeling to all who eat there.

The room grows quiet as they listen to the breaking news update from the radio playing behind the counter. "Hello, this is George Klein reporting from Graceland for WHBQ-AM. The "King", Elvis Presley, was taken to Baptist Memorial Hospital yesterday afternoon. He was admitted after suffering a stroke at Graceland.

"The word this morning is that Elvis has slept comfortably through the night. He is conscious, and the prognosis is that the "King" will eventually be fine and will hopefully be able to leave the hospital in a few days. The concert tour that was scheduled to start today has been cancelled until further notice. Even though many fans across the country are disappointed, good wishes for the "King's" speedy recovery are pouring in. That's all for now from here at Graceland. This is George Klein reporting, so it's back to our studios at WHQB-AM."

~ * ~

Colonel Parker arrives at Graceland in a cab, wearing his normal loud Hawaiian print shirt and chewing his trademark cigar. As he walks up the stairs to the mansion, Billy is coming out the door. "Oh. Hello, Colonel. You're here."

"Hello, Billy. How are things here?"

"It's been crazy."

"How's the boy doing?"

"I haven't seen Elvis since yesterday morning, but Joe talked to Marion today and she said he was doing well for what he has gone through. Larry paid him a visit this morning and I am going over this afternoon to see him."

"Larry was there and saw Elvis? Was there anyone else in the room with him?"

"I don't know, Colonel."

"I'll be going over to the hospital as soon as I finish talking to Vernon." The Colonel says walking up the stairs, "Where is he?"

"Oh, he's in his office. I'll take you back to see him."

Billy and Colonel Parker walk through the mansion on their way to Vernon's office. Just before they reach the back door, the Colonel sticks his head into the kitchen on the left to say, "Hello, Mary."

Mary Jenkins started working for me as a maid in 1963. She later took on the role as cook and has become part of my extended family.

She returns his greeting and asks, "Hello Colonel, have you seen Mr. Elvis yet?"

"No, I'm going to talk to Vernon first, and then I'm going over to the hospital. I'll see you later, Mary, and let you know how he is doing" the Colonel says as he and Billy head out the back door.

As they enter the office, Billy says, "Hey Vernon, the Colonel's here to see you."

"How are you holding up, Vernon?" The Colonel says as he walks past Billy. Billy goes to his office to leave the two men to have their conversation in private.

"I'm doing better. It looks like Elvis is going to be alright."

"I'm so glad to hear that. I know it was quite a shock to you. I'm going over to see the boy right after I finish here."

"Well, Colonel, the biggest thing now, after Elvis' health, is dealing with all the promoters. They are going to be worried about their financial out lay and the sudden lack of return on their investment."

The Colonel shakes his head, not wanting to discuss these details with Vernon. "Tell them to call me and I'll handle their issues. We need to find out how long the boy is going to be out and when he will be able to start touring again."

Vernon has a doubtful look on his face. "The way the doctors are talking it's going to be at least a year or more before Elvis will be able to tour again."

"Damn, that's a long time. I guess we're just going to have to deal with it. I'll put the promoters off and make them understand that it's going to be awhile before the boy can be back on the road again."

Vernon nervously rubs his hands together, "I've been thinking about that. We're going to have to lay off the TCB band and the Sweet Inspirations. We just can't afford to pay them while Elvis is in the hospital and during his long rehab."

"Yes I agree. I'll give the band and the support staff an indefinite layoff. What about the Memphis Mafia?"

"I think those boys are going to have to find real jobs, too. They can't keep hanging around Elvis while he's recovering," Vernon says with his head down looking for a list of employees on his desk. "But I don't want to do anything about that without talking to Elvis first." He says looking back up at the Colonel.

"Believe me I know what you mean. But, I'll be glad to see some of those boys go." Then the Colonel shifts his focus, "Now, Vernon, I spoke to Tom last night and told him to issue a press release that we were cancelling the tour."

"I forgot about him. I know I shouldn't have but with so much going on around here, I just forgot."

"That's why I'm here; to take care of things like that."

"Thanks for that, Colonel."

"That's alright," The Colonel's voice takes on a different tone. "Listen Vernon there is one more thing I want to discuss with you."

Vernon hesitates, "Oh yeah, what's that Colonel?"

"Since we've had to face this tragedy I was thinking you should sign over the control of Elvis' career to me. God forbid, if Elvis dies, I can take care of all his business affairs."

There is a long pause before Vernon answers the Colonel. "I don't know about that Colonel. I need to talk to Elvis and his attorney before I can do something like that."

"Well, you let me know and I can draw up the papers for you and Elvis to sign, if you think it's a good idea for me to handle his affairs on his passing."

"I'll have to let you know Colonel."

"OK. Is there anything else that we need to talk about before I go to see the boy?"

"No, I don't think so."

"Alright then, I guess that's it for now. Take care of yourself, Vernon. I'll talk to you again soon." The Colonel heads back to the mansion to get someone to take him to the hospital.

~ * ~

Bob Ford is outside the emergency room at the Baptist Memorial Hospital reporting to his TV fans. "This is Bob Ford from WHBQ-TV with a special report. I am here at the Baptist Memorial Hospital where Elvis Presley was admitted yesterday for what has been diagnosed as a stroke.

We now understand that the "King" is resting comfortably.

"Here outside the hospital, the crowd continues to grow with fans, well-wishers and reporters arriving from all over the country and the world. Security around the hospital has been increased to keep fans and the press from Elvis so that he may focus on his recovery.

"We have learned that as a result of the stroke, Elvis has some paralysis in his right arm and his speech has been affected. Doctors are saying that with time, Elvis will, more than likely, make a full recovery. We are also told that he should be able to tour again in the future.

That's all for now, from here at Baptist Memorial, so it's back to you in the studio, for WHBQ-TV this is Bob Ford reporting."

~ * ~

Ginger Alden was born November 13, 1956 in Memphis Tennessee. I met her father when he was serving as an induction officer when I joined the United States Army in 1958. Her family had been invited to join me at the fairgrounds for a night of fun before I was shipped out to Germany.

Terry Alden, Miss Tennessee, had once been a guest on George Klein's TV show, 'Talent Party'. While on the show she had specifically asked if she could be invited to a party at Graceland. In 1976, George remembered that wish and invited Terry to visit Graceland. Terry asked and was allowed to bring her two sisters, Rosemary and Ginger with her. That is when they were re-introduced to me. I found Ginger's warmth and innocence most alluring, even though she was only 20 and I was admittedly attracted to her.

The day after my stroke, Ginger and Terry are walking down the hall of the hospital to visit me. The strong smell of antiseptic and the polite quietness of the nurses walking past makes Ginger feel a little nervous. A disembodied voice announces, "Dr. Silverstein, paging, Dr. Silverstein, please report to the ER. Dr. Silverstein to the ER."

As they quietly enter my room, Ginger says in a timid, little voice, "Hello E. how are you feeling?"

I open my eyes, startled by the break of silence in my room and stare at my fiancé and her sister trying to recognize them. "Ah… hey… ah… Gingerbread."

Ginger is surprised by the sound of my voice, "What happened to your voice?"

"The stroke… um... interferes… ah… with my brain. Makes it… ah… difficult to… talk. It's called… um… aphasia… and causes my… um… speech difficult. Also… um… paralyzed… ah… my right… arm and… hand."

Ginger, scared that such a perfect man had turned into a sick person in a hospital bed looking weak and tired, asks, "Is it going to be like this forever?"

Ah… no… but, it's… going to take… ah… time… um… to recover."

Terry says, "Hi Elvis. Man, you gave my sister quite a scare."

I find this humorous, "I didn't… um… do it… on purpose."

"I know but, it was scary to find you on the floor."

"Yeah… it was… ah… pretty scary… for me… too."

"Are they taking good care of you here?" Ginger asks with concern on her pretty face.

"Yeah… they are… doing… um… what they… can. I hope… to… um… get out… of here… um… in ah… few days. Be good… to get… back… home," trying to reassure her.

Terry asks, "What kind of rehab do they have planned for you?"

"Have… um… already seen… physical therapist… and ah… speech therapist… this morning."

Ginger takes my hand to comfort me and asks, "What can I do for you, sweetie?"

"Ah… Ginger… ah… I've been… thinking," I say with heaviness in my heart as I look into Ginger eyes. "I have… to… um… turn… my life… around. And… ah… I need… to… make some… big… um… changes… in my… life."

I pull my hand out of Ginger's grasp. "I have… to… ah… get off… the pills… ah… they have… um… turned me… into… a fat… ah… middle aged… um… entertainer."

"Oh you're not fat, you're just getting older, but everyone does," Ginger says chuckling a little, "You're still a great looking guy."

"I've lost my… um…working man's… ethic… and humility. My…ah… audience… is beginning… to… um… talk… about… what could be… ah… wrong… with me. They're starting… to become… ah… outraged… at my… um… condition… and ah… performance. The Colonel has… ah… been on… me… um… about… the shows… not being… ah… what they… use… to be. You know… ah… Ginger… I've got to… change… um… all that… around."

Ginger says "I'm so glad to hear you talk like that, Elvis. You know I want the best for you. I'll do whatever you need to do to help you. Just tell me and I'll do it."

I lower my eyes and tell her with sorrow in my heart, "Ah… well… Ginger… you know… we were… going to… um… announce… our wedding… date… but "I can't…um… marry you."

"What!" Ginger exclaims, in shock, "You can't mean that, Elvis. I love you."

"Yes… I do… mean it," I say emphatically. "Ginger… you have… um… no idea… the changes… ah… I have to… go through…um… to get… back… where I… need… to be. I have… to… make… um… major changes… in… ah… my life… to get back… um… my health… and make… ah… strong career… come back. Ginger… I must… ah… walk… this path… on… my own!"

Ginger, in disbelief, "No Elvis, you can't mean this, I love you, and you love me. You're not thinking straight right now!"

"Yes… um… I'm sorry… I do… mean it. Ah… Ginger… you are… half… my age… and… ah… you need… someone… um… more you're… own age. Yes… I like … um… younger women… in… my life… ah… but… now's not… the time…

82

ah... to be... involved... with one. It's... not fair...
to you... um... or me. I almost... lost... my life!"
"I'm... so sorry... this is... how... it has... to be."

Terry interjects, "But Elvis you promised."

I glare at Terry, "You have... no right... to
tell... me... anything... This is... between...
Ginger... and me!" I raise my voice so loudly it
could be heard in the hallway.

Stunned, Terry just stands there like a deer in
the headlights with her mouth open. Just at this
moment Marion walks in to the room overhearing
the heated altercation that was going on. She takes
my arm to check my pulse and then checks my
blood pressure. Once she gets her readings, she
says, "Ladies, I think visiting time is over. It is
important that Elvis remain calm; his blood pressure
is elevated. So, you need to leave, now."

"Yes, please... um... leave, Terry... and
take... Ginger... with you. Ginger... we'll... um...
talk later.

"I know it's not over between us. I love you.
But Elvis, what am I supposed to do?" Ginger asks.

"You need... to... be gone...um... before... I
get... to Graceland. And... ah... you... can keep...
your engagement... ring."   Ginger tries to kiss
me goodbye, but I avoid her advance.

"Please... leave now."

With tears in her eyes Ginger turns to leave,
but not before saying, "Goodbye Elvis."

She is broken hearted and struggles to hold
back her tears. As she fumbles for a tissue in her
purse, her gaze falls upon the $40,000, 11½ carat

engagement ring on her left hand and she lets out a muffled sob. She quickly turns to leave the room with Terry trailing quickly behind her.

Marian asks me, with concern in her voice, "Are you okay?

"Yeah… um… I just… broke off… ah… my engagement… with Ginger. I have to… um… get… myself back… on track. Ah… I… don't have… um… enough energy… for her… too," I explain.

"Whatever you have to do, is what you have to do, Babe. I don't have a dog in this fight."

"Sorry you… had to… um… see that."

"We're like doctors, what we hear and see we keep to ourselves. You know I won't be telling anybody what happened here today, or any other day, during your stay here or at Graceland," Marion reassures me.

"Thank you… um… darlin'… I… appreciate… that."

"Your blood pressure seems to have come down a bit, so I'd better get back to the rest of my rounds. If you need anything just push this button." Marion reminds me.

"Before you go… would you… dial the phone… for me? I want… to talk… to my Daddy… at Graceland." Marion dials the number automatically and hands me the receiver. "Thanks again… um… see you… later," and she leaves the room.

Nancy picks up the phone, saying "Hello," and is delightfully surprised to hear my voice say, "Hello, Nancy."

"Oh, Mr. Elvis, it's so good to hear from you. You had us so worried," Nancy says.

"Thank you... Nancy... um... I need... to talk... to ah... Vernon, please."

Nancy, is startled by the changes in my voice, but doesn't say anything. "Yes sir, Mr. Elvis, I'll get Mr. Vernon for you," Nancy puts him on hold and calls Vernon's office. "Mr. Vernon, Mr. Elvis is on line two for you."

"Okay, Nancy, I'll take the call."

Vernon pushes the button on the phone for line two, "Hello, son, how are you?"

"It's been... one... heck... um... of a... day," It's good to hear my Daddy's voice.

"You sound different, how do you feel?" Vernon asks Elvis.

"I feel... sluggish... and ah... slow... um... my right... arm... and ah... hands... don't move... like they... should," I explain.

"They told me you are going to need physical and speech therapy. When will you meet with your therapists?"

"I met with... um... my speech... therapist and ah... my physical... therapist... earlier um... this morning. I have... exercises... to do, um... every day... several times... a day. Dr. Francisco... um... came by... to check... on me...too.

Ginger…and ah… Terry… came by too. Ah… Daddy… um… I broke off… the engagement… to, um… Ginger… this afternoon."

Vernon sounds surprised. "You broke off your engagement? Why, what happened?"

"I need… to turn… my life… around. Ah… this… is something… I have… to do… um… on my… own, Daddy… I need… to, um… go inside… myself… and ah… get straight. I need… to… um… lose weight… and get off… these… ah… uppers… and downers. Daddy," I confess.

"This is… ah… turning point… in… my life. It's… my second chance… that… um… God has… given me. There's… no reason… um… why… I shouldn't… do… ah… something good… for the… people… in the world. Right now… I don't… know… ah… what that… looks like… but… I need… to do… something."

"Well, I'm glad you're getting off the pills and I know that whatever you do, God is looking out for you, son. So, what about Ginger?" Vernon asks.

"I've asked… her to… um… leave Graceland… before I… ah… get back. I want you… to give… her… some money… um… so she can… make a… fresh start," Elvis says. "Give her… um… fifty… thousand dollars… to buy… ah… new house."

"Elvis, that's a lot of money! Are you sure you want to give her that much?" Vernon inquires.

"Yes… um… I owe her… that much… and, ah… I did… kind of… um… upset her life."

"Elvis you're going to have to cut back on spending so much money. If you're not going to be working for who knows how long, your income is going to drop seriously."

"Yes… I know… um… but that's… the least… ah… I can do… for her," I tell my dad. "Listen… Daddy, um… I've got… to go… ah… someone just… walked in."

"Alright son, I'll see you later tomorrow."

"Alright Daddy… um… see you… then… Goodbye,"

A while later, I wake from dozing to find A.E. standing at the foot of my bed, just looking at me with a smile on her face. I smile back at her with a Cheshire cat grin on my face.

Finally, I break the long silence, "Well… what are we… um… going to… do here?"

A.E. slowly runs the tip of her tongue over her pouty bottom lip as her mouth drops open in a seductive manner. She smiles with a twinkle in her eye, "I told you I would come back today."

"Yes… you did… young lady… yes… you did," I reply.

"So let's get to work."

Chapter 8

Billy and Colonel Parker arrive at the hospital to see me. They take the elevator to get to the 12th floor. As the doors open, the security guard stationed there asks the Colonel and Billy, "Where are you going?"

The Colonel answers abruptly, "I'm Colonel Parker, Elvis's manager. I'm here to see him."

"I'm sorry sir, can I see some identification, please?"

Before the Cornel can blow up, Al, having heard his voice, sticks his head out of his room. He quickly confirms the Cornel's identity to the security guard and goes back to his game of solitaire.

"See, Cornel. Nobody who shouldn't be here is going to get on the floor." says Billy.

"Come on Billy, let's go see Elvis." They head down the hall to my room. As they enter, Colonel Parker says, "Hello my boy, how are you feeling?"

"Oh, hi… ah… I've been… better… Colonel. It's nice… um… to see… you."

Billy interjects, "Hey Elvis. What happened? Did the racket ball game wear you out?"

"Hey Billy… um… no… but it's… sure good… to see… um… both you… guys."

"Now, Vernon says that it could take a year or more for you to recover. That's a long time to be out of work," the Colonel states with concern.

"Yeah… that's what… they, um… tell me. But… I was, um… out for… three years… in, ah… Germany. Hope… ah… I can… be back… quicker."

"We had deals in the works worth a lot of money. We're going to have to postpone those deals or cancel them all together."

"Well Colonel… um… I can't… honor them… now… ah... can I? We're just… going to… um… have to… give up… the money… ah… for now."

"Yes, that's a lot of money we both could have used. This one deal I've been working on was a guest shot on all three major network variety shows, plus two of your own TV specials, one on ABC and the other NBC.

I feel sorry about disappointing the Colonel but irritated at the mercenary priority he puts on everything. "Um… I can't… help that… now. I have… to recover, ah… from this… stroke."

Billy sensing my feelings says, "Colonel, Elvis can't honor those deals now, but in a year or so…"

"Shut up Billy!" Colonel Parker barks. "You have no idea of what it takes to put that kind of deal together, and all the people that are involved in the process."

I yell back, "Colonel… don't be… talking… to my… um… cousin… that way. Billy's… been… a big… ah… help to me… over… the years… um… and he… is family."

"Elvis, Billy has no idea about what it takes…"

I interrupt the Colonel, "That may be… um… the truth… but you… don't have to… ah… speak… to him… that way."

"Elvis, you don't have to stand up for me," says Billy.

"Ah… yes… I do… the, um… Colonel has… been riding… ah… rough shod… over… a lot of… the, um… people… that I have… around me."

Colonel Parker interjects, "Elvis the only thing I was saying was that Billy doesn't understand how show business works."

"Alright… that's, um… enough… of that… I can't… do… the work, um… right now… so until… I can, ah… I'm just… going to… um… concentrate… on myself… and… ah… get better."

"That's a good idea, Elvis." Billy agrees.

"It's good to see that you have decided to get healthy," the Colonel tells me. "You know I've been telling you for a year or more that your performances haven't been up to what they use to be. So when you get your health back we can start all over again. What about those pills?"

I reassure the Colonel "Um, yeah… I've decided… to stop, ah… taking them. I've seen… what… I have… um… turned into… and ah… I don't… like it. I really… believe… that if… um… no, no, no… not if… but when… I stop… um… taking… those pills… that I'm um… destined… to do… something… ah… really great. I'm not… sure… um… what it is… supposed… to be… yet. While I… was on the… floor… ah… in my… bathroom… um… I heard… my Momma's… voice, ah… telling me… that… I needed… to stay… here and… ah… finish doing… um… what I was… sent here… to do."

"If that's the way you feel, I hope that you achieve everything you want out of life my boy. And I want you to know that I'll be there for you every step of the way."

"Yes… that is… what… ah… I have… been told. Colonel… I need… to take care… of my… health first… and ah… then… I'll be able… to help, um… other people… more um… than I have… in the past."

"God knows that you have helped a lot of people in your life, my boy."

"And… if I do… ah… what I need… to do… I can… make, ah… bigger contribution… to the um… world."

Billy interjects, "Elvis you've already done so much to help people."

"What are you going to do, buy a Cadillac for everyone?" the Colonel says laughing.

I don't appreciate the sarcasm in his question. "No Colonel… there is… um… more that… I can do… to help… ah… the world. Just what… it is… ah… I'm not… sure yet… but um… I'll know it… when… it comes… to me."

"I'm glad to hear that you have sorted things out," the Colonel says. "I'm happy to hear that you want to get off the pills and turn your life around. It will make keeping your image as clean and wholesome as is should be, not like it has been as of late."

"Well... this is... um... my second... chance... at life... Colonel... and, ah... I'm going... to make... the most... of it... I have been... truly, um... blessed... and, ah... I'm not... going... to waste... this opportunity."

"Well" the Colonel says, "I just wanted to come by and see how you were doing. It sounds like you're doing fine and the doctors have everything under control. I'll stay in touch, so if you need anything just let me know and I'll handle it for you."

"I will... Colonel... thanks... um... for coming... by."

Billy says "I'll see you later Elvis and Jo sends her love too."

"Ah... tell Jo... that she... is um... blessed to have... a man... like you... ah... in her life... Billy."

"Thanks Elvis, I will."

The Colonel and Billy head back down stairs. Billy then drives the Colonel to the Memphis International Airport so he can fly back to his office at the MGM Studios in Los Angeles.

Chapter 9

August 18th, 1977

"This is George Klein from WHBQ-AM reporting this morning to you from Graceland. Just a few minutes ago a car left with Vernon Presley, Joe Esposito and Larry Geller on their way to the hospital to see Elvis.

"There are rumors that Elvis has broken off his relationship with Ginger Alden. We don't know what has caused the breakup, but as soon as we get more information we will be bringing it to you live from WHBQ-AM.

"So keep it tuned to 560 AM for the latest information about the "King" and all the greatest hits. This is George Klein from WHBQ-AM. Now back to you in the studio."

~ * ~

It's late afternoon as Joe drives Vernon and Larry to the hospital. They are in a blue, four-door, Cadillac Seville with white leather interior. I bought it for Joe to thank him for his endless contributions and help in both my career and personal life. As they drive down the highway Vernon says, "Well, it is official. We have cancelled all further projects that were set up for Elvis to do."

"What else could we do? We really didn't have a choice did we?" Joe replies.

"No, but the promoters weren't very happy about what had to be done. All of them have lost the advertising money that has already been spent and they had to refund all the advanced ticket sales." Vernon continues, "But, while they say they understand what we are going through we have heard that some of the promoters have threatened to sue us for damages to recover their losses."

"Wow, that's something new we haven't had to deal with before," Joe admits.

"I have the Colonel dealing with those guys. He'll get them to back down and he will even get more money out of them," Vernon says laughing.

Larry chimes in, "The public has been very concerned about how Elvis is doing."

"Yeah, and the fan clubs have all been asking what's going on." Joe adds.

Vernon says, "I have my secretary talking to all the fan club presidents to keep them informed. We should put out another press release soon though."

"We can do that after we see Elvis, today. Also the boys in the band and the Sweet Inspiration are wondering what's going to happen to them?" Joe wonders out loud, as he stops the car for a red light before turning into the hospital parking lot.

"The ones that are non-essential are going to have to be laid off. Elvis can't afford to keep paying these guys just to sit around. The same goes for the Sweet Inspiration, they are going to have to go too," Vernon replies.

As the light turns green, Joe turns into the hospital parking lot.

Larry agrees, "Yes, that's going to have to be done. Part of what Elvis and I were talking about yesterday was cutting down on his entourage, having fewer hanger-on's around him. Someone in his condition doesn't need all these people around him, pulling on his energy."

They enter the hospital and pass the information desk. Vernon greets the girls sitting there, "Hello, ladies."

"Good afternoon, Mr. Presley. Hope you have good day, gentlemen."

"I'm sure we will," Larry answers.

Vernon, Joe and Larry ride the elevator up to the 12th floor. As they step out of the elevator they are greeted by the security guard. "Oh. Hello, Mr. Presley. How are you today?"

"I'm fine. Thanks."

"And you, gentlemen?" the guard addresses the other two.

Joe answers, "We're fine, thanks."

As they enter Room 1212, Joe says, "Hey, Elvis, how are you today?"

"I'm, ah… doing better… than I was… um… a few days… ago. They ah... have me… ah walking… the halls."

Vernon says, "Hello, Son, you're looking better."

"Ah… yeah… am I?"

"You look like you're making progress," Larry agrees as he stands by my bedside.

"I hope … um… that… um … I am."

Joe informs me "I spoke with Priscilla yesterday and told her what was going on with you."

"Good... um... Joe... ah... thanks... for that. How, um... is she?"

"She is fine, but she is very concerned about you. She said that she will call you and come out to see you when things settle down. And, she told me to tell you that she loves you."

"Ah... my Cilla... I miss her."

Vernon says, sitting at the foot of the bed, "I know you do son."

"We all miss her," Larry adds.

"She's... a great... um... lady... and the... mother of... my, ah... only child. How is... um... Lisa Marie?" I ask.

"Lisa Marie is doing fine," Vernon answers, "She is worried about you. She's still at Graceland with Nancy, Mary, and Minnie Mae. But everyone is spoiling her."

"Tell... her... that her... ah... Daddy loves her... and ah... I will... be home... soon."

"I will, son."

"Um... thanks, Daddy."

"Of course, Elvis."

As a thought crosses my mind, my mood changes, "You know... something that's... um... bothering me? That book... um... that, ah... Dave Hebler... and... um... Red and Sonny West... just wrote!"

Larry says "Now Elvis, you know what they wrote in that book is true from their perspective."

Joe, standing over by the window, tries to reassure me, "Look, since you've decided to clean up your act, that book is old news. After all, you are only human."

"Son, those boys were more of a problem than they were worth. The law suits we have had to deal with, due to them beating people up has cost you a small fortune. Now, I know that they have been around you a long time, but if they can't carry their own weight, what good are they?"

Larry declares, "Elvis the best thing is to forgive and forget."

"Yeah… I know… I can forgive… um… Dave. But it's Red… and ah… Sonny… They were family! I've… known them… since high school. I know… those boys… um… were ah… lot of fun… sometimes… um… but they… had become… ah… yes people… to me. They… didn't care… if, um… I was…acting… irresponsibly. They… didn't care… ah… that I was… going down… the slippery slopes… to hell… or not. Just… as long… as they… could, um… hang on… to my… coattails… ah… They… would laugh… and… cut up… as much… as I did. But … If I stopped… laughing, ah… they… would stop… laughing."

"What they wrote in the book was out of their own frustration," Joe says "and their own anger at you for having Vernon fire them, instead of you letting them go. It had everything to do with you from their perceptive."

"They wrote that book out of revenge. Their free ride was over. They wanted to get back at you and wanted to expose you so they could hurt your reputation." Vernon stated.

"I know… it just… um… bothers me. But ah… the grief… that it… caused… um… my family… and Colonel… was unnecessary."

"Elvis, you know you're going to get some good press and some bad press out of this." Joe states.

Larry adds, "And, you have never listened to the reviews before, so why start listening to them now?"

"Listen, Son, you can please some of the people some of the time but you can't please all the people all of the time," Vernon declares.

Joe says. "Elvis, you can't get caught up in their bull shit."

"I know… your right. This, ah… getting clean stuff… is harder, um… than I thought… it was… going to be. They have… cut back… ah… on my pain… medications." I reflect.

"I remember… driving around… with, ah… G.K. and Red… and ah… I wanted to… go to um… Alan Fortas's… house to get… some um… Benzedrine. Red told me… um… in no uncertain… terms… "Elvis… you know… that's… um… how… Hank Williams… died. He started… ah… messing… with those… um… damned pills."

"I told Red… um… it's what we… used… ah… all the time… in the army. They're just… ah… bennies. All they do… is um… keep you… awake.

98

"Red… ah… was persistent … about his concerns… I listened…and ah… I just… turned… um… the car… around… and ah… I didn't… say a word… as we drove back… to Graceland."

"Elvis, you've only been off them for two days now. How long did it take for you to get into this situation?" Larry inquires. "It's been years. So why do you think you're going to lick it in two days?

Joe says, "Remember, the doctor said it's going to take a year, or more, for you to fully recover from this stroke. And, the hardest part will be getting off the pills."

"I know… I am… just, um… used to… having things… like, ah… Frank Sinatra… used to sing… ah… 'My Way'"

All three chuckle at my attempt at humor. "I'm getting… ah… older… but I… don't think… it's too late… ah… to save… myself… from this… um… disaster. But, man… ah… this stroke… problem… is a… bitch."

There is more laughter as the group realizes that my sense of humor is still intact.

Larry says, "Elvis you just need to concentrate on getting yourself better."

"I know… you're right… ah… Larry. So when… um… can I get… out of here?"

"They've got you on intravenous Heparin now to thin your blood. It will dissolve the clotting in the brain, so you don't stroke out again. But the doctor said you can switch to oral Coumadin and go home in a couple of days," Joe says.

"I… can't wait… to get… back… um… home… and have… some of… ah… Nancy's fried… um… banana sandwiches."

Larry laughs and reminds me, "that's the kind of stuff you are going to have to stop eating, if you are going to lose that extra 30 to 40 pounds," poking him in the belly.

"You mean… I can't… ah… have… any more… um…fried banana… sandwiches?"

"No, you're turning over a new leaf remember. No more fried anything! We're going to have to get you a dietician to work with." Larry says.

"Ah… you're killing me… guys."

Dr. Jerry Francisco walks in to the room, "Good afternoon gentlemen, how is everyone today? Hello, Elvis. How are you doing?"

"I'm feeling… somewhat better… ah… but, the side effect… of my speech… and the, um… paralysis… in my arm…um… has me worried. Plus… the withdrawal… ah… from the pain pills… has me… um… feeling weird."

"I told you the hardest part of this treatment was going to be getting off the pills. You are going through withdrawal and that is never an easy situation for anyone. I also have an Occupational Therapist I'd like to bring onto your case."

Elvis looks at the doctor with a puzzled look on his face and asks, "But doc… ah… I already have… a pretty good… occupation. Um… Why… do I need… one of those?"

"I know you have quite a good occupation going. What an Occupational Therapist does is help with the rehabilitation of your physical needs. They will teach you exercises for the muscles in your arm to gain the strength back, so you can begin to do the things you used to do. They will also evaluate your home environment for adaptive equipment you may need and train you in its use. They give guidance and education for family members and caregivers, too."

"Okay Doc… um… I guess I can use… the help." I joke with the doctor, a wave of relief washing over me.

"And, I am also recommending a nutritionist that will put together a diet for you."

"We were just talking about that very thing," Larry advises the doctor.

Vernon asks "When will Elvis be able to see this person?"

Dr. Francisco says, "I have a call into the nutritionist to set up a time. The occupational therapist is scheduled to come in tomorrow to begin working out a program with Elvis."

Joe poses the question we all want answered, "How much longer will Elvis have to be here in the hospital?"

"I think once Elvis has met with the therapists, we can send him home to do his rehab there. So I would say, in a day or two we will be able to discharge him, depending on his test results."

"Under normal circumstances, I am sure that would be good idea. But, doctor wouldn't you agree, that taking Elvis out of his normal surroundings would help him break his old habits and dependencies? Wouldn't it be better for his rehab for Elvis to go to some place other than Graceland?" suggests Larry.

After thinking for a moment, Dr. Francisco nods, "Yes, I would agree. Those are arrangements that you and Elvis are going to have to make."

"Where would you like to go to recover?" Vernon asks me.

"Hawaii... I would... ah... go to Hawaii. It's... warm there... ah... all year. I love... um... the people... there... and the atmosphere... ah... is so calm... and relaxing."

Joe agrees, "That sounds like a good idea."

Vernon says, "You'll be a long way away from Graceland and way out of your comfort zone there."

Larry informs Vernon, "That's just the point; Elvis needs to be out of his comfort zone. He needs to set new patterns in his life."

Dr. Francisco agrees, "You're right guys. The islands sound like the perfect place for his rehab. It is calm and relaxing there. They have all the medical support that you will need there."

"It sounds like... I'm... ah... Hawaii bound... then, boys."

"So, after your appointments with the occupational therapist and your nutritionist, then we'll get you out of here," promises Dr. Francisco.

Everyone agrees that Hawaii is the place for me to rehabilitate. The next step is to get me back to Graceland, where I will begin my therapy and diet while we make arrangements for the move to Hawaii.

~ * ~

"This is Al Cosby from WHBQ-AM reporting from, Graceland. It's 6:35PM this evening and things are quiet here, except for Ginger Alden and a few other people that are moving things out of the mansion. We're not sure what is going on, but as soon as we find out, you will hear it first on WHBQ-AM.

There are more and more people gathering outside of the gates, holding a vigil for the "King's" speedy recovery. They have been here for days now, waiting for Elvis' return to his home at Graceland, as we all do. Our prayers go out to the "King" and his family tonight.

This is Al Cosby for WHBQ-AM sending you back to the studio for more hits."

Chapter 10

Upstairs at Graceland, Ginger is in her bathroom closet next to the office on the other side of my bedroom. Nancy is helping her pack clothes for her departure from Graceland. Ginger is still sniffling softly and very upset with my decision to break up with her.

"Miss Ginger, I can't believe that Mr. Elvis has broken up with you."

"Yes, it's true. I don't know what I'm going to do now. I'm still in love with him. I hope that he will change his mind. Maybe it's just because of the stroke that he is feeling this way."

"Well, Miss Ginger, I hope for your sake you're right."

"Nancy, please, hand me those dresses that are hanging in the closet. You know, I'm really going to miss Elvis. And, Lisa Marie, too. She is such a cute, sweet little girl, I just love being with her."

Nancy hands Ginger the dresses she retrieved from the closet, "I know you do Miss Ginger."

Ginger folds the dresses into her suit case. "I hope that Elvis will be alright and he'll change his mind. When do you think he will be home?"

"From what Mr. Vernon said, he thinks, Mr. Elvis will be home in a day or two."

"Elvis asked me to be gone before he gets back. I'm going to miss all of you here. Everyone has been so nice. I still don't understand why he broke up with me? Do you think Vernon can talk

104

some sense into him? Can you hand me those shoes over there, please? Do you know if Vernon is here or not?"

"No, Miss Ginger, he is at the hospital visiting Mr. Elvis with Mr. Joe and Mr. Larry. Here are your shoes. They should be back soon."

"After I finish packing, I'll check in his office and see if he's there. If not, I'll wait a little while or come back tomorrow."

"Alright, Miss Ginger, I'd better go attend to Miss Lisa Marie and start getting dinner ready for her, Mr. Vernon and Mr. Larry. Will you be staying for dinner Miss Ginger?"

"No, I don't think so Nancy, but thanks just the same. And thanks for helping me pack my stuff."

"Well you stay as long as you like and I'll make enough if you change your mind about staying for dinner."

"Thanks, Nancy. I think I'll just finish packing and come back later. There's enough going on around here, you don't need me adding to the confusion, especially, if I'm not wanted here. Please, tell Vernon that I'll see him tomorrow, if that's okay."

"Yes, Miss Ginger, I'll do that."

~ * ~

In the heart of down town Memphis, on South Main Street, next to the Orpheum Theater, is Jim's Barber Shop. It is where I had always gotten my hair cut until I left for the army.

Two guys are watching a black and white TV, waiting their turn. Jim, the owner, is getting ready to give B.B. King his haircut. From the TV, they hear, "We interrupt this program to bring you this special report from our man about town, Bob Ford."

Jim asks Little Richard, "Turn up the TV so we can hear this report." Little Richard hops up and does so.

"This is Bob Ford from WHBQ-TV, reporting from Baptists Memorial Hospital. I am here with, literally, hundreds of other people. We are outside the hospital waiting on news of Elvis' condition. From the reports I'm getting so far today, Elvis has had his initial meetings with his speech therapist and his physical therapist to map out a plan for his rehabilitation. Other than some problems he is having with his speech and his arm, his recovery seems to be going well.

"This week, Elvis' most recent release, 'Way Down', is number 18 on the Billboard charts and it's looking like it is destined to reach #1. That's all I have from here for now so don't forget to listen to our sister station WHBQ-560-AM on your radio dial to hear 'Way Down' from the "King" himself, Elvis Presley.

"This is Bob Ford once again coming to you from Baptists Memorial, now it's back to our studios at WHBQ-TV."

~ * ~

Jim asks his famous clientele who are in town for a concert this evening, "How does a white kid, like Elvis, copy your music style and then become the biggest artist of all time?"

B.B. King, a gifted guitarist and acclaimed blues singer/songwriter sits in Jim's chair and says "Elvis once told me that his music is rooted in the black gospel songs that he sang as a young man.

"He said to me, and I quote: 'I truly love and respect black musicians, I didn't start R&B music; it was here a long time before I came along.'"

Little Richard is a singer/songwriter, piano player, bandleader and recording artist. He is considered one of the key players instrumental in the transition of the musical landscape of the mid 1950's from rhythm and blues to rock and roll. He chimes in, "Yeah, black artists were performing so called Elvis style music long before it was his style. He is one of the first white musicians to get into our music. He has turned the whole white world on to our sound."

Jim says, "Well, that's what I mean, why Elvis?"

B.B. says, "What most people don't know about this boy is, he is serious about what he is doing. He gets carried away by it. He has the heart and soul of a black man. He grew up listening to Memphis black radio stations like WDIA. When I was a disc-jockey there, Elvis and I became friends. He also listened to other stations that played race records, spirituals, R&B, and blues."

"He admired black singers like Sister Rosetta Thorpe, Memphis Minnie, Louise Jordan and Arthur Crudup. He really thinks they're all great singers. Elvis grew up attending black church services, and two of his earliest hits were written by a black musician named Otis Blackwell."

Jim asked, "But Elvis must have had other musical influences. Where else did he learn music from?"

"Elvis studied music in high school, but he picks it up by ear," Little Richard said.

B.B. said, "He also loves country music. He used to spend hours in those record shops that had listening booths. Oh yeah. Elvis isn't only a musician; he has grown to become the most popular artist of his era."

Jim said "Yes, but why him? Why didn't it go to you, B.B., or you, Richard? Or, what about you Fats, why didn't you become as big as he did? You sure did, size wise," Jim says laughing, "But seriously, why haven't you gotten as big?"

Fats Domino, the New Orleans, Louisiana born and raised R&B, rock and roll, pianist, singer/songwriter, says, "Elvis has the ability to make more of a commercial impact with R&B than all of us put together. But, he knows. He once told me, 'Nobody can sing that kind of music like colored people. Let's face it, I can't sing like Fats Domino can, I know that.' I was flattered because I think he has such a beautiful voice."

"And look, there are more white people in this country than there are blacks. The numbers are in his favor. The good part of it is that when he performs one of our songs we get paid royalties from his performance."

"When Elvis was a junior in high school," B.B. shares, "I first saw him hanging out on Beale

Street. He would be checking out the wild, flashy clothes in the window of Lansky Brothers store. By the time he was a senior, he was wearing them clothes. When I was playing in Memphis with my band, he would stand in the wings and watch us perform."

Fat's said, "I've only met Elvis a few times. He told me that he would sometimes go to the blues clubs for whites, but he preferred to go to the black shows where the audience would react a lot differently than the white only audiences. He really liked the intensity that the musicians brought to their playing. And he loved how the audience would stand up and clap their hands, dance in the aisles, and get to hootin' and a hollerin'. He would also attend the monthly All-Night Singings downtown where white gospel groups performed reflecting our spiritual music."

"Y'all know my early records were produced by Sam Phillips," B.B says. "Sam owns Sun Records and back then he was looking for a white man who sounded like a Negro. He said if he could find someone that sounded like one of us and had the soul, he could make a million dollars. Elvis had done a couple of demo records at Sun but he didn't initially catch Sam's imagination. One day, Elvis was in the studio with Scotty Moore and Bill Black when Elvis broke into a rendition of Arthur Crudup's, 'That's All Right'. That was the song that caught Sam ear. It was the first single that Elvis put out for Sun."

Fats says, "Elvis once told me 'I used to hear old Arthur Crudup down in Tupelo Mississippi bang his guitar the way I do now. I felt if I ever got to the place where I could feel all that Arthur feels, I'd be a music man like nobody ever saw.'"

Little Richard makes a point, "Well, I gotta say I resented it when Elvis rocketed to stardom. There are so many talented, black musicians with a similar sound who weren't getting the same air play or money. Elvis was paid $25,000 for three songs in a movie, but I would only get $5,000 for the same work. If I hadn't broken the ice, Elvis would have starved."

Jim spins he chair around so B.B. can see the finished hair cut in the mirror and asks "So what do you think?"

B.B. replies, "Well I think it looks good for an amateur doing the cutting," everyone laughs.

B.B. tells Richard, "Since you made that big money from those movies, would you pay for my hair cut?"

"Hell no, brother, you're the one making the big money. Don't forget you're the headliner tonight."

"Oh yeah, I guess I am. Well, here you go Jim," B.B. hands Jim a $20 bill. "Thanks, I look really sharp."

Jim said, "Yes, you do!"

"Alright, boys, we have a sound check to do, so we better get going," Fats says.

They all say goodbye and head out the door.

Chapter 11

August 19th, 1977

It is mid-morning and I am awake in my bed at the hospital. Pushing the bedside table with the breakfast tray further down the bed, I roll over and reach the phone on the bedside stand. Dialing is awkward, but I am able to call my good friend and mentor, Larry Geller. The phone rings once, twice, and a third time. Just as I begin to get nervous that I won't be able to reach him, I hear the click. "Hello, ah… Larry its, um… E… how are you."

With great delight in his voice, Larry says, "Hello Elvis, I'm fine, how are you today?"

"Larry… I want you… to, ah… come in… and um… see me… this morning. As you know… I have… a meeting… with my… um… occupational therapist… at, um… 11:00AM. Can you… be here… um… with me? I want you… around, um… so you can… take notes… ah… on what… I'm supposed… to do… and ah… then make… sure I do it."

"Yes, I can be there to help you. I'm going to have my breakfast first and then I'll come over. Since you want to recover as fast as possible, it makes sense to listen and do what these people have to say. But when you get to Hawaii, you're going to have to find other Speech and Physical Therapists to work with there."

"Yes… you're right… um… Larry. So… I'll see you… soon?"

"Yup, right after breakfast."

"Good… ah… I'll see you… then."

"See you soon, Elvis."

"Okay… um… goodbye Larry." I hang up the phone and lay back down, tired out from the call.

A while later, Marion walks into my room with a blood pressure cuff, "Good morning Babe, how are you feeling today?"

"Well… you know… darlin'… ah… I've had… better days. You should… have… um… seen me… ah… 5 years ago." I laugh, "I was… a lot… um… better looking… back then… and ah… I felt… better too."

"Oh yeah, you should have seen me 10 years ago. I was a lot better looking myself back then."

"Ah… Marion… if we had… our lives… ah… to live over… again… we could have… um… made quite… a good looking… couple.

Marion smiles and laughs, "It seems that we both missed out on our time together."

"Yes but… you're in… my life now… and ah… I'm sure glad… you are… here… um… to help me… recover."

"Thank you and that's what is most important. I'm here to help get you better and to get you back on the road to even more success. So let me check your blood pressure, and really see how you're doing today."

Marion wraps the cuff around my left arm, puts the stethoscope in her ears and pumps up the pressure. With the diaphragm of the stethoscope on my brachial artery, she releases the pressure to hear the pulse beat to get the reading.

"This is… bringing us… um… to the state… of… um… sintorie. That's known… as ah… being in… the here… and now."

"What are you talking about, Babe?"

"Sintorie… It means… um… that… what is… happening… right now… ah… is important. The past… we can't… um… do anything… about… and ah… the future… is yet… to be seen. It means being… or living… um… in the moment."

Marion says, "That's a beautiful thought."

"It's ah… a Japanese… philosophy."

"Well, your blood pressure is coming down and you're heading toward the normal range." Marion writes down the reading in my chart.

"That's… the best… news… um… I've heard… so far… today. I'm sure… ah… once you leave… it will go… down… um… a little more," I says as I wink.

"Don't you ever quit?" Marion says with a smile on her face as she gets my double meaning. "You have a good day, and I'll see you later this afternoon."

"You have… ah… good day too… Marion."

As Marion leaves the room, the phone rings. I pick it up and hear Priscilla on the other end of the phone. "Hello Elvis. How are you?"

"Hello… um… Cilla. I'm doing… a lot… better, um… than I was… a few days… ago."

"Yes, Joe was sweet enough to call and tell me what was going on. Oh my gosh, Elvis. I was so upset when he told me what had happened."

"Yeah… um… Joe… told me… that he… called you. It was… pretty, ah… scary… for me… too. I've never… been… um… that close… to dying. It has… made me… a lot more… ah… aware of… my own… mortality…and more… um… humble. I guess… I'm not as… ah… invincible… as I thought… ah… I was."

"I'm glad to hear you talk like that. I knew those pills were going to catch up with you after a while. It was only a matter of time."

"Yes… you were… um… right. If I… told you… that I'm… ah… sorry… would you… believe me?"

"Yes Elvis, you know that I believe in you… unless you mess up again. But I hope that won't happen. And I know you're a man of your word, and I don't expect you to go back on those pain pills."

"Oh baby… I'm telling you… ah… I won't… use them… again. Do you… know that… they have me… um… on Heparin… to thin… my blood… to treat… my stroke…. ah… But they're… cutting me back… on my… pain pills. I want… to get off… them… ah… but it's… hard."

"I know that you can do it when you set your mind to it, honey." Priscilla continues, "How is Lisa?"

"I haven't… ah… seen her… um… or talked… to her… but I know… she's being… looked after… by… ah… Nancy… Vernon… Mary… and ah… Minnie Mea… back at the… house."

"I'll be coming into Memphis in a few days to see you if that's all right with you? I look forward to seeing you"

"Oh... that would be... ah... fine. I look... forward to... ah... seeing you... too."

"Is Ginger going to be there?" Pricilla ask tentatively.

"Ah... no... as a matter... of fact... ah... I broke up... with her... the other day."

Surprised Priscilla says, "You broke off your engagement?"

"I know... it's surprising... this has been... a serious... wake-up call... and, ah... what I... have to... ah... go through... to get myself... back into... um... shape... I can't do... with um... her hanging around... I'm going to... make... a lot of, ah... changes... in my life... Cilla. Changes that... I think you... will be... proud of. I have to... focus on... myself now... and ah... not who I'm... ah... hanging out... with. I have... to do this... um... for me. I know that... it, ah... sounds... kind of selfish... but what... I was... um... doing... just wasn't... working... for me."

"Elvis, I am proud of you. I feel like what you were doing before was selfish. I'm glad to hear you are going to turn yourself around and get back on track. You know that Gladys wouldn't have been very happy with the way you've been living. I'm just glad that she wasn't here to see you like that."

Tears welled up in my eyes as I listen to Priscilla speak. I can't help the quiver in my voice when I say, "Cilla... I now know... um... what they mean… when they say… you have to… um… hit bottom… before you can… ah… come back up… and I want to… get back up… on top… um… boy do I… want to."

"Honey, just relax and get yourself together. I know you can do it."

Feeling embarrassed, I drop my head, "I will Cilla… you just wait… and see… I will."

"I'll call Joe and he can arrange to have the Lisa Marie or Hound Dog II come and get me if that's alright with you."

"Sure… any time. When do you… think… ah… you'll be able… to come… and ah… see me?"

"I should be able to get there in a day or two. I'm trying to free up my schedule here, I'll let you know as soon as I can."

"I might… be back… at, ah… Graceland… by then… um… I'm not… sure yet."

"Well, that's good news; I'm glad that you are doing so well. I'll see you in a few days."

"Great… I'll… um… see you soon!"

"I'll talk to you sooner, and see you later."

"Thanks… for calling… ah… Cilla; you know that… I still… um… love you."

"Elvis don't start that please," she chides him.

"I'm just… ah… telling you… how I… um… feel."

"That could be, but I'm not feeling the same way, so I'm going to say goodbye for now, ok?"

"Ok… Cilla… I'll talk to… you again… soon… Goodbye."

"Goodbye."

Priscilla hangs up the phone. I pause then do the same and reflect on my conversation with Priscilla. "My God, what would Mama have thought of my behavior? I know she would have been very disappointed," I think to myself.

Larry knocks on the hospital room door bringing me back into the present. He walks in saying, "Good morning. How's it going?"

I pull myself together and wipe my eyes so that Larry wouldn't notice that I was feeling emotional. "Hey… ah… Larry… how was… your um… breakfast? What did you um… have?"

"I had two soft boiled eggs, rye toast with honey and cinnamon on it, oatmeal and orange juice."

I smile, "Ah… Larry you're… so good."

"You're going to be eating like me from now on. When does the nutritionist come to talk to you?"

"I don't know…. I don't think… they have… ah… scheduled… the nutritionist… yet."

"Okay, so we'll get you fixed up with a new way of eating when the nutritionist shows up."

"You're, ah… right… first things… first.

Chapter 12

Colonel Parker is back in his office at the MGM Studio's in Los Angeles. It is full of Elvis posters, some framed and the other posters are piled on the spare desk. There are all kind of other promotional materials ranging from lunch boxes, key chains, gold plated sunglasses, coffee mugs, commemorative license plates and t-shirts to buttons, programs, calendars and notebooks. They are stuffed in book shelves and laying on his desk top.

The Colonel is sitting with his feet propped up on his desk, cigar in hand, looking a bit like W.C. Fields. Shuffling through some papers, he finds the phone number he is looking for and dials the leader of Elvis's TCB band, James Burton. In 1969, I recruited James, born August 21, 1939 in Minden, Louisiana, to play lead guitar and help him build the TCB band.

"Hello James, it's the Colonel."

"Oh, hello Colonel how are you doing?"

"I'm doing fine. Have you seen Elvis yet?"

"No I haven't. I've been with the band doing light rehearsals just to stay in shape."

"That's why I'm calling you," the Colonel states, dropping a cigar ash on the floor. "I don't know any other way to tell you this, but to just say it. I've talked to Vernon, and considering Elvis's condition we are going to have to let the band go indefinitely."

"Wow! Colonel, that comes as quite a blow. Happy early birthday to me. I guess that means no more, 'Play it James,' solo breaks."

"No James, I'm afraid not."

"Damn, I've been with Elvis since 1969. Well, I guess I can go to work for someone else for a while, or go do some studio work. What about the backup singers? I'm guessing that they are gone too?"

"Yes, we're letting them go and all other non-essential personal until Elvis has recovered from his stroke."

"Do you know how long that's going to be?"

"We are being told it may take a year or more for him to do his rehab."

"When is he going to be back home?"

"He should be home in a day or two."

James asks "Did you and Vernon talk about any severance pay for the band?"

"Yes and we decided that a month's pay for every year that each one has worked for Elvis would be what everyone will be getting."

"Wow… well that will help, but that's going to upset a lot of people."

"Listen James, I know that this is a shock to you, as it is to all of us. But, the fact remains that Elvis is out of commission for quite some time, and he's in no need of a band right now. I'm asking you, as the band leader, to let the other band members know what the story is and to inform them that they are no longer needed."

"I hope that when it comes time to get the band back together, we'll be able to pull everyone back again," James proposes.

"It will be what it will be," the Colonel says in his gruff manner. "If you can get everyone back together again, that will be great. If not, you'll just have to find replacements. It could be bigger and better then, than it is now."

"I understand. I'll call the boys and let them know what has been decided." James shifts the phone from one ear to the other, and asks the Colonel, "So when do you think we can expect to get these checks?"

"I'll have Vernon get them out to you within the week."

"May we go by Graceland to see Elvis and get our checks?"

"I would call Vernon first and ask him if it would be okay.

"Well then, I guess that's it for now. I'd like to say it been a pleasure, but it hasn't. I understand, but this hasn't been one of our best conversations Colonel," James says.

"I know James. It's just business. I wish you and the band the best of luck. If I hear of anybody looking for players, I'll give them your name and number."

"Thanks for letting me know, and yes, I'll let the other band members know what has been decided."

"Okay James, take care of yourself, and stay in touch."

"All right, Colonel, talk to you later, Goodbye"

"Goodbye, James."

~ * ~

It's 2:00PM and I've just finished eating my lunch with Larry. As Larry moves the table away from my bed, he says, "It looks like you are still having a little trouble using your right hand eating today."

"Yes... I don't have... um... the control... that I... used to... ah... in my hand... or arm. I'm hoping... that... um... the occupational... therapists'... exercises will... ah... help me... with that."

"I'm sure they will be able to correct that problem. You just need to give it time," Larry says. "Now, that salmon wasn't so bad now was it?"

"Well... it wasn't... um... a fried banana... sandwich!" I remark in disappointment.

"No, but you're going to have to learn to enjoy eating fish, and I don't mean breaded fish sticks either," Larry says with a snicker. "That salmon was pretty good, not the least bit dry and the green beans were nice, don't you think?"

"I have to... admit... ah... I did like... the salmon."

Just then, Billy comes walking into the room. "Good afternoon Elvis, how are you doing today?"

"Oh... ah... hi Billy. Things are... um... moving... right along."

Billy perches on the foot of the bed, since Larry is sitting in the visitor's chair. I am sitting up in the bed still sporting a hospital gown.

"Oh Billy… you should have… um… been here… to see… ah… the physical… therapist. Boy… oh boy… did we… um… connect."

"Why, what happened?" Billy asks.

"Her name… is… um… A.E., she is… stunning! And…ah… Oh my God… the sexual tension… between us… was… um… at a… all-time high. I'm glad… to… um… know… that um… I still… have it."

"So, just what kind of session did you guys have?" Larry inquires with a grin.

"We got along… great. It was… almost… all business. She has… ah… background… in karate… and ah… has been doing… um… physical therapy… for over… 8 years."

Larry says "It's a shame that you may not be working with her for very long."

"Maybe… I'll hire her… and ah… have her… move to Hawaii… with me."

"Do you think she would be up for that?" asked Billy.

"I don't know… for sure… Ah… Maybe I… should wait… till after I… get to Hawaii… to see who's… available… over there first. Then… I might… ask her."

Billy inquired, "So what kind of therapy does she have you doing?"

"It's more… about… um… strength training… mobility… and flexibility."

Dr. Francisco walks into the room with a big smile on his face. He gives a nod of the head to Billy and Larry and addresses me. "Good afternoon Elvis, how are you doing today?"

"I'm doing… ah… better… and better… every day. I really… um… appreciate you… introducing me… to the… um… speech and… ah… especially the… physical therapist… I'm sure… with this… information… and their help… um… I'll be able to… um… get back into… um… great shape."

"They're both really great people, I knew they would be a big help to you."

"I was… telling… um… Billy and ah… Larry about… A.E. and… um… how hot… she is… and ah… how good… she is… at her job," Elvis tells the doctor.

"Yes, she has that effect on a lot of people," he admits. "But there is one lucky guy in her life. She has been seeing this guy for almost four years now."

A wave of disappointment washes over me. "She's serious… about someone?" I ask.

"I'm sorry to say, yes she is. There are several people here at the hospital that would like to be involved with her," Dr. Francisco reveals with a smile.

"I guess… um… I should keep… my eye on the… um… ball and ah… worry about… getting better… and um… not so much… about getting laid," I crack as everyone else in the room has a good laugh.

"At any rate, I have some good news for you today."

"Yeah… what's that?"

"All your test have come back and they look good. I'm going send you home. You are scheduled to be discharged tomorrow afternoon."

This news puts a big grin on my face. I reach out with my left hand to shake hands with Dr. Francisco, "Oh… that's great news… ah… Dr. Francisco. I'll call… um… my daddy… and have him… make arrangements… to, ah… get me home. Ah… what time… can I… um… get out of here?"

"If everything goes right, and no problems come up between now and then, you should be able to get out of here between 1:00PM and 3:00PM."

Billy tells the doctor, "We normally try to move Elvis at midnight or after. It's safer for him to move around in the early hours. There are fewer people out on the streets looking for Elvis at that time."

"Yes, I'm sure that it's safer to move him then, but that is going to throw off his sleep schedule and start him back into living the life of a vampire again," Dr. Francisco explains.

"Okay… I know you're… um… right… so when I call… I'll tell them… um… to come… get me…at… um… 2:00PM… would that be… okay? I'll have… Vernon… um… call you… to, ah… make the… arrangements."

"Alright, that'll be fine. We can take you out through the delivery supply entrance in the back of the hospital. There will be fewer people there, so you can get out of here with less trouble."

"Thank you... for all your... um... help doctor."

"Elvis, it's been an honor to be your attending physician and a pleasure to help you get on track to achieve good health. If you need anything, just give me a call, and I'll do whatever I can."

"I will."

"Alright then gentlemen, have a nice afternoon, and I'll see you again tomorrow," Dr. Francisco says as he leaves the room.

I ask Billy to dial the phone so I can talk to Vernon. As the phone is ringing, Billy says to Larry, "This is great news, getting Elvis back to Graceland tomorrow!"

"Yes, but keep in mind, the work has just begun. Elvis still has to find the right therapists to work with."

"Hey... you guys... um... can you stop... talking about me... um... like I'm... not here?" Larry and Billy laugh.

Through the phone I hear Vernon, "Hello."

"Ah... hello... Daddy... how is you?"

"Hello Elvis, I'm fine, how are you doing?" Vernon asks, excited to hear from me.

"I'm doing, ah... well... and, ah... Dr. Francisco... just told me... I can... come home... tomorrow!"

"That's great, son. What time do you get out of there?"

"Dr. Francisco… and I… agreed… that I can… ah… leave at… 2:00PM tomorrow. I need you… to have… um… Joe… or you… give… um… Dr. Francisco… a call… and ah… work out the… details."

"I'll give him a call after we finish talking."

"All right… um… Daddy… I'll leave it… up to you."

"Don't you worry about it. I'll get it organized, and let you know how we're going to move you back here to Graceland."

"Thanks… um… Daddy… I'll talk to you… um… soon. Oh… by the way… um… how is… Lisa Marie?"

"Oh, she misses you and wants to know when she can see you. But, she is fine. She will be so happy when I'll tell her she will see you tomorrow."

"Great, Daddy… Thanks… um… for taking care… of this… and ah…tell… um… Lisa Marie… I love her… and ah… I'll see her… tomorrow."

"OK son, I'll see you then."

"Goodbye Daddy… I love you."

Vernon was a little taken aback by my expressing my love for him, but he likes the way it sounds. "Have a good afternoon, Elvis, and get some rest."

"I will… Daddy. Bye."

~ * ~

126

"Patti!" Vernon hollers.

Patti Perry was born in Stanford Hill, London. She came to the United States in 1953 at the age of ten. Seven years later, she was driving down Santa Monica Boulevard and I pulled my Rolls Royce up next to her and asked her to stop. We chatted for a while, and just clicked. So, I invited her up to my Perugia Way house where she met some of the guys in the Memphis Mafia and got on well with them, too. They adopted her like a little sister and she became the only female member of the Mafia. Since she had gone to the same Beauty School as Larry Geller, I would occasionally have her cut my hair.

Vernon instructs her, "We're bringing Elvis home tomorrow. Go ask Mary to make sure his room is ready. It will be good to have him back, but there will be some changes around here."

Patti heads out to tell Mary about my expected arrival.

Vernon then dials the hospital.

"Baptist Memorial Hospital, how may I help you?"

"Hello, may I speak to Dr. Francisco."

The receptionist asks, "Who may I say is calling?

"Tell him it's Vernon Presley."

"Oh yes, just a minute Mr. Presley, I'll get him for you."

"Thanks." Vernon waits patiently.

Dr. Francisco answers the phone at the nurse's station. "Hello, Vernon. Wow that was quick, I just left you son about three minutes ago."

"Hello, Dr. Francisco, I guess my boy is in a hurry get home. Elvis tells me we can get him out of there and back to Graceland as soon as tomorrow."

"Yes, I've talked to Jose De Jesus, or "Papi" as he is known around here, who is our Head of Security; he will make arrangements to get Elvis out through the delivery supply entrance at the back of the hospital."

"I'll arrange to have a car there to pick up Elvis at 2:00PM tomorrow."

"Mr. Presley, you will need to talk to Papi, about making the arrangements to pick up Elvis."

"Ok, I'll call him. And, thank you for looking after my son, doctor. I really appreciate what you have done for him. You and your staff have saved his life."

"That's what we're here for, and the pleasure is ours."

"Well thanks again. Can you put me through to Papi now?"

"Sure. I'm going to put you on hold and the next voice you hear should be Papi."

Jose "Papi" De Jesus is from the Dominican Republic. He is a tall, spindly man with short, dark, curly hair. He looks good in his uniform, and his personality exudes a quiet authority. He answers the phone. "Good afternoon, this is Papi, may I help you?"

"Hello Papi, this is Vernon Presley and I just spoke to Dr. Francisco. He tells me I need to talk to you about getting my son out of the hospital tomorrow."

"Oh, yes sir, Mr. Presley, whatever you want. I think maybe we should use a panel van so that Elvis can be loaded into it while on a gurney. It will look like a delivery truck making another delivery. I'll make sure that it gets done from this end. Not to worry!"

"That's a good idea, Papi. I'm sure it will go just fine. I'll send Billy, Charlie and Lamar over to assist you in moving Elvis. And, I'll have Joe and Marty come in the front door to cause a distraction at the same time."

"That sounds good, Mr. Presley," Papi says. "I'll make all the arrangements from this end, we will be ready tomorrow. Do you know what time you're going to have the van here?"

Vernon says, "Yes the guys will be there at 1:45PM."

"Great, Mr. Presley. We will be ready."

"Thanks, Papi, I'll talk to you again tomorrow."

"Yes, sir! May I say, Mr. Presley, I have always enjoyed Elvis's music, and it's such an honor for me to be able to help him get back home."

"Yes, thank you for your help Papi. I will see what I can do to get you a signed photo of Elvis to you and your family, if you wish."

Papi gets very excited about the possibility of having an autographed photo of Elvis. It would be quite a conversation piece hanging in his living room. "Oh Mr. Presley, if you could arrange that, I would be so thrilled and I know my wife would be too."

"Okay then, but no wives there when Elvis leaves tomorrow though, all right?"

"No sir, oh, I mean…, yes sir, it will be just me and one other security guard. But, I'm sure there will be some people from the hospital medical staff to see Elvis off."

"Okay, thanks again Papi. I'll talk to you tomorrow, goodbye."

"Yes sir, Mr. Presley. I'll talk to you then."

Patti has returned from passing along the information about my return. Vernon hands her some 8" x 10" glossy photos, "Patti, get these over to Elvis and have him sign them for 'Papi', please. Once he has done that, they need to go to Mr. De Jesus, the head of security at the hospital."

"Yes sir."

"By the way, do you know where Joe, Charlie, Lamar and Marty are?"

"I think they're in the pool room."

"So they're all over in the main house?"

"Yes, sir."

"Okay, I'm going to walk over and talk to the boys. Please, answer any calls that may come in. Use the intercom to reach me if you need me."

"Yes sir," answered Patti.

~ * ~

130

Vernon walks across the lawn to the mansion and walks down the stairs and turns left to go into the Pool Room. It is a twenty-four by seventeen foot room in the NW corner of the basement. The west wall is painted with a lightning bolt and cloud motif. This is the likeness of my personal logo with the initials TCB for 'taking care of business' over the lightning bolt. The south wall has three built in TV sets, a stereo and a cabinet with my record collection. The walls and ceiling are covered in four hundred yards of pleated cotton fabric to improve the acoustics of the room.

Vernon finds the guys playing a game of pool. "Hello boys, I have some good news for you."

Lamar Fike, a member of my Memphis Mafia, has a larger than life personality. I have affectionately called Lamar "Buddha", since we first met when he was just hanging outside the front of my Audubon Drive home. When I was drafted in 1958, Lamar tried to enlist but was turned down because of his weight problem. He would work the lights when I appeared in Las Vegas, and handles my transportation needs. Lamar has been the butt of many jokes, but with his good sense of humor he never lets it get the best of him.

Lamar asks, "What's up Vernon?"

"Well, I just spoke to Dr. Francisco and he said Elvis can be released tomorrow afternoon."

"Vernon, that's great news," says Joe.

Marty agrees, "It'll be great to have Elvis back home again."

Charlie raking up another game of pool asks, "What time can we get him out of there?"

"We're going to get him at 2:00PM."

Lamar ever worried about transportation details asks, "How are we going to get him?"

Vernon explains the plan to the group, "Well, here's what I think we should do. I want Joe and Marty to go into the hospital through the front door to cause a distraction. Joe, you're known well enough there that the press will be wondering what you are doing there at 2:00PM and will follow you and Marty.

"Meanwhile, Billy, Charlie, and Lamar will be driving a panel van to the back delivery area of the hospital. There will be a guard there by the name of Papi who will be your contact at the delivery area."

Lamar suggests, "When we get Elvis out of the hospital and bring him back to Graceland, we should bring him in through the back of the church property and into the back of the house."

"That's the idea Lamar."

Marty worries, "Vernon, what kind of shape will Elvis be in?"

Vernon tells the group, "He is doing a lot better. He still not near 100% yet. It's going to take some time for him to recover from what has happened.

"Now, I've asked that Elvis be on a gurney so he can be wheeled into the van, and then you guys can move out, and bring him home."

"I can't wait to see him," Lamar says.

Joe asks, "So, Marty and I will just go up to Elvis's room and wait for a while before coming back to Graceland?" Vernon nods.

Lamar thinks out loud, "We're going to have to get a van from somewhere to pull this off."

Vernon says, "Yes, and I know you will be able to get that done. I'd like the van to be there ten or fifteen minutes early so Elvis does not wind up waiting on the loading dock."

Charlie questions, "So we should leave here about 1:15PM, at the latest, to make sure we get there on time?"

Vernon agrees, "Yeah that would be right."

Joe says, "Ok, let's get the vehicle situation organized for tomorrow."

Vernon repeats the plan again to makes sure, "All right guys, everyone knows what they are doing, right?"

Marty reassures Vernon, "Yes Vernon, we'll get Elvis and bring him back home to you."

Vernon smiles and says with great enthusiasm, "Thanks, boys, I can't wait."

Joe echoes Marty, "We'll get him Vernon, don't worry."

Vernon heads up stairs to the kitchen.

Charlie says, "Well, boys, since I've already racked up the balls, let's play one more game. Then, we'll go find a van."

~ * ~

133

Vernon sits on a wooden stool at the white counter top in the kitchen. He picks up the phone and dials the hospital. As the phone rings, Vernon looks up at the clock on the wall which reads 4:30PM.

The receptions answers, "Hello, Baptist Memorial Hospital, how may I help you."

"Hi, can you put me through to room 1212?"

"Oh, is that you, Mr. Presley?"

"Yes, how are you this afternoon?"

"Fine, thank you, sir, I'll put you through now."

On the other end, I pick up the phone, "Hello."

"Hello, son. I wanted to let you know that some of Mafia will be there to pick you tomorrow to bring you home."

"That sounds... um... great."

"There is a security guard everyone calls Papi, and he will be organizing things from that end. He's going to get you down to the delivery entrance at the back of the hospital. Billy, Charlie and Lamar will be there with a van to pick you up. I'm also sending over some photos for you to personalize for him and his family. I've written out whom to make them out to."

"Okay. I'll see how that goes."

"I asked that when you leave, they keep you on a gurney, so they can wheel you right into the van."

"Thanks again… um… Daddy… I'll see you… ah… at home soon."

"Yes, you will, and I'll be glad to see you back here at Graceland."

"How's my… um… little girl doing?" I ask.

"She is doing fine. She is glad to hear that you will be home tomorrow."

"Okay then… ah… I'll see you… soon. Goodbye."

"Have a good night, son. We'll see you tomorrow."

Vernon hangs up the phone and turns in his seat to see Nancy standing in the kitchen. "Hello, Mr. Vernon. Patti tells me that Mr. Elvis is coming home tomorrow."

"Yes, Nancy, he will be home about 2:30PM or so."

"Oh that's great Mr. Vernon. I'll be sure and have some of Mr. Elvis' favorite ugly steak, potatoes and peas with plenty of salt and pepper, cornbread and a large glass of buttermilk ready for him when he gets home."

Vernon says, "Thank you, Nancy. But, no, I don't think that's what he is going to need. Could you fix him baked chicken with no skin, green beans and a salad?"

Nancy looks at Vernon like he is crazy, "What, no fried bananas sandwiches either?"

"No, Elvis is not allowed to eat fried food anymore. We have to find a nutritionist to work with you to develop a new diet for Elvis that he will be able to eat. He has to change his diet, so he can lose weight and get his health back."

"I'm in favor of getting Mr. Elvis healthy, but I'm gonna have to find out how to cook these things to get him that way."

"Yes, you will get to work with the nutritionist. They will give you new recipes to cook and help alter the meals that you already prepare so they are healthier."

"Well I'm going to like learning a new way of cooking healthy for you and Mr. Elvis."

"I'm not so sure that I'm going to eat like Elvis has to now. I still love your fried banana sandwiches. I haven't had a stroke yet, so I'm still good. As a matter of fact, will you make one for me now?"

"You know it'll be my pleasure, Mr. Vernon."

~ * ~

There's a car parked on lover's lane just after sunset outside the city limits. Inside, two teenagers are making out while listening to the radio. The announcer says. "Good evening Memphis this is Al Cosby from WHBQ-AM radio reporting from Graceland. I was informed today, that Elvis met with a Speech Therapist and a Physical Therapist. From what I hear the Speech Therapy went well and the meeting with the Physical Therapist went even better. I have also been told Elvis will be on his way home to Graceland early next week.

"And don't forget that WHBQ-AM starts the new count down to the top ten hits in Memphis tonight at 9:00PM. This is Al Cosby for WHBQ-

136

AM radio, that's it from here and its back to you in the studio."

The girl in the car says, "How cool is that Elvis will be getting out of the hospital soon."

"Yeah, that's really cool. Now where were we?" replies the young man who now has his arm over his girlfriend's shoulder as he leans in for a kiss.

"Don't you care about Elvis?"

"Yes, but I care more about you," as he tries again for another kiss.

"Oh yeah, sure you do! If you really cared about me, you would take me to the hospital tomorrow to see if we can see Elvis."

"What, are you kidding me, what for?"

"Well, if you cared about me you would do it!"

"Okay, okay! Fine. I'll take you there."

"Oh thank you! I love you so much."

So now can we get back to what we are doing?" She smiles and they do.

~ * ~

After finishing their pool game, Joe, Marty, Charlie, and Lamar go upstairs to meet in the Jungle Room. Located behind the kitchen, the Jungle Room was named because of the fieldstone waterfall inside and the furniture. The couch has hand carved dragons' heads as arm rests. It is where Marty and Charlie choose to sit. Lamar and Joe sit in a couple of the overstuffed chairs.

"Getting the van to transport Elvis may be a problem," Joe admits.

Marty suggests, "Vernon said to use a van, what if we used an ambulance to move Elvis?"

Charlie says "That would be all right around the hospital but when we get back to Graceland it will cause a lot of media attention."

"Yeah, you're right. So what kind of van do we get?" says Marty.

Lamar, who is always coming up with good ideas to move me, says, "Why don't we get a delivery van? You know a bread truck or something like that, so it wouldn't raise suspicion at the hospital or here."

Joe agrees, "That sounds like a good idea. What company do we use that makes deliveries to us and the hospital?"

Charlie says, "What about the cleaning contractor. Don't we use the same company for our supplies as the hospital?"

Joe replies, "Yeah, I think we do. I'll call and see if we can hire one of their trucks for a day."

Lamar asks, "Do you think they will let us use it?"

"We won't know until we ask," Joe chuckles.

Marty says, "Well then, we need to give Ace Cleaning Products a call."

Joe asks, "What's the phone number?"

Charlie says, "Let me get the number from Patti, she'll know."

Charlie picks up the phone, "Hello Patti, I need the phone number of Ace Cleaning Products."

"Let me see," Patti says and looks up the phone number in her roll-a-dex. "It's 615-555-2011."

Charlie asks, "Who do we deal with over there?"

"It's Ed Flarity, why?"

"We're going to see if we can pick up Elvis in one of his trucks, so it will look a little less obvious."

"Yeah, okay, that sounds like a good idea. . Ed should be able to arrange that"

"Thanks Patti, I'll talk to you later."

"Okay Charlie, 'bye."

Charlie gives Joe the name and phone number, and he places the call.

"Hello, may I speak to Ed Flarity?" Joe says.

The receptionist says, "Just a moment, please."

"Hello this is Ed, how can I help you?"

"Hello Ed, my name is Joe Esposito. I'm calling you from Graceland."

"Hi, Joe. How are you? Everything OK with your supplies?"

"Fine, thanks. Supplies are good. Listen, Ed, you probably know that Elvis is in the hospital."

"Sure. Who doesn't know that?"

"Well were going to move Elvis from the hospital back to Graceland, and I was wondering if you could help us? Can we hire one of your trucks, or even better yet, one of your vans, to move Elvis home?"

"You want to use one of my vans?"

"Yes. If you have a van that has doors in the back like an ambulance, it would be less conspicuous for a cleaning van to pull in and out of the hospital and make a delivery to Graceland."

"Yeah, I don't see why not," Ed tells Joe, "But, because of my insurance, I can't let a non-employee drive it. But, I could drive it."

"If that would seal the deal, then I'll say yes. You would claim no knowledge of what happened after words, or I'd have to kill you," Joe tells Ed laughingly.

"Got it. I've always wanted to meet Elvis."

"Yes, but I don't want you to make a nuisance of yourself. I'll just need you to drive. There will be two or three other Mafia members in the van besides you and Elvis."

"That would be alright."

"Don't speak to Elvis unless he talks to you. I don't know what condition he will be in, so if you can do that, we have a deal."

"Yes, I'll go along with that."

"Can you be here at Graceland at noon tomorrow?"

"I sure can."

"We're not going to leave for the hospital until 1:15PM. I want you here early so you can meet our guys, and be in on any last minute details that may come up."

"Great, I'll see you at Graceland at noon tomorrow right?"

"Yup. I want you to come in through the back entrance. Do you know where that is?"

"Yes, I've made deliveries out there before."

"Ok then, Ed, we'll see you tomorrow and, by the way, make sure you have enough gas."

Ed says laughing, "Oh, I will."

"Thanks. I'll talk to you later."

"Goodbye, Joe."

"Bye, Ed."

Joe relays the conversation to the rest of the guys. "As you heard, we have Ed the owner of Ace Cleaning Products driving one of his vans. He will be here tomorrow at noon."

Lamar says "Good, it sounds like we have everything covered on this end."

Chapter 13

August 20th, 1977

The phone rings in Vernon's office. He answers, "Hello."

"Hello, Mr. Presley, this is Dr. Francisco here."

"Hello, Doctor. How is Elvis doing today?"

"He is doing just fine, but I need to ask you a favor. We have found that your son has been hooked on prescription drugs which predisposed him to this stroke. What I would like for you to do is clean out all the drugs that Elvis has there at the house. This will reduce his temptation to start taking them again. I have talked to Dr. Nick and he agrees. I have written new prescriptions, but I don't want him to take any other drugs than what I've prescribed for him."

Vernon gets up and starts pacing the floor, "I understand your view point about getting rid of the drugs Elvis has here. But, I'm not sure how happy he would be if he finds that I have gone through his stuff and thrown away all his drugs."

"Mr. Presley, I know you want the best for your son and you know he has been a drug addict for years. I have spoken to Elvis, and his knowledge of prescription drugs is very impressive. However, your son has been walking a fine line and that line was crossed when had his stroke."

"Elvis has been very careful taking his prescriptions, but you're right he has taken them far too long. He has told me that he wants to stop taking the pills," Vernon confesses to Dr. Francisco.

"He has spoken to me about the same thing, Vernon. I just need you to not enable him and take temptation out of his reach."

"Alright, I'll do it! Is he still being released at two?"

"Yes, that is still the plan."

"Alright, the maid is preparing Elvis's room for his arrival and we'll throw out all previous prescriptions."

"Thank you. I know that this is a hard decision for you to make, but you have made the right choice for Elvis' wellbeing."

"I know that is what he told me, but if it is just the drugs talking, then there is going to be hell to pay." Vernon squirmed.

"I truly hope that Elvis has seen the opportunity he has here to turn his life around and become even a bigger, better person than he was."

"Thank you for calling, Dr. Francisco, and for your concern about Elvis."

"Vernon, I don't have to tell you, you have a tremendously talented son. I want him to continue to improve and do what we both know he is capable of doing."

"You're right, thanks again. I'll get on it as soon as we hang up the phone," Vernon tells the doctor.

"I'm glad we had this talk and I'm sure I'll see you again in the near future."

"I'm sure we will. Goodbye doctor."

"Goodbye."

Vernon sits back down at his desk and hits the intercom button on the phone to call Nancy. "Nancy, can you come over to my office, please."

"Yes sir, Mr. Vernon. I'll be right there."

Nancy leaves the kitchen and heads out the back door. She enters Vernon's office, "Yes Mr. Vernon, what do you need?"

"Nancy, I just spoke to Dr. Francisco. He has asked me to clean out all the old prescription medications that Elvis has around the house."

Nancy's eyes open wide in surprise on her face, "You want me to go throw out all of Mr. Elvis' old prescriptions?"

"Yes, he wants to start Elvis on a new drug regime and feels that if Elvis is exposed to his old prescriptions he may start using them again and possibility have another stroke."

"I don't want to upset Mr. Elvis. And, I sure don't want to get into trouble!"

"You won't Nancy. I'll tell Elvis that I did it if he asks about where they went."

"Okay Mr. Vernon, if you're sure. I'll go right now and make the 'vitamin packets' disappear."

"Okay Nancy, I'll be up to help in a few minutes."

"Alright then, I'll see you over there." Nancy returns to the mansion.

Bob Ford is standing outside the main entrance of the hospital. With microphone in hand he does his broadcast.

"Good morning Memphis, Tennessee. Bob Ford here from WHBQ-TV, it's 10AM and I am, once again, outside Baptist Memorial Hospital. We are on day four of Elvis Watch. The crowds are getting bigger each day with fans hoping to hear news or get a glimpse of Elvis. The pile of get well cards and flowers being left for the King by his fans continues to grow. All that we know at this point is that Elvis has met with a Speech Therapist and a Physical Therapist yesterday to talk about his rehabilitation plans. We believe that he will be going home at the beginning of next week. As more details are available we will report them here first on our Elvis Watch.

"This is Bob Ford, live from Baptist Memorial Hospital on WHBQ-TV."

~ * ~

Vernon, Joe, and Lamar are sitting in the dining room at Graceland. There are round fronted curio cabinets in both corners at the north end of the room. The three windows in the room are adorned with royal blue curtains. There is a black china cabinet between the two windows on the west wall. Hanging over the middle of the brown wood dining room table is a gold chandelier. Under the table is black marble flooring with a white carpet around the perimeter. Nancy is serving breakfast to the guys.

Vernon asks Joe, "Are we all set to bring Elvis home, today?"

"Yes, sir, we have Ed Flarity coming over from Ace Cleaning Company. He is providing one of his vans to use to move Elvis."

Vernon loves the choice, "Oh that's great. I know Ed. He's a good guy."

Nancy brings out more toast for Joe. "Thank you, Nancy."

Lamar adds, "He'll be here at noon with one of his vans that will let us roll the gurney right into the back."

Vernon sips his cup of coffee, "Where are Marty and Charlie?"

"They're out washing and gassing up the Cadillac," answers Lamar

"I heard from Larry that the meeting with the Physical Therapist went well," Joe smiles, buttering his toast.

Vernon tells Joe, after a bite of scrambled eggs, "Yeah, Elvis said he was quite taken by her. I think her name is A.E. It was just a flash in the pan. She been seeing someone for quite a while, and I don't think Elvis was quite up to doing anything about it any way."

"Yeah, but he told Larry that he was thinking of having her move to Hawaii."

Lamar asks, "Elvis is going to Hawaii? Where have I been?"

Vernon says, "Yes, as soon as he gets back here and is able to travel, we are going to make the arrangements to have him do rehab in Maui."

"Who's going to Maui with E.?"

"We haven't decided yet, Lamar," Vernon tells him.

"Vernon, how long do you expect Elvis to be over there?" Joe asks. He then takes a sip of his orange juice.

"We don't know yet, Joe. It depends on how the rehab goes."

Joe says, "Well, I know a real estate person over there in Maui. I can call him and have him start looking for a house to rent. Elvis knows this guy, too. We were all in the Army together over in Germany."

"Let's not get ahead of ourselves," Vernon suggests. "When Elvis gets home we can talk about what the Hawaiian trip will look like."

Lamar pushes himself away from the table, "I'm going to see how Marty and Charlie are doing. I'll see you guys later." He yells out, "Thanks for breakfast, Nancy!"

Nancy yells back from the kitchen, "You're welcome, Mr. Lamar!"

~ * ~

Colonel Parker dials his phone to place a call. The receptionist on the other end answers, "William Morris Agency, how may I help you?"

The Colonel demands, "Yes, get me Harry Kalcheim."

147

The receptionist asks, "May I tell him who's calling?"

"Tell him it's The Colonel."

"Just a moment please."

Harry Kalcheim is the rep who handles things for me at the agency. It's not like I need the agency, but the Colonel uses it as a front for his business. Harry is the agent in name only. He answers the phone, "Hello Colonel, how are you doing today?"

"I'm fine. I just wanted to update you on what's going on with Elvis. He should be coming home today. We expect he will spend a few days there, and then he is going to Maui for rehab."

"That's great news Colonel, but I've had several promoters ask what is going to happen to the promotional material and the merchandise that was put together for the cancelled tour?"

"The stuff that's date sensitive will become collector's items, and the other stuff we'll hold and use at a later date."

"That sounds like a good, Colonel."

"So what else have you heard from them?"

"They all wish Elvis well, and want to know where to send the cards, letters and gifts?"

"Have them sent to Graceland."

"Alright, I'll have them do that. When do you think Elvis will be able to return to work?"

This question really pisses off the Colonel. "God damn it Harry, it's going to be quite a long time before Elvis can work again. Haven't you heard the news? He's had a fucking stroke. He is partially paralyzed in his right arm and he can hardly get words out when he speak. I don't want you to promise anyone, anything until you hear from me."

"Okay, okay, Colonel, I was just asking. I understand. If you can let me know when I can see Elvis, to pay him a visit, I would appreciate it."

"Harry, I'll let you know when it would be appropriate to do that."

"So with Elvis out for a while are you going to pick up any other acts?"

"No! The boy is who I'm going to work with," the Colonel answers indignantly.

"If you sign anyone, please, let me know. I would like to handle them, also."

"Don't hold your breath Harry! If there isn't any other business we need to take care of, I'll say goodbye."

"Ok Colonel, I'll talk to you later."

"Yes, you will Harry." The Colonel hangs up the phone, and under his breath mutters, "Ass hole!"

Chapter 14

Larry and I are sitting in a front pew, facing the plainly dressed alter of the Baptist Memorial Hospital Chapel. There are stained glass windows along the chapel walls with soft lighting coming from behind. It's a very small space, where maybe 4 people can sit in each pew. There are four rows of pews on each side of the center aisle and aisles up either side.

Larry hands me a brown envelope, "Here Elvis, Vernon asked me get these photo's signed for Mr. De Jesus, the security guard and his wife. All the information is in there."

"Okay… I'll ah… do that later… but Larry… um… I still can't… figure out why… um… God has… put me here… and ah… what I'm… supposed to do? There's… got to be… a reason why… ah… I was chosen… to be Elvis Presley. I swear to God… no one knows… how lonely… I get… and ah… how empty… I really feel."

Larry answers in a reflective way. "Elvis, that's a question that everybody asks themselves. 'Why am I here and what is my purpose?' You can answer that question through reflection on your inner thoughts. Then you'll begin to understand what God's plan is for you."

"Yes… I know… but I'm just… um… a rock & roll… singer. I have fans… that idolize me. Everything I touch… ah… seems to… turn to gold. I'm feeling… like, ah… King Midas. You know… what I mean. I don't… understand… what my… um… Mama meant… by saying… um… to me… 'Go back… ah… you're work isn't… done yet?'"

"Through the connection you have with your mother, God is telling you that you need to stay here and keep on working. Doing what you do best. That's making people happy with your songs, your shows and your movies. Yes, you get paid very well from the people that idolize you, but how you use that money to effect other people's lives is what's important," Larry explains.

"And who is God? Was he Jesus... or was he... ah... Buddha, Muhammad... Zeus, Allah... um... or Mother Earth? What form... does He take? And ah... why are there... so many different... um... religions? How does anyone... know which... one is right? The Jews... the Catholics... um... the Baptist... the Protestants... or um... is it... the Buddhist... um... or the Hindu's. How... do I know... how does ah... anyone know?"

This is an area that Larry is well versed, "Who's to say that any one of them is right? They may all be right. The people that believe in God think that their God is the only one. The Native American Indians believe in Great Spirit. The Aborigines believe in a mythology called, 'Dreamtime.' Their religion is similar to that of the Hawaiians. All are right; the people of each culture who have their own belief know it to be true for them.

"Where I think things start getting out of hand is when people kill one another if they don't convert to a belief in a particular God. That's when people lose touch with God and their own Spirit."

I pause for a moment and then ask, "Do all religions... have the... equivalent of... ah... the Ten... Commandments?"

"I think for the most part that they do. It may not be the exact same wording, but the meaning will be the same. In Islam, despite the Ten Commandments not being mentioned in the Qur'an, there are texts in it that are substantially similar to the Jewish rules and the numbering of the Commandments.

"The important thing is for you to believe in one thing. Be the best person you can be and treat everyone as you would like to be treated. That's the 'Golden Rule.' It reflects the Ancient Egyptian concept of Matt that appears in the story of The Eloquent Peasant."

"I don't... um... know that story." Elvis admitted.

"The quick and the short of it is what goes around comes around. It's if someone does you wrong, and causes you to suffer, then justice comes along and makes things right for you, and makes the other guy suffer for harming you."

"I'll have to... read... ah... that story."

"Yes it's a good story. It's short and won't take you long to read at all."

"Thank you... um... Larry for... shedding light... ah... on what I've... been thinking... about."

"Elvis, just believe in yourself," Larry says, with a big smile. "Trust your instincts. You are a very spiritual, caring, and giving person. Spend more time doing what you do best, and God will take care of the rest for you."

"Oh brother… um… I hope so. His… got me… in a fine… ah… pickle right now… though."

"No, you got yourself into this pickle. God just gave you a wakeup call to get out of it! And yes, you will get through it. But that is enough to give you something to think about for now. Are you ready to go back to your room?"

"Yes… let's go. It's getting close… um… to time… for me to get… checked out… of here."

"You have about two hours yet. I'm sure it will be good to be getting out of here though."

"You can… say that… ah… again, son."

We stand up and head back to the rear of the chapel. I stop to light a candle and say a quiet prayer. Larry stands there watching me in admiration and silence, as I pray. When I finish, we leave the chapel.

~ * ~

Priscilla is sitting at her desk in her home office in Beverly Hills. She is looking out the window over the back yard garden which is in full bloom. The pool is being vacuumed by a young, tanned, muscular pool boy who is not wearing a shirt. He is tempting, but she knows better, and just enjoys the view. Coming back to reality, she picks up the phone and calls Joe.

The phone rings several times before she hears Joe say, "Hello."

"Hello, Joe. It's me."

"Oh, hello Priscilla," Joe answers with great delight in his voice. "How are you doing?"

"I've been swamped with reporters and photographers since Elvis had his stroke."

"Well you of all people know too well what it's like, having been married to the King."

"I had my press agent release a statement, and I have been very low key since then. But, you know how those reporters can be. I'm calling to let you know that I'll be coming back in two days."

"Do you want me to send the *Hound Dog II* to come get you?"

The *Hound Dog II* is a Lockheed JetStar aircraft that I bought on September 2, 1975 for $899,000 while I was waiting for the completion of the *Lisa Marie*. Milo High was going to pilot them back to California.

"No, there no sense in having them dead head here and then fly right back again. I'll just take a commercial flight from L.A. to Memphis. Once I get the flight details, if you could have someone from the Mafia pick me up at the airport that would be helpful."

"Sure. That will be no problem. Do you want me to let Elvis know or are you going to tell him when you're coming in?"

"No, keep this between you and me for now. Don't even tell the Mafia that I'm coming in until the day I'm to be picked up. You can tell Elvis the same day that I'm coming in, so it's one less thing he'll have to worry about."

"Ok, just let me know your flight details and I'll take care of it from here."

"Thanks, Joe you're great. I really appreciate everything you do for me and for Elvis."

"Oh, that's okay. You know that I love the guy. You know what I mean, not love the guy but love the guy. And, I respect you and love helping you out, too."

"Well, I appreciate it and thanks again. I'm going to let you go for now. I'll call you or the travel agent will call to let you know when I'll be coming in."

"All right, we'll talk later. Goodbye, Priscilla."

"Goodbye, Joe."

~ * ~

It's about 11:55AM. An Ace Cleaning Products truck is driving down the church service road that runs along the Graceland property line. It pulls up to a gate in the white fence. Dick is there and opens the gate to let the van come through, eyeing the driver, assumes, "You must be Ed."

"Yup, that's me." Ed replies, as they shake hands.

Dick slides into the passenger seat, points to the back of the mansion and tells Ed, "Go right down through the pasture and past the Oak grove."

As Ed drives to the back of mansion he asks, "Is Joe here? Where do you want me to park the van?" Dick directs him to park by the kitchen door.

"He's here. Come on inside I'll take you to him." They walk through the mansion to the Jungle room where Joe, Vernon, Billy, Charlie, Marty & Lamar have gathered, to get ready to retrieve The King.

Vernon seeing Ed says, "Hello Ed, it's good to see you."

"Hi, Mr. Presley, it's good to see you again too."

"Just call me Vernon. Have you met everyone yet?" Vernon motions toward Joe, "This is Joe."

"Yes, we spoke on the phone yesterday," Ed remembers.

"Hi. You look familiar; have I seen you on the property before?"

"I've been here before making deliveries. I still like to keep my hand in for special customers."

Vernon continues, "You have met Dick our head of security here at Graceland. This is Billy, Elvis's cousin. And, Charlie, Marty and Lamar are all part of the Memphis Mafia."

Ed says "Hi guys, it's nice to meet you," as he shakes their hands. "Gee, does this mean I am one of the Mafia?"

Vernon emphatically informs Ed, "No you're not a member of the Memphis Mafia, and I don't think you ever will be one."

Ed feels a little deflated being put in his place like that until Joe says, "Don't take it personally, Ed. We are cutting down on the size of the entourage, not adding to it right now."

Vernon lays out the plan, "All right guys. Let's go over it one more time. Joe and Marty, I want you to take the Cadillac and pull up to the front of Memorial, as big and bold as you can. You are the distraction, so get as much of the press to focus on you as possible. Ed, Charlie, Billy and Lamar, you are in the van. Back it into to the shipping and receiving entrance at the rear of the hospital where you will meet with the head of hospital security. His name is Papi. As soon as Elvis is brought down, get him into the van quickly and back here to Graceland A.S.A.P."

Joe asks, "How will we know when the van has left the hospital?"

"Okay, good point," Vernon says as he scratches his head. "This is what you need to do then. Once Elvis is in the van, Charlie you go and find Joe and Marty. Let them know, to coin the phrase, "Elvis has left the building." There is laughter amongst the group. "Billy and Lamar, you bring Elvis back to Graceland with Ed's help. Then Charlie, Joe and Marty you can come back to Graceland."

Charlie asks, "Where will I find you guys?"

"Meet us on the 12th floor, at the nurses' station." Marty replies.

"We'll head back as soon as you find us," Joe adds.

"Don't forget to come back through the back gate and Dick will let you in again," Vernon reminds Ed.

Ed reassures Vernon, "I'll remember that."

"Good, I'm counting on you."

157

Joe asks, "Once we get Elvis back home is he going right upstairs to his bedroom or can we have a welcome home party for him?"

Vernon counts heads to figure out how many people will be there, "I'll tell Mary to fix a nice meal for let's say um… twelve of us."

Billy grins, "It sure will be nice to have Elvis back home again."

Vernon tells everyone, "Now you all know that Elvis is going to be on a new diet, so it's going to be a different kind of meal than what we would usually have around here."

"What do you think that will be?" Lamar asks.

"I don't know, but if Nancy fixes it, you know it will taste good," answers Vernon.

Marty testifies, "Amen, to that brother."

Vernon directs everyone, "All right, you guys, get ready to leave. But before you go, let me know so I can call the hospital and let them know we are on schedule."

Chapter 15

Dr. Nick and Dr. Francisco, find me sitting on my bed, dressed and ready to go. Larry is sitting in the visitor's chair. Dr. Nick greets us, "Good afternoon guys, how are you?"

Larry says, "I'm doing fine thanks."

Dr. Francisco adds, "How are you feeling Elvis?"

I give Dr. Nick a thumbs up sign and say, "I'm feeling… um… pretty good. But… I'm ready… to go… um… home… Dr. Nick."

"Well your tests confirm that too, so you're on your way home."

"Great… I can't… um… wait."

Dr. Francisco asks, "Elvis, are you still planning to do your rehab in Hawaii?"

"I'm going to… move to… ah… Maui… as soon… as I can. I'll do what… your um… people have… shown me to do… um… until then. I plan to… spend um… all my time… rehabbing… ah… in the islands."

Dr. Francisco comments, "That sounds good. If you need anything or have questions, feel free to contact me. We're going to miss you around here."

"Thank you… for everything. I'll miss the… folks here … but… I think I'll… be better off… doing… my recovery… ah… in Maui."

Dr. Nick asks, "Have you made arrangements with the rehab people over there?"

"No… um… not yet. I'll start… working on that… ah… when I get back… to Graceland."

Dr. Nick offers, "I'll give you some referrals, so you can have names to contact as soon as you get there."

"Would you… give that information… to um… Joe or… Vernon, please?"

Dr. Nick nods in agreement.

"We're just waiting to hear from security to tell us when the van has arrived. Then we'll get you down stairs and on your way," Dr. Francisco informs us.

I laugh, "Good… I'll be glad… to get back home."

Dr. Nick agrees, "I'm sure you are."

~ * ~

Vernon places a call to the hospital. The receptionist answers the phone, "Good afternoon, how may I direct your call."

"Hello, this is Vernon Presley, may I speak to Dr. Francisco please."

She asks Vernon to hold. Using the hospital intercom, she announces, "Paging Dr. Francisco, paging Dr. Francisco, please call the operator. Dr. Francisco, please call the operator."

Dr. Francisco hears the page and picks up the phone in my room. "Hello, this is Dr. Francisco."

The receptionist tells the doctor that he has a call from Vernon Presley. "Please put him through. I'm in room 1212 and thank you." There is a click on the phone and he says, "Hello Vernon, I'm here with your son."

Vernon asks with concern, "Is he okay?"

"Oh yes, he's fine and can't wait to get home."

With relief in his voice, Vernon says, "Oh. Okay. , I just called to let you know that the Mafia is on their way. They will be there to pick up Elvis in 25 minutes. Please have him ready when they get there."

Dr. Francisco assures him, "Yes, Vernon, we'll be ready and waiting for them. Do you want to talk to Elvis?"

"No. But, tell him, 'I love him.' and I'll see him in about an hour."

"All right then, we'll talk to you later, goodbye for now."

Vernon hangs up the phone.

~ * ~

Vernon goes outside and addresses all the guys that are a part Elvis' Coming Home mission. "Okay, so are you guys ready to leave?"

Joe answers for the group, "Yes sir, we're all ready."

"Well then go ahead and get going. I've just called Dr. Francisco and told him you are on the way, so he's is going to move Elvis now."

"Then we're out of here."

Vernon bids the guys farewell, "Be safe Joe, and that goes for the rest of you guys too."

There is a collective agreement from every one as they all nod.

Vernon then goes into the mansion and asks, "Mary, what are you fixing for the arrival party?"

Mary answers, "I'm fixing to do some grilled salmon and green beans."

"And what's for desert?"

"I got Mr. Elvis some sherbet; lemon, lime and raspberry, your choice."

"We're on a new path now aren't we Mary."

"Yes, we are, Mr. Vernon."

~ * ~

Dr. Francisco is at the nurses' station finishing up the paperwork on my discharge. He uses the phone to call down stairs. "Hello Papi, its Dr. Francisco. I just got off the phone with Mr. Presley and he informs me, 'The Mafia' is on the way to pick up Elvis."

Papi replies, "I'm at the loading dock right now and it's quite down here."

"Alright then, we'll bring Elvis downstairs to where you are. We'll see you in a few minutes then Papi."

"Okay doc, I'll see you soon."

Walking back to my room, Dr. Francisco tells the orderly to come with him and bring a gurney. As he enters the room he says, "Well Elvis, it's time for you to go home."

"I'm… really ready… um … now."

"We're going to take you downstairs to the shipping and receiving platform where Papi is waiting to help get you into your transportation."

Dr. Nick tells me, "We're going to have to move you onto a gurney to get you out of here."

But... I can walk. Ah, I have... been practicing... um... in the hallways."

Dr Francisco smiles, "But, Elvis, you know we have a policy that no patient walks out, they have to take a ride to get out of the hospital. Insurance requires it."

"Ok... let's do it!"

The orderly pushes the gurney closer to the side of my bed. I protest, again, saying that I can get there myself, but Dr. Francisco tells me, "I'm sure you can, but for your safety and hospital rules we must do it this way."

The orderly, places his left hand under my right armpit and grasp my right arm gently guiding me onto the gurney. Happy to be on my way, I expresses my excitement, "It's show time... boys... let's go!"

Dr. Francisco smiles as he tells the orderly, "Go ahead. Take Elvis down to the elevator."

Dr. Francisco follows the orderly with Larry and Dr. Nick in tow. As they get to the elevator, Larry pushes the down button. Marion comes up to the group and speaks to me. "Well, I guess this is goodbye."

I reply with a grin, "No darling... um... it's just... till I see you... next time."

"I want you to recover, and be even better than you were 10 years ago."

"Why… um… ten years ago?"

"So you can be on the same page with me," we laugh at our personal inside joke as the doctors and Larry look on in puzzlement.

I ask Marion, "I'll need you… to do your… private nursing… duties… you can do that… can't you?"

"Yes I can."

Dr. Nick tells me, "I also have Tish Henley for private nursing duties when Marion is off."

"Yeah… just… um… work out the… schedule with… Joe," I instruct Dr. Nick.

The elevator door opens and the orderly pushes me in as the doctors and Larry follow. I call out to Marion, "Okay child… ah… stay well." Marion waves as the elevator doors close.

~ * ~

Joe and Marty walk up to the front entrance of the hospital and find themselves surrounded by a group of reporters. They walk into the lobby with the reporters hot on their heels firing questions at them.

Jim Kingsley says, "Joe, how's Elvis doing?"

Clark Porteous asks, "Marty, why has Ginger only been to see Elvis once?"

Alanna Stills calls out, "Joe, when will Elvis be released? Will he be going back to Graceland?"

Jim Kingsley yells, "Joe is there any truth that Elvis has broken off the relationship with Ginger Alden and the wedding has been canceled?"

Joe and Marty look at each other wondering how that story got leaked but stop long enough to make a quick statement. Joe says, "Look, the doctors are planning to release Elvis when he is healthy enough. If that is in two days or two weeks, I don't really know. We are just here to visit and keep Elvis' spirits up."

The two men start moving through the lobby again, ignoring the new barrage of questions. Joe waves to receptionists as they makes their way to the elevator, "Good afternoon ladies, how are you doing today?"

One of them replies, "We're doing just fine thank you Mr. Esposito. Are you here to see Elvis?"

"Who else would I come here to see, other than you darling," Joe replies.

The second receptionist tells Joe, "Oh Mr. Esposito you're so funny. Are these gentlemen with you?" pointing to the press that have followed then into the hospital.

"Just Marty today, the other can't come up."

The second receptionist comments, "Well, you know where he is."

"Yes, and I'll be back to say goodbye to you later."

The first receptionist says, "We'll look forward to it. Now, the rest of you guys please go back outside so I don't have to call security to remove you from the lobby."

Joe and Marty get into the elevator and push to button for the 5th, 8th and 12th floors. "That will confuse them for a little while," Joe remarks.

~ * ~

As Joe and Marty are going up in their elevator, another elevator door opens in the basement. The orderly is pushing me into the hallway of the shipping and receiving area with both doctors and Larry close behind.

"Oh, hello, Dr. Francisco, Dr. Nick, how are you?" Papi asks.

"We're all just fine," Dr. Francisco tells Papi. "Are we all set to say goodbye to our patient?"

"The van is just now backing in, so we'll be ready in just a moment, Doc."

A second security guard comes up to the group and tells Papi, "The van is here and in position for the package."

"Great, then if you're ready doctors, I guess we can head out." Papi, looking like Barney Fife waving his arms, directs the orderly and his security guard with military precision.

I exclaim, "Wow… when did I… um… turn into… a package? Don't I get any… um… say… as to what's… going on here?"

Papi says, "Sure, yes, of course you do Mr. Presley, I'm sorry, I didn't mean to…."

"Stop… ah… wait a minute… Papi. I spoke with my… um… father and… he asked me…. to

166

give this… ah… to you… and your wife." I hand the brown envelope to Papi who opens it, to find the autographed photos.

Papi exclaims with great delight and excitement, "Oh my goodness, I can't believe this. There are three autographed pictures of you in here! Let me see, there is one made out to me and another made out to my wife and then one to both of us! Oh thank you Mr. Presley. I don't know how to thank you."

"You just did… but you don't… have to," I reply. "Papi… you're making my… ah… escape possible."

There is laughter among the group standing around my gurney.

"I wish you… and your… um… family all… the best. God bless!"

"Oh yes sir, thank you so much," Papi replies.

Dr. Francisco says, "Okay, I guess this is it for now, Elvis."

"The next time… I'll see you… um… doctor… you will be… in the front… ah… row when I play… my first… um… show… after I recover."

"Yes you will, and I'll be glad to be there," Dr. Francisco agrees.

Dr. Nick says, "Elvis, I'll see you back at Graceland."

"Okay… Dr. Nick."

Charlie, Lamar and Billy come up to me and the others. Ed has parked the van and is waiting in the driver's seat. I am sitting up on the gurney. Charlie is excited, "It's good to see you boss."

Lamar says, "We're taking you home, E."

Billy greets me, "Hey Elvis, it's good to see you again."

I get a big smile when I see the guys.

"It's good to… um… see you guys… too. Now get me… ah… out of here… will you?"

Charlie says, "I'm going to go find Joe and Marty and we'll meet you back at Graceland later.

"Are they… here?" I ask.

"Yeah, they are here. They're up stairs. They are making it look like you are still here, so you can quietly leave here with Billy and Lamar to go back to Graceland. Joe, Marty and I will wait a while after you have safely left the building to leave. We'll catch up with you back there."

"Ok Charlie… um… I'll see you… back there."

The orderly pushes the gurney toward the van. The back doors are already open. Billy and Lamar help the orderly put the gurney safely into the van. Once I am in the van, Billy and Lamar climb in too.

Before the doors are shut Larry leans in and says, "That's the kind of thing that makes a difference in the world."

Puzzled, I ask, "What… are you… um… talking about… Larry?"

"Giving the autographed pictures to Papi, that's what I'm talking about."

"That wasn't… anything um… Larry. What did it… cost me… ah… in time or money… nothing."

"I know, but that's what we were talking about earlier in the chapel. God has truly blessed you, my friend."

He gives me a wink of acknowledgement and I just curl my lip… we both smile at each other.

"See you back at Graceland my friend," Larry tells me, as he closes the van doors.

Larry taps the roof of the van three times to let Ed know that it's okay for the van to pull out, sending me on my way back to my beloved Graceland.

Back at the loading dock, Dr. Nick says, "Thank you, Dr. Francisco, for all your help and assistance."

"You're quite welcome."

Papi with great enthusiasm tells everyone, "Boy, oh boy, did you see what Elvis gave me? Not only one, but three autographed pictures, wow!"

Dr. Nick comments, "It sounds like Elvis has made your day, Papi."

"Oh you can say that again," he responds.

Dr. Nick says with a slight laugh, "I don't think I will, but I will say goodbye to you all now."

Billy asks, "Will we see you back at Graceland, Dr. Nick?"

"I have to go to the office first. I'll come by later."

Dr. Francisco, Papi and the orderly head back to the main part of the hospital.

"Okay, I'm coming with you guys so I can go up to the 12th floor and find Joe and Marty. Then I'll head back with them," Billy says.

Larry says, "I'll come over to Graceland later. I have some shopping to do, first."

Having gotten me out of the hospital without an incident, everyone relaxes and heads off in separate directions.

~ * ~

With the van safely heading back to Graceland, I ask Lamar and Billy, "So… what have… you two… ah… been up to… since I've… um… been gone?"

Lamar replies, "We've just been dealing with the press and all the people outside the gates."

"Has there been… a lot of… um… people there?"

Billy explains "Oh yeah, it's hard to get in and out because of so many people leaving flowers, candles, teddy bears, cards and just hanging around waiting to see if anything is going to happen."

Lamar says, "We pick up the cards about every twelve hours and take then back to Vernon's office."

Billy informs me, "Yeah and we pick up the flowers and take them to the local nursing homes and hospital to give to patients. Of course, that's after we've pulled the cards out of them and sent them back to Vernon office."

"That's a great… um… idea, who came up… with that?"

Lamar says, "Larry did."

With admiration in my voice, I tell the guys, "Why am I… not ah… surprised. I have to thank… um… Larry… for being so thoughtful… with my… ah… flowers."

I notice that someone new is driving the getaway van. "Who's the new guy?"

Billy answers, "Oh, this is Ed from Ace Cleaning Products. His company services the hospital and we get our cleaning products from his company too."

Elvis asks, "Ed… do you mean… to tell me um… I'm in one of… your ah… company cleaning vans?"

"Yes, that's true, Mr. Presley."

"Just call me… Elvis, ah… or… you can call me… the um… King," with a little laughter, "Just kidding… um… you can just… call me Elvis. Well damn… this is… um… a first. Here I am… ah… riding in a… cleaning van. I've slipped… um… a long way.

"Did you know… um… I used to drive… a truck ah… for a living? I ah…delivered electrical… parts." I say in a matter of fact voice.

"Well, if you ever need a job driving a truck, Elvis, just let me know," Ed offers. We all laugh together.

Lamar let's Elvis know, "We did it this way for your security. We checked with Dr. Francisco and he told us you would be safe to ride back to Graceland in a van."

Billy says, "Yeah as soon as Charlie finds Joe and Marty, they are on their way back to Graceland too."

I laugh, "Sounds like… you guys… ah… have worked this… plan out. It's like… um… a James Bond… mission."

~ * ~

Charlie steps out of the elevator onto the 12th floor and heads over to the nurses' station to find Joe and Marty talking to Marion. He says in low tones, "We have gotten Elvis out of here with no muss, no fuss."

"Good. As soon as we say our goodbyes to Marion and her staff lets stop at the cafeteria for a cup of coffee. Then we can head back, too."

"I guess we will be seeing you later, Marion. Thanks for taking such good care of Elvis," Joe expresses his gratitude.

Marion tells Joe, "Elvis has asked me to come back to Graceland to do private nursing duty."

"You should check with Dr. Nick and see how you can work around your hospital schedule. And, you and your staff did a great job. Thank you again, for everything."

Marion responds, "It was our pleasure. That's what we're here for, Joe. Besides, you know that Elvis is always welcome and we love having him anytime. Of course, we prefer that he not need us."

Charlie agrees, "We would prefer that, too."

Marty, getting anxious, suggests, "Alright gang, let's get out of here."

"Okay let's go," Joe says, as he pushes the down button for the elevator.

Marion waves to the guys as they get into the elevator, "Goodbye, guys."

Chapter 16

Back at Graceland, Vernon is standing at the kitchen counter talking to Mary as she's sitting on a stool. "Is Elvis' room ready, Mary?"

"Yes sir, Mr. Presley"

"No, what I mean is, are all the pills gone?"

"Yes, sir. I looked high and low and I think I found all the pills he had up there and around the rest of the house too."

"Good girl, Mary. So how's the dinner coming?"

"All I need is about 15 minutes, and I'll be ready to serve as many people as show up."

"Thanks, Mary. You are a God send."

"Oh Mr. Presley, you sure know how to make me blush," Mary says bashfully.

~ * ~

As the van pulls up to the back gate, Dick, who has been waiting there, swings it open wide. Once they drive through the gate, he locks it up again. Dick then jumps into the passenger seat and rides down the hill to the back door.

Feeling the slow down, I am like a little kid, asking, "Are we… here, yet?"

Ed tells Elvis, "Yes we are, Elvis."

I am excited to be home and I urge the guys, "Good… get me… um… out of here!"

Dick jumps out and runs around to open the back doors. Billy and Lamar start pulling the

174

gurney out of the van, but I can't wait. I get off the gurney and carefully climb out of the van. Dick greets me, "Hello, Elvis, you're looking good."

"Uh… Thanks, Dick … but how… um… are you?"

Dick shocked to hear Elvis speech says, "Wow what happened to your voice."

"It's not just… my voice… um… it's my right… arm too!"

Dick asks, laughingly "Does your arm sound as funny as your voice?"

"No… smart guy… um… it's partially paralyzed."

"Damn Elvis, I'm really sorry to hear that. But, the word around here is you're going to rehab in Maui and will be as good as new."

"That's the plan… um… Stan… ah… that's the plan."

Once the gurney is on the ground, I tell the guys, "Listen boy's… um… I'm going… to have to… ah… get off this thing. If it hasn't… attached it's self… um… to my ass."

Vernon and Mary come walking out of the house. "Oh, my son, my God, it's good to see you standing here," Vernon comes over and we hug each other tightly. After a long moment, we separate.

"Daddy… I'm glad to see… um… you too."

Mary, standing just behind Vernon steps up and says, "Oh, Mr. Elvis, I'm so happy to see you."

I hold out my left arm, "Come here... Mary... and give... ah... Elvis a... big old hug."

"Oh my goodness yes, Mr. Elvis." She gives me a hug as tears of joy start rolling down her cheeks.

Seeing this Ed says, "Well it looks like I've intruded on this family reunion long enough, so I better get going."

"Where do you... think you're... ah... going?"

"I'm sure you have a lot to do and I..."

I interrupt, "No... you're staying to eat... ah... right Mary?"

"Yes sir, Mr. Elvis."

"Then... that settles it... Ed, you're... ah... staying for a while... we'll throw you out... um... before I go... to bed."

Ed responds, "Okay, okay. Thank you, it will be my pleasure."

"Sure it will... but... um... it will be... mine too! I'm going up stairs to change my clothes. Billy... come with me. Why don't... you guys go... to the TV room... I'll catch up... with you there."

We all enter the house through the back door. Lamar and Ed head to the TV room and Vernon and Mary return to the kitchen.

As Billy helps me up the stairs to my bedroom, Lisa Marie is coming down. Elvis calls out to her, "Where is... my baby... um... girl? There... she is."

"Daddy!" Lisa Marie squeals with delight, seeing me. She throws her arms around my waist and gives me a hug.

"What have you… been doing… um… Buttonhead… since I've been… away?"

"I've been looking after the horses and playing tricks on the gardeners."

As I continue up the stairs with Lisa Marie at my side, I say to her, "Are you… going to be… ah… champion… horse woman?"

"Yes, I'm going to ride and win lots of first place ribbons. I might even go to the Olympics. How are you feeling Daddy?"

"I'm feeling… ah… a lot better… now honey."

"You're not going to die are you?"

"No… I'm not going… to die, honey. Are you… going to sit… next to me… um… when we eat?"

"Yes, Daddy."

"That's… my girl. Now daddy… um… is going to change… um… his clothes… so why don't you… go out and… um… play… I'll call you… when we're… ready to eat."

"Okay." Lisa Marie hugs me again. As she goes running down the stairs to head outside to play, she calls out, "Bye, Billy!"

"Bye-bye, Lisa,"

We continue up stairs to my bedroom.

~ * ~

Vernon tells Mary, "I'm going to be in my office, so call me when it's time to eat, will you?"

"Yes sir, Mr. Presley."

As he turns to leave the kitchen, Joe, Marty, and Charlie get back from the hospital. Joe asks, "Hello Vernon, did Elvis get here without any trouble?"

"Yeah, he's fine. He just went upstairs with Billy to change. The other guys are in the TV room, so go on down there. We'll be eating soon."

The three go to the TV room joining the other two.

Joe greets them as he enters, "Hey you guys."

"Hey, guys, it looks like we pulled it off. We got Elvis home without so much as one press person noticing," Lamar relates.

"Well, that's not the first time we have snuck him out of a building unnoticed," says Marty. "But, I wonder what's going to happen when Elvis goes to Hawaii?"

Joe ponders the question, "I don't know. Why? What are you thinking, Marty?"

"We don't know how long Elvis is going over there for rehab."

Charlie replies, "We'll probably go over to Hawaii with him. You know that he likes having us around and he's going to need us to take care of him and be his body guards."

"Yeah, Elvis needs us to watch his back. Someone has to keep that boy from getting into trouble," Lamar says, laughing.

Joe, remembering there is a stranger in the group says, "Well, let's see what happens. Anyway, I see we have a guest here tonight."

Ed responds, "Hi. I'm Ed. Elvis invited me to hang out with you guys."

"Hi, Ed. I'm sure he did. But, now is not the time to talk business. Let's just be happy that Elvis is home." Joe states.

~ * ~

Vernon is in his office on the phone. "Hello, Colonel. I just wanted to let you know that Elvis got home just a few minutes ago."

"That's good news, Vernon. I'll come over tomorrow and see the boy. There are few items of business to go over with him."

"We're about to have a get together here if you want to come by and say hello."

"Thank you for inviting me. But, I have other plans, but I'll see him tomorrow."

"Okay. I just wanted to let you know. We'll see you tomorrow then."

"Thanks again, Vernon. Talk to you later."

"Goodbye," Vernon says to a dial tone.

~ * ~

Meanwhile, Billy and I are upstairs in my bedroom. I change into a black pair of pants and a purple shirt.

"Ok Billy… let's get down stairs… and ah… see what's… going on."

"Are you sure you're up for this?"

179

"Oh yeah… I'm ready."

"Okay then, let me call down and tell Mary we're on our way." After making the call, we head down stairs to the dining room. As I pass by the kitchen, I call out, "Hey Mary… are we ready… to eat?"

"Yes sir, Mr. Elvis."

"Great… then um…. let's do it! The food… at the hospital… um… was some of the… worst… I've ever had."

"Okay Mr. Elvis. You and Billy go in the dining room and I'll call Vernon and the boys in."

I ask, "Have you seen… Lisa Marie?"

"Yes sir. She is outside."

"All right… I'll ring the bell… um… to call her in." I head over to the back door and open it. Hanging just within reach is a western dinner bell made of iron. I pull the cord of the ringer with my left hand, calling Lisa Marie in. In the distance, I hear her answer, "Coming!"

Mary has picked up the intercom. "I'm about to serve, Mr. Vernon, come and get it."

"I'll be right there."

Mary redials and calls the boys in the TV room. "Hello Lamar, let everyone know the food is ready, and to come on up to the dining room."

We'll be right up."

Billy and I go to the dining room and sit down. The dining room table has all its leaves in it to accommodate everyone. Vernon and Lisa Marie arrive at the same time.

I get a big smile when I see my daughter, "Come here... Buttonhead... and sit... ah... next to daddy." Lisa Marie skips to the seat next to me. "Vernon... why don't you... sit at the... um... other end... of the table?"

"All right, Son."

The gang from the TV room comes in and sits down around the table.

Vernon stands up holding his glass in a toasting manner and raps his folk on it, "I have something I would like to say. I want to toast to my son, Elvis Aaron Presley. We almost lost him, but thanks to God we have him back. Elvis has made a commitment to turn his life around. So here's to Elvis, long may he live." Everyone at the table holds their glasses up and agrees in unison.

I smile, nodding my head in acknowledgement, "Thanks... um... Daddy. I have made... um... somewhat of... a fool of myself... um... over the past... few years. And... after going through... ah... what I've just... been through... um... I see the... ah... future as... my second chance... I've decided to... ah... turn my life... around... and to ... stay off the pills... to live a clean... and ah... sober life. It's to you... my family... and ah... friends that I make... this pledge."

Standing in the doorway between the kitchen and the dining room is George Klein. I gave George the nickname GK, back in 8th grade music class and we've been friends ever since. GK is a member of the Memphis Mafia and has his own career in the music business as a DJ and TV dance show host in

Memphis. He has total access and is always welcome to see me, anytime, anywhere.

GK claps his hands and says, "I've been waiting to hear that from you for a long time, Elvis. I'm sure that everyone in this room is glad to hear it too." They all agree and applaud their approval of what GK has just said.

I greet my old friend, "Boy… am I glad… to see you. Come in and… sit down." He walks into the dining room as I extend my left hand to shake. Another chair is brought in and GK is added to the mix.

The talk around the table takes a more general turn when Billy asks, "Have any of you seen the new 1978 Corvette?"

Joe responds, "No I haven't."

"Oh baby, it's a hot looking car. The Corvette is 25 years old this year. To celebrate, Chevrolet is placing a commemorative badge on the front nose. It comes with a special two tone paint job with dark silver on the lower body and light silver above."

Charlie says, "Yeah I've seen it. It has a new 'fastback' design which gives it more luggage space."

Lisa Marie wants to know, "What are we having for dinner, Daddy?

I tell her, "I don't know… darling, ah… Mary is fixing… something special."

Ed responds to Billy, "Yes, but one of the drawbacks to the new design is that the interior heats up on sunny days, and places more demand on the air conditioning."

"Yes, but the new spare tire has made it so that they have enlarged the gas tank from 17 to 24 gallons to increase the driving range between fill-ups." Billy explains.

GK adds, "They've upgraded the interior. And, you can also get AM-FM stereo radio with a CB feature for only $638.00, 'good buddy.'"

Joe says, "Ouch!" There is laughter among the group.

Mary wheels in a cart and starts serving everyone. I say to her, "Mary… this looks… um… delicious."

Lamar asks, "Elvis, have you heard Donna Summer's new song, 'I Feel Love?'"

Billy asks, "Is this salmon?"

Mary says "Yes, its grilled salmon."

I turn to Lama, "Yeah… it's her new… um… disco record."

Joe, after a mouthful of salmon, "Mary, this tastes great!" Mary thanks him.

Lamar says, "It's the single from her new LP, 'I Remember Yesterday.' It is a concept album. "

Joe remarks, "Yes, it's considered a pioneer work. The entire album uses electronic backing tracks."

George informs the table at large, "Most disco records are usually backed by acoustic orchestras, but not this one."

"I don't like… that electronic sound… and ah… I like the sound… of a real orchestra… behind me… um… and the sound of… a real band. That electronic stuff… will put… um… musicians out of business."

Billy says after swallowing a mouthful of green beans, "The German band, Kraftwerk, pioneered the all-electronic music. That's what Donna has is using."

George says, "Yeah, her song is the first disco style record that uses an entirely synthesized backing track. That robotic bass line really makes the song popular."

Taking a sip of filtered water Joe says, "David Bowie said that Brian Eno told him, 'I have heard the sound of the future.' "After playing 'I Feel Love' for David, Brian then said, 'This song is going to change the sound of club music for the next fifteen years.'"

"Well… that's why… um… Brian… isn't producing… my records. There's no room… for that kind of… um… sound… in my life. I'm not doing… ah… disco songs. My music is… blues, R&B… um gospel… country and pop."

Lisa Marie asks, "What's disco, Daddy?"

"It's dance music… um… for night clubs… where people go… to dance."

As everyone finishes eating, I see Larry walking into the dining room and give him a great big smile, "Hey… um… old buddy."

Billy and Joe say, "Hi, Larry."

Larry greets everyone, "Hello Elvis, GK, everybody, it looks like I missed the food."

Mary tells Larry, "Oh no, Mr. Larry, there is more if you want some."

"No that's okay, Mary. Thank you, but I ate earlier."

"Are you sure? Really, it's no problem."

"Yes, I'm sure. I just came by to see our patient."

"I'm doing fine. As you can see... um... I've had my... first healthy... um... meal outside... the hospital. And ah... I loved it... Mary."

"Thank you, Mr. Elvis."

"Oh, no... thank you. Um... Larry... come up stairs... with me... will you?"

"Yeah, sure, I will."

I tell everyone, "I'm going... to lie down... and talk to... Larry for a bit. It's been a... busy... ah... day.

Lisa Marie who is used to taking naps says, "Good night Daddy, don't let the bed bugs bite," as she hugs her daddy.

"I won't... Yisa. I'll talk to... you later... um... Daddy."

"Rest well, we have a meeting with the Colonel tomorrow, and we should have another press conference."

"Ok... we'll do it... um... but for now... ah... thanks everyone... for your help... today. Larry... ah... come with me."

We go upstairs to my bedroom, where I start rummaging around looking for my stash of drugs. Larry asks, "What are you looking for?"

"I'm looking for… my um… pills.

"The ones they gave you at the hospital?"

"No… my… ah… other ones."

Larry is astonished, "And why are you looking for them?"

"Because… I want you… to get rid of them… for me."

"Elvis, you must know that someone who cares about you has already gotten rid of them. We all know that they are what caused most of your problems. Someone has done you a big favor by moving them out of your reach."

Elvis exclaims, "Oh… I didn't realize… how much support… I really have."

Larry asks, "So you're not upset that the drugs aren't here? You really are an ex-drug addict?"

"Yeah… um… I'm not upset… and I am… always going… to be… um… a drug addict. Just one… that takes it… one day at… ah... a time."

"You had me worried there for a moment," Larry says laughingly.

"I've told you… that… um… I'm not taking… those pills… um… any more. I'm just taking… the medications that… um… Dr. Francisco gave me… to treat my… condition."

Larry tells me, "You know that prayer has played an important role in your life. Like the prayers that have helped many people that go to

Alcoholics Anonymous. Now, I know that you can't go to AA meetings, but if you continue to pray, prayer will strengthen your spiritual life. Through prayer, hard work and self-sacrifice, you will be able to survive any trials and tribulations that may lie ahead of you."

"Yes… I understand… um… I think of myself… as more… ah… spiritual than religious. You know… I've studied… all kinds of… um… religions… and I take from… each of them… ah… what I think applies… to me… and leave… what I don't… believe in. I think… that gives me… a more… um… intimate relationship… with God. I don't have… to go to a church… and ah… listen to… some preacher… tell me what… um… God thinks… I should be doing… When God himself… is guiding… my every step."

Understanding, Larry says to Elvis, "So the basis for your belief is that Jesus came to free man from those rules, and traditions. And gave you the ability to walk in his spirit and live through a one on one relationship with God."

"By actively… connecting to… um… the force… the power… and the energy of… um… Mother Earth… I can feel… spiritual energy… that has nothing… to do with… religion. You have helped… teach me about… um… mind-body-spirit energy… through, Eastern… and Western… philosophies."

"What I've introduced to you, is the ability to enhance the quality of your life as you explore your desire to remove blocks that inhibit the full expression of your life force. This is done through clean living and the personal education of knowing ones true self."

"And I… um… thank you… for that. You're… the only person… that I can… talk to… ah… about this kind… of stuff. You understand… what I'm talking… about and… ah… you teach me… and point me… in the right… direction," I say gratefully.

"Yes, and that comes with a price to me. Because of our spiritual studies, Colonel Parker and the Mafia view me with suspicion and contempt."

"Larry… don't you… worry about… them. Um… I just told you… you're the only… one… um… that I can… talk to. I will always have… room in my… ah… heart for what… you have taught me."

"Thanks for that my friend. You've had a full day and need to rest, so I'd better get going. We'll talk again soon."

"Okay… take care… Larry… ah… I'll see you later."

"Yes you will, Elvis," Larry then leaves me reflecting on my thoughts and a second chance to the start of a new life.

~ * ~

"Good evening this is Al Cosby, here outside Graceland for WHBQ-AM. There has been a lot of activity in and around Graceland this afternoon. The Memphis Mafia has been moving cars and running in and around the compound. Larry Geller was let out of the gate here at Graceland just moment's ago.

"Good evening this is Al Cosby, here outside Graceland for WHBQ-AM. There has been a lot of activity in and around Graceland this afternoon. The Memphis Mafia has been moving cars and running in and around the compound. Larry Geller was let out of the gate here at Graceland just moment's ago.

"We have been told that Elvis is resting comfortably and he has only seen family and the closest of friends at the hospital. Like you, we are eagerly awaiting a sighting of Elvis here or at Baptist Memorial Hospital. It has just been announced, that there will be a press conference here at Graceland tomorrow afternoon. But the scheduled time is yet to be announced.

We have been lead to believe that Elvis will be coming home sooner rather than later, so we will keep you posted as we continue day 5 of Elvis watch. That's all from me, Al Cosby here at Graceland on WHBQ-AM."

Chapter 17

August 21, 1977

Its mid-morning and I have just walked from the mansion over to Vernon's office. Seated at her desk, I see Loanne Parker. Loanne, a native of southern Ohio, first met the Colonel in 1969 in Las Vegas. She was employed by the International Hotel, where I sometimes played. When I started to tour live again, Loanne was hired by RCA Records as the tour secretary, and has traveled with my show ever since.

"Good morning... um... Loanne... how are you... today? It's nice to... um... see you."

Looking up from her paperwork, Loanne says, "Good morning, Elvis. I'm doing fine, but how are you feeling?"

"Hey... I'm walking and... um... I'm talking... well, sort of," I chuckle.

"I'm glad that you are up and around. You sure gave us a scare."

"Yeah... I gave myself... um... quite a scare."

Just then Vernon walks out of his office, "Hey... um... Daddy... how are you doing... today?"

"I'm doing good, but look at all this fan mail," as he points to the stacks of mailbags holding thousands of letters and cards that have come in wishing me well. "It's going to take us months to reply to all of these cards and well-wishers,"

"You need to… put on… um… additional people… to help sort through… ah… all of this. Call Jo in… and call Joanne… Joe's wife… to see if they can… help… um… Loanne out."

Vernon says, "That's a good idea Elvis. We'll call both of them and ask if they can come in and help."

Loanne picks up the phone to make the call.

I asks his father, "You wanted… to talk to me… about… um… a press conference… today… ah… to let everyone know… ah… that I'm going to be… um… alright. I don't want… to do the… um… press conference… because of… the way I… um… sound."

"Well who do you want to give the statement, and are you going to be there or not?" Vernon asks as he tucks his shirt tail into his pants.

"You… can do it… or have… um… the Colonel… do it," I suggest.

Vernon goes and sits at his desk, "The Colonel is on his way back home already. We had our meeting earlier this morning. He said to say hello, and he would talk to you later."

"That's like him… to be… um… always out there… in advance. Then you… or Joe… um… can do it. I understand that… um… Al read… the one that was… given at the hospital… ah… maybe he could… do it."

"I can do it," Vernon volunteers. "It will be a lot easier than the one I did from here, when you were in the hospital. Do you want to be there when I give the statement?"

"I don't know… I want everyone… um… to know… that I'll be okay… but to see me… and ah… hear me… like this… is going to put… a lot of fans off. Maybe I could just… um… stand there… next to you."

"That would be a little strange! You're not saying anything at the press conference?"

"Well… I'll be there."

"You know there will be hundreds of fans and press people there, and they are all going to want to ask you questions. And for you not to say anything would be really strange."

"Look… you do the… um… statement… and I'll stand… next to you. You just say… there will be… no… um… questions… at the end. I'll wave… with my left hand… and ah… we'll come back inside."

"Okay, we'll do it that way if you want. I'll set it up for later this afternoon. Let's say, 3:00PM?"

"That sounds… fine to me," I change focus. "But… I wanted to… um… talk to you… about my going… to Hawaii, to… ah… do my rehab. I want to buy… a, um… sugar cane… plantation in Maui. And… I want to put in… a recording studio… in the house… um… so I can work… on a new album," I say with enthusiasm.

Vernon raises his eyebrows, "You want a sugar cane plantation? And, you're thinking about recording a new album?"

"Well yes… um… but not… right away, um… it will be… part of my rehab! With a… studio there… ah… when I get… inspired… um… I

192

can put down… some tracks. I can… record the… rhythm tracks now… and ah… do the vocals later. I know I can't… do the vocals… um… right away. But, maybe… I can do… before and ah… after tracks… so you can hear… how I sound… um… now… and what I… sound like after… um… my recovery. Great idea…right?" I say laughingly.

"Oh my gosh, son. You've gone from bad to worse. Now I think you've totality lost you mind," Vernon says, glad that my sense of humor is intact.

With a smile, I tell him, "All right… um… maybe that wasn't… such a great… um… idea, but… I do want… to buy ah… sugar plantation. And… I want you… to talk to… ah… Joe. He knows someone… over there… that does… um… real estate… We were all… in the… um… service together. He can find… ah… the property… for me in… Maui."

"So you are going to Maui to do your rehab? I thought that was you just talking."

"No, Daddy… I really think… going to… um… Hawaii… will be a good… thing for me. The weather… over there is… ah… great… all year round. I won't have… as many… um… people trying… to get to me. You have to fly… um… almost 2,500 miles… just to get to the island ah… from the main land."

"So what kind of house are you going to want over there?"

"I want… a mansion… um… with lots of rooms. Lots of bedrooms… lots of bathrooms… you know that… um… Lisa Marie needs… her own bedroom… with a bathroom. It has to… have a…

um… master suite. It should have… a modern kitchen… and ah… den… a TV room… and a gym/dojo… type area… um… for my rehab. And… it has to… have… um… ah a three car garage. There should be… um… several guest houses… with at least… ah… two or three bedrooms… or two or three… bungalows. You know… the workers… have to… um… live somewhere. The grounds… should be gated… and ah… it should… be on the beach."

Vernon asks, "How soon do you want this mansion?"

"I know that… it may take some… um… time to find… the property I want… It has to be… um… an income producing… property. It will make money… um… while I'm doing… my rehab… ah… when I'm on the… road it will… um… keep making… money for me… and ah… the family. I'll have to hire… a great um… foreman to… run things… for me."

"Your right, this could take some time to find or develop a property like that. Where are you going to stay until you get this property?" Vernon asks.

"I'll move into… the um… Wailea Beach Resort. I'll need… their best suite… and ah… two or three… of their deluxe… suites also. I'll order… um… other rooms after that… as I need them… and ah… when people come over."

"When do you want this booked?"

"The sooner… um… the better! There's no sense… in wasting time… here I've… ah… been doing the… um... exercises they gave me… at the hospital. But… I want to… get started on… my full… rehab program… um… as soon as… I can. "

Vernon asks, "Who's going over with you?"

"Lisa Marie… and… ah… maybe Nancy… or Mary… will have one of… the deluxe suites. I'm going to ask… Billy and Jo… Joe and his wife… and of course Larry… if they will… ah… come over… full time… with me. The other Mafia members… um… I'll invite on a… as needed bases. I must… take this seriously. I need to recover… ah… from this… and I don't want… um… any distractions."

Vernon asks, "So what's going to happen to Marty, Charlie, Lamar and the others?"

"Dad… can you… use them… around here on… ah… full time… or part time… bases? Maybe… keep one or two… ah… you may have to… let the others go. I don't know… you'll have to… um… work that out. I don't want… to lose any… of them… um… but if I'm not… working… I can't afford… to pay them… um… to just sit around… and keep me… company… um… while I recover. I'll tell you what… um… call the Colonel… and ask… ah… his advice. He will help you… figure it out."

"It sounds like you want to cut back on who is hanging around."

"Daddy… this is one of… the most… um… serious times… in my life. It's a cross roads… and ah… I have to make… the right choice… um… for me to gain… my strength back… and recover… from this stroke. When I come back… um… from Hawaii… I'll be better than… I ever was. Then

195

if… they are available… and ah… I'll put them all… back on… but until then… um… I'm going to have… to cut back. I hate doing it… but, ah… I'm not going under… just to make them… happy."

"I know. The Colonel and I have talked about cutting back on the Mafia. The Colonel has already let the band and the backup singers go."

Elvis answers with surprise, "He has? I didn't know… um… that. I don't disagree… but I wish… um… I would have known… um… about it… before he did that. What kind of… ah… severance pay… did he give them?"

"I think he said one month's pay."

Elvis emphatically says, "Oh no… I want them to get… um… one month's pay… for each year… they have been… with me… paid out… on a monthly basis… um… not all at… one time."

Vernon expresses surprise. "Elvis, I didn't know that the Colonel hadn't talked to you about what he was doing."

"No… I didn't know… and ah… this sort of stuff… is really starting… to um… piss me off. The Colonel… has been holding… me back… um… for years. I swear to God… um… I'm going to find… another manager." I say in frustration.

"Elvis, you know that the Colonel has been very good to you, and to us. He really pushed your career and helped you become as popular as you are."

"I know… but on the other… hand… um… I haven't toured… outside the United States… just because… ah… the Colonel… doesn't have a passport. He couldn't… get back into… the United

States… without one… um… and I have… to suffer? You know how well… I do in… um… Europe… Asia and… Australia… and ah… I've never… toured there. Yeah… I spent time… in Germany… in the… um… Army… but the Colonel… told me… um… I couldn't perform there. And… ah… I think the Army… would have had… something… um… to say about it."

Vernon advises, "Just be very careful who you pick as your next manager."

"The deal I cut… will leave everything… um… in place that… the Colonel has done… with ah… record contracts… and movie contracts. And… he will get… his cut… um… on all of that. The new manager… will start out… um… fresh and… get a smaller percentage… than the… um…Colonel did. The merchandising deals… will be much… ah… more in my favor. I'll be going… with the industries… ah… higher end percentages… paid to people… for their services,"

I slow down, "Wow… you've really got me… worked up and… ah… we've only talked… about two subjects… Is that all for now?"

"That'll do it for now," Vernon tells me. "But don't forget we're doing the press conference at 3:00PM today."

"Yes… I remember… ah… 3:00PM today. Where… are we going… to do it?"

"We'll do it from the front steps. That way we can just make the announcement and go back inside the house after we're done. Then Dick and the Mafia can make sure that everyone leaves."

"Ok… is that it… then? I'm hungry… um… I'm going to… get something to eat. Do you want me… to ask… um… Mary to fix… you something?"

"No, I'll get something later. I have a lot of work to do here."

"All right then… ah… I'll see you… later. Loanne… do you want… um… something to eat?"

"No thanks Elvis, I've eaten already."

"Alright then… um… I'll see you… later too… Loanne."

"Yes, you take care of yourself Elvis."

"Yes ma'am… um… I'm doing my… best."

~ * ~

Entering the house through the back door, I find Mary in the kitchen where the phone is ringing. Mary answers the phone, "Presley residence."

Mary Jenkins has been with our family since 1963. She was born in 1921 in Hernando, Mississippi, just south of the Tennessee border. She started out as a maid and then became a cook three years later, just around the time when Priscilla moved in to Graceland. She is more than help, she has become family.

The friendly voice on the other end of the phone says, "Hello Mary, its Priscilla."

"Oh Miss Priscilla, how are you?"

"I'm fine thank you. How's Lisa Marie doing?"

"She's doing just fine, Miss Priscilla. She's growing up to be such a big girl."

"I know that you're looking out for her while she's there. Thank you for that, Mary. How are you holding up?"

"Oh I'm doing just fine. I've had a cold, but I'm okay now that I'm getting over it. I'm learning a new way to cook for Mr. Elvis. I've only had a couple of complaints about this new way of cooking, but I know that they will get used to it. Or, I'll just have to fix the meals for Mr. Elvis and the regular food for everyone else."

"I'm sure you're doing a good job and the ones that are complaining can go to McDonald's for their food, if that's what you want to call it."

"Oh, Miss Priscilla, you're so funny. I know that you're right, so the next time they give me any guff, I'll tell them to do just that."

"Good for you, Mary. Is Elvis there?"

"Yes Miss Priscilla, he's right here. Mr. Elvis, it's Miss Priscilla, she wants to talk to you."

I tell Mary that I'll take the call in the Jungle room and head off in that direction. Mary speaks into the phone, "Miss Priscilla, Elvis is going to pick it up in the Jungle room, so I'm going to put you on hold. It was nice to talking to you again."

"It was nice talking to you too Mary, thanks I'll hold."

"Goodbye."

"Yes. Goodbye, Mary."

~ * ~

199

By now, I am in the Jungle room sitting on the couch and pick up the phone, "Hello, Cilla… um… how are you?"

"I'm doing well, thanks. What's going on with you?"

"I got out… of the… um… hospital yesterday. We had a… nice meal with the… boys in the Mafia… ah… Lisa Marie and Vernon… it was a… welcome home… party. After that… Larry stopped by… and ah… we had a… long talk about… the meaning… um… of life. When he left… ah… I went to bed… and took a nap… for a while."

"Wow, I'm impressed. Did you take anything other than what Dr. Francisco had ordered for you?"

"No… I only took… just what I was… supposed to take. All the drugs… that I had… ah… stashed in… my room… are gone."

"Someone had the good sense to clean out your stash?"

"Well… I do admit… um… I was a little… upset… but ah… I got over it. Larry really um… helped me out… with that. He's… um… a smart guy. I've learned so… much… ah… from him… over the years. The other guys… don't get… him, so they… don't really get me… either… um… sometimes."

"You have always liked him and I know he's good for you."

"Yeah… um… you're right… about that, Cilla.

"Elvis, I want to come back and see you and pick up Lisa so she can spend some time with me."

"When… do you want… to um… come in?"

"I was thinking tomorrow or the next day."

"I'm planning… to go to… um… Hawaii… in the next… few days, ah… so why don't… I stay over… in… ah… L.A. and bring… Lisa Marie back… since I'm… um… coming your way? That way… you don't have… to interrupt… um… what you're doing… by traveling… um… back and forth… but we can… see each other."

"That sounds like a good idea. Where will you stay while you're here?"

"I'll stay… at the… um… Beverly Hills… Hotel… for the night… and ah… then fly out… to… Maui… the next day."

"How about I meet you at the hotel after you get in, and maybe we can have dinner?"

"I'd like that! Let's plan on… doing that… ah… I'll call you… when I get… into… um… the Santa Monica… Airport."

"Okay, so let me know when you're coming exactly so I can make my arrangements and I'll plan to see you then to pick up Lisa Marie."

"I'll call you… as soon as… I um… know more… details."

"I'll talk to you later, see you."

"Yep… I'll see you… soon… 'bye."

"Goodbye, Elvis."

~ * ~

In Vernon's office, he and Joe are putting the finishing touches on the statement that they are about to make on my behalf.

Joe tells Vernon, "That sounds good, Vernon."

"Let's go and do this then. Where is Elvis?"

"I think he is in his private office."

Vernon dials the intercom to my office and gets no answer. Vernon then dials Mary in the kitchen and finds out that I had just headed up the stairs to my office. So he dials the number again and this time I answer. Vernon asks, "Are you ready?"

"Yes, I am… Are you… down stairs… um… yet… or are you… still in your… office?"

"I'm still in my office, but I'm coming over in 5 minutes."

"I'll meet you… at the bottom… of the stairs… then."

"Okay."

Joe places a call to make sure that everything is ready to go. He dials the kitchen, and Mary answers the phone. "Grand Central Station," she says with a laugh.

"Hi Mary, is Dick out front on the portico?"

"Yes, I think he is, Mr. Joe."

"Would you ask him to come in, I need to talk to him for a minute."

"Yes Sir, Mr. Joe." Mary goes to the front door and finds Dick standing there with Marty and

Charlie. "Mr. Dick, Mr. Joe wants to talk to you on the phone."

Dick heads to the kitchen and picks up the phone, "Hello Joe."

"Hi Dick, is everything over there ready?"

"Yes it is. We're just waiting for you guys."

"Okay, Elvis should be coming down the stairs any time now. Vernon and I will be there in a minute."

"Okay Joe, we'll see you soon."

Vernon, Joe and I all meet in the foyer of the mansion, and walk out the front door. We see what looks like a thousand people, filling the driveway and spreading across the lawn, patiently waiting to hear what Vernon has to say. There is applause and cheers from the crowd as they see me for the first time in five days.

Vernon takes a deep breath and starts to make his announcement, "Good afternoon. I'm glad that all of you could be here today. As you know my son has suffered a stroke. It has left him with a speech impediment and partial paralysis of his right arm."

I interrupt, "Hold on a second… um… Daddy… I have something… I want to… um… say… to these people."

I move to the microphone, "As you… can hear… um… I have trouble… speaking, and… ah… my right arm… is partially paralyzed. It happened…because I was… um… using pain pills… and other drugs…

"Dave Hebler... Red and Sonny... West... and ah... Steve Dunleavy... wrote about me... in their book... ah... 'Elvis... What Happened?'... Most of... what they wrote... was... um... true, but... not all... of it.

"I was... going to... um... stand here... and let my... um... daddy... do the talking... for me. But I just... decided that... it's... um... best for you... to hear it... from me. What I... have done... in the past... has... um... affected me... but I am... going to be better.

"I'm leaving... for... um... an undisclosed... location... day after tomorrow... for my rehabilitation... both speech... and physical therapy. I don't want... to take any... um... questions... but I do want... to thank you all... um... for coming out... and wishing me... well... I ask for... your continued prayers... and patience... while I recover. I love my fans... and I know... that I have... let... um... you down. I will be back... um... sounding stronger... and healthier... ah... than I've been... in a long time. Thank you again!" I turn to go back into the mansion.

As we turn to go back inside, tremendous cheers go up. The crowd cheers, there are cries of "We love you Elvis." Then they change to, "El-vis, El-vis, El-vis," over and over again.

Once back in the house, Vernon questions me, "I thought you wanted me to make the statement?"

"I did... um... until I heard you... start talking. Then I thought... um... I'm going to... tell the people... the truth... ah... about what's... going on... with me."

Joe comments, "I don't know how wise that was."

"Joe… um… you'll have to… trust me. It will be… alright."

Joe says, "You just surprised us. That's all. You're the boss."

I smile at Joe, "Yes… I am."

Vernon asks, "Joe, I understand that you know someone in Hawaii that is in the real estate business."

"Yeah, an old army buddy of mine is over there, and he's doing very well at it."

"Call him and let him know that Elvis is looking for a sugar cane plantation to buy in Maui, and see what he can find for us."

Joe asks, "A sugar cane plantation? Wow, I'll give him a call now and see what he can find out for Elvis. It's only 10 am in Hawaii. I'm sure he can get started right away."

Elvis tells Joe "Yeah… I want… um… 15,000 or… 20,000 acres… with a big mansion and… ah… houses for the workers… and it has to be… gated."

Joe says, "I'll give Fred a call right now," as he goes to make the call.

Vernon asks, "What are you going to call the property?"

"I'll think… I'll call it… um… EPP… for Elvis Presley… Plantation. I'll make it… the finest… um… sugar plantation… in the islands."

"I'd better have Joe call and make reservations for you in L.A. for the day after tomorrow and then in Maui the following day."

"Ok… um… Daddy… I'll catch up… with you… later."

Vernon heads back to his office as I head to my office upstairs.

~ * ~

Back in his office, Joe dials his old Army buddy, Fred, in Maui. It's been years since they have talked, and he is excited to be talking to his old friend.

"Hello, may I speak to Fred?"

"This is he. Can I help you?"

"Fred, this is Joe, Joe Esposito, your old buddy from the Army days, how are you?"

"Joe! Oh my gosh, Joe. Wow! It's great to hear from you!"

"It's been a long time, I know."

"Wow, I hear about you every once in a while. Are you still working for Elvis?"

"Yes, I am, and that is one of the reasons I'm calling. Besides finding out how you are, I've heard you're doing pretty well in the real estate business over there."

"Yes, I do alright for myself."

"Well, Elvis asked me today to find a plantation on Maui to buy, and, of course, I thought of you."

"Elvis wants to buy property in Maui? What's he looking for?"

"He wants a sugar plantation on about 15,000 to 20,000 acres with a mansion and other houses on the property. Some of the land has to be ocean front and it needs to be a secure property so people can't bother him while he is there."

"I don't know of a sugar plantation that's for sale, but I've heard there is a pineapple plantation that has been on the market for quite a while. I'll check on it, and let your know."

"Great, Fred. I'll let Elvis know you are working on it."

"I understand he had a stroke, or something, how is he doing?"

"Yes, he had a stroke, and he's planning on doing his rehab in Hawaii. He really loves the islands. The weather will be better for him there than here in Memphis, especially in the winter."

"Boy oh boy, I'm sorry to hear about the stroke, Joe."

"Oh, don't be sorry, he's more determined than anyone I know. When he wants something, he gets it, or does it."

"When will Elvis want to move in?"

"Well Fred, not to put any pressure on you, but Elvis will be in Maui the day after tomorrow."

"What! Joe I'm good, but I'm not that good. It's going to take some time to go through the listings and see what we have in inventory."

"Relax Fred; he will stay at the Wailea Beach Resort until you can find what he is looking for."

"Well that does take some of the pressure off. Okay, so he will be here in two days, I assume you will be coming with him?"

"Yes, I'll be coming too. I look forward to seeing you again, Fred. And, even though you two weren't that close in Germany, Elvis is looking forward to seeing you, too."

"Let him know that it will be my pleasure to see him again. I'll do everything I can to find the property he is looking for."

"I sure will Fred," Joe says. "Ok then. It was good to talk to you again. I'll keep you in the loop about what's going on from this end."

"Great Joe, I'll wait to hear from you, and thanks for thinking of me to help Elvis out."

"Hey, we're part of the Army team; we look out for each other."

"Yes we do! I better get right to work on this so I'll say aloha for now."

"Aloha, to you, too. We'll talk soon, goodbye."

Joe heads back over to the house and comes upstairs to my private office. I am sitting at my desk as he comes in and sits down on the couch across from me. "Elvis, I have great news! I just spoke with Fred in Maui. He doesn't know of any sugar plantations for sale, but he said there is a pineapple plantation that has been on the market for several months. Does it have to be a sugar plantation?"

I think for a moment, "No… it could be… um… a pineapple plantation. When can I… see it?"

"He's not sure it's available. If it is, you can see it any time you want to."

"Great, set it up for as soon as we get there."

"Elvis, I'll call him right back, and see what we can do."

Joe heads back downstairs as I pick up the phone and call Priscilla. "Hello Cilla… um… it's me."

"Hello, Elvis. How are you?"

"I'm doing… ah… well. I just wanted… to let you know… um… I'll be in L.A…. with Lisa Marie… the day after… tomorrow. We'll be coming in… um… around 4:30… in the afternoon."

"I'll look forward to seeing you and Lisa Marie then."

"Okay… I'll call you… when… um… we get in."

"Talk to you then. See you soon," Priscilla says.

"Alright… goodbye," As I hang up the phone I sit back to reflect on what is happening in my life, and I like what I see.

Chapter 18

August 23th, 1977

It's late afternoon, we are at the airport, standing around on the tarmac, outside the Lisa Marie. We are about to leave for Los Angeles. I call to Joe, "Okay… um… Joe is everyone… here?"

"Yes we're all here."

"Come on… um… Lisa Marie… it's time for us… ah… to go see… Mommy."

"Where is she?"

"She's in… L.A."

When Lisa Marie and I reach the top of the stairs, Elwood is there to greet us with a big smile. "Good afternoon Elvis, How are you Lisa?"

Hey… um… Elwood… how are you doing?"

"It's really great having you back on board sir. We're expecting no problems getting to Santa Monica Airport today."

"It's great… um… to be back… in your hands again."

"You couldn't be in any better place."

"I'm counting on it… um… Elwood…," I give him a wink as we move into the cabin. The rest of my entourage, Joe, Billy, Jo, Charlie, Larry, Lamar and Marty follow. The cabin door is closed, we all get settled in and the plane taxies down the runway for takeoff. Four hours and nine minutes later the *Lisa Marie* lands at Santa Monica Airport and we all are able to stretch our legs and get off the plane.

It's a beautiful day in Santa Monica. The sun is bright and the temperature is in the high 70's by the ocean. As I step out of the plane, walking down the stairs with Lisa Marie in tow I say, "Larry... and Joe... come with me." The others gather the luggage and take town cars to the hotel. The four of us get into a limo.

The limo leaves the airport and heads north on Bundy to Beverly Hills, then makes it way east on Sunset Boulevard until it turns left into the driveway of the Beverly Hills Hotel, stopping at the front door. The doorman comes down to the limo and opens the door. As I get out of the car, the doorman greets me, "Hello Mr. Presley, it's nice to have you staying with us again."

I return his greeting as I take Lisa Marie by the hand and walk into the hotel. The lobby has a great circular crystal chandelier, hanging from the ceiling and overstuffed chairs arranged in a circle around a glass table holding a magnificent arrangement of flowers.

Joe takes care of getting me checked in. He gives me a key for the Presidential Bungalow Suite. I am registered as 'Jon Burrows', the code name that I use when on the road. The bellman shows Lisa Marie, Larry and me to the bungalow, while Joe finishes the registration.

Larry gives the bellmen a tip for their help with bringing our luggage in. Lisa Marie and I check out the suite. There is a living room with a fire place. There is a fire burning which reflects off the hardwood floors accented with white carpet. In the corner stands a Baby Grand Piano. To the right is the dining room, overlooking a private pool. To the left, French doors lead into the master bedroom suite.

After a quick tour I sit on the couch and call Priscilla. Lisa Marie turns on the TV as Larry sits across from me waiting for Joe to show up. "Hello… um… Cilla… we're here… at the hotel."

"Great, I'll be right over."

"We're in the Presidential Bungalow Suite."

"I'll see you in about a half hour."

"Wait… there is… someone here… um… who wants to… say hi… to you." I call to Lisa Marie, "It's… your mommy."

As she takes the phone from my hand, Lisa squeals with delight, "Hi, Mommy!"

"Hello sweet heart, how are you?"

"I'm fine. I'm here with Daddy. Are you coming to see us?"

"Yes sweet heart, I'll be right over to see you. I love you."

"I love you too, Mommy! Bye." Lisa Marie hangs up the phone and turns to me, "Daddy, Mommy is coming over to see us."

"I know… honey… um… she'll be here… soon." There's a knock on the door, and Larry lets Joe in.

~ * ~

Priscilla drives to the Beverly Hills Hotel and hands off her keys to the valet. She walks through the lobby and out the back to the secluded Presidential Bungalow located in the rear of the property. Priscilla rings the doorbell and is greeted by Larry who invites her to come in.

She gives him a big hug. "Hello Larry, how are you?"

"I'm doing fine. Elvis is out on the patio with Joe, watching Lisa Marie in the pool."

"Thanks Larry," Priscilla says as she heads out to the patio and stands next to me. We both watch our daughter playing in the pool. Lisa Marie doesn't notice her mom right away. Joe says 'hello' to Priscilla.

"Hi, Joe!" Priscilla answers. She then directs her comment to Lisa Marie, "Hello honey, it's so good to see you."

Feeling slighted, I playfully say, "It's good... to see you... too... um... just kidding."

Lisa Marie gets out of the pool, grabs a towel and runs up to her mom for a hug, "Hi Mommy, I'm so glad to see you."

"Well, I'm just as happy to see you too."

Then Pricilla is directing her attention at me with a smile, "Hello Elvis, it is good to see you too."

"Hi... Cilla," I stand up and hug her with my left arm and she hugs me back. "Listen... we didn't... have much to eat... um... before getting here... so why don't... we go and get... um... a bite."

"Do you want to order room service or do you want to go to the restaurant?" Priscilla asks.

"Let's go… to the restaurant… and ah… get out… of this room."

"That sounds good to me. Okay, Lisa Marie, honey, go get changed. When you're ready we'll go to the restaurant."

"Yes Mommy." Lisa Marie goes to her room to change out of her bathing suit into dry clothes.

I tell Joe and Larry, "Come along … you guys…But … ah…you have… to sit at … another table, okay?"

Joe answers, "Sure thing, Elvis."

After Lisa Marie changes, the group leaves the Bungalow and walks over to the hotel restaurant. As we enter, I ask the maître d' for a table for the three of us. The maître d' leads Priscilla, Lisa and me, to a widow table overlooking the garden. Once seated, I observe, "This is… a very nice… um… table."

Priscilla remarks, "The garden is beautiful."

Larry and Joe are seated near us, but far enough away not to hear our conversation. I tell Priscilla, "You're looking… beautiful."

"Thanks, I've seen you look better."

"I guess… um… I deserve… that," I say with my feelings of shame coming out in my voice.

"I'm not saying it to be mean; I'm just telling you the truth," Priscilla says.

"I know, I know. You always do. But, there is… something I… um… want to tell… you," I pause for a moment, then say. "I'm going… to buy… a working… um… pineapple plantation… as

214

an investment... ah... to live in... while I'm in... Hawaii."

"A pineapple plantation?" Priscilla says with surprise.

"I've been... told... um... I'm going to... have to work...at my rehab for... ah... a year... or more. So I thought... um... why not buy... something that's... um... going to bring in... an income. It will be... a great place... for Lisa... to grow up... during her... summer breaks... and holidays."

Priscilla asks, "Isn't Graceland enough for you?"

I tell her, "You know that... I bought Graceland... um... for my mommy... and my daddy. I've always... loved Hawaii... and now is... the perfect time... for me to buy... something there... because I need... a nurturing place... in order to heal... myself."

The waitress comes up to the table. "Hello Mr. Presley, my name is Betty, and I'll be serving you and your guests this evening."

"Hello... um... Betty... I'm not sure... we know what... we um... want... do you Priscilla?"

Lisa Marie says "I know what I want. I want chicken fingers and French fries."

Priscilla tells Betty, "I'll have a Chicken Cacsar salad with no croutons, plcasc."

"That's what I like, women that know what they want. I guess... I'll have the... um... Salmon grilled... and a side... of broccoli."

Betty asks, "What would you like to drink?"

Priscilla says, "I'll have a glass of white wine and Lisa Marie will have a glass of milk. Elvis, what are you having?"

"I'll have a… bottle of… um… Perrier… in a glass… um… with no ice… and ah… lemon wedge please."

Priscilla says with surprise, "What, no Pepsi?"

"No… water is just… um… fine."

Betty wants to know, "Would that be a small bottle or a large bottle?"

"I'll have… the large… um… bottle please."

"I'll be right back with your drinks."

Priscilla says, "Thanks Betty," as the waitress goes to place the order.

Priscilla, picking up the prior conversation, asks, "So you want to buy a plantation? Who is going to run it for you?"

"I'll hire… the best foreman… to um… handle the job… for me. This… isn't just… a business… opportunity… ah… it's a great place… to live when… um… the weather is… miserable in Memphis… um… which is in the summer… and ah… the winter."

"What else are you getting yourself into?"

"Like I told you… um… I'm going to… do my… rehab there… and ah… I'm going to… be working on… a new… um… album… as my ability… improves."

Priscilla asks, "Elvis, you're going to be working on an album while you sound like this?"

"Well… I don't think… um… the property will have… um… a recording studio… in it yet… ah… so I'll have… to put one in. By then… I'll be able to… um… at least lay… rhythm track and… ah… do the vocals… later… after my… um… rehab has… worked its magic… and ah… I can sing… again."

"You know I want the best for you, and if that is what you want, then go for it."

"That's… just the… beginning… Cilla. I'm really… changing… um… my life. I've stopped… doing all those… crazy things… and ah… the drugs… are out."

I look over at Larry sitting with Joe, "Larry has… been a big… help… um… to me… in that matter."

Lisa Marie wants to know, "What crazy things, Daddy?"

"Oh… just some… stupid stuff… um… your daddy used… to do."

"When is my milk getting here?"

Priscilla tells her, "The waitress will bring it in just a minute, honey." Just then Betty shows up and serves us our drink order. She tells us that their dinner will be out in just a few minutes.

"Cilla…When… um… I woke up in the hospital… ah… I thought to myself… this is a… wakeup call… for me. Not being able… to talk normally… or… um… move my arm… really upset me. I finally realized… how badly… um… I have screwed up… my life.

217

"I heard… um… people talking… at some of my… ah… shows. They were saying… um… how bad… I looked… and ah… how I would… ramble, and ah… laugh on stage… in my own little… um… dream world. I thought… I was… ah… invincible. But… when I woke up… in the hospital… I had a whole new… prospective on… life."

"Well, I'm glad you survived your wakeup call Elvis. I've been telling you for years that those pills would cause you more harm than good. I lost you to the fog those pills put you in a long time ago. You weren't the same person I met in Germany. That's why I left you."

"I know Cilla… I know. Like I said… I fucked up… my life… and ah… in turn… your life… um… and our life… together."

Lisa Marie exclaims, "Daddy, you said a bad word!"

"Oh… Yes honey…um… I'm sorry. Your right… ah… I shouldn't have… said that word."

Priscilla scolds me, "Please Elvis, I hope you don't use that kind of language around her all the time."

"No Cilla… I don't. I'm just… um… that upset… with myself… and ah… I'm passionate… um… about what's… going on… in my life… right now… and ah… in the future. I have a lot of… um… work to do… um… on myself. I need to… um… concentrate on me. I know… that may sound… um… selfish… but I only have… so much energy… and ah… I need to… use it to… heal me," I tell Priscilla.

"I understand, and I know that you can do whatever you set your mind to," Priscilla tells me, "And, now that you are getting clean it's going to be easier for you to do. You are a very powerful man, and if you focus your energy in the right direction you can accomplish anything you want."

"Thanks… for that… um… I thought you… had… ah… lost faith… in me."

"No Elvis, I have never lost faith in you, you lost faith in yourself. And now you're on the way back. You had to sink to the bottom, before you could return to the top."

Betty returns to serve the meals. "Here are the chicken tenders, young lady, the Cesar salad with no croutons for you ma'am, and grilled salmon for you, sir. Is there anything else I can get for you?"

Priscilla asks Betty for some ketchup. "Yes, ma'am, I'll be right back with that for you."

Priscilla turns back to me, "Like I said, I'm proud of you and I know you can do it. Let's eat dinner and enjoy the meal."

"Thanks for… um… believing in me… Cilla. You don't know… um… how important… that is to me!"

Betty comes back to the table and puts the ketchup in front of Lisa Marie. "Is there anything else you need?"

I reply, "No… thank you… um… we should be… fine." We proceed to enjoy a delightful dinner together.

After dinner, all five of us walk back to the bungalow together. Joe opens the door, walks in and Larry follows. I ask Lisa Marie to go inside and get her suite case so she can go home with her mother. Standing at the door, Priscilla tells me, "Okay Elvis, be safe in Hawaii."

"Yes… I will… um… Cilla, I'll be… just fine."

When Lisa Marie comes back to the door with her suite case, I hug her saying, "Goodbye… um… Yisa… You be good… for your mommy."

"I will."

"I love you… both. I'll see you… again soon."

"I love you too, Daddy" Lisa Marie says as she hugs me tighter.

"Alright, take care, and stay in touch. When do you think we will see you again?" Priscilla asks.

"You're going… to have to come… to um… Hawaii… to see me. I said I… love you… Cilla," I remind Priscilla.

"I heard you; you said 'I love you both.' You know I love you too, but not in that way anymore."

"We'll talk… again soon,"

"Goodbye Elvis," Says Priscilla. "Say goodnight, Lisa Marie," Priscilla reminds her.

"Goodnight Daddy." Lisa Marie gives me another hug and kiss.

"Goodbye… sweetheart."

Priscilla steps forward and gives me a hug, "Goodbye Elvis take care of yourself."

"Goodbye… Cilla."

They turn and head back to the lobby. I stand in the doorway watching them walk away. Once they are out of sight, I close the door and pause to reflect.

Larry notices me looking down, "Are you alright?" he asks.

"No… the two women… um… in my life… just left me."

"Elvis, they haven't left you, they are just on their journey and your paths will cross many more times in this life."

I look at Larry wistfully, "I hope… you are right."

Chapter 19

August 24, 1977

My entourage and I are on board the *Lisa Marie* waiting for our departure from the Santa Monica Airport. Elwood makes an announcement over the intercom, "Alright, ladies and gentlemen, we're ready for takeoff, so for your safety, please, fasten those seat belts. Thank you for choosing to fly the *Lisa Marie,* sit back and enjoy the five hour and forty-five minute flight to Maui."

Elwood pushes the throttle all the way forward, and the roar of the engines lets everyone know they are taking off. Joe and I are sitting together at the glass top conference table that is surrounded by six tan leather chairs.

Joe reports, "Fred will meet us at the airport."

"Good… it will be nice… to um… see him… again. So… he has this… um… pineapple plantation… for me to see?"

"Yes, and we can go to see it as soon as we get there, or if you want to check into the hotel first we can do that."

"Let's see… how I feel… um… when we get there. I'm going back… and take a nap. I'll see you… in a few hours."

I get up, and move to the back of the plane which houses my penthouse bedroom. It is furnished with a custom-made queen size bed. I take a drink of water before heading to the bathroom. Coming back, I remove my clothes, crawl into the bed, fluff up the pillows and pull the covers up around my shoulders. Within a few minutes, I'm in dreamland at thirty-two thousand feet over the ocean on my way to Maui.

Just as Elwood said, it has been five hours and thirty five minutes gate-to-gate as the *Lisa Marie* lands at the Kahului Airport, the primary airport on the island of Maui.

Fred, accompanied by four hula girls dressed in flowered sun dresses with leis around their necks, carrying armfuls of sweet smelling leis wait on the tarmac at the bottom of the ramp to greet us. The door opens and I emerge. Then I am followed down the stairway by my entourage. Fred greets me with a big smile as he offers his hand.

"Wow, it's been a long time Elvis. I know how you've been doing. You're all over the news lately."

"It's good... to see you... um... Fred... my old friend. So what... have you... um... been up to?" The hula girls dance up to me and throw their leis around my neck. Laughing with pleasure I bend down to let them kiss me on the cheek.

"After getting out of the service, I decided to come back to Hawaii. It's paradise here. I did my R&R in the service here and fell in love with the place. When I got out, I came back here and went into the real estate business and I've done very well since."

Distracted by the hula girls, I tell Fred, "Ah... you have to... excuse me... I have to... thank these... um... charming hula girls... for a minute."

Directing my attention back to the hula girls, I say, "Thank you... um... thank you very much...

ah… young ladies… for this… um… warm welcome." The hula girls giggle, and whisper comments among themselves.

"Hopefully… um… we'll see you… again ah… while we're here," I joke with the girls as I pat one of them on the butt.

I wave as they leave to greet the other passengers. "See you later… ladies." I turn back to Fred, and continue the conversation. "Well… you know… after talking with… um… Joe… I'm here to… buy a… little piece of… um… paradise for myself."

Joe comes walking up and greets Fred, giving him a big hug. "Hey, old buddy, how's it going? It's good to see you."

"I'm doing just fine, Joe," he says hugging him back. "Thanks for thinking about me when Elvis decided he was looking for some property here in the islands."

"Hey, that's alright. Elvis wanted to see you anyway, so why not do a friend a favor."

"I have the limos you asked for over here, so are you guys ready to go?"

I nod, "Yes… um… I'm ready. Can we go… and ah… see that plantation… now."

Fred is happily surprised. "Why sure, why not?"

"Joe, you… ah come with… Fred and me. Send the rest… of the guys… um... on ahead to… the hotel. The three… of us have… um… old times to… talk about, um… and a property to see."

224

Fred and I climb into one of the limos as Joe gets the rest of the guys organized. "Hey, you guys, Elvis and I are going with Fred to see the plantation, so you go on ahead and check into the hotel, and get Elvis' suite ready for when he gets back. Okay?"

Marty tells Joe, "Yeah sure, we can take care of things, we'll see you later."

Sounding slightly childish, Lamar asks, "Why do you get to go, and see the plantation?"

Joe just looks at Lamar with a grin and says, "Ok guys, see ya' back at the hotel." He joins Elvis and Fred in the waiting limo.

After accepting their leis from the Hula girls, the Memphis Mafia piles the luggage and themselves into the remaining limos and head to the hotel.

There's a lot of catching up going on in the limo. Fred tells me, "After I got discharged, I came back here, and married a Hawaii girl. Her name is Anumea, which means 'cool mountain breeze.' We have a son named Eric, but his Hawaiian name is Elika."

Elvis replies, "That's great… of course… you remember… um… Priscilla… I married her… and we have… um… a little girl… named ah… Lisa Marie. She's… nine years old… now."

"I know. That's who you named the plane after, right?"

"Right… As you know… um… Joe came back… after we got… discharged and… has been with me… ever since."

"Joe, that must be something, hanging out with, 'The King of Rock 'n' Roll' for a living?"

They all laugh.

"It's been a blast, and very interesting. I wouldn't change what I'm doing for the world," Joe says.

The three Army buddies continue to reminisce as they ride together taking in the sights. The limo drives along the two-lane road with guard rails or lava rock fences protecting the car from the edge of the cliffs. The terrain is very steep, wrapped in lush green plants for as far as the eye can see.

I remember my earlier days in Hawaii and recognize the foliage. I begin to identify the large trees in my mind: Rainbow Eucalyptus, Palm trees, African Tulips, Avocado, Banana and Halo trees. Then the variety of flowers captures my gaze. The Protea flowers, Orchids, Tropical Splendor, and Red Anthuriums begin to make me feel at home.

I ask the limo driver to pull over for a couple of minutes. The limo slows and pulls into a turn-out. Joe, Fred ad I get out and look over the vast landscape before them. The fragrance of the small flowers carpeting the land at our feet is heady and there are bee's flying from flower to flower. Various song birds, crickets and katydids create a symphony of nature's delight. The Three Bears Water Fall, running down the side of the mountain close by, adds its glorious percussion.

After enjoying the sights, sounds and smells for a short time, they get back into the limo and continue their journey down the mountain. I smile to myself as I enjoy seeing cows in the tall grass and a distance group of people riding horses through the surf on the beach.

Suddenly, Fred points. "Oh, look we're coming to the plantation."

"I love… the country side… so far. I just hope… ah… this is what… I'm looking for… um… Fred."

They ride down the long winding driveway a half-mile to the master-craftsman-built home. The limo stops near the front door. We get out and stare at the magnificence of the structure.

I look at the two story mansion, and comment, "Wow! This is bigger… um… than I was… thinking… and that's saying… something." We laugh as Joe, Fred and I walk up to the front door.

Fred tells me, "Yes it's quite palatial and is designed so many people can enjoy its quiet privacy. As you can see, there are hand carved Indonesian temple entrances framing the front door, and the garden gates.

"It has fifteen bedrooms and twelve bathrooms. The grand master suite also has a small kitchen off to one side as well as a sitting area for total privacy. Off the master suite, there is a covered, outside sleeping area with a magical courtyard, dramatic oceanfront setting and Koi ponds that give a feeling of serenity."

Fred waves his arms around in expansive gestures as he goes on describing the property. "There are two living room areas, and a dining room that can seat twenty-five to thirty people. It also has a huge, over-sized gourmet kitchen with an eat-in area, plus a walk-in pantry that will accommodate any professional chef."

"There is a library, an office, a private gym, and a spa, all with state-of-the-art equipment and technology. There is a fire pit overlooking the ocean's captivating views, and lush tropical gardens on the grounds. It has a home theater room, and get this; we're getting cable on the island this month," Fred turns back to us with a huge grin.

"And, as an added bonus, you can take possession of the place as soon as the papers are signed."

I say to Joe, "Listen to this... um... guy. Do you think... he knows... ah... this place... or what?"

"Fred's just doing his thing, and he does a great job of it,"

"Hey, that's my job, and I like what I do. I happen to know this property. I have often wondered who would pick it up."

Fred gives us a tour of the spacious house and grounds. I look around and nod in appreciation, "Okay... so what else... does it have... to offer?"

Fred laughs. "Well, there is an Olympic-sized infinity pool, with a pool house that has two bedrooms and a kitchen. There's also a five-car garage, and a wood shake roof which accents the house design. It sits on just over eighteen thousand acres, and it produces the finest pineapples you have ever tasted in your life. There are worker quarters in and around the plantation so there are people here on the grounds twenty-four hours a day seven days a week."

I ask, "Do you have… the keys?"

"Yes, sure, would you like to see the inside?"

"Fred," I say with a chuckle, "I didn't come… all this way… um… not to!"

"Okay, let's go inside."

~ * ~

Billy, Lamar and Marty are in Elvis's suite at the hotel making sure that everything is right for Elvis' arrival. Billy says, "Everything looks good here. The hotel even put fresh flowers and bowls of fruit everywhere."

Marty exclaims "This is one of the nicest suites I've ever seen. Check out this TV, it's huge."

"It's one of those new Sanyo's." Lamar says.

Billy wants to know, "Let's finish putting everything away for Elvis"

Marty answers, "Yes. Then we should go down to the pool, and see what kind of women are staying here."

Lamar agrees, "I'm up for that."

A little later, Billy wants to know, "Now that we have that done, should we check with the front desk to have them notify us when Elvis gets here? How is it going to look if he needs us, and we show up in our bathing suits?"

Marty defends the motion, "Oh come on, Billy, we're in the islands now. We'll just be dressing like the natives do."

"Do you think that will fly with Elvis?"

"Well, I think he would find it funny."

"Let's hope so!" Lamar exclaims, "Last one in the pool is a rotten egg."

The guys go racing off to change into their bathing suits and head to the hotel swimming pool.

~ * ~

Joe, Fred and I arrive at the hotel, and get out of the limo.

"Fred… Find out what… their… um… absolute, rock bottom… price is. I think… we can make a deal. Call… um… Vernon… and ask him to… work out the deal… to get the paperwork… in order."

"Great Elvis, I can fax the papers to Vernon."

"What's… a fax?' I inquire.

Fred explains, "It's a machine that copies pages and sends them over the telephone lines to another fax machine to be printed out at the other end."

"Where… is there ah… fax… um… machine in… Memphis?"

"I'll have to find the phone number for someone that has a fax there and send it to them. Then they can give the pages to Vernon. It takes only minutes to send pages."

"Wow… new… um… technology. I'll have to… um… get one… of those things," I say in wonderment to Fred.

"If there is anything else I can do for you just let me know."

"I sure will… um… Fred… Thanks again!"

Fred throws an idea out, "I have a friend that owns a restaurant in Paia. We could go eat at the EZ Café. It's a hippie health food haven; that's right in line with your new healthy diet.

"Then we can go to a night club in Lahaina, called The Blue Max. There is a conga player by the name of Joe Cano. He is better known for his guitar work. He's fucking great! There is another guitar player, named Peter Moon, who wrote a hit song called, 'Fire Came,' and he may be there too. Are you up for it?"

"Yeah… I got some sleep… on the… um… plane coming over… um… so I should be… all right."

"Great, then I'll arrange for us to go there. How many will be in your party?"

"Joe… how many… will be with us?"

"There could be as many as eight of us."

"Alright! We'll go out tonight and I'll arrange for nine of us, counting myself," says, Fred.

Joe suggests to Fred, "Why don't you make the reservations for ten that way they won't try to put us at a table for eight. We always round up for table reservations."

"Good idea Joe, thanks."

I put a hand on Fred's shoulder, "Great Fred… ah… I'll look forward… to it then."

"I'll be back at eight-thirty for you guys. And, I will bring you the numbers. See you later."

Joe shakes his old friend's hand and tells him, "Yes, we'll see you then."

Fred tells me, "It's good to see you again. Thanks for the deal. I'll see you tonight."

"Yeah... I'll see you... um... later," I say as I wave goodbye. Fred gets back into the limo and is driven way, as Joe and I walk into the hotel lobby.

Joe picks up the suite key from the front desk. We take the elevator to the top floor and cross the few steps to the suite's front door. Joe uses the key and pushes the door open.

Without a moment's thought, I go to the phone to call my father. The phone rings several times before a sleepy voice answers, "Hello."

"Hello... um... Daddy... it's me."

"What? Elvis, do you know what time it is here?"

"Oh, shit...sorry... um... I forgot... about that!"

"Well, now that I'm up, what can I do for you, son?"

"I had... um... Fred... take me over... to the plantation... it's beautiful... and the price is right. It has been... on the market... um... for, nine million... ah... nine hundred... ninety -five thousand... but I got it... for, ah... eight million dollars. I can't... um... believe it. I'm not here... less than... um... five hours and... ah... I found a place... to live."

232

"What did you say? Was that eight million American dollars?" Vernon says in disbelief.

"Yes… I know that… it sounds… um… like a lot… but ah… you should see… the place, um… it's gorgeous. You're going… to love it. Fred… is going to… um… fax over… the paper work… ah… to you. So… I need you… um… to take them… to my attorney… um… Ed Hookstratten. Have him… go over the details… and ah… get back to me. I want this deal… Daddy. You won't believe… the house… um… it's bigger than… Graceland."

Vernon asks, "What's a fax?"

"It's a machine… that um… sends pages… over the phone… line. Check with… um… Ed… and see if… he has… ah… one of those… machines to receive… um… the pages… in his office."

"Are you sure you want to do this?" Vernon questions his son.

"Absolutely… sure! I have… um… thirty years… to pay for it. And it's… a working… um… pineapple plantation… and ah… the income from… the property will… um… help cover… the cost. Don't worry… about it… Daddy."

"Should I have the Colonel look at the paper work?"

"No… I want this house… and ah… I'm going to… do it… without him. I can do this… um… on my own."

"Okay, I'll check with Ed and see if he has one of those machines. And, Elvis, do me a favor. Call earlier next time." They both laugh.

"Sorry… Daddy, I'll be better… um… about that… in the future. I'm just so excited… about this deal."

"All right, son, I'll talk to you later. Goodnight, Elvis."

"Good night… Daddy." And I hang up. Then reality clicks in about where I am now and asks Joe, "Where are the guys?"

Joe, standing at the window looking down and says, "If you come over here, I think I can show you where they are."

I go over next to Joe and look out. Joe cracks, "It looks like they're at the pool."

"I don't see… um… Larry… um… or Marty."

Joe laughs, "It doesn't mean that their not down there."

"I would expect… to see… um… Marty down there… but… um… not Larry," I say half-heartedly.

"You're right about that," Joe agrees.

I turn and sit on one of the couches in the living room, "So, Joe… um… what do you think… about the… um… plantation?"

Joe comes over and sits on a couch across from me, "The mansion is amazing. I can't believe all the bedrooms and bathrooms, and the home theater is incredible. It sure puts the TV and the Jungle rooms to shame. I really like the lush tropical plants, and the feeling of serenity."

"Well it's… um… a working piece… of property too. It should… be able to… um… pay for itself. I hope… you like… um… pineapples… for a… Christmas gift," I say, laughing.

"I love pineapple upside down cake."

I pause, collecting my thoughts, "Thanks Joe… for remembering… Fred… and staying in touch… with him. He was… a big help… to me… today."

"That's all right, boss, I was glad to do it. It sure was good seeing Fred again."

"Well… you know, um… now that we're… going to be… ah… living here… for a while… we'll be seeing… a lot more… um… of him, I'm sure."

"Yeah, I guess you're right."

I ask, "Can you… go get the guys… and ah… let them know… that we're going out… um… tonight… ah… so they can… be ready?"

"Do you need anything before I go?"

"No… I just need… some um… quite time… before we go out… tonight."

"I'll be back in a little while."

"All right. Um… I'll see you then."

Joe leaves the suite to round up the guys. I get up, go lie down on the bed and try to go into a meditative state.

~ * ~

Joe takes the elevator down to ground level. He walks out to the pool area and finds some of the guys playing around. He announces as he walks up to the group, "Well, I hope you're having fun!"

Charlie answers, "Why, what's up?"

"We're all going out tonight with Fred and Elvis for dinner and a night club to hear some hot guitar players."

Lamar questions, "Hot guitar players, here in Maui? And who's Fred?

Joe tells Lamar, "Fred, the real estate guy. He has lived here for years, and he just wants to show us a good time."

Billy wants to know, "Where is Elvis?"

"He's up in his room."

"I guess I'd better let Jo and Larry know to get ready too," Billy announces.

Joe asks, "Where are they?"

Billy, drying his hair with a towel, gives a muffled reply, "Jo's up in our room."

Charlie answers "I guess Larry would be in his room."

Joe informs the merry pool goers, "All right, you guys, get ready. We're being picked up at 8:30PM. I'll tell the others what's going on." Joe heads back into the hotel to find Larry and give him the heads up for the night's festivities.

~ * ~

While Joe was at the pool informing the guys, Larry dropped in to see me. Larry and I are sitting on the balcony of my suite, taking in the view while

236

talking. "You will get to see… the um… plantation tomorrow."

"Boy you didn't waste any time finding a place."

"Um… God was looking… out for me… Larry," I said with a grin.

"You can say that again."

"We're going out… um… to dinner… with the realtor… tonight. His name is… um… Fred. Then we're going… to a night club… um… to hear some… guitar players."

"You mean we came all this way to see guitar players?"

"Fred… does have a… pretty good ear… ah… as I remember… um… so I'll trust him… this time. But if he fails… um… at least he will… have um… real estate… to fall back on."

There's a knock on the door of the suite. Larry goes through the sliding glass doors from the balcony and opens the door to let Joe in.

"Hi, Larry, here you are. I was looking for you. I left a message for you in your room," Joe tells him as they both walk back through the suite and out onto the balcony.

"I've been here talking to Elvis."

"We'll, we're going out with Fred to have dinner, and then to a night club."

"That's what Elvis just told me."

"Great, Fred will be here at eight-thirty with the car to meet us in front of the hotel. I've got to go get ready. You two can finish talking about whatever you guys were talking about."

"Yeah… you haven't… um… even been to… your room yet… have you?"

"No, I'm off to do that now. I'll catch up with you guys downstairs at eight-thirty."

"Okay, we'll see you then," Larry assures Joe.

~ * ~

Billy and, Jo, meet Charlie, Lamar and Marty in the lobby. They check out each other in their new Hawaiian shirts and Bermuda shorts.

Fred walks into the lobby. "Hello my name is Fred," he says extending his hand to each. "I'm the real estate broker who is working with Elvis.

Billy shakes Fred's, and says, "Oh, I've heard about you. You were over in Germany with Elvis and Joe, right?"

"Uh huh, that's where I first met them both."

Billy makes the introductions, "This is Charlie, Lamar and Marty. They are part of the Memphis Mafia. This lovely lady is my wife, Jo."

They all shake Fred's hand, "I've heard about you guys. It's nice to meet you. And, a pleasure to meet you too, Jo," He sees me coming off the elevator, "Oh, here comes Elvis now."

Joe and Larry and I walk to the group and I greet my friends, "Hello… um…Jo… boys… are you ready… to hit the town… um… tonight?"

Joe notices that guests checking into the Hotel have recognized me, pointing and whispering. He is anxious to avert a mob scene so ushers our group along, "Let's get in the cars and get going."

So we all head out of the lobby to the waiting limos. As we get in, I ask, "Fred... did you say... the name of the... place we're going to... is the... um... EZ Café?"

"Yes, that's where we're going. It is just a short drive from here along State Highway 36 and to 89 Hana Highway."

It's a beautiful evening and I pause a moment to enjoy the warm ocean breeze. Taking a deep breath, I feel even more relaxed.

We go into the café and are greeted by Marty and Mary Blechta, the club's owners. Fred makes the introductions all the way around. The group is seated at a large round table with more than enough room. The menu is filled with fresh, healthy dishes.

Over our meal, the discussion ranges from how the trip went to how different the food is from the fried food that they were used to back in Memphis. Almost everyone enjoys the food. Lamar complains, "Hell, I had to drown my sandwich in enough ketchup so I couldn't taste the tofu burger."

The entourage finishes their meal, complimenting and thanking, Marty and Mary for the good food and drinks. I, too, thank Marty and Mary, "The EZ Café... is... um... a great little place... to eat... ah... when you're in the... neighborhood and... hungry. I'll be back again."

It's a short drive to The Blue Max, a night club on Front Street in Lahaina. With very little fanfare, we are taken to a restricted seating area.

The show is going on as we arrive; both Joe Cano and Peter Moon are on stage performing with the band. As we settle in to watch the rest of the set, Fred, Larry and I order fresh fruit smoothies while the rest of the group orders something stronger.

Joe and Peter finish their set and come over to the table. Peter greets Fred, "Fred, my kaikunane, how are you doing? Who do you have here with you, as if I didn't know?"

"Peter, Joe, I want you to meet, Elvis Presley. Elvis, this is Joe Cano, a conga player who picked up the guitar and hasn't looked back since. And this is another good friend of mine, Peter Moon, one of Hawaii's greatest slap guitar players."

"Hello um... Peter... Joe... you guys sounded... um... pretty damn good... up there. You have... um... a sound... that's all your own... and that's good. What do you call... that kind of picking... Peter, slap guitar?"

"Yea, finger picking with the left hand, and thumping the beat with your right hand rather than the usual strumming style of playing the guitar."

"That's very cool... I'm moving here... to do... um... rehab. In a few months... I'll be working... on an album. Can I... stay in touch... um... with you... and maybe use... you guys... on the next album?"

Peter's excitement practically fills the room. "Sure, sure. I'll give you my number and we'll get together and jam. We'll see if you can work it into your style or not."

Elvis addresses Joe Cano, "Joe... I'd like to... use you... um... also... if you're available."

240

"Yeah, I'd love to work with you."

"Give your… phone numbers to… um… Joe here… and ah… I'll stay in touch," I say as I nod toward Joe sitting next to me.

"Yeah, that sounds great, Elvis," Peter says.

Peter addresses Joe Esposito "Here's my business card. If you lose it, you can always get my number from Fred."

Peter tells me, "It was great meeting you! We're going out back to cool off. We have one more set to do."

"You guys… are really talented… and ah… I enjoyed it," I tell them.

"We'll stay in touch with you. Mahalo ukulele," Joe Cano chuckles. "That means goodbye."

"Yep… take care… you guys. Mahalo… ukulele… to you… too."

They both head off through the club.

Fred says, "I told you, you would enjoy their style of music."

"The times… I've been here… before… um… I heard Hawaiian… steel guitar… um… but this… 'slap guitar'… is a first… for me… and I like it. I can see… using them… um… on an album… with the right song."

"They are good guys to work with, and they have the Aloha spirit."

Suddenly, there is a small commotion as another party is brought into the restricted seating area. It turns out to be Elton John who is requesting to play a solo set. Bob Lozoff, the manager of the club says that he will have to check with the owner.

After Bob leaves, Elton notices me and approaches the table. "Elvis how are you? Imagine meeting you here at The Blue Max."

"Elton... it's good... um... to see you... again."

"The last time I spoke to Tom Hulett, he told me you were still in hospital, recovering from your stroke. Tom is one of your biggest fans."

"Yes... um... Tom is a... great guy. I got out... um... a few days... ago. I'm moving... over here to... do rehab... and ah... to get... my life straight."

"Where are you staying?" Elton inquires.

"We're at the... um... Maui Inter-Continental... Resort... in Wailea."

"I'm staying over at the Wailea Beach Resort. The band and I head back to L.A. tomorrow, but I want to play a few songs tonight. I'm sure I'll be able to talk the management into letting me play."

"You're... um... going to play... here tonight?"

"I'm here with nothing else to do. I like the club, and if the fans would be into it, why not?"

"Sure... why not. Um... that would be... very cool," I nod in agreement.

John Lawrence, the owner of the club comes over to the table where Elton and I are talking. He says to Elton, "Elton, we'd be thrilled to have you play a set!" John then turns his glance to me and asks, "Would you do a short set?"

"Ah… no… um… I can't… perform. I'm just… getting over… ah… stroke."

"Yes, I heard about that. We'd love to have you play a set. Any time you want to play the club, you have a standing invitation to do so."

"Let Elton… have the… um… spotlight tonight… please."

Elton asks John, "When can I go on?"

"You can go on now if you like."

"Good one. Elvis, I'll see you after my set."

"Yeah… I'll see you… then… um… have a good… set."

John gives the thumbs-up signal to the club announcer. An announcement comes over the PA, "Ladies and gentlemen, it is The Blue Max's pleasure to present to you… Elton John."

The audience erupts into an enthusiastic round of applause at the unexpected appearance.

Elton goes up on stage, sits at the piano and opens his set with, 'Your Song.' When the applause dies down, Elton addresses the audience. "There is another special guest in the house tonight. Let me introduce to you, Mr. Elvis Presley." The audience applauds and whistles wildly. Most of the people jump to their feet in appreciation of what I have done as an entertainer. "I know that he's recovering from a stroke, but let's bring him up here on stage. Come on, let me hear it." The audience applauds even wilder.

I shake my head no, and think to myself '*I would love to get on that stage, but I don't know how it's going to sound?*'

Elton continues, "Come on, Elvis, your fans want to see you. Come on up here."

Knowing things will not calm down until I do; I slowly head to the stage with Elton, and wave to the audience.

The audience is standing, applauding, whistling and stomping their feet even more ferociously. You would have thought a riot had broken out.

"I know you said no, but I would like you to play a song with me," Elton says, as I make my way across the stage to Elton at the piano.

"Oh no… I'm sorry… ah… I can't."

"I know that you can't sing right now, but I think you could play the guitar even with your right hand slightly paralyzed."

"No… I don't think… um… I can do it."

The audience breaks into a chant 'El-vis, El-vis.

I reluctantly shake my head no, and think, '*What if I bomb? My arm doesn't work right. Can I hold the pick, and strum the guitar? My left hand can make the cords. I don't know maybe I can do this. God, I'm in your hands, help me get through this.*"

Elton cajoles me, "Come on, I know that you can do this!"

Elvis gives in. "Alright... I'll try... um... just... one song."

The audience goes absolutely crazy. While the audience is going wild, I pick up a guitar. Elton and I put out heads together to come up what song we are going to do and decide on 'Hound Dog.' I count off the song and Elton does the vocals and plays piano, while I play rhythm guitar. The Blue Max Club is rocking as we play.

At the end of the song, I am glad that it's over, but excited that I still have the crowd, I was only playing rhythm guitar on one of my earliest hits and the performance was pretty rough. But, it gave me the reassurance that I can still thrill the audience. There is a sense of inner satisfaction: *I am still "The King of Rock and Roll."*

"This is the... first time... ah... I've ever just... um... played guitar... on that song. Elton... you rocked it!"

Elton stands and joins the audience in applauding my effort.

"No, man, you're still The King of Rock and Roll." Elton turns and announces to the audience, "Ladies and gentlemen, The Blue Max has just given you Mr. Elvis Presley!"

I step down off the stage and return to my table where the group is still standing and applauding. Larry has tears in his eyes and the mood of the Mafia has never been higher than it is tonight.

"That's it... it's time... for me to leave," I tell the group. I lead the reluctant entourage out of the club as the audience continues to go wild.

Back inside the club, Elton announces, "Ladies and gentlemen, Elvis has left the building. I've always wanted to say that," he says laughing.

~ * ~

Back in the limo, the group is discussing the unexpected events of the evening.

"I wasn't sure… I could do that… ah… I think I… played it… fairly well."

Larry reassured me, "Yes, you did. I was nervous when you went up on stage, but I've been around you long enough to know that you know what is best for you. And, by the way, Elton really did a great job singing Hound Dog."

"Yeah… he did… ah… good rendition," I admit.

"Well, it looks like you enjoyed yourself on stage tonight." Fred says.

"Yes… I did… thanks um… Fred. I knew that… you were… a good… um… real estate… person… but… I didn't know… how much fun… it is to… hang out… with you."

"Thanks, Elvis. It was a pleasure to party with you and the rest of the gang."

"You mean… um… the Memphis Mafia."

Fred replies, "I'm from East Lansing, Michigan, back home they call them gangs."

There is laughter from everyone in the limo.

"Yeah well… they are… my guys."

Joe says to Fred, "We all had a good time tonight. Thanks, Fred, for showing us a part of the night life in Maui."

"You guys are most welcome," Fred replies with a grin, as the limo cruses along the coast road on its way back to the hotel.

Chapter 20

It is late morning. Members of the Memphis Mafia are having breakfast on the lanai of the hotel restaurant while enjoying the amazing ocean view.

Billy, spreading strawberry jam on his toast, asks Joe, "Where is Elvis?"

"He's upstairs, with Larry. They're having a serious discussion about what is important to Elvis, and what he is going to do with the rest of his life."

Charlie says, "Boy, Elvis, and Larry can really get into some heavy discussions, when they get going," as he pours syrup over his buttermilk pancakes.

Marty adds, "They are on another level when they go there."

Jo, thinking about last night's performance, says, "I'm still amazed at how well Elvis did at The Blue Max last night."

"I am, too." Billy pauses, "It was like the early days. It had the same energy as the recording session Elvis did with, Jerry Lee, Johnny and Carl at Sun Studio back in December of 1956.

"The crowd really seemed to be into it," Charlie reflects, wiping his mouth with his napkin after finishing his over-easy eggs.

Lamar pours cream in his coffee, "So, Joe, do you know what we're going to be doing today?" He then adds three packets of sugar.

Joe answers, "I think we're all going out to the plantation today. Elvis wants everyone to come with him to see the place."

Charlie says to Joe, "You were out there yesterday. What does it look like?"

"The mansion is huge, and it has a very spiritual feeling and look to the place." He paused for a moment, thinking. "Oh, and the smell of pineapple fills the air... It's a beautiful piece of property."

Lamar states, "Elvis wants to put a studio in to work on a new album."

Marty says, "This is going to be a nice place to work out of for the next little while."

Just as Marty finishes saying that, Larry and I walk up the table. I address the guys, "Hello boys... ah... are you ready... to go see... the plantation?"

Billy says, "I can't wait to see the place."

Joe says "I haven't finished my breakfast yet."

Elvis tells everyone, "That'... ah... okay. When Fred gets here... he's going to... ah... take us all... out to the... plantation, ah... there's plenty of time... to finish eating."

A few minutes later, Charlie, who always sits in a position to see who is coming in and out of the room announces, "Here comes Fred now."

Fred asks with a big smile on his face, "Did everyone have a good time last night?"

Joe says, "Oh yes, we were just talking about all the excitement last night."

Larry says, "Yeah, it's been a long time since the energy was at that level when you preformed. It was raw, and the feeling really came out in the performance. It was amazing."

"Are you saying… um… that when I… performed with… ah… Elton… I did an… okay job of… just playing?"

Larry shakes his head. "It wasn't your best playing ever. But, that wasn't it at all. It was because you were up there playing after everything you have been through lately."

Billy adds, "Elvis, you were just playing and you let it all hang out. It was great seeing you up there and performing again."

Having heard enough accolades, I ask, "Is ever body… um… ready… to go?"

Lamar says "I need to finish my coffee."

Marty tells Lamar, "Just get it to go."

Fred says "Great. Let's get going?"

~ * ~

The two limos make their way up the driveway to the mansion. Everyone is very excited about seeing the place, and they are acting like kids at Christmas time. They can't wait to see the compound.

The limos pull up to the front of the mansion and stop. Everyone gets out and stares in amazement at the mansion. Just then, a figure comes out of the front door and stands with his hands on his hips, in a pose reminiscent of Superman. It's the plantation foreman, Bumpy.

Fred calls out, "Aloha, Bumpy."

Bumpy, a native Hawaiian, is a big guy. He looks like a Samoan football player, standing six foot three inches tall with thick muscles. He weighs in about two hundred and forty-five pounds, all muscle, with only five percent body fat. He comes down the steps, and up to Fred. "Aloha, Fred. Who is this?"

Fred answers, "This is Elvis Presley. He is buying the place. Elvis, this is Bumpy, he is the foreman who runs the plantation."

Elvis holds out his left hand to shake Bumpy's, "Aloha... um... Bumpy... it's nice to... meet you."

"Aloha, Mr. Presley, so you're interested in owning a plantation?"

Elvis feels the power in Bumpy's handshake, and realizes that he has just met a Hawaiian gentle giant. "Yes... I guess I am, um... as long as... the paperwork... goes through. The rest of... these guys," Elvis motions to acknowledge the entourage with him, "are my... friends. You'll get to... know them... as time goes on."

Bumpy nods his head to the group and says, "That's fine, Mr. Presley."

Elvis tells Bumpy, "Please... call me... Elvis."

"Thank you, Elvis. I understand you were out here yesterday. Did you get a chance to see much of the property?"

"No... um... Fred... Joe and I... walked through the... house... and ah... I'd like to... see it again. I'd also like... to see the... rest of the... um... property."

Fred says, "Great. Let me take the Mafia through the mansion, and Bumpy why don't you take Elvis, and Joe around the property."

"Sure, let's… go," Elvis says.

The three of us get into Bumpy's pick-up truck, as the Mafia go into the mansion to look around with Fred.

Bumpy drives along a dirt road that is really only two tracks worn in the growing grass. He stops along the side of one of the pineapple fields that extends for as far as the eye can see. Joe and I gaze at the field in awe of its size.

Bumpy asks, "Do you know how pineapples are grown?"

I have to admit, "No… I've never seen… one growing."

Bumpy raises one eyebrow, and launches into a dissertation about pineapples. "Pineapples are herbaceous short-lived perennial plants. In about twelve to twenty months they grow to about three, sometimes four feet tall. They have thirty or more long narrow leaves with sharp spines along the edges that measure one to three feet long surrounding a thick stem. The stem then grows into a spike like flower that can vary from lavender to a light purple or even red in color. Each plant produces only one fruit before it dies.

"Pineapple is a good source of manganese, and contains significant amounts of vitamin C and vitamin B12. It also contains the proteolysis enzyme, Bromeliad which breaks down proteins which means the juice can be used as a marinade to tenderizer meat. The enzymes in raw pineapple can interfere with the preparation of certain foods, such as making jelly and gelatin based desserts. The nutritional value of Pineapple breaks down during the cooking and canning process, so they are best eaten raw or juiced.

"Customers have reported they have benefited by using pineapple for intestinal problems and others believe it aids in pain relief. Women on the islands insist that pineapple helps to induce childbirth when the baby is overdue."

"Wow, Bumpy, you really know your stuff about pineapple." Joe says impressed with the big man.

"Yes, I grew up on this plantation, and have worked the property all my life doing every job from picking pineapples in the field to running the whole operation." Bumpy laughs "I even use to give guided tours and that's why I sometimes sound like an encyclopedia of pineapple."

I immediately realizes what a valuable person Bumpy is to this plantation, "Yes... but you... obviously have... ah... good education. Where did you... go to school?"

"I was schooled right here on the island. I went to Saint Anthony's from Grade School through Senior High thanks to the Harry C and Nee Chang Wong Foundation. If it weren't for the foundation's contribution, I wouldn't have been able to go there. That is why I tithe10% of my wages back to the school."

Hearing that, I know in my heart that Bumpy is surely the right man to run the plantation for me when the deal goes through. For now, I just nod my head in acknowledgment, and grin at Bumpy, knowing I have just found the pearl of Maui.

Back in the truck, we drive to the pineapple packing plant and warehouse. The entrance is through a small, unassuming door. We put on white dusters to protect the pineapple from being contaminated by any particles carried in on our street clothes. "Now, you are in for the full tour." Bumpy winks.

Walking along the processing line Bumpy starts, "When the fruit is ready for harvest it is picked and delivered here to us at the packing plant. The different growers on the island have crops harvesting at different times. And since we here don't harvest all year round, other growers have contracted with us to process and package their harvest for a fee."

I look around trying to take everything in and ask, "How do you know... um... how much a grower... ah... brings in here?"

Bumpy explains, "The packers have a built-in system that allows the full bins to be weighed when they are brought in and once emptied, reweighed so the grower is given credit for every pound of fruit they deliver."

Bumpy continues, "The pineapples are then placed on the packing line and graded for size and placed into tight fill cartons by a sizing machine. The pineapples are labeled during this process and the sizer insures not only that the correct number of pineapples are packed into the cartons by size, but also that the weight of the carton is correct."

Joe asks, "I suppose there is some sort of quality control?"

"Yes, indeed. All the cartons are inspected once more by a quality control person before the carton is sealed. The cartons are then stacked on pallets and placed in insulated refrigeration units.

"How am I doing on my memorized speech, Elvis?"

Laughing, I say, "You sure know… um… what you're… talking about. How do you… ship… um… the pineapples?"

"Pineapple produce is moved many times; from harvest, through the processing and distribution process before the consumer buys, and eats them. Pineapples require particular temperature, humidity, moisture and ventilation conditions. Once the cartons are in the refrigeration units, they are maintained at about forty-six degree Fahrenheit with forced air cooling where fans pull the cool air through the pineapple packages. We also ventilate the air exchange anywhere from forty to sixty times per hour with a fresh air supply.

"To move our crop, we use everything from off road vehicles to deliver locally to refrigerated trucks and cargo ships to deliver worldwide.

"Traditionally, pineapples are used fresh or canned. But, as we broaden the pineapple market, it becomes a good strategy to increase consumption in the main markets of the world. Therefore, pineapples are now consumed single strength, or as concentrated juice, dehydrated, sugared, and/or canned as slices or cubes.

"I'd like to talk with you about new developments in the pineapple market such as; dried chips, cocktail-type drinks, dried powdered, isotonic mixtures, and wines, as well as, whole fruit bars, flakes, and cubes. This is an area of the business that could be developed to increase the plantation's profit."

"So you think…ah… there is room… to um… increase the plantation's… production… and sales?" Elvis asks.

"Yes, but the present owner doesn't understand the new business and how the world is 'locals on the island.'"

"I don't know much about pineapples other than I like it on my banana splits, but the way you explain it, there sure is a market out there to deal with," Joe says.

Elvis asks Bumpy to explain what else could be done to increase profits.

"Essentially pineapple pulp is perfectly suited for conversion to frozen juice, nectar, drinks, jam, fruit cheese, or concentrate to be had by itself, or with cream. It can also be used in puddings, bakery fillings, and fruit meals for children. The raw fruit is utilized for products like chutney, pickles and sauces. We could also make a pineapple beverage with ripe pineapples such as nectar. Ripe pineapples can be quick-frozen whole, or peeled, in a moisture-proof container."

By now, we have walked through the entire plant, and are taking off their protective attire before going back out to the truck. Bumpy continues, "The diced flesh of ripe pineapple,

256

bathed in sweetened or unsweetened lime juice, can prevent discoloration, and can be quick-frozen also. Half-ripened, or green pineapples are peeled, and can be sliced into pie filling, used for jelly, or made into pineapple sauce."

As we drive back to the mansion, I think to myself, *"I don't know much about pineapples, but I'm very impressed with Bumpy's knowledge of them, and the marketing and distribution ideas he has."* Elvis has great plans for Bumpy once the plantation is his.

~ * ~

As we pull up to the mansion, Billy and Lamar are coming out the front door. "So… ah… what do you… think, um… Billy?"

"Oh, my God, Elvis, this place is beautiful! You've taken us to some nice places, but this has to be the best one ever."

"Elvis, the kitchen is so much bigger than you have at Graceland," Lamar says.

Charlie, Marty, Jo, Larry, and Fred emerge from the house into the Hawaiian sun, each having something wonderful to say about it as well.

Fred asks me, "Well… what do you think about the property?"

"I am impressed… with um… the property… and even more so… with Bumpy's knowledge… of it."

"Thank you, Elvis. I love this land, and what we do with it," Bumpy says.

Joe addresses Fred, "You should have heard what Bumpy had to say about the property, and what can be done with it."

"I have. I have. And, more than once," Fred laughs.

"After listening… to you… ah… Bumpy… ah… if I have… anything to say… about it… um… I'm going to give… you the chance… um… to do that."

Fred tells Elvis, "I've known Bumpy almost ever since I got here. I have found him to be an upstanding young man, and he continues to grow in knowledge and dedication."

"You don't… have to… um… sell him… to me, Fred… um… I'm a pretty good… judge of character… and ah… I know… that he will be… my guy… um… when I get… this place."

Fred replies, "I have been on the phone with your father and I'm pretty sure we are going to get the paperwork done today or tomorrow morning at the latest. I would like to suggest that we have a luau here tomorrow evening."

I agree to the idea, and am excited about spending time in what I hope will become my new home.

~ * ~

It's a warm evening on the grounds of the plantation. The sun begins to set, slowly disappearing into the Pacific Ocean. The lush tropical plants are swaying in the breeze, as big puffy Max Parish clouds float by. Behind the house, there are two tents decorated with ferns and red ginger.

Yesterday, employees began cooking a pig in the fire pit for the luau, in honor of me, hopefully, becoming the new 'po'o a hale,' or 'head of house.' Picnic tables adorned with flowers are scattered across the lush green lawn interspersed with tubs of ice brimming with soft drinks and beer. The serving table of the Luau is set to hold the pig once it has finished cooking, flanked by long tables set buffet style, filled with a vast array of beautifully arranged food that create a feast for the eyes as well as the palate.

Dressed in my favorite Hawaiian shirt, Bermuda shorts and flip-flops, I find the organizer, "Bumpy... this is quite... ah...a Hawaiian feast."

Bumpy explains, "This is called a 'luau.' We serve Hawaiian foods including hors d'oeuvres we call pu-pu's, poke, poi, kalua pig, ahi tuna, coconut shrimp with red pepper chili sauce, tomato cucumber papaya salad, macerated honeydew cantaloupe, watermelon with iced pineapple wine, lomi lomi salmon, sugar cane skewered shrimp, Kauai shrimp mango and hearts of palm salad, coconut water, pineapple juice and beer. There will be Hawaiian music with hula dancing."

I wink and say, "I'm up for... the um... hula dancing. I might learn... ah... new move for... my stage shows. Bumpy... um... you don't... do this... every night... ah... do you?"

"No sir, just for special occasions, and you buying the Hala Kahiki plantation is as special for us as it is for you."

"What is... um... 'Hala Kahiki'?

"'Hala Kahiki' means pineapple."

Fred comes up to us and asks, "I'm not interrupting anything am I?"

Elvis replies, "No... um... we're just... talking about... the luau... and ah... what... Hala Kahiki... means."

Fred says, "Well Elvis, my office just got the papers back from Vernon, and it looks like if you want the plantation... it's yours!"

I am so excited, I practically shout, "Yes... I want the... Hala Kahiki... Plantation!"

"Great, then we can sign the paperwork tomorrow, and your attorney says the plantation will be yours."

I loudly proclaims to everyone, "Boys... I just bought... the um... Hala Kahiki... Plantation... so let the luau... begin. And ah... we'll deal with... the paperwork... tomorrow."

Everyone claps and cheers upon hearing my good news. A couple of the native men dig into the fire pit; shovel the coals aside to pull out the pig and remove the banana leaves. They carry it to the serving table to officially start the luau, serving guests and employees. The celebration goes well into the night and everyone has a great time congratulating me, the new owner.

At 2:00AM, I have had a wonderful time at the luau, but I am ready to go back to the hotel. I ask Joe to get the limo. As he goes to get the car, he also lets the other members of the mafia know that I am getting ready to return to the hotel. If they want they can wind things up and ride with me, or stay and take the other limo when they are ready.

After I thank Bumpy for organizing the luau, I walk to the front door to meet Joe and the limo. Billy, Jo, Larry, and Charlie are walking out as well, just as the limo pulls up. Joe opens the limo door for me and everyone gets in for the ride back to the hotel. I ask, "Who else... is left here?"

Billy tells me, "Marty and Lamar are staying for a while longer."

Elvis says "Okay... let's go, then."

Charlie tells me what a wonderful time he had at the luau, and everyone else chimes in with their remarks on what they enjoyed most about this terrific evening. I listen as I settle back into the leather seat with a smile on my face, and gratitude in my heart.

Chapter 21

Its 9:30AM and I am sitting at the desk in his suite at the hotel. I pick up the phone and dial Colonel Parker. The Colonel answers his own phone, "Hello."

"Hello… um… Colonel… it's me."

"Hello, Elvis, how are feeling today?"

"I'm feeling… ah… fine thanks. I'm in Maui… staying at the… Inter-Continental Resort… and Colonel… I've just bought… um… ah pineapple plantation," I blurt out.

"What? Have you lost your mind?" the Colonel inquires.

"No… Ah… why do you… say that?"

"What are you going to do with a pineapple plantation?"

"Colonel… I'm going to be… um… living here… in Maui for a year… ah… or more. I love Hawaii… and ah… it's a great… second home… for me, and… ah… Lisa Marie."

"I understand that you like Hawaii, and it's a good place to raise Lisa Marie, but why the hell a plantation? What did you say it grew? Oh yeah, pineapples? You don't even eat pineapple!" Colonel Parker exclaims.

I cut the Colonel off, "Listen… um… Colonel… this is… ah… money making… proposition… um… for me. I have a… great foreman… named… ah… Bumpy… to run the… plantation… and ah… it's my little piece… of paradise."

"You have some guy named Bumpy running the place for you, and you did this deal without informing me?"

"Wait a minute… Colonel… I don't tell you… um… every time I buy… ah… something… do I? No. When I buy… someone… a car… or go and buy… the guys um… motorcycles… I don't tell you. If I buy… a house… ah… for someone… I just do it! So why… is this… um… any different?"

"Listen my boy, you're out of work now, and there is nothing coming in except for record sales and movie royalties. Buying a plantation just isn't a good idea. But you've already gone and done it, so there isn't much I can say about it now. You are just going to have to get well as soon as you can, and get back to work to start paying for it."

"Look um… Colonel… I just wanted… you to know… um… what I was… up to… and ah… for you to be… happy for me. I can hear… that you're not… so I'm going… to say goodbye."

"Elvis you know that I'm happy for you, but I just think it's not a timely deal."

"You know what… um… Colonel, whenever someone… says the word… but… what they say… ah… before the word… doesn't count… or… they don't mean it. And, um… what they say… after the word… but… is how they… really feel. So you must think… um… it's not a… good time to buy… the um… plantation. Well… I disagree… um… I have to get going… ah… I'll talk to you… later. Goodbye… uh… Colonel."

"All right Elvis, I'll talk to you later."

We both hang up the phone frustrated with each other.

~ * ~

Fred calls me at the resort. "Hello Elvis."

"Hello… Fred. Do you have… the um… closing documents… together?"

"Yes I do. I have the lending agent here with me, so why don't we come over, and you can sign the paper work. Then I can drive you out to your new home."

"That sounds… um… like a good plan. Yes… come on over. While I'm waiting… ah… for you… I'm going to… call Bumpy… because I want him… to find me… um… a personal chef… and nutritionist."

"I'm sure he can help you find someone. We'll be there in about fifteen minutes, see you then."

"Ok Fred… um… I'll talk to you… soon."

I call the plantation, and after a short wait on hold, Bumpy answers, "Aloha, Hala Kahiki Plantation."

"Aloha… Bumpy… it's Elvis."

"Aloha, Elvis, what can I do for you."

"I need you… to find me…a chef… and ah… nutritionist. You said… you ah… knew someone."

"Yes I do," Bumpy says, "I have a cousin, we call her Ali'i which means chef."

"Do you think… she is… um… available?"

"I pretty sure she is. I'll call her, and have her come out here so you can meet with her at your convenience,"

"Good... call her... and ah... have her come out... this afternoon... um... if she can. Fred is... um... coming over... in about... 15 minutes... and ah... it will take us... um... about an hour... to get out there. I will have... um... signed the loan... documents so ah... the mansion will be... officially mine."

"That is great news. I'll let the staff know that we have a new owner. I look forward to working with you Elvis."

"Thank you... um... Bumpy. I know you're... going to be... um... a big part of... the success... of the plantation now. We'll talk more... about that... um... later. Just know that... I have big plans... for you and the... plantation."

"Thank you, Elvis. I'll see you in about an hour and a half and I'll make sure that Ali'i is here."

"Thank you... um... Bumpy... I'll see you... then," I disconnect from the call.

Joe is the next person I place a call to, "Hello Joe... um... can you come up... here, ah... I have... um... Fred coming up... for me to sign... the, ah... loan documents... um... for the plantation... and ah... I need a witness."

Joe says, "That's great news, Elvis. Yeah, I'll be right up."

"All right... then um... I'll see you... in a few minutes,"

There's a knock at the door. I get up to look through the peephole before answering the door, just to be on the safe side. It's the waiter with my breakfast. "Come on… in," and the waiter pushes the cart through the door, into the living room.

"Do you want this here, or out on the balcony?" the waiter asks.

"The balcony… thanks."

"Yes sir," the waiter pushes the cart out to the balcony and I follow him. He takes the food from the cart and sets it up as I sit down.

"Can you please sign for this," the waiters ask handing me the bill. Just then there is another knock at the door. I say "Sure… if you'll answer… the door." As the waiter turns to get the door, I tell him "Ask who… it is, if it's… Joe let him in… kid."

"Yes, sir." I sign the receipt for my breakfast as Joe and the waiter come back to the balcony.

With a surprised look on my face, I look at the waiter and say, "Who is this guy?" The waiter looking very confused says, "He said his name is Joe."

"This isn't… the um… Joe… I was looking… for. Then I begin to laugh cutting the nervousness in the air.

"Oh, you're having fun with me aren't you?" the waiter asks.

"Yes… the look on… your face… um… was priceless," I hand him the receipt for breakfast.

"Elvis quit messing with the kid," Joe says.

"Oh that's alright; I'll have a story to tell the rest of the staff down stairs. And, I'm not even going to turn in this receipt for the meal because I have your autograph."

Joe asks, "But if you don't turn it in you have to pay for it don't you?"

"Yes, but it's worth it to me."

"Listen kid… um… do you play… guitar?"

"Yes sir I do, not very well, but I play."

"Joe, will you please go get the… guitar that's… in the living room… and bring me… a black sharpie."

Joe goes and comes back with a Martin D28 guitar, and a sharpie, and hands them to me.

I ask, "What's… your name?"

"It's Michael. In Hawaiian it's Mikale."

"Okay… how do you… um… spell that?"

"M I C H A…"

"Oh… um… you're a… wise guy! How do you… spell Mikale?"

Laughing he spells it out, "M I K A L E."

I open the sharpie and write on the body of the guitar, 'To Mikale, God Bless, Elvis Presley' on the front and then put the top back on the sharpie. "Here you go… um…Mikale… turn in that receipt… and now… ah… you really have… something to… um… talk to the… staff about," I say handing him the guitar.

"Are you kidding me?" Mikale exclaims wide eyed and in disbelief.

"No… um… that's for you… and as long as… I'm here… um… I want you… to serve me… um… up here… in the suite… okay?"

"Oh yes sir! It will be my pleasure."

"All right… now… um… get out of here… my food… um… is getting cold," I say with a smile.

Mikale takes his new prized possession and leaves the suite.

Joe shakes his head and smiles. "You just made that young man's day."

Taking a bite of my egg white omelet, I say, "He wasn't… going to turn in… that receipt… just to get… my autograph. How many guitars… can I play… at one time?"

"That was every generous of you, Elvis."

"He seems… like a nice… um… kid. Oh, wait… a minute… um… there's a tip… on that receipt… and ah… he's going to get… that too," I laugh.

There is another knock at the door which Joe gets up to answer. Fred and his lending agent come in and join me on the balcony. "Hi Elvis, how are you today?"

"Hello Fred… I'm doing well… um… thanks."

"Elvis this is Kale, he's the lending agent."

"Hello… um… Kale… it's nice to… ah… meet you. You have some… um… papers for me… to sign?"

"Yes sir, I do," Kale says.

"Let's go back… um… inside and… ah… I'll sign them… at the desk. Do you guys… um… want anything… to eat or drink?"

Fred speaks up and says, "I'll have a cup of coffee please. Do you want anything Kale?"

"I'll have a cup of coffee too, with cream and sugar please."

I ask Joe to order a pot of coffee and whatever he would like. Joe picks up the phone and places the order as the signing begins. Fred, Kale and I go through the paper work page by page.

~ * ~

About three hours later, I am at the desk in my new office at the mansion. Sitting across from me is Bumpy's cousin. Ali'i is 27 years old and apparently I have been her idol since she was a young child so she is nervous about meeting me for the first time.

"So, Ali'i, you know um… I've had a stroke… and… ah… I need to change… my eating habits. Bumpy tells me that you are a good chief. But, I need a chef who understands my nutritional needs."

"Yes sir, Mr. Presley. I have dealt with several stroke victims in my time. I have my MHNE which means, Master of Science in Health and Nutrition. If are willing to maintain compliance and adhere to my recommendations, you and I will get along just fine."

I am surprised by her answer, raise my eyebrow and say, "That's… what I like… um… a take charge… kind of woman. You fix what… I'm supposed to eat… and… ah… I'll eat it."

269

Ali'i put out her hand to shake his and says, "Deal."

"Deal. Um… when can you… start?"

"Right now. The first thing I'll have to do is get some sort of idea how many people I'll be feeding and what food is already in the house."

"Ok… you're on. I want you to… find um… Bumpy, have him… introduce you… to ah… Joe, and ask him… what you … um… need to know."

"If I have other questions who do I talk to?"

"If it concerns me… talk to… um… Joe, if it concerns… the house… um… then talk to… Bumpy. As you… get to know me… um… I'm sure… you'll know… what to do."

"Thank you, Mr. Presley. I know that I'll do a great job for you."

"I'm sure… you will, and… ah… you can call me… Elvis."

"Thank you, Elvis. I'd better get going."

"When you are … um… finished with… Joe, ask him… to come… see me, I need… to talk to him."

"Yes sir," Ali'i leaves the room as Larry comes walking into the office.

Larry turns to watch Ali'i walk away and then faces me raised eye brows, "Hello Elvis, I just got off the phone with Ed."

Ed Parker was born in Honolulu, Hawaii on March 19, 1931. Well known as Senior Grand Master of American Kempo, Ed trained and awarded me my black belt while working as my bodyguard and as stunt man in some of my movies.

"Ed said he would be happy to come over and work with you. He also said that he would coordinate with the local rehab center for your physical therapy."

"Okay Larry… would you please… give him… ah… call back and… um… tell him to… get here… ASAP."

"Sure, I'll do that right away."

A short time later, Joe walks into the office, "Hey, Elvis."

"Joe, I just… um… hired the Chef."

"Yes, she told me you wanted to see me."

"Do me… a favor. Would you… and um… Bumpy interview… one or two housekeepers… for me? I want you… and Bumpy… to do it… because you know me… better then Bumpy does… and ah… Bumpy knows the locals… better than… you do."

"Sure Elvis, I'll get right on that."

"Thanks… Joe."

~ * ~

The shift from living at Graceland or out of hotels to the mansion has begun. I make arrangements for certain things to be sent from Graceland to the new home in Maui.

The house is now fully staffed with the addition of Ali'i, housekeepers, and security people to protect the grounds and my privacy. With Ed's help a complete rehabilitation staff has been hired, with a speech therapist and a physical therapist on call to work with me during my recovery.

One, sometimes two, of the therapists come in every day to work with me. Ali'i has me on a very strict nutritional régime for weight loss and good health. I have truly started to turn my life around.

Chapter 22

I am walking slowly along the beach, by myself, with my pants legs rolled up to just below my knees. My head is down in serious thought as I reflect on my life. I hardly notice the surf washing in around my bare feet. I feel like I a fog has been lifted and there is a lot to think about.

I realize this is my opportunity to turn my life around and have my second chance. Giving up the pills has been harder than I ever thought it was going to be, but so far I haven't fallen off the wagon. With the support of my rehabilitation team, and the encouragement of the house staff, I've been able to stay drug free. Being new to Maui, I haven't had the need to search for local doctors to help feed my old drug habit.

I wonder about my career, what am I going to do. Thoughts about producing a new record run thru my mind. Being on the island has made getting new material more difficult than I thought it would be. I guess I am going to have to make a phone call to Hill & Range Music back in the states or get song writers who have written hit songs for themselves or others to help me. I'm going to have to pay more attention to what is happening out of England because of the British invasion. Although Lennon and McCartney are huge fans, they are writing a great deal of hits for the Beatles, and other singers are covering their songs in their own style. Even Keith Richards of the Rolling Stones has written some great songs with Mick Jagger. There

273

is a lot of great material out there; I worry about what is going to fit my style.

Touring is another thing that occupies my mind. What kind of show should I produce? What would the stage look like? What kind of sound system and lighting would should there be? Oh… and where to tour? I have always wanted to tour internationally, but because of the Colonel that's never happened.

But, the first thing I have to concentrate on is getting over these physical ailments, especially this speech problem, before any of this can become a reality. It's not so much the quality of my voice, but the stutter that's the big problem, everything else can be worked around. Getting my voice back, without the stutter is the most important thing right now.

Thinking about all of these things, putting them in order of importance in my mind, helps me sort things out. Thank God, I am able to think more clearly than I have in years!

I head back to the house, walking up from the beach through the backyard and into the house. Ali'i greets me with a freshly made pineapple smoothie. "Thank you… Ali'I that's just what… I needed,"

"How was your walk on the beach?"

"I have a lot… um… on my mind, but… uh… things are okay." I nod and take a sip of the smoothie and give her a big grin in appreciation. "Yes, everything… is going to be… um… all right. I have even learned to enjoy pineapple!"

~ * ~

274

November 24, 1977

In the past, we would have a very traditional Thanksgiving dinner: roast turkey, stuffing, mashed potatoes, turkey gravy, green bean casserole, cranberry relish, butternut squash, buttered rolls, cornbread with honey butter, and for desert, pumpkin pie, pumpkin cheesecake, pecan pie, mincemeat pie and a bowl of Devonshire cream to top everything off.

However, on this first Thanksgiving in the new house, Ali'i is preparing a very traditional Hawaiian luau in the garden with a carving station, featuring roasted kalua turkey cooked in a Polynesian style underground oven. Other main dishes included prime rib, Mahi Mahi, with toasted macadamia nuts and paella bamboo steamed fish. She has also created side dishes of macadamia nut dressing, cranberry pineapple relish, and Molokai sweet potato Palau, along with tofu with black mushrooms and vegetables over chow main noodles. Other stations included a salad station, appetizer station, iced seafood station, and the dessert station featuring flavored sherbets, and custard, with just enough pumpkin pie to be a little bad.

Everyone is sitting at picnic tables scattered on the lawn. Joe and his wife Joanie, along with Billy and his wife Jo, are sitting with me. And, much to my delight, so are Priscilla and Lisa Marie, who have come over to visit for the Thanksgiving holiday. Others who are filling their plates and sharing our day are Larry, Charlie, Marty, Lamar, Al, and Dr. Nick. The Colonel and Vernon are filling their plates and laughing over some personal joke with Tom Hulett and Pat Kelleher from RCA

Records. Elwood, Ron and Jim, the flight crew who brought everyone over from the main land are sitting on the lanai. Hawaiian music, played by a local band is wafting on the warm tropical breeze off the ocean, as is the sweet fragrance of plumeria.

There is a bar set up to serve traditional Hawaiian drinks such as Banana Mango Smoothies, Blue Hawaii cocktail, Pink Mai Tai, Piña Colada Smoothies, Pineapple Iced Tea and Lava Flows. There are soft drinks for the kids and the adults who prefer not to drink alcohol.

I may no longer drink, but I have come to realize that all people are not the same. I have learned tolerance and honoring other people's choices. I no longer feel the need to have everything my way. It is a very happy time for me. My friends and family are together and everyone is having a great time.

I stand up at the head of the table and tap the side of my water glass with a folk. "Excuse me! Um… I'd like… your attention please. I'd like to thank… um… you all for… your help… ah… over the… past few months. Without… your love and support, I would not… have made it… this far. I have a… long way to go… and um… I'm on the road… to recovery. I want each… and every one… of you to know… uh… that when I… make my come back… um… I'll be bigger, and uh… I don't mean… size wise… and uh… better… than I ever was." There is applause, and shouts of "We love you, Elvis!" Lisa Marie hugs her Daddy (me).

I raise my glass again and everyone else follows suit in a toasting gesture. "I love you… all… and your families… God bless you… and uh… now enjoy… your Thanksgiving dinner." Everyone takes a sip of what they are drinking to complete the toast and the conversations pick back up. I sit, lean back and reflect quietly on all the things I have to be grateful for.

~ * ~

December 14, 1977

I am sitting in an overstuffed chair in the library, when Larry comes in and notices the book I am reading, "The Masters and the Path" by C.W. Leadbeater. "So what do you think about the book?"

I am startled out of my concentration, "I can see… why they say… Leadbeater was… ah… one of those early… um… theosophists… who seem to… have had a… um… profound influence… on the thinking… of the New Age… and ah… Spiritual Philosophy… movements… um…. of today."

Larry nods, as he takes a chair near me. "Many of his books are considered landmarks for introducing new ideas into the West. But, Leadbeater had quite a falling out with parts of the Theosophical Society over his ideas. He has never been forgiven by some of the theosophists. It was several years after that break when C.W. wrote this book."

I brush my left hand over the page I've been reading. "Yes but… his spiritual, and uh… qualities are what um… shine through… in this book. This book contains uh… an array of… Spiritual truths, and uh… is the only book… that gives real insight um… into his spirituality… as he um… moves forward… on his spiritual path. It's an invaluable… source of information… for the true seekers… like myself, of um… spiritual wisdom."

Larry lays his hand on my arm. "That book is both inspiring and uplifting; every page contains priceless gems to meditate on." His expression reflects his sincerity as he continues. "I think it's better than all his other books, and shows his truest contribution to the spiritual cause. I'm glad you're getting a lot out of the book."

I sit up straighter in my chair. "Oh yes… it's been an eye opener, and uh… it's helping me a lot."

Larry asks, "On another subject, do you have all your Christmas presents yet?"

"No… not yet, um… I have most of… the presents I want… to get, but uh… I still need… to get something… for um… Lisa Marie… Al and Billy. I also need… to get something for… the um… field workers."

"Well, if you need me to get anything, just let me know and I'll be glad to pick them up for you, unless you want to go into town, and pick out some stuff yourself?"

"I'll let you know… if I need… um… any help, thanks."

"Do you have my gift already?"

"Yes… I have a case… of um… pineapple with… your name on it," I laugh as Larry cracks up at my answer.

~ * ~

December 25, 1977

It's a beautiful day in Hawaii. Maui winter has begun to make its presence known. The temperature has dropped to the high seventy degree range.

Along the driveway to the Hala Kahiki Plantation, blue lights start from the main road all the way up to the mansion. The house itself is bordered on all corners and along the roofline with the same royal blue lights.

A life size Nativity scene is visible from the main road. There is an area that is scattered with a dozen of aluminum Christmas trees, each decorated with red, blue or green lights. They surround a single Christmas tree that is twice their size and covered in the same brilliant royal blue lights as the mansion. Santa and his sleigh with eight reindeer appear to be coming through the Christmas tree forest heading toward the house.

Close to the road is a sign that spells out "Merry Christmas to All, Elvis" in white lights. Nearby is similar sign that reads, "Merry Christmas, Peace on Earth."

Inside the mansion, each room has its own ornately decorated Christmas tree. I have brought in a touch of Graceland by adding traditional red velvet drapes over the windows, replacing the blue ones that normally hang there. In the main living room, a white tree with red bulbs reaches the ceiling. Another room has a real tree with colored lights, ornaments and tinsel hanging from its boughs. It fills the room with the fragrance of Christmas pine. Evergreen garland adorns the fireplace mantels and surround all the doorways complete with mistletoe. Beautifully wrapped packages are under all the trees in the house for family and friends, including gifts for the staff and field workers.

I am not subtle when it comes to decorating for the Christmas season.

Priscilla and Lisa Marie are spending Christmas with me. I enjoy catching them under the mistletoe to give my girls a big kiss. My grandmother, Minnie Mae Presley, even in her frail condition, has come to Hawaii to celebrate my first Christmas in Maui with the family. Vernon and all the members of the Memphis Mafia have come also.

Everyone is truly enjoying the holiday season, being able to go to the beach during the day where the water temperature is sixty-eight degrees. The weather back in Memphis is a miserable forty-one degrees, cloudy and rainy. What a great way to spend Christmas!

~ * ~

December 31, 1977

New Year's Eve is being spent with just the family. Priscilla, Lisa Marie, Minnie Mae and Vernon are still here to bring in the New Year with me. This is the first time in a long, long time I have had such a small group around me at any time, let alone during a holiday. Only my family and the house staff are here. The Mafia and other people in my entourage are spending time with their families at my request. Instead of a wild and crazy time at a New Year's Eve party, it's a quiet family dinner with light conversation at the dining room table.

I talk about how my life is changing and how much I appreciate the support of the family. I also talk about the future and how I would like it to be, describing the recording studio I plan to put in the house, and the new album I will start working on as soon as it is built.

Of course with a new album, a tour would be put together to support the album and I want it to be a worldwide tour this time. I know how the Colonel feels about touring internationally, however, I explain that this is something that I really want to do. I want to perform for the fans that I have never been able to meet before and to see more of the world.

After diner, we all retreat to the music room where I play the piano, and try to sing some old gospel songs as my family chimes in with harmony. We sing, *How Great Thou Art*, *Amazing Grace* and *Take My Hand Precious Lord*. My left hand is playing the bass line well enough, while my right hand stumbles over some of the notes. But it's my stutter that causes me the most challenge.

Frustrated, I stop singing, and just play the piano instead. Vernon steps up and takes the lead vocal as the family enjoys the private show, even though it's far from my best performance. As the countdown begins for the New Year of 1978, Vernon opens a bottle of champagne and pours out five glasses as he says, "Lisa Marie, you only get a taste, not as much as everyone else." I too, only take a small sip.

I turn on the TV and tune it to KGMB-TV, the CBS station out of Honolulu. The six-hour delayed broadcast features Victor Lombardo. He is the brother of Guy, the original band leader of the Royal Canadians, who died this past November. As we watch the ball drop, we all begin to count down with the broadcast. "Six, five, four, three, two, one. Happy New Year!"

I kiss my daughter and my grandmother, wishing them a Happy New Year. Vernon gives Priscilla a kiss on the check then bends down to gave Lisa a hug and a kiss. He then, hugs his mother and gives her a Happy New Year's kiss.

I lean in and give Priscilla a kiss on the lips, something that hadn't happened in years. When the kiss ends, we hold each other and look into each other's eyes lost in the moment, Hearing Auld *Lang Syne* being played and sung by the people at the Waldorf Astoria Hotel in New York City brings us back to reality.

We sing along with the people on TV to a rousing chorus of *Auld Lang Syne*. Then Lisa Marie asks, "Daddy, what does, 'For old ang zine mean?'"

Elvis chuckles and tells her, "It isn't 'For old… ang zine', it's… 'Auld Lang Syne,' um… the translation of the words mean… um… 'times gone by.' So when… you sing it… uh… what you are actually saying is… uh… "We'll drink a cup… of kindness yet… for times gone by."

Priscilla chimes in, "I didn't know that! Anyway, I want you to have a wonderful New Year, Elvis, and I hope that all your wishes will come true."

"Thank you… um… 'Cilla" I reply as my eyes mist up, "I'm sure with… God's help and the support… of my family, friends and fans, ah… I will. I'm going to… stay clean and off drugs… and continue to… regain my health." I decide that makes for a very good resolution for the upcoming year.

~ * ~

February 12, 1978

I am standing in my library before a full length mirror working hard to perform my vocal and diction exercises. I am working with my speech therapist, Kawika Ailaausd, whose name means David Fire God. "Very good Elvis, you're getting better at this. Okay, I want you to do Peter Piper now."

"Peter Piper uh… picked a peck of um… pickled peppers… A peck of pickled peppers um… Peter Piper picked. If um… Peter Piper picked… a peck of uh… pickled peppers, how many… pickled peppers did um… Peter Piper… pick?"

"Elvis, when you speak, I notice that when you say someone's name, you say 'um' first. Try to go right into the person's name without stopping. Try saying, it's nice to see you, Cilla."

"It's nice to see you, um Cilla."

"No, you did it again. Try saying it again."

"It's nice to see you…Cilla."

"There, that was much better. But you paused before you said her name. Try it this time using a different phrase. Say, 'Go get the accountant, Larry.'"

"Ah… go get the accountant… Larry.

"That's a little better. Now, do the woodchuck exercise."

"How much wood um… would a woodchuck chuck uh… if a woodchuck could chuck um… wood? A woodchuck would um… chuck as much wood as a woodchuck could, if a woodchuck um… could chuck wood," I finish up.

"Elvis you're doing a lot better than when we first started doing this exercises." Kawika reassures me, sensing my frustration. "I want you to practice as often as you can, whenever you can. That's it for now, but, I'll be back in two days."

"Okay, Kawika, I'll see you then."

"Now, did you hear that? You said it without stuttering!"

A big smile breaks out on my, "Yeah, I'm coming along."

Kawika leaves and I start going through the Peter Piper exercise again.

~ * ~

April 23, 1978

Ed Parker, my physical therapist, is here. We are working to restore the function and improve the limited range of motion and strength in my right arm.

Ed tells me "Your stroke caused partial paralysis and restricted range of motion. So, today I'm going to add new exercises to your curriculum. Using your arm to do these exercises will help improve your forward extension, your ability to lift your arm above your head and the bending of your elbow. The diagonal extension and flexion

284

exercises are going to strengthen your shoulder muscles, maintain flexibility and increase your range of motion.

"These small exercises focus on your motor skills. They will help maintain the function of your arm. I'm going to show you how to convert daily tasks like twisting off a jar top or picking up a three pound dumbbell can improve your ability to grasp, twist and the turn your wrist and elbow joint to improve your range of motion.

"Now, let me take hold of your elbow and wrist to move your right arm above your head. That's it, now we're going to move your arm until the inside of your arm touches your ear like this, and then slowly lower your arm back down. Yes, that's good! Now, I want you to repeat this exercise several more times."

As Ed continues the stretching he tells me, "This stretch won't build muscle but will help to increase your ability to move your arm up-and-down as well as side-to-side. This will prevent contractions and continue to promote your mobility.

"Okay, Elvis, let's move on to another exercise now. It's called the 'empty the can' exercise. It will increase your hand and wrist flexibility as you rotate your hand. Pick up the dumbbell with your thumb pointing up, and rest your elbow on the table top. Then extend your arm away from your body."

I pick up the three pound dumbbell and follow his directions.

"Okay, now I want you to turn your wrist so your thumb is pointing down.

"You are to do this exercise five to seven times, in sets of three. This exercise will work the muscles, ligaments and tendons in the wrist, forearm, elbow and shoulder."

I try to do as I am asked, "Wow, I really feel that working."

"The benefit of this movement will give you more flexibility, toning and strength in your affected arm. However, it would be good for you to add a few reps of each exercise on your unaffected side to keep your body tone balanced."

June 23, 1978

Joe and I are playing ping pong and Joe remarks that my game is coming along nicely.

This gets my ego going, and I try even harder to score points against Joe. "Take that, Joe!" I exclaim, as I hit the ball back to Joe.

"Right back at you," Joe says as he volleys the ball back to me.

I return the ball and Joe comments "Your right arm has improved so much you'll be beating me at this game pretty soon."

"Today's the day um… my friend. Today's the ah… day." We play the game up to twenty-one, and I finally win the game against my old friend, twenty-one to nineteen.

"A-ah, you finally did it, you beat me!" Joe teases. But I can tell Joe was please to lose the game fair and square.

~ * ~

August 10, 1978

It's been almost a year since my stroke. Priscilla and Lisa Marie have come over to spend a few weeks with me for the end of summer. I am driving the girls in a golf cart, taking them up to one of the highest points on the property where we stop to look out at the vast view.

"Elvis, this is gorgeous!" Priscilla exclaims.

"Wow, Daddy. This is so beautiful!" Lisa Marie proclaims.

"Yes, this is surely one of…um God's most lovely places on earth," I share my opinion as we look out across the valley below. From the cliff covered with huge lush trees and wild flowers, we can see some workers checking on the growth of the pineapples in the fields that stretch all the way to the edge of the ocean.

"Elvis, you have made a wonderful decision to buy this plantation. It's a beautiful place and it produces income," Priscilla comments.

"Yes, I love um… this place. I really feel at home here. I love Graceland, but this place ah… is special in a different way."

I put my arm around Priscilla's shoulder in a friendly way. "I'm glad that I can share this um… with both of you. You are my favorite girls in the whole world."

"You're my favorite Dad in the whole world," Lisa Marie teases.

I laugh, "Thank you sweetie."

As I gaze with loving pride into my daughter's face, Pricilla says appreciatively, "I am so glad we have this wonderful child together. And I hope you appreciate as much as I do, the close relationship we share even though we are divorced."

October 31, 1978

Lisa Marie and Pricilla have joined me for Halloween. Lisa Marie is dressed up to look like Rizzo from the film Grease. She feels she relates to Rizzo as she also enjoys being a free spirit and follows her own rules. She is wearing a black top, black skirt, a pink satin jacket with the words "Pink Lady" embroidered on the back and black boots. Her eye liner, dark green eye shadow, black eyebrow pencil and mascara along with red lipstick create a striking resemblance to Rizzo.

Lisa Marie runs up to me, a bundle of excitement. "I'm ready Daddy."

"You look great… um… Lisa Marie, all grown up, maybe too much so!"

She flounces her skirt, tossing her curls. "Look daddy, I am growing up."

"Yes that's what I am afraid of. I'm going to have Bumpy, and… ah… Lamar take you to the local um… neighborhood to go trick or treating."

"But Daddy I want you to take me trick or treating."

"Buttonhead, you know I can't go out… um… in public, and… ah… walk around."

"But, Daddy, pleeease."

288

"Well, it is… ah… Halloween and it will be dark out. How about, I get dressed up… um… like Count Dracula? I can wear a black cape."

"What if you went as the Werewolf?" Priscilla suggests. "We could cover your face with hair so no one would recognize you."

"That sounds um… like a great idea… Cilla. Come on, help me put the uh… hair on my face and pick out um… the clothes I need to wear."

The three of us go up to my bedroom and proceed to turn me into a werewolf. After they are done, Lisa Marie and Priscilla agree that their makeup job on me really does look like a werewolf.

The three of us along with Bumpy and Lamar take Lisa Marie out trick or treating in the local neighborhood. I can't believe how much fun it is being out with my daughter this evening. One of the best parts was that nobody recognized me. Lisa and I had a wonderful time together running from house to house, trick or treating as Priscilla, Bumpy and Lamar looked on.

Lisa came back to the house with a bag full of candy and was on a sugar high for a week.

~*~

December 31, 1978,

I am spending New Year's Eve, with Priscilla, Lisa Marie, Vernon and his girlfriend Sandy, Minnie Mae, Larry, the Memphis Mafia, and Bumpy, much like Thanksgiving and Christmas earlier in the holiday season. It's a beautiful evening, just before midnight, out on the lanai. There is a bonfire in the fire pit, and a festive atmosphere is in the air. Everyone is enjoying a fabulous luau feast that Ali'i has put out for this holiday.

As I hold up a glass of champagne I announce, "It's almost midnight and I'd like to tell everyone how thankful I am for all your help, um… over this past year. My last year's resolution was for me to continue to regain my health, and ah… to stay off the pain pills. Well, I've been off the pills now for over a year, and… ah… with my physical therapist, and speech therapist working hard with me… ah… I'm seeing the improvement every day. With Ali'i's help, I am eating right and have lost most of the excess poundage. I want to wish everyone um… a Happy New Year, and remember: Dream big!" I finish up by taking a small sip of champagne.

Vernon raises his glass. "Elvis, I want you to know how proud I am of you. You have done an amazing job of turning your life around, so here's to you!" Everyone raises their glass in agreement with him.

"Look, it's almost midnight," Joe exclaims. He starts the countdown. "Ten, nine."

Elvis and Priscilla join in, "Eight, seven."

The Mafia and Larry raise their glasses, "Six, five."

"Four, three," Vernon and Sandy add their voices, as Bumpy, Lisa Marie and Ali'i chime in, "Two, one."

"Happy New Year!" they all cheer.

The revelers start blowing their horns as Vernon and Sandy and Priscilla and I exchange New Year's kisses. Everyone else hugs, shake hands and wish each one another a Happy New Year.

~*~

February 12, 1979

I am sitting at the full-sized grand piano in the recording studio I have had built in the mansion. My right arm is feeling stronger and my hand is playing the melody line with relative ease. The cord progression is the typical one, four, five, four, one rock progression. I am having a problem with the lyrics of the song I am working on. So, I keep going over the same passage as I play, singing, *"You lied and I still love you anyway. I hear your lies and I can't live without you. I heard your lies and I'm going to live without you.* No, No, that sucks*. I'd rather go on hearing your lies, than to go on living without you.* Yes that's it!"

"That last track sounds great Elvis," Felton Jarvis tells me from the sound booth. "Yeah, those lyrics flows a lot better on the last take and the meaning. Wow! They're strong."

I smile knowing that I am on track writing a great song. I keep working on it as the tape machine continues to roll, recording everything that I sing and play in the studio. It amazes me how being back in the recording studio has helped my recovery process.

~ * ~

March 16, 1979

Spring has arrived. Out in the back yard, I am quarter-backing the Memphis Mafia touch football team in a game against the house and grounds staff.

291

I am running around and throwing passes, feeling like, if not actually performing like Roger Stauback.

I get behind Lamar, who's playing center. "Ready, blue twenty-four, blue twenty-four, hut, hut, hut." Lamar, because he is too large to snap the ball between his legs hands off the football to me. I drop back looking for my receivers. Both front lines push each other around, trying to get at or protect me.

Joe and Marty are running down either side of the "field". I see Joe is in the open about fifteen yards down the field and toss the ball in his direction. Joe is looking over his shoulder and sees the ball coming toward him. He reaches up and pulls it in. Out-running his defender, Joe crosses the goal line for the touchdown. My team starts jumping up and down in victory raising their arms in the air cheering. "Yeah, that's what I'm talking about," I shout.

Joe comes running back, "Great pass Elvis; that means we win the game 28 to 14." The score really should have been 24 to 12. But, since we don't have any goal posts to kick the ball through, we agreed before the game started that a touchdown would score 7 points.

They players from both teams congratulate each other on a game well played. Then we all head back to the mansion for some well-deserved pineapple smoothies.

~ * ~

May 16, 1979

I am at the beach putting my windsurfing board in the water. I hold the boom with both

292

hands, and let the wind fill the sail. It lifts me up onto the board allowing me to sail away from the shore.

Joe, Larry and Billy are on the beach watching me as they throw a Frisbee back and forth. Billy asks, "How did Elvis learn to windsurf?"

Joe answers, "Elvis learned the basics of sailing and steering from a young kid named Mike Waltze. Mike moved here a few months ago, and has become one of the pioneers in the windsurfing community."

"He was the first person to windsurf the Hookipa Beach, putting Maui on the map for windsurfing," Larry adds.

"Elvis has been surfing for years and he is just getting into windsurfing. He really seems to like it, even though there is a big difference," says Joe. It's basically a combination of surfing and sailing.

"You should have seen Elvis in the beginning. Between learning new skills and developing his balance and stability, there were some pretty funny moments."

Billy muses, "Who would have ever thought Elvis would become a board head?" They all laugh as I tack my way back to the beach.

Chapter 23

June 23, 1979,

"Would you listen to yourself? You don't have that awful stutter anymore," a delighted Priscilla points out. Priscilla, Lisa Marie, Larry, Joe and I are in the dining room, having breakfast together.

"Yeah, I feel like I sound like my old self again, have almost full use of my arm and I can still curl my lip," as I demonstrate and everyone laughs.

"I feel like the bionic man. There are a few crows' feet around the eyes, but that makes me looked distinguished don't you think?"

Priscilla replies, "You are an older version of the man I fell in love with."

"Thank you, thank you very much." I mimic myself.

"So, what is on the agenda for today?" Larry asks.

"Johnny Cash and Kris Kristofferson are flying in today to help me work on a song."

Priscilla asks, "What kind of song are you guys working on?"

"It's a cross between country and spiritual. I've wanted to work with these guys for quite a while now."

Larry asks, "What time do they arrive?"

"I think it's about 3:00 PM."

"They are actually coming in at 2:15 PM," Joe corrects me. "I'll pick them up, unless you want to?"

"No, I want to get back to work on in the studio, so, please, go ahead and pick them up."

"J.D. Summer is coming in, too." Joe adds.

"We'll all be glad to see J.D. again," Priscilla says, vocalizing everyone's feeling.

~ * ~

I am sitting in the studio control room with Felton Jarvis, my producer and engineer. Ronnie Tutt, my drummer, is with us, too. The door opens and Johnny, Kris and J.D. come in. Felton, Ronnie and I greet the guys. There are handshakes and hugs all around.

"Hey, you guys, it's good to see you", I say.

"Hey, old buddy, how the heck are you?" Johnny says.

"I am truly blessed."

"Hey, E." says J.D., "Man, it sure is good to see you."

"It's good to see you to, J.D."

Kris is the last one to greet me. "Damn, son, you are looking good. This Hawaii stuff sure seems to work for you."

"I just love it here. This is such a healing and relaxing place to live,"

"Yeah I haven't seen you with this much color… ever," Johnny kids me.

"I do spend a great deal of time out in the sun. Like I told Kris, I love this place."

"So you have become quite the gentleman farmer, growing pineapples," Kris says.

"It's a good business to be in," I explain, spreading my arms in an expansive gesture. "But, enough about that. Are you guys hungry or tired; do you want to get some sleep? What do you want to do before we get into this song I've been working on?"

J.D. is the first to chime in, "I think we could all do with something to eat first. You know how wonderful that airline food is. Then we can get into this song of yours after."

"Okay, let me introduce you to my chef. Ali'i. She makes the best lomi lomi salmon you have ever eaten."

Kris grins, "That sounds good to me; I'm in."

~ * ~

After Ali'i's delicious lunch, we all go back into the studio. Fulton explains "I've done some work with Elvis, and we have already put down some rough tracks. But Elvis and I know it is not right yet. We are looking for your input to polish it up."

Let's play them what we have already done, even though it is only a piano and rough vocals. I'm not sure I want to use it the way I have it arranged. We can tear it apart and put it back together with the right chord progression and hook. So that's not too much to ask for, after feeding you guys now, is it?" My smile shows I am kidding around.

Kris makes us all laugh by replying, "If I had known that, I would have had seconds."

Johnny gets down to business, "Ok let's hear what you have. Then we'll play with it and figure out the missing parts."

They listen to it several times over and start throwing out ideas. After about 45 minutes of brainstorming, it's time to stop talking and try things out.

Johnny gets toe organizing everyone "Kris, you play lead guitar and J.D., you sing the harmony and I'll play rhythm guitar. We can switch it up later."

Fulton tells the guys, "Alright guys let's jam to start, just to see where we're going to go with this."

Everyone finds their place in the studio. Fulton hits the start button on the recorder and they hear, "One, two, three, four, one, two, click, click." The track begins playing and Elvis starts singing to it. And so the session begins.

We have a great time over the next two days, enjoying each others company and cutting up when we are not making good use of the studio.

~ * ~

June 26, 1979

The song is finished. Priscilla and I are listening to the track when the phone rings in the control room. I pick it up.

"Hello, Elvis, can you hear me?" It's Billy on the other end of the line.

297

"Yes, sure I can hear you, Billy. What's up?"

"Elvis… it's about your father." Billy's voice cracks. "Elvis, your Daddy had a heart attack this afternoon."

"Oh my God! Daddy! What happened? How is he?" I can hardly get the words out.

"He was out in the paddock, cooling down your palomino, Rising Sun, and collapsed. We got an ambulance here as soon as we could, but there was nothing we could do to save him. I'm so sorry, Elvis. He died. I can only imagine what you're feeling right now."

I feel the blood drain from my head. I have to grab onto a control board, feeling as though my world has just dropped away as I hear the news. Priscilla grabs my arm and I feel her support keeping me from losing it completely.

"I'll be home to bury my daddy as soon as I can get the *Lisa Marie* in the air. Billy, I have to go now. I'll be there as soon as I can. Don't do anything until I get there."

I hang up the phone, slump to the floor, put my head in my hands and I begin to sob. "Oh my God, what am I going to do? Priscilla, both of my parents are gone now. You, Minnie Mae and Lisa Marie are the only family I have left."

Priscilla sides her arms around me, in a genuine effort to console me. "Oh, Elvis, that's terrible. I am so sorry."

"I have to get back there right away."

"Of course you do. Do you want me to pack anything for you?"

"I'll just take one small bag, and whatever I need that's not at Graceland, I'll just get while I'm there."

"Do you want Lisa and me to go with you?"

"Oh, course I do. Yes, please. Will you tell Lisa that her granddaddy has passed away? I don't think I can do that," I sob.

"Yes, I can do that. Elvis, if there is anything else I can do, just ask."

"I need to have Larry and Joe come back with us to Memphis, too."

"Don't you think Charlie, Lamar and Marty would want to be at the funeral?"

"Yes, I guess so. I'm not thinking straight. Yes, of course they would want to be there and should be there. Tell them to get ready and have Joe get the *Lisa Marie* ready as soon as possible."

Priscilla hugs me and gives me a kiss on the forehead. Looking into my teary eyes, she promises, "Everything will be alright, I promise."

~ * ~

The *Lisa Marie* is ready for takeoff from the Maui airport. I buckle myself into my seat, "Okay, let's get this thing going. Joe, did you call Dick?"

"Yes, Elvis, I let him know when we'll be getting there and he will have cars there to pick us up."

The flight back to Memphis is quiet as everyone reflects on the loss of Vernon.

~ * ~

June 27, 1979

Two limos pull out on the tarmac and drive out to where the *Lisa Marie* has just landed at the Memphis airport. The door opens as Priscilla, Lisa and I exit the plane and are followed by the entourage.

Dick greets us in a very somber mood, "Hello Elvis. Priscilla. Hi, Lisa Marie." He turns and leads us to the first limo. Joe and the others gather the luggage and follow in the second car.

Once in the limo, Priscilla asks, "Dick how is Sandy dealing with this?"

"She has just cried and cried over Vernon's death. I've never seen a woman cry so much. She must really love him."

"I'm sure she does," I say. "We all loved Vernon, and now another big part of my life is gone."

Priscilla reminds me, "We're all going to miss him, Elvis."

"I know, but Mama went in 1958, now my daddy is gone. I don't have anyone left except my grandmother, Minnie Mae. She's all that is left of my family, except for you and Lisa Marie."

I feel the reality of my words begin to sink in, as the limo leaves the airport. My brooding puts a damper on any conversation and the drive back to Graceland is completed in silence.

~ * ~

In the kitchen at Graceland, Colonel Parker is talking to Mary. "Mary, Elvis and the rest of his party should be showing up here soon."

"I know, Colonel Parker. I have enough food to feed everyone. I spoke to Ali'i from the island, and she told me what to fix, and how many people were coming. Some of Elvis' friends have been bringing dishes of food by to help feed everybody."

Al walks into the kitchen. "Colonel, it looks like Elvis has arrived, and will be coming in the through the front door."

"We better get in there, then," The Colonel, Al and Mary go to the foyer to greet me as the door opens and we come in.

"Hello Elvis, I'm so sorry about your daddy," the Colonel says as we hug each other.

Al hugs me, and says, "Elvis, man, I don't know what to say. We're going to miss your daddy."

"Yes, we're all going to miss him," I say mournfully.

Mary comes up, and gives me a big hug. This makes me to break down into tears.

"Mr. Elvis, you know that your daddy was very proud of you, he loved you very much."

Sobbing, I say to Mary, "I know Mary, but I didn't get a chance to tell him that I loved him before he left. That's what hurts so much."

"Oh, child, I know. You're the man of the house now. Not that you weren't before, but now with Mr. Vernon gone, it's all on you."

"Mary, I need to get up stairs and pull myself together. Is my room ready?"

"Yes sir, Mr. Elvis, it's always been ready for your return home."

The Colonel watches me go up the stairs to my room. Mary greets Lisa Marie. "Hello Miss Lisa, come here and give Mary a hug, will ya."

The foyer becomes crowded as the rest of the group comes in bringing the luggage with them

~ * ~

Later on in the day, I am sitting in my office upstairs with Larry. "Larry, I'm a mess. I can't believe that Daddy is gone. I've relied on him for so much. He ran everything here at Graceland. I feel so bad. I'm over in Hawaii getting my life together, and daddy's life was slipping away. I didn't even notice it was happening."

"That's what happens when you are away from the people you love. I know you had Vernon come over at the holidays. But, with so many other people around it took up much of your time that could have been spent with him. It's not that you were wrong; you spent quality time with him. It's just what happened.

"It's hard, being in the moment all the time. When you think back, you kick yourself for not having done something else at that time." Larry paused and then added, "If you had done something else it would have affected the outcome and the future. You might be even sorrier about that outcome."

"Yes, but he was my daddy. He raised me. He's part of what made me who I am today, with my Mama's help. God, Larry, I miss them both."

"Of course you are. The sadness you feel is the sorrow that everyone feels when they have lost both of their parents. You're no different than the rest of us; your feelings are your feelings. Everyone has two parents, and misses them when they are gone. It's the sense of loss that people feel and it's different for everybody but the same feeling of loss. It's your turn now, and you will get through this.

"Just think about Lisa, when you and Priscilla are gone, how is she going to feel? Elvis, now is the time to stay close to her and to Priscilla--they are the only family you have. Let them know how much you love them, often. Every time you leave to go somewhere, be sure to tell them that you love them. It should be the last words they hear from you, and they will remember you that way."

Looking me in the eyes, Larry continues. "And, you know, you still have your grandmother, Minnie Mae. Think what she is going through right now. She just lost her son. I would think now is the time for you to honor her, in her grief."

"Thank you, Larry. You are a Godsend. I feel better knowing I may be able to help the other people touched by Daddy's death," my voice softens. "I'll look in on Minnie Mae, and see how she is doing." I stand up and start to pace, "I also need to find out what has been done about Daddy's funeral arrangements and when they are planning to bury him. I need to talk to Sandy Miller, to see what she needs."

Larry leans over and gives me a pat on the shoulder. "I'm going to leave now, and give you a chance to collect your thoughts and change your clothes."

"I'll see you later."

"Thanks again, Larry."

~ * ~

Priscilla, Billy and Dick are in the music room at Graceland . Priscilla asks. "When have they scheduled the funeral? And, who will preside?"

Dick answers, "Vernon's body is at the funeral home. They are waiting to hear from the Colonel to make the final arrangements."

Billy says, "Elvis told me he wants to have Vernon buried next to his mom. I think C.W. Bradley will be performing the service."

I join them. "I need to go over to the funeral home and see Daddy. I have to make the final arrangements."

"I'll go with you," Priscilla volunteers.

"Billy, get Joe and Lamar to come with us too," I say.

"Are you ready to go now?" Billy asks.

"Yeah, get the guys together, we'll meet you at the car out front and then we'll leave."

"See you outside" Billy says on his way out.

Dick informs me, "I think the Colonel has already made arrangements for your dad's funeral."

"Well it's not his daddy, now is it?" I say, raising my voice in irritation.

"No, it's just that I think it has already been done," Dick says, sheepishly.

"Well, guess what, I'm going to bury my daddy the way I want to. Not how the Colonel thinks it should be done."

Priscilla tries to reassure me, "Honey, I don't think the Colonel was trying to do anything other than help you."

"I don't need his help. I can do this on my own. I'm sick and tired of him telling me what to do. I almost died, and now my daddy is gone. I've had to put up with his rules and ways of doing things long enough. I'm going to take control of my life and stand up for myself."

"Honey, you're just upset."

"Yes, I am. And this has been coming for a long time. Let's go. Dick, stay here and hold down the fort, we'll be back later."

Dick folds his arms and nods. "I'll look after everything, Elvis."

~ * ~

June 30, 1979

My Daddy is laid to rest at Graceland, in the Meditation Garden, beside Gladys, his wife and my mother. The mourners are a relatively intimate group of family and close friends.

C.W. Bradley, the pastor of the Wooddale Church of Christ, is finishing up the graveside funeral service. "We are gathered here to say farewell to Vernon Elvis Presley, and to send him into the hands of God. In the name of God, the merciful Father, we commit the body of Vernon Elvis Presley to the peace and final resting place of this grave.

The reverend continues to pray with his head bowed, "May the Lord bless you and watch over you. May the Lord's face shine upon you and be gracious unto you. May the Lord look kindly upon you and give you peace. In the Name of the Father, and of the Son, and of the Holy Spirit, Amen."

Sitting graveside, I am crying and Priscilla puts her arm around me, pulling my head onto her shoulder, patting my arm. Everyone files by the grave and lays flowers on the casket. After paying their respects to Vernon, they come by to say a few words to me.

After the funeral, I retreat to my Graceland office to pull myself together. My reverie is interrupted by a knock at the door. Without waiting for a response, Colonel Parker barrels in saying, "Elvis, I'm working a deal with the new Merv Griffin Resorts hotel that has just legalized gambling in Atlantic City. They want you to open the resort for them."

I glare at him, "Not now!"

"But we need to make a decision…" the Colonel says ignoring my response.

"I said, not now!" with anger resonating in my voice. "The answer is no, I'm not interested in opening another casino!"

"Elvis, this would be a great comeback for you to open Merv's new casino. You're ready to go back to work, aren't you? Merv has asked for you specifically to open the resort. I'm asking that you do one show a night, Tuesday through Thursday and two shows Friday to Sunday."

"Colonel, I said no." I am adamant and shake my head. "Have his people call Tom Jones to do it. I'm not doing any more casinos. I'm not some lounge lizard. I want to get out on the road, and see my fans and they want to see me. Not everybody can afford to come to Vegas, or Atlantic City, to see me. I want to tour, and I don't mean just the United States. I want to do a world tour."

"My boy, do you have any idea how much it would cost to tour around the country like that, let alone the world. You would have to move the equipment and the personnel, the constant changes in hotels and fights. It would be a logistic nightmare."

"Colonel, I have been thinking about this for a long time. Other acts do it all the time. If you can't hear me and do this for me, then I'm going to find someone else who can! To be clear, I am talking about new representation that can manage me the way I want to be handled."

"Now, listen my boy, I know you. You have threatened to fire me before, and you're not going to do it now."

"Colonel, that's where you are wrong, I'll honor the agreements that are in place. But as of now, you no longer represent me. I have a new manager, and everything that I do will go through the new management company from now on."

The Colonel gets red in the face, "Well, we'll just have to see what you come up with. You think that there is someone better at managing you than me?"

"Yes, I've been talking with him for months and I think it's time to put my plan into action," I calmly say. "I'll have my attorney contact you and we'll settle just how we're going to move into the new arrangement."

The Colonel clenches his fist in anger, and shouts, "We'll see about that, you ungrateful son of a bitch."

"You do what you have to do. I truly thank you for everything you have done for me in the past, but it's time for me to move on. I'm getting the next part of my life together and new management is a part of that. They will be able to take me to higher places than you have been able to. I don't want to part as enemies, but it is time for a change. I'll talk to you again, but it won't be about new business."

"If you're going to fire me, you're going to have to pay me what you owe me, and you don't have the money to buy me out. So, goodbye Elvis, you'll hear from my lawyer." The Colonel stomps out of the office in a huff.

I pick up the phone, and dial Tom Hulett. "Hello, Tom, it's Elvis."

"Oh, hello Elvis. How are you holding up? I thought the service today was very nice."

"Thanks, Tom. Listen, I just had it out with the Colonel, and I fired him. It's time to put into motion what we have been talking about."

"You mean that you are ready to have me manage your career now? Wow! That must have been some conversation."

"You know that things haven't been going well between the Colonel and me for quite a while. It's time to make the change. I want you to come over to Maui, and we can start making the moves to create my future like we talked about. I'm leaving for the island tomorrow. Can you come over A.S.A.P.?"

"As you know, we've been talking about me opening Tom Hulett and Associates, a management company. I guess this would be the perfect time for that," I can hear his smile through the phone. "I can come over in two days, and we will finalize things."

"I'll see you in Maui then. Aloha."

"Aloha," Tom laughs, "I'll see you there, goodbye."

~ * ~

July 3rd, 1979

Back at the Hala Kahiki Plantation, Bumpy is talking to Ali'i and Anake Malia, "Elvis is coming back today, and I want to make sure that everything is to his liking."

Ali'i teases Bumpy, "Don't worry, Bumpy. I'll be ready to feed him, and whoever is with him."

Anake Malia chimes in "I'll make sure the house is in perfect shape. I just have to clean all the bathrooms; everything else is in order."

"O.K. ladies, I don't know how Elvis is going to be feeling after burying his dad. So, please make sure that everything here in the house is in order. I have to go check on the plantation to make sure production is up to speed." Bumpy leaves to check

309

in with the plant manager and Ali'i returns to the kitchen to ready the preparations for Elvis's arrival.

~ * ~

We fly from Memphis to Los Angeles, where we drop off Priscilla and Lisa Marie. Joe, Al, Billy, Lamar and I head on to Maui. When we arrive back in the islands, a limo is waiting to drive us back to the plantation. When it pulls up in front of the mansion, Anake Malia comes out the front door to greet us.

"Aloha, Elvis, it's good to have you back home."

"Aloha, Anake Malia, it's nice to be back."

"I'm sorry for your loss, Elvis."

As we walk into the mansion, Anake Malia brings me up to date on what's been going on. "Everyone on the plantation met the day you buried your father, and we held a traditional Hawaiian paddle-out ceremony to return your father's spirit to the Hawaiian water at dusk.

"We had two paddle boats, side by side. All of your father's friends, and people he met while he was here on the island gathered on the beach. Bumpy and Ali'i paddled out with the Hawaiian Kahuna, and Fred and I were in the other boat. The Kahuna chanted a prayer, and your father's spirit was released into the ocean. Bumpy blew a conch shell, and one of the workers blew an answering call on another conch shell from on the beach. We then threw flower lei's into the water. We paddled back in to join everyone else on the beach for a gathering where we had food and drinks with everyone. We remembered your father with our stories of him."

I am touched, "Thank you Anake Malia, that was very kind. And thank the field hands for me also. I'm sure I'll see Bumpy and Ali'i, so I'll thank them myself."

"Yes sir." As they pass through the front of the mansion, Anake Malia continues, "There are several phone messages for you, but there is one particular phone message from Tom Hulett, that says he will be arriving this evening around seven-fifteen P.M. I thought you should know about that right away."

"Oh that's good news, Anake. Find Joe and ask him to make arrangements to have Tom picked up from the airport."

Joe comes in right behind me and overhears what I just said. "No need to find me. I'll be happy to make the airport run.

"Thanks, Joe. Let me know as soon as you get back here with Tom. We have a lot of business to go over."

"I'll bring him right to you."

"Anake, will you please ask Ali'i to fix some salmon? And, I could use some water. I'll eat in my office. Ask her to fix something for Joe and anyone else who is hungry."

I turn to Joe, "I need to get ready to meet with Tom."

Joe flashes me a smile. "Sounds like you have big plans set up with him."

"Son, you don't know the half of it."

"Well I guess I'll know when I know."

311

Chapter 24

In my office, I sit in the black leather chair at my beautiful distressed Tamarind finished desk made of solid mahogany and American maple. The solid brass hardware finished with aged bronze and copper undertones glistens in the sunlight. But the surface is covered with notes and piles of papers. So is the three drawer credenza. There is a pair of wicker chairs in front of the desk and blooming Hibiscus plants filling the room that offset the heavy look of the desk, credenza and matching hutch. The light green walls accent the floral colored patterns of the light breezy curtains blowing gently in the open sliding glass wall leading to the balcony inviting the outside world in. I am focused on a thick stack of papers.

Lamar comes in, "Elvis, Joe's coming up the driveway right now."

"Great, have Tom come right up to see me, will you Lamar?"

"Sure will boss," then Lamar returns to the front entrance to wait for them.

"Hi, Joe!"

"Hi, Lamar"

"Hello Tom, Elvis is expecting you. He's up in his office. Let me show you the way. Joe, will you please take Tom's bags to the guest room overlooking the pool in the south wing?"

Surprised at Lamar's request, Joe is a little taken aback, but does as he is asked.

"Tom, come with me, I'll take you to Elvis."

Tom is very excited about being hustled in to see Elvis right away, "Yeah sure, lead the way Lamar."

As they come through the office door, Lamar announces, "Elvis, Tom is here."

I get up to greet Tom with a hug, "I hope you had a good flight."

"Oh yes, it was fine."

"Great. Sit down, do you want anything to eat or drink?"

"I understand your pineapple smoothies are the best on the island."

"Oh just you wait, Lamar would you ask Ali'i to make two pineapple smoothies."

"Sure will," Lamar says, heading out of the room.

"So, here we are at the starting line for a whole new opportunity for the both of us," I say to Tom.

"I intend to announce the formation of, Tom Hulett and Associates, as a management company. My first acquisition will be you, and I can't think of a bigger name in the business to start out with."

"Tom there is so much I want to go over with you."

"That's fine. Let's start with your recording contract. I've been on the phone with Pat Keller, and without mentioning any names I know that I can get you a better deal than what you had with the Colonel."

"I thought we had a great deal with RCA?"

"Well you do on the domestic side of things. It's the international side, where they're screwing you."

"What do you mean?"

"When most companies negotiate a deal for international sales, they say that because each country is so small they can't pay as much for the royalties. That's just bull shit. Two thirds of your total royalties should come from foreign sales. And you have never paid any attention to the international market."

"The Colonel never wanted me to tour internationally. It's like the world didn't exists outside of the States. That's why I did so many movies."

"Look Elvis, I've known that you've wanted to tour internationally, and for whatever reason the Colonel didn't what you to. I've been setting up international tours for Led Zeppelin, Jimmy Hendrix, The Rolling Stones, Frank Sinatra, the Eagles and Elton John for years."

"I ran into Elton one of the first days I was on the island."

"Yeah, he told me he ran into you. It sounded like you guys had a great time together. But back to the world tour... I can set one up for you that would break all attendance records. If we put together an international tour, and get the record and the publishing companies to kick in funds to help support the tour that will lower our expenses for touring and mean more profits for us."

"You mean to tell me you can do that?"

"Yes! Like I said, I know how to do it, and I have been doing it for years."

"My new album is coming together and should be done in a couple of months. Since RCA was sticking it to me what if we went to another company, and raised the stakes on them?"

"When I announce the formation of my new company, and that I have signed you as my first acquisition, every major label will be at my door wanting to do a deal. So yes, we should shop around and get the best deal. Don't feel like you have to rush the album. Take the time you need."

"Thanks, Tom. I think I will take a little more time than I originally planned. I miss my daddy so much. And I think I want to add a number to honor him.

"When the album is almost done, I want to take it to Los Angeles. I'll sweeten it and do the mastering there. Then it will be time to put the band back together and start rehearsals."

"Ok Elvis, take your time. We are going to have a long and successful partnership. Why not spend Thanksgiving and Christmas here with your family. I will get the office set up and put things in motion to get your new record deal. And, I'll start working on the international tour. Come over in January, master the album, and start rehearsals with the band.

"I have a stage manager named Jason Doyle that I want you to meet. He has put me together with a new light designer by the name of Marc Brukman and I'd like to use Paul Staples to do the set design. The sound system will be a quadraphonic speaker system that will have more power than any PA system you've ever heard. It will fill any auditorium or stadium, and be bigger and better than anything that has ever been done before. I'm still working on who will be good to build this system for us."

"What about the mafia, I'm still going to need them. I don't want a lot of strangers around."

"Don't worry. There's plenty of room for the Mafia. I know that they are your security guards, and that's fine. These other guys are pros. This is what they do for a living. Their job is to get the stage, sound and lights set up so you can concentrate on your performance. Afterwards they break it all down, and move it to the next site. There will only be a hand full of new people that you will have to deal with in order to make sure everything is the way you want it. The rest of the stage hands are roadies, they do the grunt work. You won't have to deal with them.

"If you can get the album mastered by the end of January or early February we can schedule the release for March. Before then, I will have contacted the major labels and ask them to put together a proposal of how they are going to support you, and the album release. The best deal wins."

"What about me doing movies?"

"You should do movies. But, not right away. You have enough on your plate for now with finishing the album, rehearsing the band and being on the road for 10 to 12 months touring the world. In the meantime, I will keep my eye out for a script that I think would be good for you. I don't see you having the time to do a movie for about two years from now, to be honest with you."

"What about merchandising?"

"When the album is finished we'll incorporate the art work from the album cover and have one of the major merchandising companies put their people out on the road to deal with sales and we'll collect our share of the profits from them. Even if we get a bad deal, you will make more money than you have ever made with the Colonel."

"That sure sounds good. You know Larry Geller, don't you, Tom?" Tom nods. "I've been talking to him about giving back, tithing. I want to share what I make from ticket and album sales, to be able to feed hungry kids around the world."

Tom pauses for a few moments and then says, "That is a very noble thing to do Elvis. Most artists want to make as much money as they can and invest it to make more. What they do with their money is their business. That is a personal thing that I don't get involved in. I will make a lot of money in our dealings, and if that's the way you feel, I will contribute to the cause 10% of my earnings to honor you, and help in the effort to feed the kids as well."

"I like your style Tom. Thank you for your offer. You think big, and I know that you can deliver what you say you are going to. I've got a feeling you're going to push me in directions that I want to go, and beyond what I've believed was possible."

"Well, Elvis, I think this was a very good first meeting. We both seem to be on the same page. I'll get the contracts drawn up, and sent to you.

But, what I want to know is, where is that pineapple smoothie you promised me?"

Elvis looks back at Tom, "Once I get the contracts, I'll sign them as soon as Ed Hookstratten, my attorney, has had a chance to review them. Now, let's go to the kitchen and see what is going on with those smoothies. Then you can get settled into your room."

Both men shake hands and head down to the kitchen.

~ * ~

Over the next several months, I work on the album using local musicians. A variety of song writers and other artists come over from the mainland to help put the album together. I call it, "My Second Chance" to celebrate surviving and overcoming the effects of the stroke.

My life has turned around, and I live a cleaner, healthier lifestyle than I ever have. The future looks bright and I can't wait for the first of the year to come.

Chapter 25

January 9, 1980

The *Lisa Marie* lands in Los Angeles, delivering me and my new album. Joe meets us with a limo and drives to 1174 Hillcrest Drive, in the Trousdale Estates sub-division of Beverly Hills, California. This is the house that I bought back in 1967 for $400,000. I am making it my home and headquarters while working in Los Angeles.

As I walk into the house, Tom is there already, "Hello, Elvis, was the flight, a good one?"

"Yes, I slept most of the way, it was a smooth ride."

"Things are falling right into place here. Just like I told you, I have five of the major labels bidding on a contract with you. The two best, so far, are Capitol and CBS. I'll tell you what the other offers were, but we have preliminary talks with Capitol and CBS scheduled for tomorrow."

"If you're happy, then I'm happy. It's just a formality for me to show up anyway. Most of the executives just want to say that they have met me."

"Is the album done?"

"No, I need to put some little finishing touches on it, and then it will be ready."

"So, you will have it ready in a few days, right?"

"Yes, as soon as it's finally mixed, I'll have it sequenced then mastered. That's when I want you to hear it. Then I'll be ready to start rehearsals."

"When you're ready, I'll rent the big room at S.I.R. Studios in Hollywood.

"That sounds great. What's happening with the stage and PA system?"

"Oh just you wait and see. I've rented an airplane hangar out in the valley. Not just one stage but two stages are being built and the sounds system is ready to go into place."

"Two stages?" I raise my eyebrows.

"Yes, it takes so long to set up the stage; it is more efficient to have one stage in route to the next show while you're performing on the other one. And wait till you see the lighting design and fireworks that Marc Brukman has put together. Oh my God, I've never see anything like it."

"Have you seen it working yet?"

"No, but I've seen the plans, and had Marc explain how everything is going to work, it sounds amazing. Marc has everything that he needs now, we're just waiting for the stage to be set up, and when the PA system goes in, the lights will go up at the same time. You're not going to believe the stage. It's the biggest stage you've ever worked on."

"I can't wait to see it," I say, anticipation causing a flutter in my gut.

"When you have finished mixing the album, and get it mastered, we'll go over and I'll show it to you."

"You're going to make me get everything done, before I can see the set up?"

"Yes, consider it motivation. You have to finish your work before you get to see your big surprise," Tom kids.

"Like I'm not excited enough: getting a new album out, and the thought of touring again, this time internationally? I'll have the mixing and mastering done by the end of the week."

Tom tells me, "I'll ask Joe to call the band and the other musicians to schedule rehearsal a week from today."

"No, I want to call the boys and I'll tell them myself, that it's time to TCB again."

"That sounds like a good idea."

~ * ~

Since this new tour is so different from the Las Vegas style act I had been doing, it needs a wardrobe update.

I have decided to wear black pants, white shirts with French cuffs and Spanish boots on stage. And, I will still be sporting my signature scarves that the fans love so much.

To finish off the look, I go see Nudie Cohen for my new stage duds. He is the tailor who made my gold lame tuxedo back in 1957. He has made a name for himself producing iconic clothing for performers from Roy Rogers, Dale Evans and Hank Williams to Robert Redford in the *Electric Cowboy*.

Together we design western style riding jackets to wear on stage. One is black leather with rhinestones creating the TBC logo below a lightning bolt on the back and there are rhinestone accents on the pocket flaps. While I have changed greatly, I still am "Taking Care of Business".

A royal blue jacket sports a phoenix rising from the ashes created from a combination of embroidery and multi-colored rhinestones. On the lapels are embroidered Egyptian crosses, known as Ankhs. These symbolize my new lease on life.

Another one is white leather with embroidered anemones and forget-me-nots on vines going up the sleeves and a large single red rose accented with red crystals on the back. This is the one that has a special message for Pricilla in the language of flowers.

There are two others that will be completed after the tour has started.

~ * ~

January 22, 1980

I am holding rehearsals with the band in the airplane hangar with full light and sound. We are performing a new song off the album.

At the end of the song, Tom comes walking up to me, "That sounds great. Your vocals are strong, the band is tight and the lighting effects really give the show a whole new dimension. When you're playing to a 100,000 seat stadium even the furthest person in the audience will be able to hear and see everything."

"You're right, this stage is huge. I'm walking my ass off to get around this stage. I feel like I'm traveling from one zip code to another!"

"The video cameras will follow you anywhere you go. And moving around the stage like this will help you keep the weight off." He says with a wink.

I chuckle at this last comment.

~ * ~

"By the way, we have an appointment tomorrow with Bashkir Menon, Chairman of EMI Music Worldwide, and Rupert Perry who is Vice President of A & R at Capitol Records to sign a new deal with them," Tom informs me as we sit in my den overlooking the pool. "They have heard all the tracks, and they think it's the best thing you've done to date."

"Did we get the points we were talking about?"

Tom gives me a sly grin. "Yes, it's the best deal I've ever gotten for any artist," Tom says with pride.

"What time tomorrow are we meeting them," I ask getting ready to write myself a note to tell Joe.

"The meeting is set for 11:00 AM at the Capitol Records Tower." The Tower, a landmark building in Hollywood, California, houses Capitol Records headquarters.

Writing down the time, I ask Tom, "Can you have the car pick me up so that I have enough time to be there to meet with them?"

"I'll come over and pick you up myself, so be ready to leave at 10:00 AM."

"I'll be ready and I'll let Joe know when we're leaving. I want Al and Joe to come with me as security. Besides, they want to see the inside of the infamous Tower."

Tom nods in agreement. "Not a problem. That was a great rehearsal today. I'll see you tomorrow,"

Elvis walks Tom out, "Thanks for everything Tom. I really appreciate your help in all that you are doing."

As we walk toward Tom's car, Tom informs me, "I've been working on the tour dates, and it looks like you're going to be out on the road for nine months. I have dates starting here in the U.S., then going to Europe, Asia, Australia, New Zealand, then to South America and back to the States. The first show will be on March third."

"Where will that be?"

"We're doing three shows here at the L.A. Coliseum. That way we can check to make sure everything is working the way it should. If we have to replace anything or change anything we're still here in Los Angeles. Then it's off to San Diego for two dates starting March seventh. I'll give you the full itinerary tomorrow. I'm going to show it to Bhaskar and Rupert. As I recall, we'll be hitting fourteen major countries under EMI International structure, so sales worldwide will be tremendous."

"I can't wait to get back out on the road."

~ * ~

The next morning, Tom, Al, Joe and I step off the elevator on the ninth floor of the Tower at 11:00 AM. Tom leads the way into the conference room to meet Bhaskar, and Rupert. Also in the room is Bruce Martin, International Promotion Manager for Capitol Records.

Tom greets Bhaskar first, shaking his hand, "Hello Bhaskar, I'd like you to meet Elvis Presley. Elvis this is Bhaskar Menon."

I shake Bhaskar's hand and am surprised that he is a brown skinned, East Indian gentleman with a mustache, who is dressed in a beautifully tailored western three-piece suit. He is the first Chairman & Chief Executive Officer of EMI Music Worldwide.

"Hello, Bhaskar, it's a pleasure to meet you."

Bhaskar replies in a slight Indian accent, "It's my pleasure, Mr. Presley. I've been a big admirer of your work for years."

"Well, thank you, Bhaskar, thank you very much."

Tom continues making the introductions, "And this is Rupert Perry." Rupert, a medium built Englishman with dark curly hair, a bushy beard and mustache, is wearing dark pants, a white shirt and a blue pull-over sweater.

As Rupert smiles, I notice he is a victim of the English dental system. "Welcome to the Capitol Record family, Elvis. We look forward to working with you for the next five years and, I hope, even longer."

"Thank you, Rupert, I looking forward to working with you guys, too."

Tom turns to Bruce Martin, an American born, younger man with long dark hair, naturally highlighted with streaks of silver. He stands at an even six feet tall, has a well-trimmed beard, and is wearing sunglasses, blue jeans, cowboy boots and a western shirt. "And this is Bruce Martin; he is the International Promotion and Marketing Director for

Capitol Records & EMI. He will be the liaison between you and the local companies anywhere outside the United States. He's your go-to guy to help you deal with the cultures and customs of every country you're going to visit and answer any questions you may have." Elvis shakes Bruce's hand saying, "It sounds like you and I are going to become good friends."

Bruce nods and returns Elvis's grin. "I look forward to working with you. I will be there to be your go between with label managers and executives and media persons in our efforts to increase your record sales internationally."

"You can start with these other two guys I just met." I say laughing, with a big smile on my face. This breaks the tension in the room as everyone else laughs too.

Tom finishes his introductions, "This is Al and Joe they are part of the Memphis Mafia, and Elvis' security." They shake hands with everyone as they all sit down at the conference room table.

Bhaskar says, "I can't tell you how excited we are to have you signed to Capitol Records, and its worldwide family of companies, Mr. Presley."

"Thank you, but, please, call me Elvis."

Bhaskar slides the contract over to me, "Here is the contract that we have worked out with Tom. It's very generous in percentages to you, and gives you a major presence in the world market place. It has been reviewed by both your lawyers and ours. If it is OK with you, I'd like to have a photographer come in and document the signing of the contract."

"Sure that would be fine,"

Rupert picks up the phone and talks to Bhaskar's secretary. "Betty, have Steven come in, please."

Steven Pebbles comes in with his camera and takes pictures of me signing the contract and everyone shaking hands. Betty comes in with a tray holding bottles of Chardon Champagne and glasses for everyone to toast this momentous occasion.

After the champagne is passed around, Bhaskar holds up his glass and says, "Welcome to the EMI family. We look forward to a long and prosperous time together, and if there is anything that you need, please feel free to ask and we'll do whatever we can to accommodate you."

I thank Bhaskar and add, "I'm sure that our new relationship will be mutually beneficial, but I don't drink champagne any more. Perrier water would be fine for me." A momentary sense of awkwardness comes over the room, but Bhaskar calmly asks Betty to get Elvis a bottle of Perrier.

Rupert deflects the situation. "Elvis, we really love "My Second Chance" and we think it is the best work you have done in years. Your time in Hawaii has made a big difference in your sound. You have reinvented yourself, with a new sound and style."

"Yeah, it took me a long time to do this album," Elvis admits to Rupert. "When I started it, I was still dealing with a stutter and paralysis in my right arm, so I got off to a slow start."

Bruce remarks, "Well, this new sound is just what we are looking for. I think that between our support and your touring, "My Second Chance" will be your biggest album to date."

Bhaskar addresses me, "Tom tells us that you're getting ready to go out on your first worldwide tour. Two thirds or more of your income will come from international sales, and it is Bruce's job to make sure that happens."

Tom says, "I have the tentative itineraries here," as he hands out the schedule to Bhaskar, Rupert and Bruce.

"Elvis, when you are out on the road, I assume that you will be available to do interviews for radio, TV and press?" Bruce asks.

Tom jumps in, "Except for travel days, and performance days, Elvis will be available to do interviews in most cases."

I tell Bruce, "I'll be glad to do interviews. But, if you can have them come to me at the hotel or set up a studio where we can do several sound and video interviews, it would be better than having to drag me all over the place. I also want to have a few days to see parts of the counties I'm visiting."

Bruce reassures Elvis, "I'll be out on the road with you. So, if there are any interviews to be done, that information should come through me. I'll make sure that it gets organized through the proper people at the local label. Tom, who should I contact to coordinate with Elvis, to do interviews while were out on the road?"

"That would be Joe, here."

"Great, I'm sure that over the next few months we will get to know each other very well, Joe."

"I look forward to it."

Rupert adds, "Our National Promotion Director, Bruce Wendell, is in Atlanta right now. He will be working with our local Promotion Managers throughout the US, and will be the liaison between you and the local promotion guys to do interviews and get other things done. Joe, I assume that you will be the contact for Elvis domestically, as well?"

Joe confirms that. "Yes, I'll be the main contact for Elvis when we're on the road. Everything goes through me while we're on tour."

Bhaskar mentions, "We will direct information to you, too, Tom, to keep you in the loop as to what we're doing with and for Elvis."

Joe jokes with the group, "Oh, Tom and I have a great working relationship and we are in constant contact with each other. I'm the hand and he's the glove."

I say, "Wow, I've never heard that analogy before."

Everyone laughs.

Bhaskar moves the meeting along. "I'd like to take you down and introduce you to Roy Kohara, the head of the Art Department. He will show you the artwork we have put together for the "My Second Chance" cover art, and present the way we are going to use it. We will make posters to use in promoting the album and the tour. We have other promotional ideas that we will run by Tom, and you, to make sure we are all on the same page."

Bruce adds, "Roy is of Japanese descent, and he is a Grammy award winner for his work as album art director, and design."

"Bruce, it sounds like I'm going to need you to meet with this guy," I say. "Where is Roy located?"

Rupert answers, "His Art Department is downstairs on the seventh floor. Would you like to go down there now, and see what we have put together?"

I standing up, stretch and say, "Yeah, let's go down there."

Rupert continues, "The Press Department is headed up by Oscar Arslanian, and it's on the same floor. I'm sure he would like to meet you and get a better feel for who you are and what we are going to be dealing with."

We get up from the conference room and head downstairs.

~ * ~

Tom, and Roy and I are standing at a light box in Roy's office. Roy says, with pride in his voice, "Elvis, this is the cover art we came up with for "My Second Chance."

Elvis bends over to look closely at the image projected on the light box. "Hmmm, I like the photo, but I don't like the font you used. Can you change it to something a little more uplifting, and not quite so dark Gothic-looking?"

"Yes, sure, good call. We can do that, no problem."

Tom asks, "What does the back cover look like?"

Roy pulls the artwork out of a pile of cover art that is on his deck. "Here's the back cover. We'll put in the song titles and the running times as soon as we get them."

Rupert tells Roy, "We'll get you the song titles by tomorrow."

"That would be fine," Roy says.

Oscar, a dark, swarthy Greek, Jim Croce look-alike kind of guy, barrels into the room radiating energy. He is greeted by Bhaskar and Rupert. Bhaskar makes the introductions all around.

"Hello, Elvis, Tom, I'm glad to meet you." Oscar said extending his hand to me. "When you get some time, would you come to the publicity department? I'd like to get as much information from you as I can about what you're going to be doing in the next few months."

Tom fields this one, "I don't know about today. But, we can set something up for later or have you come to one of the rehearsals and see the show, to get the information first hand."

"How do I get hold of your people to make the arrangements to do that?"

"You can call me," Tom says. "Or, you can contact Joe. We will set it up for you."

"Great! Here is my business card," Oscar says, as he hands one to Tom and then one to Joe, "It was nice to meet you, and we'll get together soon."

"I'll look forward to it," I say.

Tom adds, "We'll talk later."

Oscar talks as fast as he walks. "Like I said it was nice to meet you guys and we'll talk again soon. I've got to run; I have a staff meeting that I have to attend." Oscar leaves the room in the whirlwind that he came in on.

Bruce gazes after Oscar, shakes his head with a smile. His expression changes and he says, "I just had an idea." There is excitement in his voice. "Your opening night is March 3rd at the L.A. Coliseum, right? What if we had a free concert on March 2nd, and invite press from around the world to come in and see the show? We could invite under-privileged kids and their guardians, and church groups to the show. You know, people of lesser means that wouldn't be able to see the show ordinarily."

Bhaskar jumps on the idea, "The publicity would be incredible. Do you think you would have time to pull it together?"

Tom expresses his concern, "That means we would have to push our schedule back by a day."

Elvis adds, "Do you think you can get ninety thousand plus people, and the press from around the world to come in to do that?"

Bruce tells the group, "Yes, if I can get your okay, I'll get this ball rolling. I will let Oscar know to get the national press from the States here. I can invite the foreign press to come in to see the show. We can have the local sales branch here at Capitol invite the audience, as a good will gesture. It would build a great amount of publicity for the tour, and mark the return of the 'King of Rock and Roll'."

I have been nodding with enthusiasm all along; agree with the idea, "I think that's a great idea, Bruce. Let's set this up." Tom nods his head in approval.

Rupert, in his English manner that always seems a bit stuffy, says, "If you can pull it off, it will be unbelievable." He might sound stuffy, but they can all tell he is enthusiastic too.

Tom adds, "Bruce, I need to check and see if we can get the Coliseum a day earlier and make sure that everyone else can be ready to make this adjustment."

"How soon can you let me know?" Bruce asks, as he writes down some notes.

"Hopefully, by this time tomorrow."

"I'll wait for your call then. Tom, don't forget, it's already tomorrow in Australia."

"Now that's the way to kick off a tour." I say, thanking Bruce for the idea. "Well, we all have work to do, so, I'm going to get out of here. It was a pleasure to meet you all, and I look forward to working with you in the future. Al, Joe, we're off."

Tom, shaking hands as he leaves, says sincerely, "Thanks Bhaskar, Rupert, Bruce it's been a pleasure. Roy, we'll see you later, too."

I reflect that it was a good meeting and I'm pleased that everyone seems to get along with each other.

Chapter 26

March 2, 1980

In the Los Angeles Coliseum, the stage is set and it's early evening as Klieg lights search the evening sky. Backstage in my dressing room is set up like a living room with couches, coffee tables and chairs, plus a pinball machine, and a food and drink spread from craft services. Priscilla and I are sitting with, Lisa Marie talking. "Priscilla, I can't believe this is the opening night of the biggest tour I've ever done. I'm almost a nervous as those early days."

She gives me an encouraging smile. "Yes, and I'm sure you will do just fine."

"I'm going to be out on the road for almost a year. I want you, and Lisa to be there with me."

"Elvis, Lisa has school, and I have my work, so we can't be there with you for the whole tour."

Looking over at Lisa I begrudgingly agree, "I know, but I want Lisa to come on the road when she is out of school, or on vacations. I want her to see the world like you and I did in Germany. It would be a great education for her."

I continue, "What am I going to do on the road without you, Priscilla?"

Lisa Marie adds her thoughts to the discussion, "I want to see Daddy do his shows Mommy. I want to see the world."

Priscilla, the voice of reason, says, "Yes, and you will be able to go on the road, and see your

Daddy, but you have school and you can't go for the whole time."

"Cilla, please make as many shows as you can. You know that I love you, and we have grown so close during the last year or so."

"Elvis, you know that I love you, too. I'll come to as many shows as I can. I've always wanted to see South America, and Australia, so you will see me then, for sure."

Holding Lisa Marie as she sits in my lap, I ask, "And, will you let Lisa Marie come whenever she's out of school or on vacation?"

"Yes, I'll let her come. And maybe, just maybe, I'll pull her out of school if you're playing a really exciting place that I think she would love. I know that it will be a better education than she would get just reading a book about the place."

With a big smile on my face, I tell Priscilla, "You're the best, baby."

Joe comes into the dressing room, and gives me the high sign and says, "The shows about to begin."

"Well, it's time for me to TCB," I say as I move Lisa from my lap and stand up.

Priscilla says, "Have a good show. I'm going to get us out of here, so you can finish getting ready." I give Priscilla a hug and a quick kiss on the forehead. "All right, my queen and my princess, I'll see you after the show."

"Goodbye, Daddy, we'll see you later." Lisa Marie gives her daddy a big hug and she gets a big kiss too.

Priscilla says, with a wink of her eye, "Enjoy yourself out there tonight. We'll see you later."

"Okay, I'll see you. Priscilla, do me a favor, if you see Larry, and the others have them come in please."

"All right," says Priscilla as she and Lisa Marie leave the dressing room.

"Bye, Daddy, break a leg," Lisa Marie calls out.

Tom, Larry, Al, Billy, Marty and Charlie all come into the dressing room to assist me with my last minute preparations.

Tom tells me, "Tonight's the night you have been waiting for. This is the biggest opportunity of your life. There are over ninety thousand people out there, and press from around the world. Elvis, this is your time to shine again."

"I know and I'm nervous," I admit.

Larry grins and says, "Come on, you know that if you weren't nervous there would be something wrong."

Joe reminds me, "I can't believe there are that many people out there. It could be one of the biggest crowds you have ever played for."

"This is the new phase in my life, boys. The crowds are going to be bigger, and that means your responsibilities are going to increase also. Get used to it guys."

Billy proudly tells me, "You have jumped into the stratosphere. The buzz about this concert is amazing. You're even bigger than you used to be.

I can't tell you how proud I am of you, and the success you are having."

Al comes up behind me and says, "Let me fix your collar and straighten out your belt. You're looking good tonight, E."

I ask the guys. "Are you boys ready to do this?"

There is a collective, "Yes."

I give a thumbs-up. "All right then, let's get this show on the road."

We head for the stage. Joe gets on his walkie-talkie to tell the stage manager Jason, "Cue the lighting guys, hit the fog machines, and have the band start with the opening number. The King is about to hit the stage!"

The lights go out in the Coliseum, the stage lights come up and the opening song begins to play, "A Space Odyssey/Opening Vamp." I stop at the bottom of the stage staircase for one last moment with Larry.

I privately confess to Larry in a whisper, "I've waited for this night for over two years. I'm nervous and there are over ninety thousand people out there waiting to see if the 'King of Rock and Roll' still has it."

"Elvis, you've never lost it and you have never sounded better. You're not going to know that until you get out there and start singing. The shock wave of energy from your fans will hit you and it's going to be unbelievable."

Larry leans forward and says, "You still have what it takes, and you always did. Look at yourself.

About two and a half years ago you were on the bathroom floor about to die. You're now in the best shape of your life--" he laughs a little under his breath, "for a man of your age, and the world is waiting to hear the King of Rock & Roll again."

"Larry, my insides feels like all my organs are trying to trade places."

"Elvis, you're doing God's will. He has made you strong again, and has put you in this place to do what you do best. God loves you, your fans love you, and I love you. Everybody is rooting for your comeback to be a success. So, go out there and have a great show. I know you can do it!"

I nod in agreement, and close my eye for one last moment of silent prayer, then burst into action. After a quick run up the stairs to the stage, I proudly stride out to center stage, and stand there bathing in the adoration that the capacity crowd is bestowing upon me. The spot light blinds me for a moment. I feel tears welling up in my eyes. I try to speak, but the cheers and the applause are deafening.

"Thank you, thank you very much." I turn to the left and repeat, "Thank you, thank you very much." I wave and make another turn and walk to the other side of the stage. "Thank you, thank you very much." I pivot back to the center of the stage, and look straight out at the audience and bow. "Thank you, thank you very much. Thank you and goodnight." I start to walk off the stage and the audience goes even crazier with more cheers and laughing at my sense of humor.

I return to center stage and say, "Hello, Los Angeles." The audience continues with more cheers and applause. "Thank you so very much.

It's been a long time since I've been on the stage. Will you look at this stage, is this something or what?" I say as I sweep my arm around to show the audience the stage. The cheers and applause continue. "And, how does it sound all the way in the back of the Coliseum? Can you guys see me all right on the big screen?" as I looks up at myself on the screen.

The audience in the back of the Coliseum goes wild with applause. "I had a stroke a couple of years back and it's taken me this long to get myself back together. I hope you think it was worth the wait for the new and improved me." The audience cheers and wildly applauds again.

"I have a new album being release this week called, 'My Second Chance'. The King is now on Capitol Records, where he belongs. They are the ones who suggested that I open my tour with this free concert to say thank you to the people of L.A. Of course, now all the other cities on the tour are going to be mad at me for not giving them a free show. But, I want you and the other cities to know that I'm giving back ten percent of my earnings from each show to a local charity of the city the show is in, to help feed the underprivileged children.

"I am back and we will be playing songs from the new album as well as some of my old favorites. So are you ready to rock?" raising my fist in the warm California evening air.

"Yes!" the crowd roars.

"I said are you ready to roll?"

"Yes!" Again the crowd responds enthusiastically.

"Well, let's get this party started!" Elvis gives the down beat to queue the band to start playing, "C C Rider."

~ * ~

The "My Second Chance" North American tour dates broke my previous records.

3/2-4/1980 Los Angeles, CA @ L.A. Coliseum 94,000 X 3 = 282,000 one night free attendance.

3/7-8/1980 San Diego, CA @ Jack Murphy Stadium 84,000 X 2 = 168,000

3/12-13/1908 San Francisco, CA @ Candlestick Park 79,000 X 2 = 158,000

3/16-17/1980 Seattle, WA @ Kingdome 69,000 X 2 = 138,000

3/19-20/1980 Vancouver, Canada @ P.N.E. Coliseum 17,000 X 2 = 34,000

3/23/1980 Tempe, AZ @ Sun Devil Stadium 70,000 X 1 = 140,000

3/26-27/1980 Houston, TX @ Astrodome 72,000 X 2 = 144,000

3/30-31/1980 Dallas, TX @ Cotton Bowl 92,000 X 2 = 184,000

~ * ~

March 31, 1980

Bruce and Oscar are back stage in my dressing room on the last night of the Dallas, Texas shows, talking with the guys and me.

Oscar tells us, "The press we have been getting since the beginning of the tour has been unbelievable. I've never see anything like it before."

I say, "Well that's all well and good, but I'm not interested in what the reviewers have to say."

"It's more than just reviews, Elvis, it's articles about you, and how you have recovered from your stroke, and how great you sound these days."

Tom makes an impatient gesture with his hand. "Oscar, Elvis really doesn't care to hear what is being said about him in the press. He knows what's going on in his life, and what the truth is. He knows if he has had a good show or a bad show. It's all subjective. He really doesn't care what the press thinks."

Bruce with an enthusiastic nod says, "Well, the anticipation for the tour from around the world has been great. The albums sales have already gone gold and platinum in several countries. The single has hit the top ten in most of the countries we're released in."

Oscar continues, "The single is number one in Billboard, Cashbox, and Record World. The album is also number one in all three trades and the sales have gone platinum for the album and double gold for the single."

Joe jokes, "Elvis you're going to have to start a new trophy room in Maui for your awards from Capitol Records."

Lamar, laughing says, "Now that's a good idea."

Uncomfortable with the conversation, I change the subject, "Did you guys hear that Nancy Lopez won the LPGA at the Kemper Open yesterday? The event was moved to the Congressional Country Club in Bethesda, Maryland this year."

Larry helps shift the conversation, "Yeah, I had heard that she won the tournament."

I continue, "We're going to be in Maryland in June, aren't we? I'd like to play that course when we're there."

Tom interjects. "I'm sure I can make those arrangements for you."

"That would be great Tom. Well, if we don't have any more business, I'm going to ask you guys to leave now, so I can get ready."

Bruce says goodnight, "It was good to see you again, and to be able to give you the good news. I'll say in touch with Tom about what's going on in the international scene."

Oscar ads, "I'll keep in touch with Tom, too. We have some important interviews coming up; "60 Minutes" wants to do a segment on you for the current tour."

I nod, "That's fine you guys. Catch up with Tom, and make those arrangements with him."

Oscar says, "All right then we'll see you later. Take care, you guys. I'll give you a call next week."

Bruce waves on the way out with Oscar, "Have a great show Elvis, see you."

~ * ~

The tour continues:

4/4/1980 New Orleans, LA @ Louisiana Superdome = 88,000 X 2 = 176,000

4/8/1980 Boulder, CO @ Folsom Field 68,000 X 2 = 136,000

4/13/1980 Pontiac, MI @ Pontiac Silver Dome 76,000 X 2 = 152,000

April 14, 1980

Before the second show at the Pontiac Silver Dome in Pontiac, Michigan, I am inside my dressing room with Joe, Larry, Lamar and Marty going through the pre-show routine. They are getting me ready for the concert, physically checking my clothes to make sure everything is in proper order, and that I am emotionally ready.

Oscar comes in with a home town hero and proudly makes introductions, "Elvis, I'd like you to meet Bob Seger. Bob this is Elvis."

As Bob extends his hand, he says, "Elvis, it's a pleasure to meet you. Welcome to the Pontiac Silver Dome. I've been a big fan of yours for years."

I return the compliment. "Oh, and I've been a big fan of yours, too. You have written some really great songs like, 'Travelin' Man,' and 'Turn the Page.' Oh yeah, then there is always 'Hollywood Nights,'… I've had a few of those nights myself." Everyone in the room laughs. "But my all-time favorite is, 'Old Time Rock And Roll'."

Bob, surprised, says, "Wow, I had no idea that you knew so many of my songs."

343

"Oh, sure I do, and as a matter of fact if you would let me, I'd like to do 'Old Time Rock and Roll' in tonight's show."

Bob, tucks his long hair behind his ears, stunned, but agrees to my request, "Sure, if you know it, go for it."

"Oh, I know it; I told you it's one of my favorite songs."

Bob grins, "It would be my pleasure to hear how you do it."

Lisa Marie comes dashing into the dressing room, "Hi Daddy," and hugs me.

"Hey, sweet cheeks, I want you to meet someone. This is Bob Seger."

"Hello, Mr. Seger, how are you?" Lisa Marie says with a warm smile.

Bob responds to how polite Lisa Marie is and says, "Hello, Lisa Marie, I'm doing fine, thanks. How are you doing?"

"Oh, I'm fine. I'm here to see my Daddy's show tonight."

"You like to hear your Daddy sing?"

"Yes, he's the best singer in the world."

"Well, you know, you're not the only one who thinks that. So do I."

"You do? Lisa Marie exclaims, "Me too!"

Bob laughs, "Yes, I really like your Daddy's singing." Turning to me he says, "She's adorable, how old is she?"

I replies, with my fatherly pride showing, "She's eleven, going on twenty-one."

We both laugh.

Bob knowing that the show is about to start, tells me, "Well, I don't want to take up any more of your time, but it has been a real treat to meet you. I'd better get going, and get to my seat."

"You have a seat in the audience? Wouldn't you rather watch the show from the stage or how about the sound booth? You'd hear everything a lot better, and be able to see everything as well."

"I have twelfth row center seats, but I'm sure that hearing it from the sound booth would be a lot better, and dealing with the crowd can be such a hassle. But, I have my wife with me too."

"Where is she? Don't I get a chance to meet Mrs. Seger?"

"She very shy and told me to come meet you."

"Hey, Joe," I call, getting his attention, "Take Bob, and his wife out to the sound booth, so they can watch the show from there, and give them the information where we are staying tonight so we can catch up with each other after the show."

I tell Bob, "I want to meet your wife, come up to the suite tonight after the show, so we can all hang out. Do you know any gospel songs we can sing later?"

Bob's face lights up. "Yeah I know ah few. Elvis, it's been a real pleasure meeting you. Have a great show, and I guess we'll see you after the show."

"Thanks, Bob, for welcoming me to Pontiac, and coming by to say hello."

Oscar asks if the photographer can take a few pictures of the two stars meeting.

We agree and stand together, with Bob's arm over my shoulder and me with my arm around Bob's waist. The photographer takes their picture for posterity.

Oscar says, "That's a great shot, you guys." Bob and I shake hands again.

Bob says, "Goodbye, Lisa Marie, it was nice to meet you."

"Goodbye, Mr. Seger." she replies, not looking up, while she makes a sandwich at the craft services table.

Bob leaves with Joe, to get ready to watch the concert.

Oscar stays behind, "Thanks for meeting Bob."

I nod and confide to Oscar, "He has gotten better and better at his craft over the years. I think his best songs are yet to be written. But he needs to work on his lyrics."

Oscar agrees and says, "Thanks again." and leaves the dressing room.

Larry, Lamar, and Marty, continue to get me ready for the concert. I do the show and rock, "Old Time Rock And Roll," much to Seger's surprise.

~ * ~

346

And the tour continues.

4/18/1980 Cedar Falls, IA @ Unidome 16,000 X 1 = 16,000

4/21-22/1980 St. Louis, MO @ Checkerdome 20,000 X 2 = 40,000

4/25-26/1980 Kansas City, MO @ Kemper Arena 20,000 X 2 = 40,000

4/30-5/1/1980 Lexington, KY @ Rupp Arena 24,000 X 2 = 48,000

5/4-6/1980 Rosemont, IL @ Rosemont Horizon 19,000 X 3 = 57,000

May 8, 1980

I am having dinner in my hotel room, when Joe comes in with his shoulders slumped and a long look on his face.

"What's got you down, Joe? I ask. "Everything's been running smooth as silk."

"E, I'm so sorry, but I got word from Graceland earlier that Minnie Mae, passed away today."

I feel the breath leave my body and I cannot speak. While it is not totally unexpected at the age of 89 years old, it saddens my heart, that another piece of my family is gone. I am a little comforted knowing that my Daddy is there to meet her on the other side.

Joe continues, "We have already made arrangements to reschedule the Ottawa date to the end of the North American leg of the tour. We will fly back to Memphis tonight on the *Lisa Marie*."

"Oh, Joe, thank you. Send the *Hound Dog II* for Lisa Marie and Pricilla. I have calls to make for the arrangements to have Dodger laid to rest in the Meditation Garden at Graceland."

~ * ~

After the funeral, I go back on the road:

5/17-18/1980 Hartford, CT @ Hartford Civic Center 17,000 X 2 = 34,000

5/22-23/1980 Cleveland, OH @ Richfield Coliseum 20,000 X 2 = 40,000

5/27-29/1980 Philadelphia, PA @ JFK Stadium 100,000 X 2 = 200,000

5/31-/6/1/1980 Buffalo, NY @ Rick Stadium = 89,000 X 2 = 178,000

6/4-6/1980 E. Rutherford, NJ @ Meadowlands Sports 80,000 X 3 = 240,000

6/9-10/1980 Syracuse, NY @ Carrier Dome 59,000 X 2 = 118,000

6/14-16/1980 New York City, NY @ Madison Square Garden 20,000 X 3 = 60,000

6/20-23/1980 Largo, MD @ Capitol Center 18,000 X 4 = 72,000

6/27-29/1980 Hampton, VA @ Hampton Coliseum 14,000 X 3 = 42,000

7/3-4/1980 Memphis, TN @ Liberty Bowl 110,000 X 2 = 220,000

~ * ~

July 4, 1980

It is the last day of the Liberty Bowl shows. Back stage is set up like a Fourth of July picnic area

348

with everyone and his brother partying and barbequing before the show that evening. There are balloons for the kids, games like horseshoes, croquet, badminton, and lawn darts. There's a pool for the kids, and lots of food. I can eat some of the picnic food, but there's also a lot I choose to stay away from.

The party started at twelve noon and goes on until seven P.M. an hour before the show is supposed to start. There is another great fireworks display planned for the close of the show, even better than the one the night before.

The mood is very festive and everyone is having a great time. Priscilla and Lisa are there with the Memphis Mafia and their friends and families. Larry, Tom, Oscar, Bruce, Rupert, and Bhaskar are also there enjoying the festivities.

Tom comes up to me as I walk by myself through the back stage area enjoying seeing my friends around him having fun. "Elvis, I think I've got it for you."

My curiosity is piqued, "What have you got for me?"

Tom replies with a wink, "What have you been waiting for most of your life?"

I guess with great hope, "The script?"

"Yes sir and it's a great one. It's called, 'An Officer and a Gentleman'."

"What's it about?"

"Here's the plot summary. It's about Zack Mayo, the lead - that's you, a young man who is a loner, and has to rely on himself. After graduating from college and trying to find himself for a few years, Zack shocks his father, a career Navy man himself, by telling him that he has enlisted in the Navy, and wants to enter training as a Naval Aviator.

"Zack brings along the loner attitude he has had all his life. He meets a local girl named Paula, an attractive young woman who often attends base functions in the hopes of nabbing a young naval officer. The training is difficult, but not as difficult as having to deal with his training officer, Gunnery Sergeant Foley, who is there to train and evaluate the trainees. Gunnery Sergeant Foley teaches Zack a lesson in the importance of relying on your friends and colleagues. Zack gets Paula. The End."

Elvis asks, "What did you say the name of it was?"

"The working title is "An Officer and a Gentleman.""

"That's a great title and the script sounds interesting too. But, when could I do this?"

"I talked the people over at Paramount into holding the movie until after you finish your tour. They really want you to do this movie, Elvis."

"That's what, six months from now, if I don't take a break before shooting the movie?"

"Elvis, I got Paramount to hold up production until the first of February. You finish the tour New Year's Eve in Hawaii. You have all of January to take off or start studying the script, and they want to start shooting principal photography the beginning of February."

I ask Tom, "When can I get the script?"

"I'll be able to get a copy of it to you when you're in Europe. They are doing a second writing on the script as we speak."

"Tom, you just gave me the best Fourth of July gift ever. I know I can really get my teeth into a role like that. Me, becoming a fly boy in the Navy, being a loner, a dark and brooding kind of guy, and I still get the girl in the end. What a great script. No songs or corny dialogue. It sounds like a really good movie, Tom."

"I thought you would like it. But we have to get you through the rest of your tour first, Elvis. You have about six more months before you can really start working on this script."

"Yeah I know, but, it's the carrot on a stick. I'll go for it. I think you know how much I've wanted to do a really good movie. I'm a much better actor than I am a singer believe it or not. Even those silly movies I had to make for the Colonel, I would have all my lines down for the days shoot, and I'd also know everyone else's lines."

Tom says, "I know. I remember seeing you on the set, and how professional you were when the cameras were rolling. But with as much fooling around that went on, I was surprised that any of those movies ever got made."

"Tom, those were the bad old days."

"I know you and the Mafia have really been good out here on the road. It shows in your performances every night."

Larry comes strolling up to Tom & me, "Elvis do you want something to eat?"

351

"Yes, I do, and I have some great news that I want to share with you. Tom, get that script to me as soon as you can, will you?"

"I will. I have to check on the gate receipts, so I'll catch up with you later."

Larry and I walk off together toward the craft services area.

"So, Elvis, what is this great news you have to tell me about?"

"Tom has found a script that sounds like it could be a great role for me."

Larry raises his eyebrows, "When will you be able to shoot it?"

"A month after I finish the tour. That will be in February."

"The Lord works in strange ways, my friend."

"Yes, he does, and with Tom's help I think we are going to shift my energy into becoming a serious major film star."

The evening's show goes off without a hitch and the final night's crowd loves it. The fireworks display afterwards is a great way to end the show, and celebrate the 4th of July. While the audience is watching the fireworks, the entourage and I head back for a precious stop over at Graceland.

7/7-8/1980 Orlando, FL @ Tangerine Bowl 71,000 X 2 = 142,000

7/11-12/1980 Ottawa, Canada @ Ottawa Civic Center 10,000 X 2 = 20,000

The rescheduled Ottawa shows wind up the American part of the tour. Total attendance of all sixty shows was, three million, two hundred nine thousand people with the tour grossing over forty-two million dollars for all of the shows and merchandise sales. I made donations to charities in each of the city's I played. The total donations have been over four million dollars.

~ * ~

The tour ships the equipment over to Europe for the second part of the tour.

7/18-19/1980 Rome, Italy @ the Palazzetto DelloSport 11.000 X 2 =22,000

7/22/1980 Genova, Italy @ Palasport di Genova 10,000 X 1 night

7/25/1980 Milan, Italy @ Stadio San Siro 80,000 X 1 night

7/28/1980 Stafford, England @ Bingley Hall 11,500 X 1 night

7/31/1980 Chester, England @ Deeside Leisure Center 4,000 X 1 night

8/3-5/1980 London, England @ Wimble Arena 12,500 X 3 = 37,500

~ * ~

August 7, 1980

There are a couple of days before the Frankfurt, Germany show. Priscilla and I are driving Lisa Marie out to visit our old stomping grounds. We are in the front seat with Lisa Marie in the back. After a while we pull up in front of a two story white house with white waist high fence around it at Goethestrasse 14, Bad Nauheim.

Priscilla tells Lisa Marie, "This is the house where you're Daddy and I first met. He was in the Army and rented this place. I came to Germany with my parents and used to hang out at the Eagle Club, where I would listen to the juke box while I wrote letters to my friends.

"One day while putting money in the juke box, I met a guy named Currie Grant who said he knew Elvis Presley asked if I wanted to meet him. I said, 'Of course I want to meet Elvis Presley!' He was famous even then, chic-a-dee.

"Currie drove me here to Bad Nauheim, where your Daddy lived, off base. When we met, there was an instant attraction between us and over the next few months we talked and saw each other frequently. By the time six months had passed, we had become inseparable and I went everywhere with your Daddy. Then came the day he had to go back to the States to be discharged. My heart was broken when I had to say goodbye to him at the airport. I went home and closed myself in my room where I cried for three days."

Lisa Marie, wide-eyed, exclaims. "What happened? How did you get back together?"

Priscilla smiles and strokes her daughter's hair, "Three months later, I got a phone call from your daddy; he wanted to see me for the summer, so your grandparents agreed that I could go back to the States to see him. We went to Las Vegas, and the more time we spent together the closer we became.

"After coming back to Germany from my summer vacation, I missed him so much; we spent hours talking with each other on the phone. For Christmas that year, he bought me a ticket back to the states to be with him for the holidays at Graceland. One of my Christmas presents from your Daddy that year was a poodle that I named, Honey. Do you remember her?"

"Yes I remember her. We use to put bows on her ears," Lisa says, picturing Honey in her mind.

"That's right. Well, after the Christmas holidays, your daddy said he couldn't bear to live without me, so he convinced your grandparents to let me live at Graceland with his father and step-mother, in their house. I finished the rest of my junior year and my senior year of high school, at a private Catholic all girls' school. It was named Immaculate Conception High School. When your Daddy was off in Hollywood making movies, I would hang out with his cousin Patti and we became good friends."

"When he was at home, we had so much fun together. We would rent out the movie theater after hours and invite people to come to the movie with us. Or, we would rent the Memphis fairground and ride the roller coaster all night. Although, what I enjoyed the most was being alone with him, when other people weren't around, because we were in love and just really getting to know each other."

Lisa Marie giggles. "Oh, that is soooo romantic!"

"One evening shortly before Christmas in 1966, your daddy got down on one knee and asked me to marry him. We decided to have a short engagement and were married in Las Vegas on, May 1, 1967. Nine months later you were born."

Lisa Marie says, "So that's how you and Daddy met. It was really nice of Grandpa and Grandma to let you stay with them at Graceland."

Priscilla replies, "Yes, it was. If it weren't for them, you may not have been here with us now, sweet heart."

I tell Priscilla, "I love the way you told our story. You have such a kind and gentle way about yourself. I love you." We look into each other's eyes lovingly and I slowly lean in for a kiss.

Lisa Marie pretends disgust, "Eweee, my parents are kissing!"

This changes the mood and I laugh and start the car. As we drive back to Frankfurt, I hold Priscilla's hand the entire way.

~ * ~

And the tour goes on:

8/8-9/1980 Frankfurt, Germany @ Festhalle Frankfurt 13,500 X 2 = 27,000

8/12/1980 Dusseldorf, Germany @ Philipshalle 7,500 X 1

8/15-16/1980 Nurnberg, Germany @ Messehalle 12,000 X 2 = 24,000

8/19/1980 Stuttgart, Germany @ Hanns-Martin-Schleyer-Halle 15,500 X 1

8/22-23/1980 Munich, Germany @ Olympiahalle 14,000 X 2 = 28,000

8/25/1980 Brussels, Belgium @ Forest National 8,000 X 1

8/28/1980 Lyon, France @ Palais Des Sports de Gerland 5,900 X 1

8/30- 9/1/1980 Paris, France @ Palais des Sports (Paris) 4,500 X 3 = 13,500

9/3/1980 Basel, Switzerland @ St. Jakob Halle 51,000 X 1

9/6/1980 Cologne, Germany @ RheinEnergieStadion 50.000 X 1

9/9/1980 Hannover, Germany @ Ernst-Merck-Halle 5.700 X 1

9/12/1980 Rotterdam,Netherlands @ Ahoy Gebouw 10,000 X 1

9/15-16/1980 Stockholm, Sweden @ Globe Arena 16,000 X 2 = 32,000

9/19/1980 Gothenburg, Sweden @ Scandinavia 14,000 X 1

9/22/1980 Copenhagen, Denmark @ Valby Idrætspark 12,000 X 1

9/25/1980 Oslo, Norway @ Jordal Amfi 7,500 X 1

And the last day of the European tour is complete.

~ * ~

September 26, 1980

We are at the Capitol Records European label manager's conference. All the European countries label managers, Bruce, Joe, Al, Lamar, Billy, Marty, Charlie and I are in attendance

Bruce opens the ceremony, "Good afternoon, ladies and gentlemen. You all know why you're here. Six months ago, I told you on a conference call that Capitol Records was going to sign the world's biggest recording artist… and we did.

"Now, we are here to present to him the gold, diamond and platinum awards that you and your countries have been able to achieve, because of this man's efforts. He has overcome a stroke, paralysis, and worked for two and a half years to make this album. When he came back, he came back with the best album of his career." He takes a deep breath, and extends his hand toward me. "I am pleased and proud to introduce to you Capitol Record artist, and still the 'King of Rock & Roll', Mr. Elvis Presley." The label managers stand, applaud and cheer.

I address the group, bow slightly from left to right acknowledging the applause. I am wearing blue jeans, a royal blue shirt, with my black Spanish style boots. "Thank you, thank you very much. Please, let's get to the award part of this program."

Everyone laughs.

"Even though this is the first time I have toured Europe, it has been one of the best times I've had in my life touring. I have met most of you, and I want to thank you again for the tremendous work and effort you and your staff have put into making, 'My Second Chance,' album the biggest hit I have ever had in the European market." I put my hands together in a prayer motion and bows again to the group. The European Label Managers respectively stand and applaud.

"Okay, Bruce, so what's going to happen now?"

"Elvis, I can't tell you how happy I was, when you told me back in my L.A. office that you were going to tour Europe. I told you then that this would be your biggest album in Europe to date and what these label managers and their staffs have done since the release of the album is nothing short of amazing. You have just finished touring ten countries, selling out thirty-one shows in just sixty days. On non-show days you took the time to do radio, and TV interviews, and met with the press as often as we asked you to."

"For the effort you put into the album, during such a difficult time in your life, and because of the hard work you did for our European staff, I want to present to you the awards for each of the counties you visited on this tour, and some of the other countries in the European market as well."

As Bruce finishes saying this, the curtain behind Elvis and Bruce opens to reveal a wall of gold, diamond and platinum albums along with singles for the European countries. The label manager, the staff and even my guys break into spontaneous applaud and cheers. I stand there in amazement looking at all the awards.

"Oh my, look at all that gold and platinum. Thank you so much. Thank you." The label managers keep applauding. I say again, "Please, Thank you, thank you very much."

"Just about three years ago I thought I was going to die. Then, God gave me my second chance, hence the name of the album. I told God that I would turn my life around if he would show me the way to help as many people in the world as I could."

David Munns, the English Label Manager yells, "We love you Elvis."

I acknowledge his comment, with a nod, and continue. "It was because of people like you, that allowed my 'Feed the Children Foundation,' to raise over five million dollars, to be divided up among the charities in each of the towns and cities that I played in the States. I will be giving ten percent of the house receipts from each of the countries that I played in Europe to help feed the children here. It's been because of your hard work that I am able to do this, so I thank you, from the bottom of my heart."

The label managers applaud again.

Bruce announces, "There is champagne for those of you who want it, or there are other beverages if you prefer something else."

The hotel service staff comes out with champagne on silver trays and serves everyone. A beautiful young waitress comes out with a glass of Perrier water, and serves it to me.

Bruce raises his glass and gives a toast. "Elvis, here is to a long and prosperous relationship, and many more gold, diamond and platinum albums in your future. To Elvis!"

The label managers hold up their glasses and repeat in unison: "To Elvis!"

~ * ~

The tour moves the equipment to Southeast Asia for the third part of the "My Second Chance" world tour.

October 13th, 1980

We land at the Tokyo Narita Airport in Japan. After I move through customs and enter the main part of the airport, I'm blinded by flash bulbs going off and have to work my way through the crush of press and fans. It is overwhelming.

The sheer number of security guards, and barriers used to help control the crowd and allow me to move through the airport is amazing. I am used to fans, and the adoration a crowd can exhibit, but I'm amazed at the Japanese fans' enthusiasm. They reach out offering gifts, flowers and good wishes, spoken in broken English. I am a little fearful for my security and that of my entourage. I smile and wave to the crowd as I move toward the exit and the waiting limo. Outside there are even more fans behind the security barriers, also bearing gifts and good wishes.

I walk over to a section of the barriers, and shake hands with several of the fans, which makes the crowd scream even louder. Joe comes up and lets me know that it's time to go. I turn, and get into the limo. The police escort leads the way out of the airport to the hotel.

We arrive at the Peninsula Tokyo Hotel which is located in the prestigious Marunouchi district. It is opposite the Imperial Palace and the Hibiya Park, and just a three minute walk to the shopping capital of Ginza.

As the limos pull up to this gracious free standing hotel, I am amazed to see a contemporary modern building, with Japanese accents. After checking in, I go to my suite on the top floor.

I find the living room offers a breath taking view of Tokyo below. There is a marble bathroom, with mood lighting, double vanities, and a rain shower. The suite has a spacious self-contained dressing room with a full length mirror and a room safe and a valet box for shoe polishing and laundry service. A bedside panel is outfitted with remote controls that adjust the environment thermostat and humidity with the touch of a button. The accommodations include a kitchen area large enough for fixing meals with espresso, coffee, tea, and a fully stocked mini-bar.

Everyone meets in my suite about an hour after we all get checked in. As the guys are talking and goofing around with each other, there's a knock at the door. Lamar answers it. "Hello Tom, how are you doing? Come on in."

Tom nods, "I'm doing just great thanks. What's everyone up to?"

"We're just taking it easy before Elvis has to do his interviews downstairs with the press and TV, about an hour from now."

Tom enters the living area, "Hello, Elvis, boys, are you over the jet lag yet?"

I reply, "Oh yeah, it was nice to go back to Graceland for a few days to recover from the European trip, but the flight over here takes forever. We left on a Saturday and arrived on Monday, what happened to Sunday? What's up with that?"

Larry, laughing, tells me that we will make it up on the return trip home, "We'll leave, let's say Monday evening, and arrive back home in the morning the same day we left."

Al tells us that he had gone to Los Angeles on his days off, and picked up a couple of new Nudie coats, and some additional shirts and pants for Elvis, and they, "sure are pretty."

I acknowledge, "Well a few new things for the last part of the tour should look good."

Billy adds, "You can't have too many stage clothes with all the shows that you've been doing."

Tom stands in front of me, holding an envelope in his hand just out of my reach. "Well, I have the script you been waiting for."

I grab for it, and Tom pulls it back.

Don't be like that," I tell Tom. He holds out the envelope and again I try for it, as Tom pulls it away. "One more time and you're fired, Tom," I joke. I get a big grin on my face once Tom gives up the envelope to me.

I tear open the envelope, and start reading the script. "Oh, this is going to be great. I start shooting this in February right?"

Tom reminds me, "Yes, when you've finish touring Japan, Australia and New Zealand. That will take you to the end of November. Then in December you have four shows in Brazil, some time off for the Christmas Holidays and two shows in Hawaii, the last one being on New Year's Eve."

I say, "This has been so much fun touring around the world, getting to see places that I never have been before. The work has been hard sometimes, but the shows are getting better and better each time. When we played the Dallas shows I thought the show couldn't get any better than that. But now it's running like a well-oiled machine."

Tom agrees, "Well, now everyone, the light guys, the sound guys and the stage hands all know what they are supposed to be doing, and the band just keeps getting better. You're right, it's incredible."

"Not only is it incredible, it requires much less of my time than it did in the beginning. I have free time that I can now be studying this script," I say holding it up in the air.

Larry asks, "Is that the script for the movie you are going to do?"

"Yeah, An Officer and a Gentleman." I answer, ruffling though the pages, stopping here and there to read a particular passage.

Lamar wants to know, "What's it about?"

"It's about a guy named Zack--that's me, and he tells his dad that he wants to become a Navy Aviator. Zack meets a local girl that he's attracted to but doesn't want to be tired down. His drill sergeant doesn't believe he has what it takes so he's riding him constantly. Zack becomes a Navy Officer, and gets the girl in the end."

Lamar says with amazement, "What, no more beach movies?"

"Nope!" I say emphatically, "This is a serious movie; I'm going to win an Oscar for this one!"

Tom mentions, "By the way, the studio has come up with one more request."

I groan, "Uh-oh, what's that?"

"They want you to sing the title song for the movie. It's called, 'Up Where We Belong' and it's a duet."

"I don't know," I hesitate to commit. "I haven't heard the song and I haven't even read the whole script yet."

Tom advises me, "Don't get all wound up in this movie yet. I knew I shouldn't have mentioned the title song to you so soon. You have another month and a half before you even have to start thinking about the script. You wanted to see the script early, so I got it for you, but don't lose focus of the task at hand, which is the tour."

I nod and agree, laying the script aside. "All right, I'll stay focused on the job."

"Good, we'll talk about this again next year," Tom says with a chuckle, as he leaves the room.

~ * ~

10/15-17/ 1980, Tokyo, Japan at Budokan
14,000 X 3 = 42,000

I open my first show at Budokan, a two minute walking distance from Kudanshit Subway Station, near the Yasukuni Shrine. I walk out on the stage and holler, "Konban wa Budokan." The crowd goes wild... but politely. Their response throws me off and I wonder about my ability to read the audience's reaction. Then I remember Bruce telling me about audiences in Japan. They sit very attentively during the songs, and applaud politely at the end of each song. There was no swooning during the show as there was at the airport or the hotel. At the end of the show I hollers, "Doomo arigatoo, doomo arigatoo gozaimasu." The show ends and I head back to the hotel.

And so the tour continues:

10/21-22/1980 Osaka, Japan @ Festival Hall 3,000 X 2 = 6,000

10/26-27/1980 Kyoto, Japan @ Kaikan 3,000 X 2 = 6,000

11/2-3/1980 Perth, Australia @ Entertainment Center 8,000 X 2 = 16,000

11/7/1980 Melbourne, Australia @ VFL Park Stadium = 78,000

11/11-12/1980 Adelaide, Australia @ Adelaide Oval 33,000 X 2 = 66,000

11/16-18/1980 Sydney, Australia @ Sydney Showground 21,000 X 3 = 63,000

11/21/1980 Brisbane, Australia @ Lang Park = 52,000

11/28/1980 Wellington, New Zealand @ Athletic Park Stadium = 39,000

11/31/1980 Auckland, New Zealand @ Western Springs Stadium = 50,000

~ * ~

December 12th, 1980

The crew and I are settled in at The Fasanco Hotel, in Sao Paulo, Brazil. Priscilla, Lisa Marie, Joe, Tom, Al and Charlie are sitting with me, poolside. I am dressed in my swimming trunks, reclining in a lounge chair beside Priscilla. Tom is on her other side.

Looking past her, I say to Tom, "I would like to do something special for the shows down here."

"What did you have on your mind?"

"I was thinking about doing the song, The Girl from Ipanema."

Priscilla's face lights up, "Oh, I love that song."

Joe being an old jazz man asks, "Hey, do you think we could get, Stan Getz down here to play the sax parts on that song?"

"I don't know, that is a great idea, but the shows start tomorrow," I reply.

Tom advises, "I'd could call his people, and find out where he is, and if he has the dates open or not. Does the band know the song?"

"I'm sure James and the boys know it well enough that we could add the song in tomorrow's show, and if Stan can be added, whenever he can fit it in, that would be great. Besides, I want to do the song for my Cilla."

"Ah, that's sweet. Thanks, Elvis," as she gives me a kiss on the lips, I see the raised eyebrows in the group and can hear the unasked question, *"What's going on here? This is more than just Mr. and Mrs. Divorced Couple kissing."*

"Check into that, to see if you can get Stan or not," I instruct Tom.

"I'll do that right away. I'm getting burned out here in this sun anyway. But, first I was wondering if you have made plans for Christmas this year."

"Yup. Priscilla and I have decided to spend Christmas with Lisa Marie in Belize. I understand it's beautiful down there, up there, where ever it is, and I would stand a pretty good chance of not being bugged while I'm there. We'll be staying at a retreat on a private island." Priscilla and I exchange smiles.

"We'll be at a private resort that is three miles from San Pedro, just off the coast of Belize. There are miles of beaches, and no one in sight. Cayo Espanto sounds like my kind of place."

Charlie asks, "Where are we going to stay down there?"

"There is no "we" in this trip Charlie! Priscilla, Lisa Marie and I are going. Everyone else will be going home to their own family for the holidays."

"What, you don't want any of us around for security?" Joe asks.

"Nope, not this time Joe. We're leaving Rio de Janeiro, on December twenty-third, and staying until December twenty-seventh, when we'll be flying back to Hawaii to do the shows there. I just want the flight crew to fly us there, drop us off and leave, then come back to pick us up on the twenty-seventh."

Tom says with concern, "That sounds a little risky. Are you sure you want to do this?"

"Yes, we'll be fine. Just put it out to the press we are spending Christmas at the plantation before the last shows."

Priscilla adds, "We're looking forward to it, Joe. Just us spending Christmas time together as a family. We'll be staying on an exclusive private island where we will laze in the sun, walk the beach, dive and explore the reef. The diving there is amazing. It's the world's second largest barrier reef.

"And we won't even have to make decisions about our meals. We have already filled out a survey, so the award winning chefs can create a new menu daily to perfectly suit our tastes. I can't think of anything I'd like better than that."

I smile, gazing at Priscilla and say, "What my baby wants, my baby gets."

"Well, I guess that settles that then," Tom says feeling a little left out. "I'd better get on the phone, and find out if Stan Getz is in Brazil for the holidays, and see if he will agree to do the shows in Morumbi Stadium and Maracana Stadium."

~ * ~

It turns out as wonderful as I imagined. When I introduce, *The Girl from Ipanema*, I invite my special guest star to accompany me. Stan Getz comes out on stage, the crowds go crazy. The song becomes one of the highlights of the shows.

And the tour goes on:

12/15/1980 Sao Paulo, Brazil @ Morumbi Stadium 140,000 X 2 = 280,000

12/21/1980 Rio de Janeiro, Brazil @ Maracana Stadium 89,000 X 2 = 178,000

When we end the last show at the Maracana Stadium, I say, "Obrigado, muito obrigado. You have been a wonderful audience tonight. Thank you again. I'll see you the next time I'm in Rio de Janeiro." The audience goes wild hearing my plans to return to Brazil.

Leaving the stage, I go down the stairs and into a waiting limo as the band keeps playing *Can't Help Falling in Love.* A voice off stage announces: "Elvis has left the building!" This brings an end to the South American tour.

My next stop is our family vacation to Cayo Espanto.

Chapter 27

Priscilla, Lisa Marie and I are enjoying our time at Casa Estrella, a private villa on the island of Cayo Espanto. The second story bedroom has an open air design with brilliant fruitwood hardwood floors. The three of us, Lisa Marie in the middle, are lounging on the king-size bed that is made up with luxurious Ives De Lorme sheets. The views overlook the Caribbean.

Priscilla tells me, "I've had a wonderful time with you over these last several months."

"Oh Cilla, you know I have always loved you. I'm so appreciative that the bathroom floor was not the end of me. It was literally a wakeup call. I'm glad that I had the strength and support to change my life around, get off those pills and to get back on the straight and narrow life."

Lisa Marie says, "Daddy I'm glad, too. I was really scared when you got so sick. I didn't want you to leave me."

"I was scared too and didn't want to leave you either. But, I got better and that's behind us now. No need for you to worry. I hope you have had a good time coming to see me while I tour."

"I've had a great time seeing those different places. I liked Japan and Germany, but I liked Australia the most of all because they have kangaroos and koala bears. I liked petting them."

Priscilla brushes the hair off Lisa's face. "I'm glad you had a good time with your daddy and that you had the chance to experience the world rather than just reading about it in a book." she says then tickles Lisa Marie in her ribs.

"And I'm so glad to have the two of you in my life. I am so proud of you," I lightly touch Priscilla's face with my hand. "And you, Buttonhead," tapping Lisa Marie on the tip of her nose, "You were so well behaved on the tour. I would like to take you along the next time I go out on the road."

"Oh boy, when are we going on tour next?"

"First, Daddy has to make a movie, but I'm sure that I'll be going on tour after that. And remember, I have two more shows to do in Hawaii, with the last show on New Year's Eve."

"Can I stay up to see the ball drop this year?"

Priscilla realizing that it's getting late, answers, "Yes you can. But, now, it's time for you to go to bed. We're going snorkeling tomorrow morning, and we're going to get an early start."

"Okay Mommy, Good night," kissing Pricilla. "Good night, Daddy, sleep tight, don't let the bed bugs bite," kissing me on the cheek.

"Goodnight, Yisa, I'll see you in the morning," I answer.

Priscilla tells her, "All right, I'll be in, in a few minutes to say your prayers with you."

Lisa hops off the bed, and heads to her own bedroom. Priscilla snuggles up to me as I wrap her up in my arms.

"Elvis, you know that I have always loved you. Do you understand why I had to leave?" I nod. "Over the last two years, we've grown into a more mature relationship than we have ever had before."

"Yes, things have changed for the better for us, haven't they?"

"Yes they have, and I have something that I want to tell you."

"And what might that be, my little Cilla?"

"Elvis... I'm pregnant."

Stunned, I take a deep breath, staring at her with my eyes wide open. My hand jerks off her stomach, but immediately returns to gently caress the almost imperceptible swell. With great joy, I say "That's great news! You're not kidding me, are you?" She shakes her head no. "Oh, baby, how far along are you?"

"I was hoping that you would be happy about me being pregnant again."

"Oh Cilla, I couldn't be happier. When are you due?"

"The doctor tells me it should be some time in the first week of May."

"That means that you got pregnant... let's see, when we were in Germany?"

"Yes, I think it was the night we were in Frankfort, after taking Lisa Marie to your old house where we first met." Pricilla rolls towards me and we kiss deeply.

The three of us spend a wonderful time together and have a relaxing Christmas. I am able to recharge my batteries without any incidences from fans or photographers, let alone the Mafia and other hanger-on's.

~ * ~

12/30/1980 Honolulu, Hawaii @ Aloha Stadium 70,000 X 1 = 70,000

12/31/1980 Honolulu, Hawaii @ Aloha Stadium 73,000 X 1 = 73,000

December 31, 1980

It is the last show of this tour.

Before the show, Tom reports, "We're expecting to get over seventy-three thousand in the stadium tonight to end 1980 with another sellout and a record setting attendance!"

It's about eleven-fifty-five P.M. and I am finishing my closing song, *Can't Help Falling in Love*, which I have dedicated to my Priscilla. At the end of the song the band reverts back into playing, *C. C. Rider*.

"Thank you, thank you very much. The fireworks will start at midnight. Thank you so much for coming to the show. I want to wish all of you a hau'oli makahiki hou, hapenuia, which most all of you know, means Happy New Year, Aloha."

As I announce the arrival of the New Year, I urge the audience to count down with me, "Ten, nine, eight, seven, six, five, four, three, two, one, hau'oli makahiki hou, hapenuia! Happy New Year! Aloha."

As the fireworks go off, I run backstage to be with Priscilla and Lisa Marie. As we stand together watching the sky filled with bursting colors, the light reflects on their faces. I slip my arms around my girls, feeling the essence of a truly loving family.

Chapter 28

January 15, 1981

I am sitting in my plantation office with Tom and Michael Eisner, President and Chief Operations Officer of Paramount Pictures. Taylor Hackford, the director, and Douglas Day Stewart, the writer of the script, *An Officer and a Gentleman* are also present.

Michael says, "Then it's all set. I have the budget lined up, and the production schedule is in order, so it's a green light for us."

I stand up, and come around from behind the desk to shake hands with Michael. "Thanks Michael, I know that I'm a little long in the tooth for this part, but I appreciate you giving me this chance. I'll do one hell of job for you, you just wait and see."

"Elvis, you have made such a turnaround in your life," Michael explains. "You're in great shape, and I know you're going to be considered a great actor. I don't think I'm taking a chance. With your popularity now and your acting ability, this part is perfect for you. This role is going to make you a huge, international motion picture star."

"I like the script. I've been looking forward to doing this part for months," I tell Douglas.

He replies, "Thank you, Elvis. I'm looking forward to having you in the role. I know you will bring Zach to life on screen."

"Oh, I will, Douglas. I will."

"I love the script too, and I look forward to directing you, Elvis," Taylor chimes in. "But, on another note, pardon the pun, what about the theme song? I know some of you guys don't agree, but Elvis, I know it will be a hit."

I pause in thought for a moment, than answer, "I've heard the demo and I've decided that I'll be happy to do it. We could get Jennifer Warnes, Anne Murray, or Whitney Houston for the female part."

"We'll set up a demo with each of the ladies to decide which one will sound best with your voice," Michael suggests, as he gives me a wink.

Ignoring the wink, I continue, "I think the best choice will be between Jennifer and Anne."

"So, Taylor, what day is the principal photography supposed to start?" Tom asks.

"I'd like to have Elvis in Hollywood on February 3rd to read through the script with the other actors. We'll start shooting on the seventeenth. How does that sound to you, Elvis?"

"I'll come in on the first or the second just to get settled in, and I'll be on set by the third. But, you know, we may have some scheduling problems around the fifteenth of May. That's when Priscilla is due."

Michael's eyebrows shoot up in surprise to find out that Priscilla is pregnant as he says, "I didn't know she was pregnant! Congratulations! Do you know what you're having?"

"No, we're going to wait until the delivery to find out. So, I'm going to need a few days off. As soon as she goes into labor, I'm out of here for at least four to five days when the baby is born."

Taylor agrees, "I'm sure we can shoot around your schedule."

Douglas adds, "That's great, a new little person in your life."

"Yes, I'm looking forward to the delivery. Well, everything is signed, sealed and delivered, so let's go down stairs and have some pineapple smoothies to celebrate. And we are going to have a fabulous luau this evening before you go back to Los Angeles."

Chapter 29

We are on the set of An Officer and a Gentleman. I have become so immersed in the role; I feel I have become Zach. As Zack, I am in my father's bathroom.

Taylor hollers, "Lights… camera… action!"

Zack finds the aspirin, and downs them with a glass of water. Suddenly, Zack's father, Byron, played by Robert Loggia, comes in the bathroom and shoves Zack out of the way, and pukes in the toilet. Zack stares at him, intently, seeing more than the moment. He's seeing all the other times he's played out this scene with this man.

BYRON

"What're you looking at? Hand me that towel."

Zack hands him the towel. Byron swigs some mouthwash then turns to his son.

BYRON

"Hey, that was pretty great wasn't it? Not as great as that night with the three stewardesses in Manila… but pretty fucking nice."

Zack says nothing, but there's something on his mind.

BYRON

"So what're you doing in Seattle?"

ZACK

"Get ready, Pard, this one's goanna blow you away."

BYRON

"Zackie, nothing you do will ever surprise me, Pard, not after some of the shit you've pulled."

ZACK

"I ah… joined the Navy."

BYRON

"You… in the Navy?" (Laughing)

ZACK

"What's so funny? I'm on my way over to the officer school in Port Rainier."

BYRON

"You man. What for?"

ZACK

"Jets, I want to fly jets. I want to be the fastest motherfucker in the world. You gotta come and visit me. I'm only a couple hours away."

BYRON

"Who gave you this idea?"

ZACK

"Nobody, it just came to me." Byron starts to laugh and Zack reddens slightly.

BYRON

"I don't believe this! You… in the Navy… an officer, that's like me saying I'm running for president. Hey, man look at yourself. Officers don't have tattoos." He laughs until he practically chokes.

ZACK

"Look, I'll be seeing you, Pard. Take care."
Zack leaves the bathroom and starts putting his
clothes on.

BYRON

"Don't be pissed. I'm on your side, Pard. I
just don't want you to do something you'll regret.
You gotta give six years... that's six years with the
most uptight assholes God put on this earth.
Officers aren't like you and me, man. It's another
breed."

ZACK

"You afraid you'll have to salute me, chief?"

BYRON

"Fuck no! Why would I care about
something as dumb as that?"

ZACK

"I don't know. That's just how it sounds.
Well, I'll see you." Zack opens the door and walks
out. Byron moves to the door.

BYRON

"Hey, what did you want, a lot of fatherly
bullshit, a big pat on the back?"

ZACK

"From you Pard, never. Thanks for the
graduation present."

BYRON

"Hey Zackie, don't go away mad."

"And cut!" Taylor yells. "We need to do
another take. Robert, I need you to act a little more

hung over. That was a good take, but I know we all can do better."

Taylor walks up to me and whispers in my ear, "Good job Elvis, you looked great."

The scene is done over again, and this time Taylor likes what he sees, "Okay everybody, that's a wrap. We'll check the dailies tomorrow to make sure. Everyone be here at 7:00 A.M. to start shooting and I want the principals in make-up one hour before that. All right, kids, we'll see you tomorrow," Taylor walks off the set with me.

"Elvis, you're really getting into this part. I'm sure glad that Paramount decided to go with my recommendation to cast you in this part," Taylor confides.

"I'm glad you realized that I can do more than those vapid B movies I use to do. Thanks for recommending me for this role. I know this is going to be a winner."

"From your lips to God's ears," Taylor declaims. "From your lips to God's ears."

~ * ~

Taylor hollers, "All right everybody, is every one ready? Good then, lights... camera... action!"

Zack and Sid, his new best friend and class mate, played by David Keith, drop to the ground doing push-ups. They appear to be watching something out of frame.

SID

"Look at that hot blonde!"

But, Zack is not looking at the same thing.

And cut!" Taylor calls out. "We got it this time. You two are amazing! We had to do three takes and you are still doing pushups like is it just a walk in the park."

David laughs, "And Elvis even challenges me to push up contests between takes. We are pretty evenly matched."

"Well, take it easy for five, but don't go anywhere; we are going to bring the girls in to finish this shot."

~ * ~

Lynette, played by Lisa Blount, and Paula, played by Debra Winger, start across the street.

LYNETTE

"Far fucking out! I've been wanting to meet one of those Blue Angel pilots since I can remember."

PAULA

"Lynette, watch your mouth! Someone might overhear."

LYNETTE

"Paula, look at the new puppies."

PAULA

"Yeah, I saw 'em, poor guys."

LYENTTE (calling to them)

"See you in a month when you get liberty!"

PAULA

"Don't worry; it grows out about an inch by then," referring to their hair cuts.

383

"Cut!" Taylor hollers to end the scene. "That's a take.

"All right let's get set up for the next scene then break for lunch."

~ * ~

May 15, 1981

I am on set with Joe, Larry, and Lamar in my dressing room. The phone rings, and Larry answers it and hands it to me, "It's Michelle."

I grab the phone, "Michelle, is Priscilla all right?"

"She's OK, Elvis. But she has gone into labor. Billy's driving her to California Pacific Medical Center here in San Francisco."

"I'll be up there as soon as I can. I'll take the Lisa Marie, so I should be there in an hour or so at the most."

"Give us a call and I'll have Billy pick you up from the airport."

"I'll call you right before I take off. Tell Cilla I love her. And, Michelle, thanks for the call. I'm so grateful you're there. I'll see you soon."

I start giving orders, "Joe, please, get the car so you can get me to the airport. Cilla is in labor and on her way to the hospital in San Francisco to deliver the baby. And, please, page Elwood. Have him get the plane ready to leave right away."

"Larry, I want you to come with me. Lamar, go tell Taylor that I'm leaving for San Francisco and I'll call him to let him know when I'll be back."

Lamar leaves and Joe dials Elwood.

Larry says, "I'm so happy to be with you for such a blessed event in your life, Elvis. Mazel-tov, my friend."

"Thanks, Larry. I'm excited about having another baby. I love my Lisa Marie. But, truth be known, I'm hoping for a boy this time."

"Well, you will know in just a few hours."

Joe gets off the phone, "Elvis the car is ready to take you to the airport, and Elwood said the plane is ready for takeoff as soon as you get there."

"Okay guys, let's get out of here." They leave the dressing room, and head for the limo.

~ * ~

Billy pulls the car right up to the door of the emergency entrance of the California Pacific Medical Center and parks. He jumps out and helps Priscilla out of the front seat of the car and assists her into the hospital.

"Hello, can I get some help here? This is Mrs. Presley, her doctor is expecting her."

The nurse on duty meets them with a wheel chair. She reassures Priscilla, "Hello Mrs. Presley, my name is Lilly. I've had a call from your doctor already, and she is on her way in. I'm going to put you in a room and make you comfortable."

Priscilla smiles, "Thanks, Lilly, I sure could use a room right about now."

"I'm sure you could, let's go." Lilly pushes Priscilla down the hall.

Billy says, "I have to move the car, then I'll come back and find you."

Lilly tells Billy, "I'm going to put her in room B-12, so you can find her there when you come back in."

"I'll be right back," Billy calls to Priscilla as Lilly continues to push her down the hall toward her room.

~ * ~

Lamar finds Taylor, "Taylor, Elvis has asked me to tell you that he has left for the hospital. Pricilla is having the baby."

Taylor asks, "Has he left already? I wanted to say goodbye to him. I hope everything will be all right."

"I'm sure things will be okay. Elvis does seem to live a charmed life."

"Well, I'll have to reschedule the shoot around Elvis's schedule since he's out for a while. Stay in touch with me, so I can get him back in the schedule as soon as he is ready."

"I'm sure Elvis will let you know when he will be back. I've got to go and TCB for Elvis, so I'll catch up with you later."

~ * ~

The *Lisa Marie* is heading for San Francisco. Using my mobile phone, I call the hospital, "Hello, please put me through to Mrs. Presley, and thank you."

Elvis waits a few moments, and then hears Priscilla answer, "Hello?"

"Hello, Baby, how's my girl doing?"

"Elvis! Where are you? My water broke at the hotel when I was with Michelle, Lisa Marie, Jo and Billy. Billy drove me to the hospital. Michelle and Jo are watching Lisa Marie now. My contractions are coming every five minutes."

"Cilla, it's all OK," I try and sooth her. "I'll be there as soon as I can. I'm on my way; I'm calling from the plane."

Priscilla tells me, joking. "I'll try to hold off till you get here, but I'm not going to make any promises. I know you'll do the best you can but I'm not in control here; the baby will come when it's ready to."

"Hang on a second, Cilla." Elvis asks Larry, "Find out from Elwood when we will be landing."

"Oh Elvis, please hurry up and get here, the pain is really starting to be too much."

"Remember your breathing Cilla, I'll be there as soon as I can."

Larry returns from the cockpit, "Elvis, Elwood says we are about twenty-three minutes out. He will start his landing approach soon."

"Did you hear that Cilla? Larry said that we should be landing soon. I will be there very soon."

Billy enters Priscilla's room. She tells him with agitation in her voice, "Elvis is going to be landing at the airport soon, please go get him. And, have the nurse come back in."

"Yeah, sure, Pricilla," says Billy, as he heads back out of the room.

I reassure Pricilla, "Okay, sweetheart, I'll be with you soon. I'm going to let you go for now.

I'm going to call Sergeant Wilson for an escort to get me there quicker."

Priscilla says, kidding, "Uh… oh. Please hurry up Elvis, or you're going to miss all the fun." She laughs through the pain.

I put a call though to Sergeant Wilson, who answers after he initial hellos, "Elvis how are you?"

"Listen, Sarge, Priscilla is in California Pacific Medical Center having our baby. I'm in the air about twenty minutes out from the airport. We are landing on the north runway. We're told it's about fourteen miles from SFO. Her contractions are close and it will take us another twenty-five minutes to get there.

"If we had a police escort we could make better time. Can you radio a couple of your guys to catch up with us at the airport to provide an escort to the hospital?"

"Sure. I already have two motorcycle officers at the airport on patrol. I'll radio them and have them meet your driver to escort your car to the runway to pick you up there for a quicker exit from the airport.

"He'll be in a white town car with tag number, oh wait Sergeant, I don't know what the tag number is, it's a rental! But how many white town cars are headed in to the private jet way this time of day?"

"Elvis, you never know. Have your driver put on his hazard lights so my guys can spot the car."

"Thanks, Sarge. I'll call and tell him right away! Talk to you later to tell what we had."

"Good luck Elvis, give the missus my best, and good luck! I'll get on the radio to my guys right now."

"Thanks again. Goodbye."

I hang up the phone and call Billy to relay the instructions. Then I call the hospital again and ask, "Can you please put me through to Mrs. Presley's room? This is Elvis, thanks."

The hospital operator puts me on hold, and after a quick minute comes back on the line, "I'm sorry Mr. Presley; there is no answer in Mrs. Presley room. She must be in delivery."

I start sweating bullets, hang up, and frantically yell, "Okay, hurry up and get this thing on the ground will you? She's not in her room. She could be having the baby now!"

The *Lisa Marie* lands at San Francisco International Airport. Billy is already there with the police escort. They are waiting on the tarmac for the plane to come to a stop. The door opens, Joe, Larry and I bolt from the plane and race to the town car. As we get in, Billy takes off even before the door is fully closed; he drives like he is in a high speed chase but with the motorcycle officer escorts leading all the way to the hospital.

"Billy, did you see her? How is she doing? Is the doctor there?"

Billy answers, "Elvis, she is fine. Yes, I saw her and I drove her to the hospital. The doctor wasn't there when I left to come get you."

"I'm sorry, Cuz. I'm just excited and nervous for her."

Billy laughing says, "E, you're more stressed out than she is."

~ * ~

In the delivery room at California Pacific Medical Center, Priscilla's feet are in the stirrups and the doctor is coaching her. Dr. Epstein says, "Now I want you to breathe, Priscilla. Just breathe through the pain."

Priscilla snaps at the doctor, "I don't need you here to tell me how to breathe. You went to medical school for this?"

Dr. Epstein laughs to lighten Priscilla's mood, "You don't know how many times I've heard that before. It's a good sign when you still have your sense of humor. Now, the next time the pain comes, I want you to push."

"Doctor Epstein, I want to thank you before Elvis gets here, for helping me keep our little secret! Ooooh…oooooh, Doctor!"

Dr. Epstein encourages Priscilla, "Keep breathing and push, Priscilla, breath and push."

"Ooooh… oooooh, I am breathing and I'm pushing! I wanted Elvis to be surprised!"

"You're doing great, Priscilla. Oh, I see the head crowning. Now, take a deep breath and push hard."

"I want this over now!" Priscilla shrieks.

A nurse enters the delivery room and announces my arrival.

Priscilla gasps, "Tell him to get in here, and hold my hand. That's the least he can do." The

390

nurse leaves and I hurrying in having stopped to get dressed in surgical scrubs.

Priscilla looks at me, "I'm giving birth to your child! Get over here and hold my hand! Oh, Doctor, is it out yet?"

I go over and comfort Priscilla. I hold her hand, and talk softly to her, "Priscilla, you're doing just fine. I love you, and I love our child."

Dr. Epstein encourages Priscilla, "Keep pushing. That's it, you're almost there. Keep pushing. Here it comes. Oh look--how beautiful he is. It's a boy, Priscilla."

Priscilla exclaims, "Oh, my God, we have a boy!" Turning her attention to me, with great pride she proclaims, "Elvis, you have a son."

My voice is husky as I say, "Cilla, you gave me a son. Oh, thank you." I lean over and give her a gentle kiss.

The doctor quickly wraps the baby and hands him to Priscilla, "There you are, your new baby son. Have you thought of what you're going to name him?"

With tremendous pride, I announce, "Yes we're going to call him Elvis Jr. or EJ."

Priscilla coos, "Oh look at him……..he is so beautiful. He looks just like you at this age."

"He sure is cute. Hello, little EJ. Are you going to be an actor when you grow up?"

"Oh I don't care what he's going to be, just as long as he is happy and well." Priscilla smiles at me. Then her expression changes, "Oooh. Another contraction."

I notice the Doctor is still working behind the drape between the stirrups, "Doctor, why hasn't Priscilla's stomach gone down yet?"

"Elvis, it hasn't been two minutes, and you're complaining about my stomach not being flat enough? Is that all the thanks I get?" Priscilla asks.

Dr. Epstein says, "Yes, you would have thought her tummy would have gone down more by now, but I'm beginning to think there is more to this story."

I look at the doctor both puzzled and concerned. "What's wrong Doctor?"

"Oh nothing, nothing's wrong! It's just… there's another baby here just beginning to crown."

I stare at Priscilla with shock and delight, "Oh, my God, there's another baby? We're, going to have twins? Is that true? We're going to have twins? Oh God, I hope, and pray that everything is going to be okay, but this is too good to be true!" I exclaim.

Dr. Epstein instructs Priscilla, "Give Elvis Jr. back to the nurse, and get ready to push for the second baby."

"Yes, Elvis we're having twins. Just like you, when you were born." says Priscilla.

Fear and trepidation fill me, "Oh, God, I'm so nervous. My twin brother Jesse was stillborn, and I came along about twenty minutes later, Dr. Epstein. I've always wondered what my life would have been like if he had lived? That's not going to happen here now is it?"

"No, I don't think so, but we can't be sure until we deliver the baby. There doesn't appear to be any problems, the baby's heart rate is stable. So let's just wait and see."

Priscilla agrees, "Yes, let's pray everything is good. Ooooooh, my God, Doctor. Here we go again."

"You'll be all right, Priscilla, you did just fine with the first one, and the second one should be easier."

I encourage Priscilla, "Yeah. You'll be alright. Won't she, Doctor?"

"That's easy for you to say, Mister. You weren't here for the whole performance. Here's the encore that you never give at your shows," Priscilla jibes.

"Doctor, are you sure she's going to be all right. I mean, Priscilla is going to be alright?"

"I'm sure she is going to be fine, Mr. Presley. You can see she is very lucid, and seems to have all her wits about her."

Still concerned, I ask, "How is the second child?"

"Like the first one. I won't know until we deliver the baby."

"Dr. Epstein, please do whatever you have to do to make sure that nothing goes wrong," I plead.

Priscilla interrupts, "Oh Doctor. Oh…, oh…, oh…, I feel the pressure again it's starting all over again."

"Remember, you just told me you knew how to do this. Breathe, that's it, breathe. And when you feel the pressure, bear down and push."

"Oooooh. I feel the pressure. Oh, my God. I hope that I can do this again."

She squeezes my hand as I tell her, "Do like the doctor says, Baby. Breathe and push. Breathe and push."

Priscilla says, sounding testy, "Look who is giving directions now. I know, breathe and push. Oooooh, God the pressure! Is it coming out yet?"

"You're doing great, Priscilla. Keep it up, that's right, breathe, and when you feel the pressure, push hard. Oh that's great. I can see the baby's head, here it comes. Keep pushing. Thatta girl, push. Oh, look at this beautiful child."

I exclaim with great joy, "It's another boy? Oh, my gosh, it's another boy. And look how healthy, and strong he looks."

The doctor lays the baby on Priscilla's chest as she prepares to cut the umbilical cord. Priscilla coos, "Oh, my God, look at this beautiful child. Elvis, this is Jesse, your second son."

With tears in my eyes, I say, "Oh my God… Jesse. We are truly blessed. I can't believe it, I have two beautiful boys."

Dr. Epstein seems proud of the evening's work and says, "You are truly blessed. And look at her tummy, it's almost flat again."

We all laugh at the doctor's joke.

I express my appreciation, "Doctor, I can't thank you enough. You have delivered my twin boys, and made me the happiest man on earth."

I turn to Priscilla, "I'm so proud of you. Thank you for giving us twin boys. I love you. I know there's a song in all this emotion, but it's not coming to me yet."

Dr. Epstein says, "As soon as we get you cleaned up and back to your room, you can start letting your relatives and friends know that you are the proud parents of twin boys."

Priscilla asks the doctor, "Please let me hold them both. I want to connect with both my sons."

"Let her hold them for as long as she wants, while we get her cleaned up. When you take her back to her room, take the twins to the nursery." A tired, but all smiles, Dr. Epstein directs the nurse.

I stop by the waiting room as they transfer Priscilla to her room and tell Joe, Billy and Larry about the twin boys.

Later, in Priscilla's room, sitting by her bed as she sleeps, I am overwhelmed by a rush of emotion. I said a silent prayer of thanks that Priscilla and I were so fortunate that the births went well and everyone is healthy.

I also felt a pang of sadness for my mother and father. They weren't as fortunate at my birth, January 8, 1935, when Jesse Garon Presley, my identical twin was still born at birth.

Chapter 30

May 20, 1981

Back on the set of *An Officer and a Gentleman*, the cast and I are preparing to shoot a scene at the officers club where Zack and Sid meet Paula and Lynette at a dance. The scene is set in the interior of the Regimental Ball Room at night.

Taylor is giving everyone their directions, "Elvis and David, you guys are part of the line of stubble haired Air Officer Cadets in your dress white uniforms. You're watching the door like hawks as a parade of Puget Debs come into the club wearing satin formals and hopeful smiles.

"Then you spot Lisa and Debra coming through the door. They'll be wearing clingy little formals looking very seductive thanks to our Costume Department.

"Ladies, you look great in these formals. They really show off your cleavage well. The Props Department did a perfect job with the little gold cross that's accenting your curves, Debra," he says as he walks over and ogles her breast.

Debra indignantly says, "Taylor, do you have to be so rude?"

"I'm trying to set the mood here," Taylor informs her. "Your character is a bit slutty, so I need you to play it that way. This isn't your sweet sixteen cotillion. You're here to get yourself a Navy Officer as a husband, to take care of you for the rest of your life. So, does everybody have that?" The cast nods their heads.

"Does anyone have any questions? No response! Okay, then! Places, everybody!"

The cast and crew take their positions. Taylor waits for everyone to settle down and then yells, "Mark the scene."

A young intern stands in front of the camera and says, "Scene 32, take 1" and claps the slate down to mark the beginning of this take on film.

"Okay… lights… camera… action." The scene begins to unfold as Taylor has blocked it out.

SID

"Look, Zack. It's them. Holy shit, look at the bodacious set of tatas on her."

Sid and Zack approach the girls where they have stopped to chat with Nelli Rufferwall.

SID

"Mrs. Rufferwall, ma'am, think you could introduce us to these attractive young ladies…?"

Sid immediately fixes his eyes on Lynette. Zack and Paula size each other up as Nellie makes the introductions.

NELLIE

"Officer Candidate Sid Worley, may I present Miss Lynette Pomeroy. Miss Paula Pokrifki, Officer Candidate Zackary Mayo. Well, I hope you have a good time tonight."

Nellie slips off, leaving the foursome alone.

ZACK (rubbing his head)

"You told us it would grow out an inch."

SID

"It's grown out more than an inch, sweetheart."

PAULA

"That was you guys, huh?"

LYNETTE

"Come on, let's go dance."

Sid offers Lynette his arm, and she takes it with a little smile as they head off to the dance floor. Zack offers Paula his arm, and she takes it, meeting his eyes for an instant. Zack and Paula walk over to the refreshment table and Zack serves her some punch.

ZACK

"Hey, what kind of name is Pokrifki?"

PAULA

"Polish, what kind of name is Mayo?"

ZACK

"Italian, my mom was Irish, I got her ears, but the rest is all wap."

PAULA

"Where are you from, Mayo the wap?"

ZACK

"Everywhere and nowhere Paula the Polack."

PAULA

"Seriously."

ZACK

"My father is a Rear Admiral in the Seventh Fleet."

PAULA

"Really?"

ZACK

"Yeah, we've lived all over the world, Katmandu, Moscow, Nairobi."

PAULA (impressed)

"Really. I've never been out of Washington State, except once when I visited this aunt of mine over to Portland. I mean, over in Portland. Ain't it pathetic the way folks talk around here?"

Paula suddenly blushes.

PAULA

"You're putting me on, aren't you?" We don't got no Navy bases in Moscow."

Zack just smiles.

PAULA (returns his smile)

"You got a girl?"

ZACK

"No, and I'm not looking for one either."

Paula meets his eyes, brazenly flirting.

PAULA

"Yeah, what are you looking for?"

ZACK

"I hear most of the girls who come to these things are looking for a husband."

PAULA

"Not me."

ZACK

"Yeah, why're you here then?"

PAULA

*"To meet interesting people, improve myself.
You wouldn't believe the losers we got over in Port
Angeles."*

ZACK

"Do you go to school?"

PAULA

*"No. I work for National Paper. It's a good
job. I make $8.23 an hour and when I get enough
money saved up; I plan to go to college."*

"And cut!" Taylor yells. "Okay principals, I
need you over here, the rest take five." The five
actors come over where Taylor is sitting in his
director's chair, "Listen folks this is supposed to be
a dance. You know: happy people out to have a
really good time. David, Lisa and Debra, I need a
little more life out of your characters. I'm not
asking for much, just a little more liveliness. David,
I need you to be more seductive, you've got to have
a lustful feeling toward Lisa. And Lisa, your
character needs to be more into it. You want to
jump Sid bones as much as he wants to jump yours,
okay? Any questions?"

Debra asks, "You want a little more out of
me? What didn't you like about that performance?"

"It's not that I didn't like it, but I think you
can deliver an even better scene. After Elvis' line,

'No, and I not looking for one either,' the directions in the script call for you to look into Elvis's eyes and flirt brazenly with him," Taylor explains to Debra. "I want more flirt out of you at that point."

"Yeah darling, I can handle a lot more flirting than what you delivered," I said with a big smile.

"Well then you better watch out, Zack," Debra flirts back.

"Alright let's try this again form the top, everybody back to their places. Let's make this a good take! Makeup, take the shine off of Elvis's forehead.

A young lady from makeup comes running in and powders my forehead to cut down the shine. After she finishes, Taylor yells, "Places everyone! Slate the scene."

The intern stands in front of the camera and says, "Scene 32 take 3" and claps the slate down to mark the scene."

"Ready, Lights… camera… and action!"

The cast runs the scene straight through again. At the end of the scene Taylor yells, "Cut, cut, cut! Now that was a take! That scene just oozed with sex appeal,kids. Good work today everybody. We had so much fun today let's do this again tomorrow. Makeup, hair and wardrobe at 5:00AM and we'll start shooting at 8:00AM. Thanks everyone."

Taylor gets up out of his director's chair; he walks over to me as he is heading back to his trailer. "So, Elvis, how are the twins?"

"They are doing well, thanks."

"And Priscilla, she's doing well also?"

"She's doing great thanks. But taking care of twins is keeping her busy. Changing diapers and feeding twins that are on two different time schedules is pretty tough. I'll be glad when this shoot is over so I can spend more time at home, helping her take care of the boys."

"We'll be through shooting in a few weeks. Then you can spend all the time you want at home with the family. We'll that's until the promotion part of your contract comes into effect. You know, doing the promotion tour to hype the movie."

"Taylor, I'll be glad to do the promotional tour. I have a feeling that this movie is going to be a winner."

"The promotional touring schedule will be a little easier than the shooting schedule," Taylor tells me. "And, you'll have a couple of months between finishing the principle photography and the promotional tour, while we do the editing."

I open the door to my trailer and we both step inside and take seats. Joe joins us from the rear of the trailer and asks if I need anything. "No thanks Joe, I'm fine right now."

"How is Lisa Marie taking to the twins?" Taylor asks.

"She loves her brothers! She's like a little mama to the boys, and she is a big help to Priscilla, especially, with me being away. I can't wait for the boys to be old enough for me to play football with them, coach little league, go horseback riding and play music. Whatever they choose to be will be fine with me; I just want to help them grow up to be fine young men."

"It's good to see you so happy. And, now back to business; are you ready for tomorrow's scene? We'll be on location at the Tides Inn Motel to shoot the scene with Debra. This is the scene where you have just beat up one of the townies, and your back at the motel. You're in a dark brooding place, drinking from a pint of rum. Debra is trying to comfort you but you don't want anything to do with her. There is a lot of emotion in this scene."

"Yes, I'll be ready. Your right, it will be very emotional, it's a great scene."

"Elvis is drinking rum tomorrow?" Joe asks.

"No. We've already taken care of that. He'll be drinking sweet tea," Taylor reassures Joe.

"Oh, I was going to say, I didn't think that was going to happen."

Taylor checks with me again, "So you're up for tomorrow then?"

"I'll be ready, just wait and see."

"I don't know why I ask you, you have to be one of the most professional actors I've ever worked with. This part is going to show Hollywood what you are really capable of doing. Our budget affords us a print campaign to nominate you for best male actor. I wouldn't be surprised if you win the Oscar for best actor."

"Do you really think I stand a chance?" Elvis asks.

"Yes, you do, without a doubt, my friend."

The phone rings in the trailer and Joe answers it. "Hello, can I help you?"

"Hi Joe, it's Priscilla. Is Elvis there?"

"Yes, he is, just a second," Joe hands me the phone.

"Hello Cilla, is everything alright?"

"Yes, the boys miss their daddy though. When are you coming home?"

"I was just finishing up here. I should be home in about a half an hour or so. Do you need anything?"

"No, just your girls and the boys wanted to see their daddy before they have to go to bed."

"Okay, I'll be there in just a few minutes, I'll see you then. Love you."

"I love you too, see you then." I hang up the phone and ask Joe, "Are you ready to go?"

"Yeah, let's go."

"See you in the morning Taylor,"

"Yeah, I'll see you then. Have a good night."

The next morning, the crew, Debra and I are in the interior of Zack's room at the Tides Inn Motel. The windows are darkened out to make the scene look like nighttime. I am lying on the bed, angry and brooding, doing some serious drinking from a pint bottle of rum. Paula is sitting in a chair across the room from the bed looking at Zack.

Taylor takes command of the set. The close proximity of the room in which they are shooting prevents him yelling directions. "Mark the scene." The intern walks up, "Scene 48, take 1," claps the slate, then steps out of the scene. "Quite on the set, alright, ready lights… camera… and action," the scene beings.

PAULA

"Want a back rub? Might make you feel better."

She climbs onto the bed and tries to position herself to rub Zack's back, but he pulls away."

ZACK

"I shouldn't have done that, I should've walked."

PAULA

"He didn't give you much of a choice."

ZACK

"There's always a choice."

PAULA

"Where'd you learn to fight like that?"

ZACK (snaps)

"I don't feel like talking, if you don't mind."

PAULA (angry)

"Opening up just a little wouldn't kill you, you know."

As she hops up off the bed and starts for the door. Zack barely even looks up.

ZACK

"You want me to fuck you? Is that it? Okay, come here. Take your clothes off, get into bed."

PAULA (turns, angry)

"Where's that coming from? I wouldn't fuck now if my life depended on it!"

ZACK

"Forget it. Just get out of here."

Paula starts to leave then turns back furious now.

PAULA (explodes)

"I don't know who you think you're talking to! I ain't some whore you brought here! I've been trying to be your friend, and you treat me like shit!"

ZACK

"Be a friend, and get the fuck out of here then."

PAULA

"You got no manners, and you never tell the truth! You're nothing special. And if you ask me, you got no chance at all of being an officer!"

Zack rises from the bed and very slowly approaches Paula. Paula almost flinches as Zack stops one foot away. Then he leans forward and kisses her as gently as he knows how. Very tentatively she responds.

"And cut. Boy that was the easiest day's work ever. That was outstanding you guys. Let's just do one more for safety, and we can call this scene a wrap," Taylor says.

"Where is, Pam Eilerson, the second assistant director?"

"Yes sir?" Pamela steps forward.

"I want you to get the next shot set up so we don't waste the rest of the day."

"What scene do you want next?" Pamela asks.

"I want to shoot on top of the bunker at the gun emplacement over at the naval station. You remember, we scouted the location last month. So get over there right now, set up the shot and I'll bring the crew once we shoot this scene one more time."

"Can do, see you over there."

"Pam, don't forget to get the crane for that shot." Pamela nods as she leaves to set up the next shot.

Debra and I are sitting on the bed talking to each other. As Taylor walks up, he comments, "Elvis, Deb that was great. I don't normally like to do just one take, just to be on the safe side. So we're going to do this shot just one more time even though that was really brilliant."

"Well that's what you get when you work with professionals," I say with a chuckle.

Debra says, "I can't believe how you hit your marks every time, and you nailed the dialog with such emotion. That was incredible.

'When you came up behind me, and I was facing the door, you kind of pinned me there and then kissed me. Wow, that was hot!" as she fans her face with her hand.

"That's just what I do baby, that's just what I do."

"Let's take five minutes. Then we'll come back and do the scene before we break for lunch.

After that, Deb, you can have the rest of the day off. Elvis, after lunch, I need you to get over to the naval base. We are shooting the scene with Lou Gossett Jr. on top of the bunker.

Here's the setup: Louis is grinding on you and you finally show him that you are in the Navy Officer Candidate School because you really want to fly jets after which he begins to cut you some slack."

"Sounds good to me, let's shoot this puppy so we can eat!"

~ * ~

It's later in the afternoon at the Navy Candidate School. Lou and I are on top of the gun emplacement bunker. It's a gray overcast day with a light mist in the air. I am lying prone on my back holding my feet six inches off the ground. Louis is standing over me smiling down at me.

"Okay let's shoot this. Slate the shot."

"Scene 51, take 2," the intern intones and moves out of the way.

"All right is everybody ready? Good, let's go then, lights… camera… and action," Taylor calls out to get the scene going.

FOLEY

"Hey, what do you say we call off this little charade of yours over a couple of beers at Traders? Come on, man. You're about as close to being officer material as me."

ZACK

"Sir, this candidate believes he'll make a good officer, sir."

FOLEY

"No way, Mayo. You don't give a shit about anybody but yourself, and every single one of your class mates knows it. Think they'd trust you behind the controls of a plane they have to fly in? Hey, man I figure you for the kind of guy who'd zip off one day on my F-14 and sell it to the Cubans."

ZACK

"Sir that's not true. I love my country!"

FOLEY (Laughs)

"Sell it to the Air Force, Mayo."

Foley bends down and puts his lips close to Zack's ear and whispers:

FOLEY

"Let's get down to it. Why would a slick little hustler like you sign up for this kind of abuse?"

Zack legs are shaking wildly with the effort to keep them up.

ZACK

"I want to fly, sir"

FOLEY

"That's no reason. Everybody wants to fly. My grand-mother wants to fly. You going after a job with one of the airlines?"

ZACK

"I want to fly jets, sir."

FOLEY

"Why? Because you can do it alone?"

ZACK

"No, sir!"

FOLEY

"What is it, the kicks? Is that it?"

ZACK

"I don't want to do something anybody can do."

FOLEY

"Pity you don't have the character."

ZACK

"That's not true, sir. I've changed a lot since I've been here! And I'm gonna make it, sir."

FLOEY

"Not a fucking chance, asshole!"

Zack bolts upright suddenly, meeting Foleys' eyes.

ZACK (defiantly)

"I got nothing else to fall back on, sir. This is it for me... and I'm gonna do it!"

Foley studies him with squinty eyes.

FOLEY

"All right, Mayo. Get on your feet."

Both men get up and start walking back toward the base, the end of another perfect scene.

~ * ~

Music producer Don Simpson is at the Record Planet in Los Angeles to record the song, "Up Where We Belong." The original music score was written by Jack Nitzsche and Buffy Sainte-Marie with lyrics by Will Jennings.

Curt Sobel, the music editor for the film is in the control room at the studio directing my recording session with Anne Murray. "There is a piano intro right before you come in Anne. Elvis, 8 bars into your part the bass line and the drums fade up. At the chorus, the strings with the 'ooh' vocals come in to fill out the dynamics of the sound. Then you go back into the lyrics, the music goes back to just the piano, bass and drums until the next chorus. Alright let's take it from the top!"

After several hours, the track is recorded and everyone except Don seems pleased with it. Don, unhappy with the way the track turned out, says, "The song isn't really that great. It isn't a hit."

His demands to have the song cut from "An Officer and a Gentleman" sound track. But producers Martin Elfand, and Douglas Day Stewart insist that the song be used.

After the session Anne and I are still in the studio talking with each other.

"You know, I have most of your albums back home at Graceland," I tell Anne.

"Are you kidding me... really?" She says with surprise.

"Yes, I love the husky mezzo-soprano sound of your voice."

"That's what happens when you grow up the only girl in a family with five boys."

411

"Oh is that how you got that voice? Well, I just love the way you sing, especially Snow Bird, Danny Song, A Love Song, and one of my real favorites, "You Needed Me." I'd like to record that sometime, what do you think?"

"Yeah sure, you would do a great version of that song. It was written by Randy Goodrum. He describes it as being about the unconditional and undeserved love."

"Yeah, that's what hit home about the song and why I want to record it. Thanks so much, Anne. It was great working with you, finally, and I hope we can do something together again."

"I'd like that too."

"I've got to get going; I have an early call in the morning for the film, thanks again. See you," I give Anne a kiss on the check as I leave, leaving her with a silly smile and a dreamy look on her face as she watches me leave the studio.

~ * ~

"Alright, everyone! This is the final scene of the film so let's make this a great moment in film history. It's a great ending so let's do it right! Passion is what I'm looking for! Slate the scene," Taylor barks for the last time. The intern says, "Scene 58 Take 1" and claps the slate board together. "Okay. Cue the music, lights… camera… and action!"

As the song "Up Where We Belong" plays, Zack enters the National Paper Company striding through the ware house wearing dress whites with gold insignia. Zack walks toward Paula, coming up behind her, he kisses her on the back of the neck.

412

Paula turns around, surprised to see Zack. He takes her face in his hands and kisses her in such a romantic way it's unlikely anyone will ever forget that kiss. The other aging debs in the factory stop their work to watch. A few applaud or start to cry. Zack suddenly picks Paula up in his arms and he carries her toward the exit door.

LYNETTE (with tears in her eyes)

"Way to go Paula! Way to go!"

"And cut!" The filming is wrapped up, in the can, ready to be edited.

~ * ~

The movie takes almost a year to be edited. They make use of study group suggestions and pre-promotional movie trailer reviews. After frequent changes to the scheduled release date, the movie finally premieres on July 28, 1982. It is a date anxiously awaited by both my fans and me.

The next morning Joe goes to the Studio City Newsstand and buys newspapers from all over the country. We gather for breakfast and to read what the critics have to say.

Joe grabs the New York Times. "Here's the review from Janet Maslin. Let's see…

"The best thing about "An Officer and a Gentleman" is the level of acting that is sustained throughout, particularly in the key performances of Mr. Presley, Miss Winger and Mr. Gossett. Mr. Presley has never been this affecting before; there's urgency to his performance, some of it visibly induced by the hard physical work of the basic-training sequences, that cuts right through his manner of detachment.

413

"I guess they can see how much work you have put in to get into shape, Joe laughs.

"Oh, listen to this… 'When Zack is finally pushed to the limit by Sergeant Foley, and he must beg Foley not to boot him out of the corps, he screams: "Don't you do it! I got nowhere else to go!" If the audience doesn't believe this, the movie is lost, but Mr. Presley makes it utterly real.

He brings just as much authenticity to the love scenes.' Well, that's no surprise" Everyone laughs.

Lamar chimes in, "Hey this is from a TV Guide staff writer.

"Elvis Presley, as Zack Mayo, should be nominated for a much-deserved Best Male Actor Oscar) for his stellar portrayal in this story.

"Let's see…

"Elvis' performance is uniformly strong, with his offering some of his best work ever.

"And…

"The film's memorable theme song, "Up Where We Belong" (sung by Elvis Presley and Anne Murray), should also be nominated for an Academy Award."

There are more reviews along the same lines. We celebrate; toasting with mimosas and orange juice for me.

Chapter 31

April 11, 1983

It is the night of the Academy Awards.

Boasting one of the largest stages in the country, the Dorothy Chandler Pavilion seats over three thousand people, and is the centerpiece of The Music Center, an eleven-acre, four-theatre campus. The Pavilion's rich décor includes beautiful chandeliers in the lobby, curving stairways and tiered seating. It has proven itself an important part of Los Angeles history and the perfect setting for the Academy Awards.

Throngs of fans line the red carpet to see the parade of stars. There are hundreds of celebrities, but no one gets a bigger response when they step out of their limo than I do. I have brought Priscilla and Tom to sit with me. Joe, Larry, GK and Al will sit in the balcony for the Oscar show tonight.

Making my way to our seats on the main floor is difficult. I am stopped to greet people who have waited a lifetime to meet Elvis. I am happy to be meeting people from all facets of the movie industry.

Steven Spielberg, nominated for best picture and director for *E.T. the Extra-Terrestrial*, is one of the first to introduce himself. Julie Andrews, the nominee for best actress in a leading role for *Victor/Victoria*, seems delighted when we meet.

One of the classiest ladies in the industry, Glenn Close, nominated for her supporting role in *The World According to Garp*, goes out of her way to introduce herself to me. John Lithgow, her cast mate and nominee for best actor in a supporting role in *Garp*, proclaims that he is one of my biggest fans.

Without question, one of the greatest composers in the movie industry, John Williams, nominated for the song "If We Were in Love" and the original score for *E.T. the Extra-Terrestrial*, pushes through the crowd to meet me. We talk briefly about music, and really seem to hit it off.

I get tag teamed by Teri Garr and Jessica Lange who were both nominated for the best actress in a supporting role in *Tootsie*. Jessica was also nominated for best actress in a leading role for *Frances*. The two actresses, one on each side, gush over me, both at the same time, making this meeting awkward. All the while, Priscilla who is very comfortable in our relationship watches the familiar scene with amusement.

I am excited when Lesley Ann Warren, the nominee for the best actress in a supporting role for, *Victor/Victoria* stops by. I stand to give her a hug and experience a charge of sexual attraction between us. But, knowing that Priscilla is my true love, I know that I am not going to pursue her.

The lights go up and down, making everyone aware that the show is about to begin. I take my seat on the aisle, in the second row center, with Priscilla on my right and Tom next to her. The orchestra plays the opening number.

The evening is co-hosted by Liza Minnelli and Dudley Moore, Richard Pryor, and Walter Matthau. The four come out from behind the curtain, and are trying to sing the opening song. It is so bad that many in the audience jeer and it will be rudely panned by the critics.

The song lyricist, Buz Kohan later said, "I had written the opening number called, 'It All Comes Down to This.' They were all scared stiff, but ordinarily when you're scared, you put in the time and rehearse the number. If they had done that, things would have gone better. They unfortunately took the opposite approach. So Liza was forced to carry the number, Walter was singing in his own time zone somewhere, Dudley was just trying to walk down the stairs without falling over and Richard, well I think they told him the next day that he was there."

After the disastrous opening number, Liza went on to do the introduction for the show. "Welcome to the Fifty-fifth Academy Awards show. Tonight we will be presenting the Oscar to the best people in the industry, and in their individual categories as voted by the members of the academy. And now, on with the show!"

Billy Wilder presents the Award for Best Director to Richard Attenborough, for *Gandhi*.

Jessica Lange receives the Award for Best Supporting Actress from Sigourney Weaver and Robert Mitchum for her work in *Tootsie*.

Next up is a category that I pay close attention to, since a member of our cast is up for the award. After a warm introduction by Walter Mattheau , Sylvester Stallone does the honors:

"Good evening ladies and gentlemen. The nominees for the best actress in a leading role are: Julie Andrews in *Victor/Victoria*, Jessica Lange in

Frances, Sissy Spacek in "*Missing*," Meryl Streep for her role in "*Sophie's Choice*" and Debra Winger for, "*An Officer and a Gentleman.*"

I lean over and whisper into Priscilla's ear, "I hope Debra wins this. She worked hard, and she deserves it."

Sly opens the envelope and announces, "And the winner is… Meryl Streep in "Sophie's Choice."

I feel like a guy who just lost at the craps tables in Vegas, smacking my hands together in frustration, but then applauds for Meryl since she deserves it.

After Meryl gives her acceptance speech, she turns toward Walter and Sly and the three of them leave the stage to the audience's generous applause.

Richard Pryor comes out with a big grin on his face, and steps up to the podium. "Where the heck am I, and how did I get here from Detroit?"

The audience roars with laughter. "Oh yeah, I'm supposed to announce the next sucker to present the best actor in a supporting role. One of my brothers is in this category. He must be their token black guy for the Academy. But here to present are Susan Sarandon and Christopher Reeve."

Susan, wearing a sleeveless scoop necked brown gown with gold accented draping, begins, "It's our pleasure to reveal the winner for the best performance by an actor in a supporting role."

Christopher, tall dark and handsome in his tuxedo, continues, "The nominees are: Charles During for, *The Best Little Whorehouse in Texas.*"

Susan picks up, "Louis Gossett Jr. in *An Officer and a Gentleman*."

Chris reads the third name, "John Lilthgow in *The World According to Garp*."

Susan announces the fourth, "James Mason in The *Verdict*."

Chris finishes the list, "and Robert Preston in *Victor/Victoria.*"

Susan looks up at Chris and comments, "It's funny, Chris, but two of those performances could have been performed by women."

"Yeah. I guess you are trying to say that this year's Oscars derby is partly a drag race. Eh-hem." This exchange is met by weak laughter and a few groans.

"Okay" Chris says.

Simultaneously, Susan says, "Okay, and the winner is…"

Chris hands Susan the envelope, "You'd better do that"

"I will be glad to. Thank you very much." She replies, opens the envelope and removes the card.

Chris reads the card with Susan joining in. "And the winner is… Louis Gossett Jr."

The audience applauds enthusiastically for Louis' work as he makes his way to the stage.

"My brother, my brother," Richard screams, "The brother won!"

"I am so glad that Lou won. His work ethic is incredible and he was able to give me some great pointers to improve my performance," I tell Pricilla.

Louis walks to the podium where Susan gives him a kiss hands him the Oscar. Chris shakes his hand. He addresses the audience, "You know when you prepare a speech it's no use, cause it's all gone. I tried to get my kid to come up here to share this with me…

"But there are some special people I would like to share this with; specifically, tomorrow is the seventeenth anniversary of my relationship with my one agent, Mr. Ed Bondy. They say marriages don't last.

"I've got a spirit that guides me, starting with my great-grandmother who died at the age of 117, and my mom and dad who I know are watching, and my cousin Yvonne. Thank you, you make everything fall into place.

"I can't tell you what a privilege and pleasure it was to work with Elvis Presley. What a great performance." And all you other guys, this is ours [holding up the Oscar]. Thank you."

Louis turns and leaves the stage.

After numerous other awards are presented,, John Travolta, makes his way to the podium. "Good evening ladies and gentlemen. Of many outstanding performances by actors in leading roles in sheer brilliant movies, the five nominees are…"

You can feel the tension in the air, as the audience waits, almost forgetting to breathe. I know I was holding my breath.

"For his multilayer portrayal of the unemployed actor who becomes a better man by putting on a dress and gaining an insight into the world of women, Dustin Hoffman in *Tootsie*;

"For his remarkable recreation of the young Indian lawyer as he moved through history to become a symbol of peace and non violence, Ben Kingsley in *Gandhi;*

"For his extraordinary interpretation of the brash navel cadet who leans no man is an island, Elvis Presley in *An Officer and a Gentleman*;

"For his deep conviction as an alcoholic lawyer who comes to victorious terms with himself, Paul Newman in *The Verdict*;

"For his flamboyant caricature of a swashbuckling film star who invades television with a lunge and a thrust, Peter O'Toole in *My Favorite Year.*"

"Five outstanding performances and the winner is…" John opens the envelope and reads, "Elvis Presley, for *An Officer and a Gentleman!*" There is thunderous applause from the audience.

I am frozen in shock for a few moments. Then I jump up out of my seat, kiss Priscilla, then lean over her and shake Tom's hand with a big ole grin on my face. I run up the stairs to the stage to accept the award. The audience is still applauding even after I reach the podium. I grip John's hand, pulling him close and says quietly in his ear as the audience continues to applaud, "Thank you, you have no idea what this means to me."

John hands me the statuette, returning my smile and gives me a wink of acknowledgement.

I turn to the audience and bask in the energy of the moment before I speak. "Good evening ladies and gentlemen."

The audience continues to applaud. "Thank ya. Thank ya very much," I bow and nod my head in appreciation. "Wow, this is a great honor, after making thirty-some odd films... and believe me, some of those films made even me cringe and wonder why I even agreed to appear in them."

The audience laughs at my acknowledgment of my somewhat doubtful prior film career.

"Oh my gosh, who to thank? First I want to thank Priscilla, for sticking with me through all the good years and a few of the bad years," looking down at her from the podium, "Thank you, Cilla, I love you." The audience applauds her standing by her man, most of the time. But unlike most Hollywood marriages that break up and then get back together again, people have seen they are a stronger couple for doing so.

"My lovely daughter, Lisa Marie, is back at home, and I want to thank her for putting up with me also. Daddy loves you, now go to bed." Once again, this elicits laughter from the audience. "The boys, Elvis Jr. and Jesse are at home with their sister, and when they get old enough I'll show them a video tape of tonight's show so they will know that I was thinking about them tonight, too."

"I want to thank my manager, Tom Hulett for believing in me. Tom was the one who believed in me enough to push me beyond what I had done before. His understanding of the entire entertainment industry is incredible. He is a great captain to have at the helm of my career, helping guide me. Tom, thank you for believing in me!" Tom gives a wave of thanks, and then shakes his fist in the air in victory.

"I want to thank Larry Geller for his spiritual inspiration and guidance. I also want to thank my Memphis Mafia, Joe, Al, Billy, Lamar, Marty, G.K., Charlie and Jerry for their never ending support and protection.

"Also, special thanks go to the cast of *An Officer and a Gentleman*, who produced such outstanding performances and made me feel a part of the team from the get go. Debra, David, Bob, Lou and Lisa, your performances inspired me to do better.

"I can't forget Michael Eisner and everyone over at Paramount Pictures, Taylor Hackford, my director, and Douglas Day Stewart for writing such a great script."

The music comes up to signal my time is up. "I hear the music, which is my signal for me to get off the stage. So ladies and gentlemen, until we meet again, may God bless you as he has blessed me."

Warren and I walk off stage left as the audience goes wild. One person stands, then another, and just as I leave the stage, I turn back for one last glimpse, and they have given me a standing ovation. A feeling of humility washes over me and a smile of gratitude breaks across my face.

To Be Continued...

www.ingramcontent.com/pod-product-compliance
Lightning Source LLC
Chambersburg PA
CBHW071639260626
47170CB00001B/159